"Anna's struggle to find her place in a society that wants to constrain her within appropriate gender roles is enhanced by the author's attention to details—of fashion, culture, and even mountain climbing. **An engaging escapade with a feisty female lead.**"
—*Kirkus Reviews*

"Searching for purpose and adventure, Anna will win your heart over and then some. Filled with lessons of strength, perseverance, and audacity, In Sight of the Mountain is a beautifully written story. **A must-read** for those who are striving to fulfill their dreams."
—Kristi Elizabeth, *Seattle Book Review*

"Focusing on themes of the liberation of women, the American class system and effects of colonialism, this intelligent and heart-warming novel introduces us to Anna Gallagher at the tender age of nineteen. . . **An epic and gripping work of historical fiction**. . . Overall, In Sight of the Mountain is the perfect historical read for fans of pioneering heroes and tales of triumph over discrimination."
—K.C. Finn, *Reader's Favorite* (5 Star Review)

IN SIGHT OF THE MOUNTAIN

The Rainier Series, Book 1

JAMIE MCGILLEN

ALSO BY JAMIE MCGILLEN

In Light of the Summit

For my grandparents,
Barbara and Bob Pavitt.
For always reminding me
that my roots are in
Alaska
and in poetry.

More pleasure is to be found at the foot of the mountains
than on their tops. Doubly happy, however, is the man
to whom lofty mountain tops are within reach,
for the lights that shine there illumine all that lies below.

—John Muir, from "An Ascent of Mount Rainier"

CHAPTER ONE

THE GREAT FIRE

Seattle, Washington Territory
6 June 1889

Anna Gallagher tucked a wrapped package under her arm and escaped out the front door as a light wind rustled her favorite summer dress. It was possible Greta hadn't spotted her, so she tiptoed across the porch, but just as she reached the top of the wooden steps, she heard the familiar voice.

"Your grandfather's waiting for you," Greta called from the kitchen. "At the hardware store by the Opera House."

Anna strolled back to the front door and popped her head in. "Just need to make a quick stop at June's first."

Greta shook her head as she pulled strawberry muffins out of the oven.

"Be careful. If anyone recognizes you there, they'll think you're one of *those* girls." She eyed Anna's hair with a grimace. "Your hat, dear."

Anna sighed and grabbed her hat with a small lace veil before racing out the door again. Finally free, she didn't mind Greta's tone or her warning as much as she usually would.

To save time, she took the new electric streetcar. Usually, her grandfather accompanied her to town, but it was still daytime, so she could take liberties. She leaned out the opening to cool herself, holding the frame with one hand as they rattled past maple trees lining the street. In her memories of Ireland, it was never this hot. But that was so long ago—before her parents had died, before her grandfather had taken her and her brother to America, and before he'd married Greta.

She hopped off the streetcar at Front Street before it came to a full stop. With the scent of hydrangeas in the air, she strode south, past wooden buildings with connected, yet uneven awnings. The shared walls looked as if they'd been pushed together—smashed, even. The bustling, wood-planked sidewalk creaked below her with every step, and her low heels clicked a steady rhythm beneath her rustling skirts.

With a deep breath, she paused across the street from the brothel—June's current home. A carriage passed in front of her on Third Avenue, the horses holding their heads high as they clopped along, kicking up a cloud of dust. She hurried across the street, her face angled away from the crowds as she pulled her hat lower to obscure her features. The thrill of secrecy sent an electric jolt down her spine as the minor chords of a string quartet drifted from the second-floor windows. Still catching her breath, she hesitated, motionless before the ornately engraved front door.

The lace veil on her hat covered her eyes. Her reputation hung in the balance. She looked up at Mount Rainier, the great snow-capped mountain to the south. The rocky peak was nearly covered in snow, with dark blue ridges bearing themselves in the summer heat. It was hard to imagine snow falling so near when the warm air blew around her, making her neck sticky with sweat.

It was a sight she'd been in awe of since childhood—it grounded her. She exhaled a shaky breath, gathering the courage to enter the building. Now was *not* the time to lose her nerve and abandon her dearest friend.

But before she could knock, a muffled boom shook the air. A black-purple cloud of smoke rose from a building back the way she'd come. On the tips of her toes, she strained to see which buildings were near the explosion—if that's what it was. The blood drained from her face. Firemen flew past her, and her feet sprang into action before she could decide—she dropped the package and ran in the direction of the hardware store.

Crowds on the street drifted toward the commotion as others ventured out of stores, squinting in the bright sunlight. Anna raced past them toward her grandfather. As she grew closer, her lungs began to burn. Gray smoke swirled around her arms and legs, prickling the hairs on her neck.

She jerked to a stop before Frye's Opera House, stunned to see flames licking up the brick. Spray from a firehose rained down, misting her face and arms, before she jumped out of the way of a flaming piece of lumber as it crashed to her feet. Heat from the sun and fire gave the street an unearthly aura with sunbeams slicing through thick air.

A man with his face covered in black soot darted by. He cupped his hands around his mouth and shouted, "The tide's out, and there's no water pressure! Run to the docks and fetch buckets of water!"

Anna struggled to peel her gaze away from his grimace—the panic in his wrinkled eyes surely matched her own.

A rush of bodies raced past her, but she pushed her way to the entrance of the hardware store. She swallowed her fear and flung the heavy wooden door open. Thick smoke rolled out to meet her like trapped water. She tried to call out to her grandfather, but choked on the smoke, succumbing almost immediately to a painful coughing fit. The floor was hot, and it

3

was only a matter of time before the flames burst through the basement or the walls from next door.

Covering her face with the hem of her dress, she searched, passing by wooden buckets lining walls and filled with nails, tools, and hinges. Five empty aisles. Shelves of mirrors reflected the hazy, empty rows. There was no trace of him. An image of her grandfather—dusting a bookshelf, smiling warmly at her—filled her mind, and her chest tightened.

Confusion settled in. Could he be in the back room? Dread seeped down her arms as a muffled shout escaped the dense air.

She dropped to her hands and knees, crawling toward the sound with shallow breath, her eyes burning. There was no oxygen left, but her mouth opened wide to gasp for it as she reached her hand toward the doorknob of the back room to pull herself back up. It scorched her palm.

The ground below her seemed to sway as she struggled to stand, and her legs gave way beneath her. The last thing she remembered before losing consciousness was a pair of strong, familiar arms catching her.

⚜

HALF AWAKE, Anna felt herself being passed into someone else's arms. The sudden force of a second explosion caused the person holding her to stumble, and the jolt snapped her back to reality, sharpening her surroundings.

Where was her grandfather?

She opened her eyes in confusion. The man's carefully trimmed mustache stood out from his smooth-shaven jaw, and his light brown hair was swept to the side. One of his arms wrapped around the back of her shoulders, the other under her knees. Surprised to be in the arms of a stranger, she wasn't sure if she should be grateful or struggle to free herself.

He cleared his throat. "I'm glad to see you awake, miss. What's your name?"

He set her down carefully into a seated position on the sidewalk.

"I'm—" She coughed painfully before gathering herself. "I'm Anna Gallagher."

She glanced down at her dress with its high collar and pearl buttons and frowned as it was now covered in soot.

"I was looking for my grandfather. Did you see a tall man with a white beard?" The words burned in her throat.

"Sounds like the gentleman who carried you out." He rubbed the back of his neck and squinted at the fire. "He said to look after you—then ran. You've breathed a lot of smoke, Miss Gallagher. I'm Doctor Evans, and I'd be happy to escort you home."

Relief flooded her, and her eyes stung with tears. Her grandfather was alive.

"Thank you, but no." She paused to cough again, then cleared her throat. "I should help get buckets of water."

She took a closer look at the man's face. Although it hardly mattered in the moment, he was handsome. She felt for her hair ribbon that tickled her neck, dangling haphazardly, and she reached up to tuck loose waves of her long brown hair into what was left of a bun.

The doctor furrowed his brow. "I don't think so. I promised to keep you safe."

Anna crossed her arms and stared down the street at the fire. It was just like her grandfather to bar her from participating in something dangerous. The good doctor should move along, save someone else. Now that she knew her grandfather was safe, there was something almost enticing about the fire; a strange exhilaration flowed through her at the thought of running wildly through the streets. It would be the most independence she'd experienced in months.

"Miss Gallagher, this fire is growing fast. It's no place for a lady. It'll put your grandfather's mind at ease, as well as my own, knowing you're safe at home." He smiled encouragingly, offering his hand.

She rested her hand on his arm—no harm in letting him feel useful. But staying home with the city in flames was out of the question.

"Thank you, Doctor Evans." She raised her voice over the wailing fire alarms. "Our house is down East Madison Street, almost to Lake Washington."

"Let's go." He placed his other hand on hers and pulled her close as they hurried away.

A group of men ran by with buckets and strained faces while others darted away with their arms full of goods.

"Do you suppose those men are store owners or looters?" she asked.

Doctor Evans surveyed the scene with a wary eye. "Probably both."

"Does anyone know yet where the fire started—or how?"

With a shrug, he offered a half-smile. "I'm sorry. I'm afraid I know very little."

Ash fell like snow, landing on Anna's arms, coating her dress with grayish-white. She struggled to match the doctor's long strides.

As they passed a group of on-lookers, she recognized June's face, and they locked eyes. June pushed past the crowd and ran to her, curls wild. Anna released the doctor's arm to squeeze her in an embrace. After the hug, June set her hands on her hips and leaned forward to catch her breath.

"I've been lookin' out the window and waitin'. You're late, by the way." Her low-cut dress, supplied by the brothel, exposed her cleavage. "Goodness, you're covered in soot! What happened?"

She glanced at Anna's companion, then straightened and smiled suggestively. "Who's this fine-lookin' fella?"

"I'm fine. This is Doctor Evans. Doctor Evans, meet June. Come with us. I don't want to be worried about you along with my grandfather." Anna lifted her eyebrows and glanced pointedly at the fire, desperately signaling to her friend that she had every intention of returning.

June's hazel eyes betrayed her confusion as she glanced down at their interlocked arms. "You go ahead. I'm headin'…home."

She sauntered away, her pink satin dress reflecting the sunlight as her hips swayed.

Anna frowned. No matter—she could just find her later. "I'll see you *soon*."

June turned and blew a kiss.

Home meant the brothel. Now, she needed a polite way to say goodbye to the doctor. Her lungs felt clearer already, and she wondered how difficult it would be to slip back to town without notice.

"Let's take the trolley." Doctor Evans held out his hand to help her up.

He paid their fare, and the smoke thinned as they rattled away. By the time they made it the twenty-five blocks to the long dirt road in front of her house, the doctor had barely spoken another word—all business, this man. Anna peered over her shoulder, dull panic settling inside her now that she was distanced from the action.

A shy smile danced on his lips. "Perhaps I'll see you again— under different circumstances."

She smiled sweetly and squeezed his arm. "You've been so helpful—thank you. I can walk up the road from here."

"Are you sure? I'm happy to walk you all the way."

"I insist. I'm sure you're needed with the fire. Please."

Was he buying it? It was hard to tell from the way his jaw clenched.

He nodded solemnly, his eyes searching hers, then tipped his hat. "As you wish."

She watched him leave. He was exactly the type of man her grandfather wanted for her, and quite the opposite of what she needed. Although he was attractive and the press of his arm still lingered on her skin, she couldn't bear the thought of simply clinging to a gentleman.

As soon as he turned the first corner, she lifted her hem and started back toward the brothel.

CHAPTER TWO

THE UNDERSTANDING

O ut of breath and covered in sweat, Anna finally arrived
back at Third and Washington ten minutes later. The fire
had already spread south. With her mind spinning, she searched
the ground for the package she'd dropped and finally found it
covered in dust near the brothel's now wide-open front door.

An elegant woman leaned against the doorframe, watching
her. June had told her all about the madam—Lou Graham. She
was a businesswoman and a benefactor, and she ran a tight ship.

"Is June here?" Anna whispered. Her heartbeat hadn't slowed
since the first explosion, and things were about to get even riskier.

The madam motioned for her to follow, making no effort to
hide her amusement at Anna's attempts to conceal her face as
they passed several tables of gentlemen, many of whom stared.
Women in satin and silk evening gowns drifted around the great
sitting room, which was filled with imported European furniture
and life-size portraits of naked women in ornate gold frames.
Oddly, only a few people inside the brothel seemed concerned
about the fire.

Anna ran her fingers along the cold banister as she ascended the stairs—lavender and laughter suffused the air. She wondered if other cities had as many brothels as Seattle. She'd barely left the city since arriving from Ireland as a child, so it was hard to know.

As soon as she reached June's room, she locked the door and embraced her. An elegant oak bed stood against the wall, with a white silk canopy. The vanity table near the window was covered with glass bottles of perfumes and trinkets.

June tossed her blond curls behind her shoulders. "Two hugs in one day. Is that to say goodbye? Are you gonna use all this commotion to finally escape on some adventure?"

Anna laughed. June knew her better than anyone in the world, and she loved her for it. "With what money? Come on. Let's help fetch buckets of water."

"I'm sure our valiant volunteer fire department has it covered." June winked and blew a kiss out the window. "Plus, they'll turn us away. 'Get on along home, ladies.' We might as well stay put."

Anna stood in disbelief. "Nonsense. They'll be lucky to have us."

June flopped down on her bed. "I need a quick rest first if we're gonna be haulin' buckets all afternoon—Hey, is that for me?" She reached for the dusty package with a sly grin.

Hesitating a moment, Anna smiled. "Yes. Happy twentieth birthday, June. But we *really* ought to get out there."

June tore open the package to find a silver music box—one corner dented from when it was dropped. She turned the handle and "Für Elise" started playing. "My favorite!"

The energy inside Anna pinged around, and it pained her to do nothing. But June was nothing if not stubborn. She sighed impatiently and moved back toward the vanity table, examining her assortment of makeup and powders. "How long's it been, now?"

"Forever." June stretched her arms above her head. "Two years, I guess. And that's the last time she's spoken with me."

She shot Anna a challenging look, then settled into her seat. "I heard she's married now. Enjoyin' livin' off her husband's money."

Anna's heart sank at the hurt look in June's eyes. They'd both been close with Emily ever since they were children. Until Emily's father, the local police chief, had forbidden her to associate with June.

"The wedding was last month. I'm sure she'd have loved for you to come."

June laughed darkly. "She'd have been mortified if I'd shown my fallen face."

Anna shifted in her seat.

"Anyway, how much do you have now?" She sat at the chair in front of the mirror, her light blue eyes shining. She hated that she had no money to call her own, but her grandfather assured her she wouldn't need any once she married a successful gentleman. The way he said it made her feel helpless.

June came up behind her and applied a fresh coat of brilliant red lipstick. "Almost fifteen dollars. But I've always got expenses."

"You could buy a train ticket all the way to California!" Anna leaned forward. "You have money and freedom. You could easily walk into any saloon, and no one would care. I can't even walk around after dark without a chaperone. I'll need money of my own if I'm ever going to get out of this city."

If she married a steady, successful man like her grandfather wanted, she'd never be able to see the world. His expectations hung like a thick fog. But it wasn't just *his* expectations. Ever since grade school, she was told to keep her hands clean, braid her hair neatly, and speak softly. Luckily her grandfather had never sent her away to a finishing school, but even in their cozy frontier town, she was expected to act like a lady.

The hair stood up on her arms as she imagined the possibility of throwing all societal expectations aside—what kinds of delightfully daring things would she be capable of doing if nothing was holding her back?

June sighed and placed her hands on Anna's shoulders as they peered at each other in the mirror. A deep understanding passed between them. Neither of them was living the life they wanted.

Something had been stirring inside Anna over the last few months. She'd always wanted to travel around Washington Territory, or take to the sea like her brother Levi, even though it wouldn't be *proper*.

Every time she looked up at that mountain, it was as if it was daring her to do something great. Majestically resting on the horizon, it reminded her that there was more to life than finding a suitable husband and keeping house.

Longing to see the mountain, she stood and pulled the window's floor-length velvet curtain aside, but a menacing smoke cloud obscured the view—the fires seemed to be moving closer. She exhaled sharply.

"We need to get out of here! Bring your money just in case. The fire seems to be spreading this way."

June gathered her cash, and they ran down the stairs and out the door.

Just a few blocks north, piles of goods were stacked haphazardly on the sidewalk, and the bucket brigade and frantic shop owners filled the streets. She searched the sea of faces for any sign of her grandfather and finally spotted him outside his favorite barber shop carrying armfuls of goods with the owner. A strong wind blew against her back, no doubt assisting the greedy flames.

A few looters—she was sure of it now—were trying to make the best of the situation, and her grandfather attempted to fight them back. Flames reached an adjacent building, and Anna felt a gust of heat as a series of explosions pierced her eardrums.

Confused, she figured it must be a stockpile of ammunition going off like fireworks. She dodged falling cinders from above as they landed on piles of goods, setting them on fire. She locked eyes with June—they were in the thick of it now.

The town clock struck seven. She looked around herself in a daze, her ears ringing. Smoke erupted from the windows of the Yesler-Leary Building and the Occidental Hotel while flames moved hungrily toward the remaining wood structures in the business district. As she watched her grandfather, she hesitated. If he saw her, he'd send her home, certainly. But she *had* to help—to prove she was capable.

She rushed up to him, June trailing behind. Anna pressed a hand on her grandfather's back, and he swung around, his face filled with surprise. He kissed her cheek, then enveloped her in a hug. Being in his arms, she felt safe, like nothing could touch them, but the screams that ricocheted around the streets reminded her otherwise.

He coughed then attempted to clear his throat. "What are you doing here?"

Before she could answer, a man ran up to them. "Oscar, your shipment arrived this morning, and it's still on the docks!"

Her grandfather threw a panicked glance toward the harbor then frowned at Anna. From where they stood, it appeared that the whole city was aflame. His rebuke was coming, but now that their livelihood was in danger, she was determined to help.

"Go home. Please!" he urged, then turned and took off running to the harbor.

"He's right, let's get out of here," June pleaded. "It's gettin' out of control!"

She took Anna's hand and tried to yank her away.

Another explosion sent debris flying at Anna's face. "But the docks are on fire! That shipment's worth almost two hundred dollars."

She jerked her hand out of June's hold and raced after her

grandfather. Flames grew closer to the dock, and men rushed past her to avoid being trapped against the water. Guilt and doubt gave her pause, but losing those supplies would put them in an impossible position for winter. Her heart squeezed as she peered into the black smoke that had settled into the streets. Most of the boats had already left the harbor, away from the flying embers.

She found her grandfather pushing a large wooden crate along the groaning pier. She rushed over and gripped the splintered front end of the crate, using all her strength to pull. The dock swayed beneath her, and the sound of the nearing flames kindled fear inside her. Heaving with all her strength, Anna glanced up at her grandfather, who now appeared grateful she was there. His face was flushed with exertion, and he groaned as he shoved the massive crate, budging it only a few feet at a time, even with her help.

When they were scarcely ten feet from the street, a loud cracking noise from above startled her. She looked up just in time to see a wooden awning hurtling toward them. In an instant, she and her grandfather exchanged glances and leapt from the dock onto the street as the last of the wood planks went up in flames and crumbled into the bay—the crate of books disappearing into the lightless waters.

CHAPTER THREE

THE NEW BEGINNING

Off the Coast of Alaska
7 June 1889

B enjamin Chambers walked to the bow of the ship and scanned the billowy clouds. Fishermen were scattered around the deck. It was only halfway through fishing season, but they were sick of each other already.

A thin man joined him at the rail, and Ben clapped him firmly on the back. "You sure your family won't mind a visitor, Levi?"

"Not at all." Levi plunged his hands in the pockets of his wool pants. "It'll be fun."

"Good." Ben inhaled and folded his arms, his feet planted firmly, keeping his large frame steady on the rocking deck. "Let's pull up the line."

The night before, they had laid down forty fathoms of line, with buoys marking the anchors on either end. Now, they gripped the hefty wheel, groaning as they pulled the long line resting on the ocean floor up to the surface, heavy with halibut.

The three tall masts of the ship rose above Ben's head, the sails whipping in the Alaskan breeze. While his eyes were drawn to the rectangular gray patch in one of the sails, another man pulled Levi aside and whispered something.

Levi glanced up at Ben as he coiled a rope, nodding pleasantly. Ben's stomach dropped with worry although he was probably being paranoid. Even if the rumors about him had traveled all this way, they'd have already been around the small ship twice. But then again, that man in Oregon had deserved what he'd got, so Ben had few regrets.

He spent most of the year hunting, but every summer for the last three years, he'd joined Levi for halibut fishing. They'd spent many late nights talking and long days working side by side. If he ever did hear the rumors, surely Levi would just confront him rather than take them on blind faith.

Later, as Ben lay in his bunk, Levi turned to face him across their tiny quarters. "Can I ask you something?"

Ben glared at him. "No, I'm sleeping."

Levi laughed. "Is there anything about you I don't know? Anything important?"

"I detest olives," he said warily. "And I especially love the smell of brown Windsor soap. How about you? Any secrets?"

Levi rolled over, pulling his thin blanket up to his chin. "I hate the smell of Windsor soap. I always tell my sister Anna to stop using it. Isn't that made with olive oil? You're a walking contradiction, Ben Chambers."

Ben laughed. "What can I say?"

Relieved that Levi seemed satisfied with his response, or at least he'd decided to drop it, he stretched out on his bunk, his feet dangling off the edge. Levi would give him the benefit of the doubt, he was sure. If he'd heard anything at all.

As he tried to drift to sleep, Ben imagined the clinking of champagne flutes and soft laughter drifting around a ballroom. Although he'd never been seasick a day in his life, his stomach turned at the thought. His mind spinning, he reached inside his bag hanging on the side of the bunk and pulled out a worn letter. The words were so familiar, it was impossible to read them in order—his eyes took in the whole thing as one blow to the chest, with certain phrases jumping from the page.

Dearest Benjamin,
    How could you leave… … … … … … … ..
    … … … be ashamed of… … … … … … … ..
    … … … … come back to me… … … … … …
    … … … … … … … I'm sorry… … … … …
    … … … … … … … … my love for you… … ..
    … … … … … … … … I still think of you…

He folded it gingerly and returned it to the tattered envelope. Although the words stung, the letter brought a familiar comfort. He could hear her voice, imagine her lilac scent.

At the end of the season, their ship would stop in Seattle to let the majority of the crew off, and he planned to disembark there as well. It could be a new start—the ocean nearby, easy access to hunting, and no one expecting anything from him. The territory was still wild, in the best way, and might provide the anonymity he craved, with an ocean voyage escape available at any moment. He was certain that in the frontier town, surrounded by trees and mountains, he could be anyone he wanted to be.

CHAPTER FOUR

THE DAMAGE

Anna's eyes burned, her eyelids weighed down as she sat motionless at the window where she'd stayed all night watching the dark smoke clouds reach the sky. Greta sat across from her, knitting with all her might.

"Where is he?" Greta held her hands to her cheeks, rubbing them slightly. Her Swedish accent had faded from decades in America; her voice had morphed into a friendly, easy drawl.

Anna rested her forehead against the glass pane. For reasons she couldn't understand, she didn't always feel at ease around Greta. "I'm sure he's just helping shop owners go through their things."

The aroma of her grandfather's unfinished woodwork, the wood-burning stove, and cinnamon cloves filled the room, calming her nerves.

"Oh, dear." Greta clasped her hands together near her chest. She wore an ivory cotton dress with a pattern of small pink roses and an embroidered lace collar. Her graying hair was braided and wrapped around the crown of her head.

Soot residue still clung to Anna's clothes, so she went to her room to change. It was a small space, but it was her safe haven. The circular rug, chunky and tightly knit, covered most of the hardwood floor. White linen curtains spanned her large window, and above her pinewood bed hung a framed cross-stitch she'd made as a girl. It was an old Irish saying: "Your feet will bring you where your heart is."

She pulled out a light cotton skirt and a white shirt with tiny yellow buttons. Her mother's cameo brooch sat on her dresser, and she traced the edges with her finger. It was carved from mother-of-pearl and set in a silver oval setting. The profile of a young woman's face looked to the left, her hair swept up gracefully on top of her head, a few loose curls escaping. Anna pinned it to her collar and used her small hand mirror to check her reflection before resuming her vigil.

Around seven in the morning, she sighed with relief as the front door finally creaked open. Her grandfather's white hair was singed at the tips, and his clothes were blackened. She couldn't remember what color his suit had been, but it was impossible to tell now. Only his red bowtie appeared untouched, and the splash of color made the red in his mostly white beard stand out.

He put his hand on Greta's cheek. "Our bookstore is safe, darling, but I'm sure Anna told you..."

Greta sat, her shoulders stooped over her lap, hands limp. "She did."

Her brown eyes glistened with tears. He sat in his chair, and Greta slowly stood, smoothing her skirts, then gently wiped ash and soot from his face with the cloth hanging from her apron.

"Mayor Moran took over when the firemen couldn't put it out." He shook his head. "They tried to use dynamite to take out buildings on either side of the street to stop it, but rubble from the explosions only served as kindling. Eventually, it simply spread until it ran out of buildings to burn."

Anna lowered herself to the floor near his chair. "That's terrible."

She felt guilty for how much she'd enjoyed running freely through the streets unaccompanied.

"You shouldn't have been out there, lass." He brushed more ash out of his hair and onto the floor. "Two hundred special deputies have been sworn in, and the city's under martial law. The entire business district burned."

Esther, the cat, weaved through his legs, purring loudly. The fluffy gray cat plopped down at his feet and stared up expectantly.

He stooped down and gave her one lengthwise stroke. "I'm grateful I went back in to look for you, lassie. I asked that man to escort you home."

"Doctor Evans. He did." The thrill of holding on to his arm had been nice, but she shook the thought away. She wanted to be with the kind of man who would let her fight fires along with him.

"We'll have to thank him, then." He kissed her forehead. "I'm going to get cleaned up, then head back to survey the damage. Help out where I can."

"Let's bring sandwiches. They'll be at it all day, won't they, Grandfather?"

He hesitated. "That'd be nice. But head straight home after. Wreckage is no place for unaccompanied ladies."

Anna frowned, but nodded. It didn't seem like the time to push her luck after they'd lost the shipment.

Two aprons hung in their spots near the wood-burning stove, and she tied hers snugly around her waist. Greta followed her into the kitchen. She had taught Anna how to cook at eleven years old, and chatting in the kitchen was the place they got along best. They fell into their usual positions, Greta cutting the meat, Anna cutting the bread.

"A man escorted you home, eh?" At barely five feet tall, Greta was a few inches shorter than Anna, and appeared even shorter hunched over the table working.

As she sliced bread, Anna glanced up with a small smile. Greta would have been fawning over Doctor Evans if she'd seen him. "He was a doctor."

She hesitated, holding the knife above the loaf, remembering the look on his face when they'd bumped into June. Could he tell she was a prostitute? She felt guilty for even wondering.

Greta looked up. "Handsome?"

Anna nodded with a half-smile.

Greta finished up with a pile of large slices, then wiped her hands on the brown cloth hanging from the pocket of her apron. "Perhaps he'll come to call."

"Maybe, but I don't want to get serious with anyone yet." She set down her knife, putting one hand on her hip. "I can't settle down until I do something great. But I do want a family and children of my own. One day."

Greta's eyes clouded over. A terrible knot formed in Anna's stomach. Greta hadn't been able to have children of her own. It would be better to just move on, perhaps even share something more personal with her, but she hesitated, wondering if she should be completely open with Greta. There was no reason not to trust and confide in her—maybe if she did it more often, it would feel more natural.

"I just need a purpose for my life besides marriage. Something adventurous." She raised one eyebrow at Greta and grinned.

"It wasn't proper for you to help with the fire. Or safe. Your skirts could have caught fire."

The issue of safety was certainly understandable, but propriety during an emergency made no sense. Apparently, the only proper way for a lady to help was to serve food to men.

Once they'd finished twenty sandwiches, they left for town. Seagulls flew overhead as the last of the flames died out. Seattle had burned through the night. Dust and ash swirled through the air as store owners rummaged through wreckage. Thank goodness their bookstore hadn't burned—that was a stroke of luck. Anna's chest tensed at the memory of the crate falling into the sea.

When they'd arrived from Ireland in 1874, they'd brought three trunks full of books, which her grandfather had turned into a fairly successful business. On the Washington frontier, fishermen, loggers, and homesteaders didn't have much time for books, but they got by.

As they walked down Front Street, some areas smoldered—red embers under bent steel, too hot to walk through. The air was still thick, and it was difficult to see more than a hundred feet. She held the large basket while Greta offered sandwiches to men covered in soot.

The smell of burning wood drifted through the air, and she coughed reflexively, her lungs still achy and congested. One store owner paused below his awning to put both hands over his face, kneeling to the ground. These were the unlucky ones. She frowned at her own ungratefulness, mourning a single shipment, while these men scoured to find anything left of value. She offered him a sandwich.

He wiped his face, leaving trails of dirt behind, then stood, using his knees to hoist himself up slowly.

"Thank you kindly, miss." He turned to her grandfather. "Did you hear there's to be a meeting of residents this afternoon? To discuss the best way to move forward."

Her grandfather perked up. "I'll be there, thank you."

"There's already rumors of aid flowin' in from cities near and far, even Tacoma." The man picked up a stack of plates.

"How will the money be divvied out?" Anna asked. Would they receive any? They had no fire insurance and no savings.

His face was sullen as he glanced around the devastated street. "Not sure 'bout that. I'm sure there's already a committee workin' on it, though. For now, we just need a good rain to soak the embers and clear the sky."

He tipped his hat and turned away.

Almost out of sandwiches, they walked to where the wharf used to be; charred wood floated lazily where the docks had been. Anna peered across to Ballast Island, recalling when she first arrived in Seattle and learned about the artificial landmass near the shoreline. Illegal dumping of rocks and filler material by watercraft had created the makeshift island over the years—a floating, shiftless mass that was barely fit for walking, let alone living.

The only people willing to venture out there were the people indigenous to the area. They had few other places to go in the city and were willing to take the risk. In the distance, she saw a figure with dark skin and black hair emerge from a makeshift residence on the island. She peered sideways at her grandfather and saw him scowl.

Her mind flashed to a teenage Duwamish boy, his long dark hair matted with blood. It was a scene from her childhood she wished to forget, but it remained vivid. She squeezed her eyes shut then looked toward the sky.

Her grandfather cleared his throat and groaned with irritation. "I need a stiff drink and a card game."

Greta huffed, and Anna bit her lip. Poker was his favorite pastime, and she knew the game would calm his nerves. He was quite good, but sometimes drinking turned into bad games and bad nights. On a handful of evenings, he'd come home having lost all the money they'd made at the bookstore for the whole month.

He dug around in his pockets. "The best medicine for loss would be to double the money we have left."

Greta's eyes widened. "Absolutely not, dear."

"Just teasing," he said with a tight smile. "Let's check on Pavlov, though."

Two blocks east, they pushed through double doors leading

into a near-empty saloon. Glass bottles lined the walls, and the man behind the bar greeted them heartily.

"I'm afraid we're not opening today, Oscar. The mayor issued an order saying no more drinking or gambling for the time being." He lowered his voice and leaned in. "But we're all going to Jimmy's house tonight."

Greta snorted and reached for her husband's arm. "I'm exhausted from stayin' up all night waitin' for you. And now that the food's gone, I suggest we all head home."

Anna watched their interaction with interest. She smiled at her grandfather as he offered his other arm to her.

"Quite right," he said good-naturedly. "I'll walk you lasses home then come back to help out a few friends."

Greta was being paranoid like usual—it had been quite some time since his drinking had gotten out of hand.

When they returned to the end of their street, he kissed them both and strode away. Reluctantly, she followed Greta into the house. Proper, agreeable Greta.

Inside, Greta went straight upstairs to sleep. Anna collapsed into the chair in front of the fire, her adrenaline still going.

It was a warm morning, and a day in the forest would be a great way to expend her pent-up energy. She tiptoed out and toward the forest at the back of their property. Before heading south, she turned to take in the sight of their house and the mountain beyond, which always brought her comfort. She had always imagined that if her mother were still alive, she'd somehow find a way to climb Mount Rainier, just to say she could.

Her parents had been adventurous—all the stories she'd heard assured her of this. Once, her mother had even survived three nights alone in the woods. The scent of the outdoors had always lingered in her mother's hugs. What kind of life would her parents have wanted for her?

She had been a terrified five-year-old when her grandfather

had decided he couldn't stand Ireland after his wife and only son died. He'd bought passage for himself, Anna, and her older brother, Levi. When they'd arrived in Washington Territory, her grandfather had built a crude cabin, which had felt nothing like home. Then, he'd made a land claim, with part of the acreage in the forest and the other part nestled up against the small logging town of Seattle.

After establishing a bookstore, they'd bought machine-milled lumber and, with the help of a few generous neighbors and Woodward's "Victorian Architecture and Rural Art" house plans, they'd built their sizeable house on the edge of the woods. It was two stories with four bedrooms and a large porch wrapping around, and when it was completed, Anna had finally felt at ease in the strange new land.

She turned away from her home, with the town streets to her right and Lake Washington to her left. Soon, she was surrounded by luscious greens and browns. Weaving through settlements and land claims until she reached the southern city boundary, she saw some tree trunks as thick as covered wagons and so tall the tops disappeared in the sky. She hiked south for hours, forgetting herself.

Many of her childhood years had been spent in the forest. She and Levi had made great sport of leaping over roots and using giant ferns to fan each other, pretending they were royalty. But her grandfather's warning had always echoed in her mind: *The violent Indians are deep in the woods.* Surely, they weren't all violent. After all, some of the men in town were violent—June's father, for one—but that didn't mean each new man she met would have the same tendency.

A sudden rustling of branches behind her made her knees weak. She turned, expecting a black bear to greet her on its hind legs, but instead a fat squirrel scurried up a spruce tree.

Anna caught her breath and willed herself to relax. She soon arrived in a clearing of tall, white prairie grass, where a single fox was cutting a trail down the middle. Mesmerized, she watched the lovely creature—maroon and black against rustling plant stalks.

Consumed with the sight, she jumped when a woman's calm voice came from behind her asking, "Are you lost?"

CHAPTER FIVE
THE BOOK

Anna spun around to see a woman about her age with copper skin, dark black hair, and a baby strapped to her back, standing surprisingly close to her. Her knees grew weak when she locked eyes with the Duwamish woman. Her cheekbones lifted elegantly, delicate eyebrows scrunched upward thoughtfully above dark eyes. The baby peered around her mother, squinting at Anna, offering a shy smile.

She could feel the blood pumping in her chest. "No, I'm not lost."

The woman tilted her head with a hesitant smile. "Okay."

She swallowed. Should she run? The dangers seemed minimal. The woman's long hair was in two neat braids. She stood tall—her shoulders broader than her hips, her demeanor friendly. She pursed her thick rose lips in an impatient smile, then turned on her heel and began to walk away.

Anna called after her, "Wait!"

The woman halted, but didn't turn. The baby twisted her head around to see Anna, letting out giggles of delight every time she caught a glimpse of her.

She had never encountered another woman in the woods. It was refreshing. "Do you live out here?"

The woman turned and gave her a long, measuring gaze. "Why do you ask?"

Her mind became an empty shell, and she stared blankly at the woman before her. "I don't know. I'm sorry to bother you."

The woman's face softened. "I do. Follow me."

A tingle moved up her spine as she followed the stranger. They came to a small clearing where a log cabin stood. It looked distinctly similar to the homesteading cabins built by pioneers and immigrants years ago—like the one she'd lived in for her first years in America. They had dismantled their own old cabin to repurpose the wood, but this one must have been abandoned, deep in the woods as it was.

She wondered if she'd soon be outnumbered. "Does your whole family live here?"

"My grandmother, daughter, and me—I'm Heather." She gestured for Anna to follow. "Please, come in."

She had questions, but she pushed uncertainty aside and followed Heather into the cabin. Surely, she didn't plan to harm her with a baby strapped to her back.

Heather added wood to the already blazing fire and stirred a pot of what smelled like stew.

"I'm Anna. Thank you for inviting me in," she said, finally relaxing. She paused before adding. "I've seen Indians in town sometimes, but I've never been in their homes."

Heather frowned and looked at her hands. "Are you afraid?"

Anna's cheeks warmed.

"No. I'm glad to meet you." She settled back into a wood chair near the fire, thinking of how she might fill the silence. "From my front porch, I can see the mountain. Providing it's not raining or foggy or the air isn't thick with smoke from the sawmill. Just after the rain ends, washing the sky so there's a clear view—it's gorgeous. Such a calming sight, don't you think?"

Heather sat near her. "It's a mighty mountain. Maybe climbing it would bring you joy."

Her heart pounded at her words. "I'd love to, but it would cost a fortune."

"My people call the mountain *Tuko'bad* because it's always covered in snow. It's the mother of our waters. Our stories say when it moved into place, its head was torn off in a fight. Then, it grew to new heights." Heather paused. "You'd need better boots, a fur vest, and confidence."

Anna's wheels were turning. "And quite a lot of training, I'm sure."

"Certainly. I don't know anyone who has attempted it."

"Where are the rest of your people? Don't Indians usually live with their extended families?"

Heather exhaled and gazed out the window, which Anna was surprised held a glass pane behind its thin curtain.

"Port Madison across the bay. We were all supposed to go after the treaty. But that's not our land. That's Suquamish land. We were supposed to get a Duwamish reservation by the lake and our river. But coal was discovered, and suddenly our longhouses were burned to the ground. They told us to leave the place of our ancestors and move onto another tribe's land. They think we're all the same." She scoffed.

"That's shocking," Anna said, aghast. Could that really be true? It seemed too awful. "I'm so sorry that happened."

Heather nodded with resignation.

"So...how did you end up here?"

"Our ancestral land is nearby, along the river. I found this cabin abandoned and moved in with my grandmother." Heather paused. "She doesn't speak English very often, though."

"Well, I'm glad you speak English. I'm sorry I can't speak your language. What's it called?"

Heather laughed softly.

"That's okay. We speak Lushootseed. My father taught me

English before he died." She grew quiet and glanced toward the window again.

"Both my parents died from smallpox in Ireland. Cashel was the name of our town." Anna swallowed hard as she remembered the low, comforting voice of her father—the sweet smell of her mother's hair. "I was heartbroken to leave, but my grandfather thought it best to bring us across the sea to a new life."

"I'm sorry," Heather said thoughtfully.

"But now my family owns a bookstore in town, which works out perfectly because I love to read."

Heather sat up straighter. "When we found this empty cabin, I found a book, but I can't read. Would you like it?"

Anna grinned. "Absolutely. Thank you so much."

It must have been left by the original pioneers who'd built the cabin.

Heather turned away from the fire to sift through some items in the corner of the room, then returned with a leather-bound book, a single ribbon marking a place at the beginning. The title page read "Анна Каренина," at which Anna cocked her head.

All of the text was in another language, but the name looked so similar to her own. She gingerly opened to the next page with her thumb and saw neat handwriting in the bottom right corner in English. She read the inscription aloud:

Natalya, dear, you're smart and kind, now simply clear your mind.
Your Christmas gift is hidden well, an emerald ring you'll find.
At first, you'll need to find a block, perhaps the kind that makes
the place of occidental rest so strong against the quakes.
And then, you'll need to find a rose, but not in thorny space.
Remember well the ship that brought us to this wondrous place.
To craft with wood or game alike, a tool one can't refuse.
The tool that Raskolnikov possessed but didn't use.
The first of men discovered this, the magic orange and red

to keep it here inside the house, it's made of brick instead.
Combine these all together now—you'll need each little part
to find the emerald ring, and then, forever have my heart.

— DIMITRI, 24 DECEMBER 1880

The words sounded at once familiar and foreign. The hairs on Anna's arm stood straight up.

Heather sat beside her, glancing at the inscription. "A riddle?"

"Sounds like it, with clues leading to a ring. An interesting mystery. What if it was never found? An emerald would be valuable. You could sell it."

Heather looked at her fingernails and seemed to consider it. "I don't know. I'm sure it involves going to town. I never go there. Perhaps you find it yourself, and it will take you up *Tuko'bad.*" Heather seemed pleased with the idea and nodded once before turning to ladle herself some stew.

"You sure?" Anna asked, incredulous.

Heather dismissed the idea with a wave of her hand.

"Maybe you can give me a book in English." Heather folded her arms across her chest. "For learning to read."

"Yes! A primer. I still have my old ones. I can get it for you today."

Her heart pounded a nervous rhythm. Were Dmitri and Natalya still alive? Perhaps the ring had already been found, but why was the book still wrapped at the bottom of an abandoned trunk full of blankets? She blew out an excited breath as she thought of the possibilities that might open up for her if the ring existed, if it hadn't yet been found, and if she were able to find it.

"I never go to your town," Heather repeated, bringing Anna back to the present. "I'm not wanted there, and I do *not* want to be there."

Heather turned to the fire to dish up a large bowl for Anna. It was delicious: duck and camas root stew that tasted like it was simmered over the fire all day.

Heather took her baby out of the wrap and snuggled her close. Anna's own mother flashed across her mind and, though the image of that warm smile was enchanting, the pain of the loss ached after the memory dissolved. With a soft light shining through the window behind her, Heather sat and nursed her baby.

Anna took another bite of stew. "Is that hard? Feeding your baby…"

"It wasn't as easy as I thought. My grandmother taught me." When the baby poked her head around, Heather stood, carrying the girl on her hip. "This is Pisha. She was born last summer. Would you like to hold her?"

Heather set Pisha down on the deerskin rug in front of Anna. The baby studied her with big brown eyes. Her skin was lighter than Heather's, and Anna wondered who the father was. She wasn't sure how to pick up a child so young, so she scooped her up like a cat. After setting her on her lap, she stroked her hair, but she stopped. Babies might not like that as much as cats.

"Only your grandmother and Pisha live with you?" she asked again, hoping Heather might divulge something about a lover— she was a lovely woman any man might find attractive.

Heather pulled a long, black braid over her shoulder with an amused smile then simply nodded.

Anna fell silent for a moment as she gazed out the window, noticing the sun was moving lower in the sky. "I should start finding my way home before dark."

"It'll be dark in three hours. I'll go with you most of the way." Heather scooped up the baby and handed Anna the book. "Take it."

"Thank you." She carried her bowl to the wooden basin she hoped was the sink. "Really, thank you so much."

Heather smiled warmly, putting a hand on Anna's arm for a moment, then motioned for her to follow.

She tried her best to keep up on what turned out to be a five-mile walk while her companion strode effortlessly. Clouds blanketed the forest, and a soft breeze rustled the dense trees.

"I can teach you how to find me." Heather tossed Anna a smile over her shoulder. "If you want to visit."

"I'd love that," Anna replied with an excited grin.

They made it to a clearing near town around dusk. A crescent moon rose through the trees, and a few stars pierced the darkness. Anna's body ached with exhaustion, and she wished she'd napped before the long walk. They followed the edge of the forest until her house came into view.

Heather eyed the soft city lights with her lips pursed together.

"We fish for salmon in our river next month. I can leave a note for you in August to meet again. Then I can teach you to find me. Good?" She raised her eyebrows slightly.

"Perfect." Anna offered her a hand to shake and gave the baby's hair two gentle strokes. "Bye, Pisha. See you in August."

As Heather disappeared into the forest, Anna hesitated a moment to admire the moonlit trees, outlined in silver against the night sky. Just then, a man's figure came into view about a hundred feet away, and she grew still. How long had he been watching her? He stood in the shadow of a fir tree, a rifle slung over his shoulder, an old army-issued hat low on his forehead. A scraggly beard covered his face, but when she turned to face him, he disappeared into the forest.

CHAPTER SIX
THE PLAN

The next morning, Anna opened her eyes to loud purring. Esther was curled up against her pillow, and as she sat up, excitement flooded through her. She looked to her nightstand where the leather-bound book lay, then around her room with a satisfied sigh. Sunshine poured in through the curtains, lighting the flecks of dust in the air so they seemed to sparkle. Her childhood doll still sat on her dresser—the one thing she'd been allowed to bring from Ireland besides a small bag of clothes. It had dark ringlets, a porcelain face, and a green dress with a Celtic knot embroidered on the front.

Her grandfather had been out late so she hadn't told him about Heather. Greta never pestered her about her whereabouts, and given how her grandfather felt about the Duwamish, it just seemed easier not to bring it up at all.

She dressed and grabbed her book. As she strode into the living room, she peeked out the window, hoping to see the mountain. It was half-visible through the remaining smoke that seemed determined to hover like fog. What would it be like to climb a mountain?

And why couldn't she get the idea out of her head?

She pictured the thick woods, the ice and snow past the tree line. After talking about it with Heather, it actually seemed to be in the realm of possibilities: the thrill of mountain air, the towering glaciers, the achievement of being a mountaineer—surely her parents would have been proud of that. She had never hiked through mountainous forest or icy terrain, but she'd spent plenty of time in the snowy woods, and she could train. With the possibility of an emerald ring to be found, she could barely contain the hope blossoming in her chest. Might it be worth enough to fund a mountain expedition?

She peered up the stairs, surprised her grandfather wasn't already rushing her to the bookstore. He usually liked to get an early start.

A knock on the door prompted Greta to call from the kitchen, "Can you get that?"

She opened the door, and June flashed a smile, then dipped into an ironic curtsy. Brass filigree buttons stood out against her purple silk dress, a large bustle trailing behind her.

"I hoped you'd come soon." Anna hugged her tightly.

Greta wiped her hands on her apron and rushed to embrace her. "Good to see you, dear."

June was grinning peacefully as she held onto Greta just a moment longer than usual. "You too."

"Our usual spot on the porch?" Anna grabbed June's hand as Greta returned to the kitchen humming a slow melody.

She sat on a large reclining wooden chair her grandfather had made and grinned at June. In the daylight, her usually hazel eyes looked light gray.

June lowered herself into a chair, then crossed her legs at the knee. "Well, the finest brothel in town burned to the ground."

Anna gasped.

"What? Are you all right? I had no idea. We walked through town but didn't make it that far south." She shook her head, still in shock. "Where have you been staying? You're always welcome here, you know that."

"One of my regulars offered to put me up. Bought me this new dress and everything." June grinned. "Our services are free to government officials, you know. They spoil us to make up for it."

"Is that how the infamous Lou Graham keeps the police away?"

June laughed. "Well, luckily she had plenty saved and has already commissioned a new stone building. I'll wager it'll be the first building erected in the rubble. That woman has connections, I tell ya what."

Anna nodded, then glanced toward town. "I hope Emily is safe. Did anyone die?"

June stiffened. "They're still searchin' the wreckage. No bodies yet. But I'm sure Emily's safe and sound with her rich husband in an ivory tower."

Anna frowned.

"I'm sure you're right. She wouldn't have purposely gone near the fire, anyway." Her gaze wandered south to Mount Rainier, and she swallowed the nervous lump in her throat. "Would it be crazy to climb the mountain?"

"What? Seriously?" June shook her head, then laughed. Her dimples were visible until the smile slowly faded and worry lines deepened in her usually smooth forehead. "Sounds awfully dangerous. Why bother?"

"I think I need to. To do something wild, get out of this city. To prove to myself I can." She paused to blow out a deep exhale. "I'll need money and a train ticket."

June grinned encouragingly. "Indeed."

Anna pulled out her new book.

"I met a Duwamish woman in the forest yesterday. I also saw a strange man watching us." She paused. He hadn't frightened her as much as made her wonder who he was. "Anyway, the woman gave me this. There are clues to find a ring, but I need to do some research to figure out if it's already been found. A mystery from the past! Isn't it incredible?"

June eyed the book warily. "A mysterious woman in the woods? I can't keep up with you sometimes."

"*If* I find the ring, I could use the money to join a mountaineering group and summit Mount Rainier."

"How much do you need? I can just loan you some." June pulled out her coin purse.

"I couldn't accept your hard-earned money!" She was moved by the gesture, though. "But thank you. Don't you have expenses to keep up with?"

"Mmhmm for boarding. You know, I *am* allowed to take money directly," June said with a sly smile. "A privilege reserved only for Lou's best girls. But I also gotta order new dresses and negligees every three months from Paris."

Anna's mind raced; if she couldn't find the ring, maybe she could join the brothel just long enough to earn some cash. But then she remembered the sandy-haired doctor. Maybe he was the adventurous, mountaineering type.

"I think Doctor Evans might ask to court me." She glanced up for her friend's reaction.

June smiled. "Continue."

"But gentlemen typically don't want their wives climbing mountains or traipsing around the forest." She twisted a lock of hair around her finger, then flung it away. "Just thinking about that makes me furious. It's a new world here. Women can build houses and chop down trees. We can do anything we want, June, but not from sitting rooms with respectable gentlemen expecting good behavior."

Anna paused and leaned forward. "Would I be better off joining up at the brothel for a few months? With my own money I could do whatever I want—go wherever I want."

"I don't know, Anna . . . It's not so bad being with fancy men

37

all the time. The whole thing is over before you know it." She smiled devilishly and rested her chin in her hand. "Some are more fun than others. You're still a virgin, though, aren't you?"

Anna's cheeks flushed. She'd never even been kissed. "I can't imagine it's so difficult, is it?"

"Course not. They all want the same things." June smoothed her dress, eyes down. "You mostly lie there and act like you've never done anything so fun and interesting in all your life. Usually does the trick."

June laughed and lifted her eyes to meet Anna's—she still sat with her elbow on the armrest, chin resting on her palm.

Could it be that easy? It wasn't that Anna didn't believe her, but there had to be more to it.

June bit her lip and put Anna's hand in hers. "But I'll tell ya this: two years of livin' there has been enough time to realize it's not the life I imagined. Actually, one week was long enough."

Anna looked down at June's hand over hers, then back into her eyes. Had it really been so bad for her?

"It seemed glamorous at first," June continued, "when new girls were escorted around town in fancy stage coaches so everyone could see 'em. But here I am now, confident that no man has ever truly loved me. And it's all I ever wanted—a family of my own. I was stupid to think I could find love at the brothel."

June's eyes became watery as she glanced up.

"You took the only job you could at the time," Anna said, tears coming to her eyes as well. "I wish you had moved in with us, but I know you wanted to earn your own keep and start saving."

"It's not like I had many job and housing options after my father threw me out." Her face steeled at the memory, then her voice grew quieter. "And I hate to admit it, but some of the men at the brothel are mean. They ask me to do things I'm ashamed of, and if I say no they leave."

Dread creeped over Anna, and she shuddered. "That's just

awful."

"Two things make my life bearable. It's a respected place, as brothels go. No violence allowed, and I have money and a room of my own." June closed her eyes and leaned back against the chair. "You have a good chance at findin' real love. I'm further than ever from havin' a family."

"Don't worry about the future, June. In a few years we'll run away together and build our own house in the woods. Live happily forever." Anna reached her hand to grab June's. "And we can learn to hunt with bows and arrows."

They both smiled, and Anna watched June's face relax. She let the notion of joining the brothel go. Being forced to let any man with cash caress her bare skin didn't seem like freedom at all. She'd lose all hope of marrying honorably. And although she'd had plenty of moments longing for that kind of closeness, she didn't know the first thing about entertaining a man.

June began drumming her fingers on her lips in thought.

"So, you think the doctor fancied you. Think about it: the wife of a handsome doctor, a house in town with lace curtains and glass dishes. Dinner parties and babies—you could have it all. I get marriage proposals all the time, but not from that type of man." She smiled broadly and winked.

"It's tempting. A Faustian bargain of sorts," Anna said with a mischievous smile.

June laughed. "You and your love of literature. I can't say that story was a favorite of mine."

Anna flashed a smile and looked up to the mountain—her mountain. "I should get to know him. If he's interested. I wonder if the good doctor might want to travel with me by his side? Climb mountains? You never know."

June seemed doubtful but shrugged.

"I'll see how things go and bring it up when the time's right. Nothing wrong with keeping a little mystery."

June laughed. "Now, tell me about this ring…"

CHAPTER SEVEN

THE STAIN

"Your grandfather has lost the last of our money." Greta fumed without looking up.

June had just left, and Anna had found Greta standing at the window staring down their hill over the city, a gray apron covering her plum and white pinstripe dress.

"He missed the meeting of residents, and he just crawled into bed two hours ago. Won't be opening the bookstore today."

Anna clung to her book, aghast at the thought. "Are you sure?"

"Soon as I saw him sneak up the stairs, reeking of whiskey and tobacco, I knew."

A sudden anger filled her. "Why would you assume he gambled away all our money just because he was drinking?" Her voice cracked on the last word. Greta didn't know her grandfather as well as she did.

"Dear," Greta began soothingly, "you know he's done it before."

"A long time ago. Why can't you believe that he's changed?"

Greta sighed. "See for yourself."

She pointed toward the moneybox in the kitchen. It had been full with nearly thirty dollars the last time Anna had checked. But peeking inside now felt like a betrayal.

"Well, perhaps he moved the money somewhere else. Or needed to buy some things." She walked to the kitchen window while Greta shook her head and sat by the fire to knit.

A few minutes later, her grandfather stumbled down the stairs with a cloud of whiskey stink surrounding him. He turned the water on and put his mouth under the stream, taking great gulps. Without turning it off, he felt behind him for a chair then melted into it, resting his head in his hands.

"I was trying to get some money for us, for the family…" He trailed off, clearing his throat.

Greta didn't look up from her knitting. A tightness wrapped around Anna's head, a piercing tension. It was hard to reconcile her beloved grandfather, who smelled like cinnamon and reminded her of Ireland, with the man who did things like this.

She turned the faucet off then put a hand on his shoulder. "But you didn't lose all of it, did you?"

His bloodshot eyes stared back at her with open shame. She turned away from him and returned to the kitchen window. Although it was a warm summer's day, she felt winter steadily, inevitably racing toward them. Their summer garden only contained sage, thyme, carrots, parsnips, and pea sprouts. Over the years, their family had come to rely on the markets and stores in town for fruits and vegetables, which were stocked nearly year-round thanks to frequent shipments in a port city.

Without the lost shipment, their bookstore wouldn't bring in enough income over the winter months to fill their pantry shelves, let alone restock the bookshelves. Their inventory of books would dwindle at the same time as the bounty of their garden. Her stomach twisted at the thought of not having enough food for the winter. It was in moments like this that she questioned her own selfishness; if she were married, it would be less of a burden on her family.

She pulled out her small notebook and ink pen. Her grandfather stood and crept back upstairs, taking each step slowly, stopping to groan at the top.

Tucking a stray lock of hair behind her ear, Anna kept her hand resting on the soft skin of her neck. They needed a new plan. She wrote a list: *Seeds to Buy: potatoes, squash, cabbage, onions, tomatoes, cucumbers.* It was still early June, so if she was lucky, she might have time before the first frost to grow enough food to last the winter—but it would be close. Hopefully winter would come late.

She squinted at Greta who drifted past her toward the oven. The smell of chocolate and butter filled the room as the older woman set a pan of cookies near the open window to cool.

"Now he'll sleep the day away. Best that way," she said, wiping her hands on her apron. "He didn't do it on purpose."

Anna glanced at her without responding. The small icebox sat in the corner, and she peered inside at the butter and milk. There would be no money to buy these things soon, but if they made enough jars of blackberry jam, sweet pickles, and stewed tomatoes, she could trade. If she stayed home from the bookstore in the late summer and early autumn, and if she and Greta worked hard, they might make enough to trade or sell at the market to supplement their flour, salt, and sugar.

She took inventory of the small pantry: two rows of thick shelves lined both sides. Spices, oils, and other staples were there now, but it would only be a matter of weeks before they disappeared.

"What are you thinkin'?" Greta's eyebrows were knit with concern.

Anna hated being wrong about her grandfather, but that wasn't Greta's fault. "Remember when you first married my grandfather, and you did all kinds of canning, preserving, and pickling?"

With a far-off smile, Greta nodded. "With my first husband, I faced greater times of need than you ever will in these modern times. Your grandfather is a fool for gamblin' with our money, but he's also the most positive and resourceful man I've ever known."

Anna frowned at the word "fool," but continued. "We need to take things into our own hands. Can you teach me some of the things you used to do before the markets? If we buy more seeds and turn up more rows, we can grow enough food to see us through the winter, and maybe even extra to sell to buy other ingredients."

Greta's eyes gleamed. "A mighty fine idea."

They decided to start by surveying the garden. It was much too small at just three rows. It would only provide a few extra sides of vegetables throughout the winter. Along the woodland border, there were bushes of raspberries and blackberries, already in full bloom. Humming a tune, Anna briskly covered the length of their yard, Greta beside her, as they checked on the five apple trees and two cherry trees.

Greta had a satisfied expression. "Trees look good. And there's more berries than we can eat."

"Plenty for preserving," Anna said, grinning at Greta.

They also inspected the root cellar, now mainly used to store the wine her grandfather made. The grassy roof stood only slightly higher than the ground—a wood awning held up the ground above the door, with shallow steps leading underground. Inside, thick darkness greeted her eyes; when they adjusted, she saw empty glasses lining the shelves and old, rotten piles of turnip heads someone had forgotten to plant. Such a waste.

Back in the kitchen, Greta started a pot boiling and turned with a smile. "We can start mid-August. It'll be fun."

"I'll have to wait for an opportune moment to bring the idea up with Grandfather—he'll miss me at the bookstore."

After graduating school three years prior, she had been working full-time at the bookstore with her grandfather. He likely didn't want to lose his favorite and only employee for weeks. There was no money to hire outside help, but there was nothing else to be done.

Later that evening, she settled in by the fire to read the newspaper. As she browsed, something caught her eye. It was an offhand reference in an article, about a woman named Isabella Bird who had traveled around the Rocky Mountains and climbed Longs Peak back in 1873.

Anna grinned and pulled the paper closer to her. There were women all over the country who had wild dreams. She cut the article out and tucked it into her pocket—a story to treasure, dream about, live up to. It felt as if her world was expanding with swift momentum, pulling her away from the mundane, into a delicious kind of life.

❦

THE NEXT MORNING, Anna tucked the book inside her bag as her grandfather thumped down the stairs, his slippers tapping each step rhythmically. As Greta had predicted, he'd spent the rest of the previous day sleeping, so Anna hadn't been able to show him the book or speak with him about her new plan for the winter.

"Good morning, lassie! I'm sorry," he said, embracing her in a warm hug. "Forgive me?"

Anna smiled half-heartedly, then nodded. He was difficult to stay mad at. She hooked the gold chain of her bag over her shoulder, clicking shut the clasp and admiring the embroidered bluebird and cherry blossoms covering it.

They walked to the bookstore arm in arm. She carried a basket of Greta's freshly made cookies and muffins, which always sold well.

"Why don't we stop by that doctor's office to thank him, eh?"

Her grandfather leaned in toward her with a twinkle in his eye, and she nodded.

They found white tents set up along Second Avenue, people conducting business in the swept-up aftermath. A long line had formed in front of a tent with a cloth banner stating "Tacoma Relief Bureau" hanging across the opening.

As they passed the line, Anna listened.

A stocky man removed his hat then wiped sweat from his glistening forehead. "One committee to widen streets and another to handle donations. First Regiment is guardin' property, but I already lost everything..." He turned away, and his voice melted into the hum of voices.

Beside them, the harbor was filled with merchant ships, fishing boats, and everything in between. She surveyed the piers to see if her brother Levi was in port early, even though his ship wasn't expected for another month at least. She ducked as two men made a sharp turn in front of them, carrying a load of cedar logs tied with thick twine.

Finally, they arrived at the office and met Doctor Evans's secretary who was a large woman with glasses and a gray bun. She waved them through to his office. A little boy of about eight whimpered in a chair while the doctor sat in front of him on a stool.

"Oh dear, sorry to disturb you. Didn't realize you had a patient," Anna said, turning on her heel and nearly bumping into her grandfather in her hurry.

The boy winked at her. "Ahh, I don't mind none."

Doctor Evans shrugged and waved them inside. "I suppose there's no harm. Come on in."

Anna blushed, but moved inside the room, nodding politely.

"Won't hurt much, right Doc? Promise?" the boy asked.

"Well, either way, William, you've a mighty fine story to tell. Jumping right out of a tree to catch a raccoon!" Doctor Evans folded his arms over his chest, betraying a smile.

He stood, his eyes drawn to Anna as he shook her grandfather's hand.

"How are you feeling, Miss Gallagher?" He motioned to the boy. "William has a shoulder out of socket."

Anna waved at the boy and turned to face the doctor. "I'm just fine. Wanted to say thank you for your assistance."

He had a different air about him at work—a quiet confidence.

Her grandfather took a seat on a wooden chair near the door. "Nice to meet you properly, Doctor Evans. Don't let us stop you. We can wait."

"Please, call me Connor." He drifted closer to Anna. "Why don't you give me a hand, Miss Gallagher?"

She nodded, placing her hat and purse on a seat near the door.

"Okay, son, let's get this shoulder back the way God intended."

Connor positioned her to hold William's arm just so, popped a candy stick into his patient's mouth, then yanked the arm quickly. A loud shout escaped from William's mouth, followed by a deep exhale. He grabbed the candy out of his mouth and gave a serious nod.

"You see, I'm tough like my Pa."

"You're the bravest boy I've ever had in my office, and I'll tell everyone so." Connor patted the boy on the back.

The way the little boy peered up at the doctor—with admiration and respect—gave Anna hope. It seemed there was more to him than what she could gather from their previous encounter.

The secretary rushed into the room. "Mr. Towers has come to fetch you on account of his wife takin' a fall!"

Anna glanced at her grandfather, and they both stood.

"We'll get out of your hair. I have critical bookstore business to attend to myself," her grandfather said with a chuckle.

Connor hastily gathered supplies, throwing them in a leather satchel, but his voice was calm.

"I'm really glad you stopped by. I've been wanting to speak with you." He turned to face Anna and reached for her hand. "May I call on you at home sometime? I'd love to get to know you and your family better."

She nodded, her heart skipping in its rhythm. Hopefully, he had an adventurous spirit in addition to being a handsome doctor who was kind to children.

Her grandfather happily clapped his hands together once, then cleared his throat.

Connor smiled broadly, turning to him. "Sorry to dash, but of course Mrs. Towers is in need. I'll be in California for a residency for the next four weeks, but I'd be honored to call on Anna when I return at the end of July."

CHAPTER EIGHT

THE TELEGRAM

Anna unlocked the heavy wooden door of the bookstore and swung it open. As she and her grandfather walked in, she flipped over the sign to read "Open."

With a white rag, her grandfather dusted every corner until the books looked new and the pinewood shelves shined. He wiped his large, rough hands on the front of his suit and glanced out the window into the busy street.

Anna remembered the book. Now was her chance.

"Look what I found." She certainly couldn't tell him a lovely Indian woman had given it to her in the cabin she'd reclaimed. She hesitated then blurted out, "It was...in an abandoned cabin."

He frowned and tilted his head to the side. "Are you sure it's abandoned? Where?"

"Definitely abandoned." She nodded emphatically as she eyed a low bookshelf that needed straightening.

He turned the leather-bound book over in his hands and touched the silk bookmark. The smell of old pages surrounded them, and he sighed contentedly. "Fascinating! This looks like Russian."

"Can you read Russian, Grandfather?"

He turned to the handwritten inscription, squinting and turning the book slightly to the left. "No lassie, I can't. But did you see this?"

She nodded, remaining silent while he read. Afterwards, he peered up at her with a curious lift of his eyebrows. "I suppose you're planning to solve this mystery?"

"Isn't it romantic? I feel like I'm diving into the past. Do you think it's solvable?" A mischievous smile danced on her lips.

He cleared his throat, straightening his blue and yellow patterned bowtie. "How do you know it hasn't already been solved—the ring found?"

"It was wrapped in paper, hidden at the bottom of a trunk in an abandoned cabin. I suspect it hadn't yet been given to Natalya." She paused and clasped her hands together. "Perhaps they still live around here. Do you suppose I could search for them?"

"Lassie, you can do anything." He studied the inscription. "Raskolnikov—do you think that's a friend of theirs?"

He handed the book back. "Or could he be referring to the character in *Crime and Punishment*? That's another Russian book. Let me see if we have it."

He kneeled and dragged his finger along a row of books.

Anna's shoulders slumped when he straightened up empty-handed.

"Let's stop by Pavlov's on our way home later. He knows most of the Russians in town, and maybe he knows more about this book."

Business was slow all day, and she couldn't stop thinking about the romantic inscription.

Soon it was time to close for the evening. Her grandfather grabbed his felt hat with a green feather, offering his arm to her.

They locked up and went to visit Pavlov, who was wiping beer glasses with a cloth behind the bar.

Pavlov slammed his fist down on the mahogany bar top. "It's too early for whiskey, old man!"

Anna glanced uneasily at her grandfather's deadpan expression. "Then what would you have me do, Pavlov, drink water like a commoner?"

"Fine, I'll give you some moonshine," he said with a chuckle, then turned to Anna. "Good afternoon, Miss Gallagher."

"Good to see you, sir." Anna pulled the book from her bag. "I was wondering if you were familiar with this book."

Pavlov took it and examined the cover approvingly. "A Russian masterpiece, to be certain. This is *Anna Karenina*."

Anna beamed at the sound of her own name. What were the chances? She looked to her grandfather with a delighted grin.

"I read this years ago, when it was published in installments in *The Russian Messenger*."

"Is it a good story?" she asked, leaning toward him.

"I can't say it has a happy ending, but there are beautiful moments. Anna thinks she wants one thing then realizes it's not quite what she hoped for after all." He turned to the first page and saw the neat handwriting. "Ooooh." He pulled out the glasses tucked into his front pocket and read silently. "A labyrinth of words. Just like Tolstoy himself. Let me read you the first line of the book: *All happy families are alike; each unhappy family is unhappy in its own way.*"

Anna glanced at her grandfather and cleared her throat. "Pavlov, do you know anyone named Dmitri or Natalya here in Seattle? Or who might have lived here in 1880?"

"I don't know anyone named Natalya. I did meet an old man named Dmitri last year, but he was just passing through to Oregon." Pavlov shrugged. "Perhaps this was a secret love, or a love that wasn't meant to be. Hard to say where these two are now."

He handed the book back to her with a wink.

Her grandfather slapped Pavlov on the back and ushered Anna out the doors, glaring at a table of rough-looking men who were eying her. "Well, lassie, you've found quite an intriguing mystery."

As they left, she thought about the old man Dmitri. It probably wasn't him.

At home, there was a welcoming aroma of ham and potatoes, and she went straight to the dining room where Greta set down a serving tray.

"And now we're plumb out of meat—this is the last of the ham," Greta said, nodding meaningfully at Anna as they all sat at the table.

Anna took a deep breath. "Grandfather, we need to prepare for winter. I'm going to start gathering blackberries and raspberries to make jams and jellies. And dry some along with herbs from the garden. Greta and I can make soap. Would you mind if I stayed home from the bookstore for a few weeks in the autumn?"

"Who'll talk about books with me all day?" he asked, his voice lifting in a mild panic. "I don't think all that's necessary anyway."

He pushed back from the table and crossed his arms. "We aren't the only ones putting in for a loan, but I'm sure we'll get one soon."

Greta set her knife down and cocked an eyebrow. "You're forever hopeful, and I love ya for it, but Anna's right. As of right now, we have no cash, and a low stock at the shop. I won't even be able to bake things for the store soon. If we have a fully stocked cellar we'll have food for the winter and a bounty to sell and trade for meat, flour, and butter."

He glanced from one lady to the other then shrugged. "You're both right."

Anna smiled. "Can you clean out the old root cellar? We'll use every corner of it to store food."

He nodded.

"Can you turn up three more rows next to the garden?" Greta chimed in. "And build a three-foot-high fence around it? Our garden has just become precious, and we need to keep the rabbits and deer away."

"Yes ma'am." His face softened, and he turned to Anna. "Lassie, play your cards right, and you'll be married to that doctor come springtime. Why, you might even have a housekeeper!"

"You know I don't care about all that." Surely, he knew her better than that.

Her grandfather sighed. "I just want the best for you."

⚜

On a hot evening in July, Anna snuck into the newly constructed brothel, a gorgeous stone building, to visit June. A month of hot and dry days had passed quickly. She had spent much of her time dreaming of the mountain and trying to decipher the mysterious inscription.

Oppressively warm days with no breeze were often slow at the brothel—the stagnant heat made any indoor activity miserable, and June was usually free for a visit.

"I can't believe this place was built so quickly," Anna said as she sat at the chair in front of the large mirror. "It's even nicer than before."

"Isn't it?" June reached behind her back with a skilled hand to untie her white silk and ribbon corset, then walked behind the four-panel room divider for privacy. She returned in her favorite cotton nightgown, flinging herself backwards onto the bed.

"Two of my customers today were city council members." June's hair surrounded her in a halo, and she gathered all her blond curls in a spiral on the top of her head. "They would *not* stop talkin' about the plans to rebuild. They're both certain Seattle will become even greater. The streets are gonna be rebuilt higher above sea level this time, to prevent our sewage woes, which I'm all too familiar with."

Anna sat next to June and grabbed a brightly colored fan from her nightstand. "You meet the most interesting people."

June shrugged matter-of-factly.

"One was goin' on about new architects commissioned to create stone and brick buildings. He was borin' me to death until he mentioned about a million rats died in the flames." She threw her head back and laughed with glee.

Anna smiled. The dirty apartment of June's childhood had been crawling with rats and, whenever the tide was in, the smell of backed up sewage.

"The doctor *did* ask to call on me," she said. "I'm not sure what to make of him, but he's been out of town for weeks now, so we haven't actually spent any time together yet. I should see him soon though."

"That'll be interesting." June sat up and rubbed rose-scented lotion into her delicate legs and arms. Every inch of her skin was smooth, with only a few freckles gracing her face and neck. She pulled out her birthday music box and cranked the handle. "I imagine you'll soon be married like Emily."

"Come with me to visit her sometime," Anna said, touching the box delicately.

June narrowed her eyes and pulled it out of her reach. "Why would you even ask that? To embarrass me?"

"Of course not!" She shook her head rapidly, her mouth dry. "I just need you two to reconcile. I hate the separation. Wouldn't it be great for things to be how they used to be?"

"Honestly, you don't understand anything. I think you should leave." June strode toward the door.

"June, I didn't mean to upset you."

"Please, just go."

Anna tilted her head as she tried to read June's face, torn on whether to stay or go. She could tell it would be a while before June would be calm enough to listen, so she moved toward the door. She tried to catch her eye before leaving, but June kept her gaze fixed on the music box that had just finished playing.

As she made her way home, she felt a surge of guilt for bringing up Emily yet again and agitating June. She remembered sharing her slate and chalk with June as a ten-year-old—they'd been innocent and light-hearted then, Emily giggling beside them. The three had been inseparable until they'd grown up and things had gotten complicated.

When she reached home, there was a telegram waiting for her from Doctor Evans.

- ARRIVING SUNDAY. WILL CALL ON YOU THAT EVENING. -

Short and direct. It felt good to be desired. He'd been so sweet with his young patient—did he want a son of his own, perhaps?

She could hear her grandfather's voice coming from the kitchen, and as she entered the room he slammed a document down on the table.

"Loan declined." His face clouded, and he crossed his arms over his chest. "And it looks like the aid money is only for those who experienced a total loss."

Anna studied the document. "It says they received too many loan applications at once. I'm sure every businessman in Seattle needs a loan to get their business running again."

"They gave loans to some people. Why not me? Is it on account of me being Irish? Bloody bankers!"

"I doubt that had anything to do with it, dear," Greta said reassuringly.

His face softened. "I don't have much to leave you ladies after I'm gone. I at least want there to be a family business."

Anna said nothing. She loved the bookstore but couldn't imagine being tied down to Seattle forever. Imagining life without her grandfather was unnerving, but she knew that Greta would certainly be in a worse situation than she if they were to lose him.

CHAPTER NINE
THE APOLOGY

O n Sunday evening, a knock sounded at the door, and the doctor stood on the porch, hat in hand. Greta invited him into the house where they joined Anna near the fire.

"Miss Gallagher, you look lovely." Connor held his top hat close to his chest.

She blushed as she stood, fiddling with the tiny black buttons on the cuffs of her white dress. "Call me Anna. I'm happy to see you again."

"The pleasure's all mine, I assure you."

Her grandfather offered Connor a glass of wine, which he gladly accepted, and Greta set out a plate of cheese and bread.

Anna sipped her wine, watching Connor's hands as he sliced the bread. Afterwards, he moved toward her with a shy smile.

"So, Anna, how do you spend your days, if I may ask?"

"I work at my grandfather's bookstore." She grinned, feeling more relaxed. His dark blue eyes focused intently on her. "I feel at home surrounded by books."

She remembered *Anna Karenina* and pulled it out, showing

him the inscription. "It's interesting, right? I believe it was hidden or lost before it could be given as a gift."

She scrutinized his face to ascertain his opinion as she listened.

He lifted his eyebrows. "It could be fun to solve the riddle. It sounds like a lovely book as well; I think I've heard of it. Is it by a British author?"

She twisted a stray lock of hair in her fingers. "No, it's by a Russian man named Tolstoy. The whole book is in Russian, unfortunately."

He nodded as he finished his wine, setting the glass down on the mantle. "Would the ladies like to accompany me on a walk near the docks for the sunset?"

Greta agreed and put a light shawl around her shoulders. Anna tucked the book into her purse then positioned her hat on her head.

"Shall we take a trolley?" he asked once they reached the cobblestone road.

Anna smiled brightly. "I'd enjoy the walk."

She felt like royalty in her best white silk dress, soaking in all the looks they received. An old lady nodded her approval and waved a greeting, and a young girl gazed admiringly at her elegance, or so she imagined.

"There's a town dance in two weeks," Connor said with a small flourish of his hand. "On a Friday, the second of August. Would you come with me?"

She smiled and nodded gracefully. "I'd love that."

As they arrived at the docks, Greta found a bench. "My feet are tired. I'll wait right here and watch the sunset."

Anna gave her a grateful look, then held on tightly to Connor's arm, admiring the boats as they continued on without her. She noticed a hawk flying over the gently rippling water, its wings inches from the surface with every flap for nearly a hundred feet before rising into the sky. After a moment of silence, she pulled out the book from her purse.

"It's not the first clue, but I thought since we're at the harbor we could investigate." She studied his face.

He straightened his top hat with a distinguished nod. "If you like."

"*'And then, you'll need to find a rose, but not in thorny space. Remember well the ship that brought us to this wondrous place.'* We can read ship names to see if any might have been from the poem, or speak with captains. What do you think?"

Connor smirked and stared out at the distant water. "Yes, let's read off a few. I always find them amusing."

Anna announced the name of each ship as they passed its place on the dock. *Alki. Barbara. Walla Walla.* She didn't know how to figure out which ship might have brought Russians to Seattle in the past. Some boats were fishing vessels, and others were meant for passengers, but even if the ships were old enough, the captains might come and go with the seasons.

"I'm curious to hear your thoughts, Connor." She peered up at him expectantly, adjusting her delicate lace shawl.

He pursed his lips together. "To be honest, since you don't know to whom this book originally belonged, it would be near impossible to figure out on what ship they came to America. And that ship might not even still be in use—you know—they don't last forever. Don't fret about a childish riddle. Let's just admire the ships."

So much for the charm. A change of subject was in order. She took firmer hold of his arm. "Do you spend much time outdoors?"

"I stay awfully busy with patients. I'd love to have you stop by my office again. You could stay for the day and pass out peppermint sticks to children. Would you like to?"

"I'd love to." She glanced at him sidelong, wondering if she was misreading him about the inscription. "We should head back now."

In the distance, boats sailed away, and she looked farther south to gaze at the snow-capped mountain. As they made their way back, she pictured herself surrounded by thick, snow-covered pine trees, halfway up the great heights. Her stomach tingled with a rush of excitement, her mind imagining the view as she presided over the busy city. She longed to slip through silent alpine trees, higher and higher.

After they returned, Connor tipped his hat happily then strode away as if they'd made a great connection. Anna was more confused than ever as she watched him leave.

"How'd it go, dear?" Greta asked, concern in her eyes.

"Oh, not bad I guess," she mumbled. She cozied herself into a rocking chair near the fire and sighed deeply as Esther jumped onto her lap.

Her grandfather seemed pleased with that answer and retrieved a bottle of his currant wine from the cellar while she flipped through the pages of a book catalogue from a publisher. The coffee table was covered with newspapers and magazine subscriptions from New York and Boston. Her grandfather liked to stay apprised of the latest in the publishing industry.

"I'll put in a new loan application at a different bank first thing tomorrow. It'll be approved soon, and we can order our usual favorites, *Wuthering Heights* and *Frankenstein,* although I've seen interesting new publications as well, *The Adventures of Huckleberry Finn,* and *The Strange Case of Dr. Jekyll and Mr. Hyde.*"

Anna flipped to the back of the catalogue. "Excellent. And besides novels, we need blank books, school books, and pocket books. We're extremely low on loose paper, envelopes, pencils, and ink pens."

He sighed. "I'll bring some of our books to fill the empty shelves. For now."

She swallowed, her stomach dropping. It was the right thing to do, but it was still difficult.

"Will you work at the bookstore after you're married? I know you've loved spending all your time there since you graduated."

She smiled broadly. "I can't imagine ever quitting the bookstore, even when I do marry."

His heavy eyes closed, and he let his head rest against the chair. "I can just picture you as a young girl of eight, when you thought I was the most wonderful person in all the world. If only you could stay with me forever."

A smile danced on his lips, and he lowered his voice, peeking toward the kitchen where Greta stood in front of the sink. "Sometimes it feels like you're the last of Ireland, and my heart aches to be back, a lifetime ago, when everything was as it should be."

"I love you, Grandfather." She patted his hand before heading to her room.

Speaking of things that ought to be—it was time to write to June. Her stationery and fountain pen were on her nightstand, and she lit two candles on either side, arranging them into their brass holders.

Dearest June,

I hope you'll forgive me. But I long for things to be the way they used to be between the three of us. If you don't care to reconcile with Emily, then I'll leave it be. You're my best friend. If you forgive me, would you come over before the town dance in two weeks? We could do each other's hair. I'm nervous for the dance, and I'd love to see you.

All my love,
Anna Gallagher

CHAPTER TEN
THE HOUSE GUEST

Anna leaned against the rail on the dock, straining to see if her brother was on the boat as it sailed into port. It wasn't uncommon for Levi to be gone for months at a time, but she always missed him dearly. It was a warm Thursday afternoon, the first day of August, and the clouds had lifted, sun shining through them. Her dark green summer dress rustled in the breeze, and the silk ribbon neckline felt soft against her skin.

Her brother's figure came into view as the ship glided closer. On the tips of her toes, she waved wildly, her gathered chiffon sleeves hiking up to her elbow.

Soon the vessel found its berth on the dock, and there was a flurry of men throwing ropes and jumping ashore. The tall masts seemed to tower over them, and the boat rocked with the slapping waves. She spotted Levi running toward her and felt a leap of excitement. He was thinner than she remembered, which made him look taller. His light brown hair reached nearly to his neck with scraggly, sea-blown tangles.

Levi threw his lean arms around his sister. "You came!"

"Course I did." The overwhelming smell of old fish and

unbathed men surrounded him. She stepped back. "I got your letter from Juneau. I've been bursting to see you! How'd it go?"

"Let me show ya." He jumped back onto the boat and grabbed one end of a large wooden box; another man helped him carry it down the gangplank. "This is Benjamin Chambers, a hunter from California. And *this* is our combined loot."

Levi's green eyes sparkled under thick eyebrows, and his smile revealed the small gap in his front teeth.

"How do you do, Mr. Chambers?" Anna surveyed the box. "Well done, gentlemen."

Ben lifted his hat, uncovering dark brown hair as messy as Levi's, except his fell softly around his ears. His large, muscular arms crossed over his wide chest. "Pleasure to meet you, Miss Gallagher. I've heard a lot about you. Do you still pull Levi's hair when he ignores you?"

She grimaced. "Levi, stop telling stories from when I was a child."

"You're still my sweet little sister who hates to be ignored." He hugged her, lifting her off her feet and swinging her around, skirts flying. "Mind if Ben stays with us for a while? He might move here but wants to see how he likes it."

She attempted to wipe the fish grease off the bodice of her dress. "I don't see why not."

Levi used a long piece of iron to pry the box open, revealing four giant halibut inside, packed with chunks of glacial ice.

Her hand flew to her mouth in delight. "I'm always amazed at how big they are!"

Levi closed it, and they loaded it onto the hired wagon Anna had waiting, waving goodbye to their shipmates. Pocketing the cash they'd been given by the captain, Levi and Ben hopped up on to the wagon next to her.

"You're nineteen still, right?" Levi put his arm around her, and the wagon lurched forward.

She leaned back against his shoulder. "Twenty in a couple weeks."

"So young still. Ben's turning twenty-three in October, then he'll be as old as me." He punched Ben playfully on the arm, then turned back to her. "Any marriage prospects?"

Her heart fell. Was her brother going to start pressuring her about marriage, too? She felt enough weight attached to her romantic life already. "I did meet a man who fancies me."

Levi narrowed his eyes. "Hold on. Who's this man who thinks he can woo my sister? What's his profession?"

"He's a doctor. I can't say I know him very well yet, but he's taking me to a dance tomorrow. You should accompany us so Greta doesn't have to."

Levi looked to Ben, who shrugged.

"We'll go. I feel like the king of the world with all this fish and money in my pocket!" He squeezed Anna's shoulders with both hands. "When'd you get so pretty? Ya look just like her."

Anna blushed. "Thanks."

She only had one photograph of her mother, but everyone said how lovely she'd been. She only remembered how it felt to be wrapped in her arms, how she smelled, her smile. She played with a single brown curl that had fallen out of place.

Ben watched the movement of her hands. "I promise I won't intrude for long. Thank you again for letting me stay awhile."

"It's nothing, Mr. Chambers. Grandfather will be happy to have another man in the house."

"Please, call me Ben."

Anna took a closer look at his face. He had fine, white teeth and a long brown beard that hid much of his face. His dark brown eyes exuded an honest happiness.

"What attracted you to Seattle, Ben?" she asked.

Ben slapped Levi on the back. "Well my best friend calls it home."

Levi shrugged and stretched his legs out, crossing them at the ankles.

She watched their interactions and chuckled. "You'll like it. Did you know we'll soon be granted statehood? Then we'll be able to vote for our own governor rather than having one appointed to us."

Ben rested his elbows on his knees, leaning forward. "And that's important to you?"

She grinned with amusement. "Of course—well, *women* can't vote yet, but that's another story. As an official state, Washington can decide for itself what's essential—roads, schools, and of course libraries."

Ben listened intently. "I don't think I've ever met anyone quite like you, Miss Gallagher."

"I believe that's a compliment, so thank you." She smiled, settling back in her seat next to her brother, and began pointing out buildings damaged in the fire.

While they were busy chatting, Ben pulled a letter out, leaned back in his seat, and started reading.

Anna lowered her voice and leaned in to her brother. "We lost a shipment in the fire. There's no money to buy winter inventory, and Grandfather has already been declined a loan."

Levi's mouth dropped open, and he put his hand to his pocket. "I wonder if Grandfather would accept any cash."

"Doubtful. He'll say to put it in the bank. But don't worry. Greta and I are working on stockpiling goods."

"You'll be married soon and not have to worry about this kind of thing." Levi winked.

Anna tried to smile at him, but the muscles in her face weren't cooperating.

Their wagon turned the last corner onto the dirt path to the Gallagher house.

"Does city water reach your house?" Ben eyed the property.

Anna admired their fruit trees and growing garden with

pride. "Barely, thank goodness. It almost didn't, but Grandfather petitioned, and they laid pipes under our street. Can't say it tastes better than well water, but it's certainly more convenient."

Her grandfather and Greta were sitting on the porch waving to the wagon. A formidable feast awaited—beefsteak and potatoes, with sweet buns in the oven for dessert. They had spent some of their precious recent earnings to purchase the beef. Levi's homecoming was a special occasion. Greta opened a bottle of wine while hugs and greetings circled around. Between the smell of sweet buns baking and having Levi home, Anna felt the enchanting sense of a holiday.

Her grandfather shook Ben's hand and welcomed him to stay for as long as he needed. "You both look like you've been gone for years. Were there no scissors aboard, lads?"

Levi chuckled. "Baths and groomin' would be nice."

Greta motioned for the boys to go upstairs. "Of course. Baths first."

Levi took Ben up the stairs to show him around then trotted back downstairs. He motioned for Anna to come close, then whispered, "Don't be alone with him, ya hear?"

"Why?" She wasn't sure whether she should be curious or insulted. Ben seemed like a gentleman.

Levi folded his arms. "I mean, he's a good man—good friend o' mine for a long time. I know he's a handsome fellow, strapping hunter and all. Just don't go fallin' for him. You could easily marry up—I hope you do."

"Thanks for the warning. I'll try to save myself for someone richer." She rolled her eyes and strode back into the kitchen.

"Oh, come on..." Levi threw his hands in the air then raced back upstairs to bathe.

Later, Ben came down with one hand on the pine banister. He flashed a smile at Anna and ducked his head as he passed the threshold into the living room. His soft brown hair was combed to the side, much shorter than it had been.

With a captivating smile, he ran a hand over his newly close-cropped beard, which highlighted his square jaw. "I feel like a new man."

"You certainly smell better," Anna teased.

All at once, she didn't know what to do with her hands and so rested them awkwardly in her lap.

CHAPTER ELEVEN
THE MYSTERY

B en blushed as an embarrassed grin spread over his face. He seemed too large for the cozy living room, with his long legs and broad shoulders. He glanced to the fireplace then at the hand-crafted oak chairs. "You have a lovely home."

"Thank you. We're glad to have you...visiting."

How long was he planning to stay? She drummed her fingers on her knee and watched him adjust his shirt collar.

"Don't worry, shouldn't be in your hair too long." His lips curved up in a playful smile.

Levi came bounding down the stairs moments later.

Greta was beaming, and her voice was almost musical. "Everyone, find a place and dish up."

"This looks amazing. I don't know how I can thank you." Ben placed a napkin on his lap. "It's such a treat after being at sea. We haven't had such great-smelling food in ages."

Greta smiled bashfully. "Where are you from, Mr. Chambers? Tell us more about yourself."

"Berkeley, California, ma'am. But I spend most of my time hunting in Oregon, especially in the spring before fishing season.

I trade with Indians and at trading posts. Let's see, what else...
There's nothing I enjoy more than being deep in the forest."

Greta nodded. "Speaking of Indians, I saw Princess Angeline,
Chief Seattle's daughter, by the docks. Such a shack she lives in, I
feel sorry for her."

Her grandfather grumbled under his breath, but Greta
silenced him with a look.

Levi furrowed his eyebrows. "I thought they passed a law
moving all Indians to reservations."

"That they did, lad. Clearly, there are a few stragglers." He
rubbed the back of his neck, his face tightening.

Anna cleared her throat, hesitant to side with Greta, but
wanting to defend Heather. "I always see Duwamish people
selling those lovely baskets at the market. They're high-quality,
and the women always seem kind."

Ben sliced a forkful of steak, then paused, as if considering if
he should meddle. "I've met a number Indians in Oregon. I've
traded furs and meat. Most seem honest and good-natured."

"When I was a little girl, the Indians helped us through the
famine," Greta said, passing the potatoes to her right. "So many
men married native women back then. It wasn't until those
Mercer girls arrived—a whole slew of American and European
girls—when it suddenly became looked down upon to have a
dark-skinned wife."

Anna thought of the burned longhouses Heather had told
her about. It was so evil it made her shudder.

Her grandfather's cheeks reddened. "Well, they aren't
welcome in this house, or this city. The charter—the Fifth
Ordinance—says they cannot build houses on city land."

Greta stood and collected plates. "Who's ready for sweet
buns? More coffee?"

As Greta, Levi, and Ben had dessert, Anna pulled a large
blanket from a wooden trunk, wrapped it around her shoulders,
and sat on the floor by the fire.

Her grandfather stood at the fireplace with one hand in his pocket, sipping his wine. "Are you excited for the dance tomorrow?"

She nodded, but she knew her grandfather could see her nerves.

"I want you to be happy." He sighed, his face softening. "I'm sorry for pushing you about it. I just want you happily married soon so you can start your life as a proper lady contributing to society. Ladies will be allowed to vote soon, mark my words."

He pointed his finger toward the ceiling for dramatic emphasis, and Anna laughed.

When everyone joined them, he turned to Ben. "It sounds like you spend a lot of time hunting? What type of weapons do you use, lad?"

Ben nodded, squaring his shoulders "Mainly my bow. I hunt anything I can eat or that has good fur: deer, rabbits, squirrels, the occasional elk."

Assuming she wouldn't be invited to the hunting conversation, Anna grabbed her book off the shelf. She turned the page to the silk ribbon bookmark, enjoying the full measure of its loveliness, its history.

Ben leaned toward her curiously. "What are you reading?"

"Well, I can't actually read this—it's in Russian. It's called *Anna Karenina*." She ran a finger along the spine.

He nodded knowingly. "Ah, a Russian novel. Have you heard of Dostoevsky? There are so many wonderful books coming from Russia these days, it's hard to keep up."

She studied him in disbelief. "I did not fancy you as a lover of literature."

The man was certainly a mix of unexpected traits. This hunter—this fisherman—easy-going friend of her big brother, was surprising her in the best way.

"I went to the University of California. My father's a

professor there. He made sure his only son had a good education."

Her heart pounded, and she wished she could reveal the true history of the book.

"May I?" He held out his hand.

"Of course."

She handed him the book, and he placed it in his lap, opening to the first page.

He ran his finger along the neatly written inscription. "Any idea who wrote this?"

"No, I don't think they live here anymore. It's a list of clues, though." As she spoke, she grew embarrassed. "I've been told I shouldn't waste my time on a childish riddle. It probably leads nowhere."

He raised his eyebrows in surprise. "What in the world could be a better use of time than a mysterious treasure hunt from the past? I can't think of anything I'd rather do. Let me get my glasses from upstairs."

Anna's chest expanded as she finally inhaled, her skin tingling with excitement. Greta exchanged an amused glance with her husband.

Ben bounded back down the stairs. "I sure love a good riddle, and this has the added mystery of not knowing who wrote it, or if it can still be solved."

His enthusiasm was infectious. Maybe the riddle really would lead to a genuine adventure.

He read the first clue aloud. *"'At first, you'll need to find a block, perhaps the kind that make the place of occidental rest, so strong against the quakes.'* Hmm the place of occidental rest. Could that refer to Chinese immigrants?"

Anna shrugged.

An amused grin spread across her grandfather's face as he watched the two hunched over the book on the floor. "No. Occidental refers to the West, not the Orient."

"I stayed at the Occidental Hotel last year. The *Post-Intelligencer* said it's the grandest in town. Maybe he's referring to that?"

Anna tilted her head in thought, and her grandfather rested his wine glass on the sturdy arm of his chair. "You may be right, lad. Sadly, it was destroyed in the fire. Watched it burn with my own eyes."

Ben made a disappointed grunt. "I can't remember what it was made of."

Levi yawned and rubbed his eyes. "Stone or brick. Supposed to be fire resistant."

"Have they rebuilt?" Ben asked.

"Not sure," Anna replied. "They're mostly building on top of destroyed buildings right now, so it's possible. They've erected stilts to raise the new business district, but you still have to walk on the ground below."

"Should we explore the site sometime?" Ben's eyes danced. "There'll be remnants of the old building."

Anna nodded eagerly. "Absolutely!"

Ben held her gaze with a focused look that put a delightful chill through her, like drinking cold water on a warm day.

Levi had been staring into the fire. "Wait, what's the plan?"

He stretched his arms over his head sleepily.

"Your sister has discovered a mystery that must be solved at once," Ben said, breaking eye contact with Anna and returning the book to her hands. "The additional clues should be easier once we get the first."

He turned toward her grandfather. "Thank you again, Mr. Gallagher, for your hospitality. I'm exhausted—better get to bed."

"Happy to have you. You're welcome to stay awhile if you don't need to get home soon."

"I don't expect to ever return to California, sir." Ben's voice had gotten deeper, and he stared down at his feet. "Goodnight, all."

A gentle joy buoyed Anna as she watched him walk up the stairs. A lightness filled her chest. Finally, someone understood the significance and delight of finding an inscription that had been written but never received. The love abandoned or lost; the ring longing to be found.

She remained in the living room after everyone else had gone to bed, rocking in a cedar chair, a candle on the table beside her. Even though she still didn't know Connor all that well, she was excited for the dance the next evening—dressing up, taking a horse-drawn coach, the whole atmosphere would be electric. In the past she'd gone to dances with her brother or Emily, but never in the company of a handsome doctor. It would be the perfect time to bring up the mountain.

CHAPTER TWELVE

THE DANCE

"It looks absolutely stunning on you," the store clerk said, with a flourish of her hand.

Anna spun around in front of the tall mirror. The dress was made of pink chiffon and yellow lace, with gold trim along the hem. She had no money to buy a new dress, but she couldn't help visiting a dress shop after work anyway.

"This lovely dress was purchased from a catalog for the town dance, but the lady decided she didn't want it after all." The store clerk huffed, but quickly recovered herself.

The only mirror she had at home was a small hand mirror that had belonged to her mother, so it seemed strange to see her entire body at once, especially in such a fancy dress. Her dark hair and light eyes appeared foreign to her—she had so few occasions to see her blossoming figure in something so elegant. Connor's confident face filled her mind, as did the memory of his hands around her shoulders as he carried her.

"Do you want to try on a hat as well, miss?"

"No, thank you. I've spent too long here already."

Anna took one last glance at her silhouette as she turned

back behind the curtain to take everything off. As she pulled the curtain closed, two women strolled in wearing low-cut dresses and bright makeup. The other ladies in the shop began whispering, and the clerk retreated to the back room, mumbling about something she'd forgot. The prostitutes ignored the lack of greeting and browsed the few dresses on the rack before flipping through the catalog on the polished oak counter.

Anna hated to think of June being dismissed that way, but it was reality. The women likely had money to spend on new dresses and accoutrements, but the store's clerk seemed to care little about that. Perception was everything, and a store's reputation depended on its patronage.

At home, she chose one of the two evening dresses she owned and twirled around her bedroom in her lavender silk dress, just for practice. The white lace and ruffles at the hem whirled in a perfect circle. The shoulders had just the right amount of puffy height, with ruffles on the cap sleeves. Waves of shimmering beads sewn into the waist emphasized her curves, which were also accentuated by the corset she hardly ever wore.

When June arrived at five, Anna was overjoyed. Her friend wore a green velvet dress and bright red lipstick, pearl hair pins and comb in hand.

Anna squeezed her in a hug before searching her eyes for understanding. "I wasn't sure you'd come."

June shrugged. "Course I was gonna come."

Anna smiled and took her hand, leading her upstairs to her bedroom where Greta was helping her get ready. She had made her bed neatly—a white quilt with lace around the edges, and two threadbare pillows. June perched at the foot of the bed, smoothing her dress in front of her. Anna picked up her hair brush from the wooden dresser that her grandfather had built and engraved with ivy leaves.

"Nights like tonight are some of my busiest—" June wiggled

her eyebrows, "—with all those gentlemen feelin' lonely after a chaste evening with the most eligible young ladies in town."

Greta stood near the closet, polishing Anna's best shoes, and shook her head. "I don't know how you do it, young lady. I guess I've always wondered what made you join in the first place."

June sat behind Anna and started combing her long brown hair, the pearl comb tingling Anna's scalp. She tried to remember what it was like for her mother to brush her hair, but she couldn't recall.

June's face was melancholy. "I didn't have a loving grandfather or brother like Anna. My father expected dinner the minute he came home, but his return was always a surprise—dependin' on when he left the saloon. If his food was cold, he'd shove me against the wall, and I'd run to my room before he could do worse."

Greta shook her head, a sad look in her eye as she helped braid a few small pieces of Anna's hair. Anna was glad she hadn't seen June's father in years and hoped he'd left town.

"When I was fifteen, Billy pressured me into lyin' with him. Told me he loved me, and it was the first time I'd ever been told that. Pa never said it. Billy always snuck away right afterwards, but I didn't want to make him mad by complainin'. When he moved away to Oregon, another boy told me he loved me, and I wanted to believe him, too."

Anna squirmed against the tightness of the corset. The lace pinched the skin along her back, and she was starting to get winded just sitting there trying to breathe normally. All this for a smaller waist and a little bit of cleavage. She turned her head to look back at June and give her an encouraging nod. She was intimately familiar with the events of June's life, but she'd never heard June tell the story to anyone else, and hearing it this way made her sad.

"One night, a boy knocked and asked Pa for 'the girl who'd sleep with any boy.' Pa told him to get lost, but the boy knew my name, and I walked up to the door at the wrong moment, just as Pa started yellin' and swingin' his fists. I cried and he knew right then it was all true. Pa called me all kinds of names and started throwin' bottles. I ran for my life—left everything behind."

"Oh my!" Greta's fingers froze mid-braid. "Where'd you go? You should have come here!"

"I ran to the docks, thinkin' I might sneak onto a boat to get as far away from here as I could. I sat there, waitin' for the sun to rise, and I thought of the ladies who called themselves seamstresses and giggled. We all knew they were prostitutes, but ones who kept the highest society. People knew my reputation at that point, so I figured why not. At least I'd get paid properly and spend my days in a picturesque parlor with fancy gentlemen. I mustered all my courage and knocked on the door of the finest brothel in Seattle. Lou Graham gave me a quick tour and showed me the room I'd have all to myself. I was mesmerized. It was nicer than anywhere I'd ever lived—no varmints, cockroaches, or backed-up sewage."

June weaved small white flowers into Anna's dark hair, which she'd piled on top of her head with small braids laced throughout, then stood back to admire her work. Anna exhaled deeply, trying to shake the melancholy stealing over her.

Greta wiped a tear away. "That's quite a story, June."

A tight smile formed on June's lips as she shrugged nonchalantly. Anna stood and motioned for June to sit in the chair. It was a different color wood than her dresser and nightstand, but it had always been her favorite because of the soft red seat cushion. She combed June's hair gently, admiring her curls.

"But now June has almost fifteen dollars and exquisite dresses! Spends her evenings with city councilmen and judges."

Anna lifted her eyebrows with an encouraging smile. She didn't want June to be ashamed of her life, especially since she had few other options available. Twisting June's hair into a high chignon, she pinned it in place.

Greta nodded seriously. "Well, I'm glad you're doing well for yourself now."

She kissed June on the cheek, which finally brought a genuine smile to the girl's face.

"I'd better be going." June embraced her friend, then disappeared down the stairs.

Anna put on her shoes, then glanced in her hand mirror to adjust her dress. Her grandfather knocked on the open door lightly then strode in.

"Darling girl." He lifted her hand above her head. "Twirl, lassie."

Anna shook her head shyly, but she did. The hem of her dress twirled with her to the left, then fluttered to the right softly as she returned to face him. She reached up to touch the pearl earrings Greta had let her borrow, then tugged on the white gloves that she'd had since she was ten. They still fit, but were no longer as high as was proper.

Her grandfather had a radiant grin on his wrinkled face. "You're the most beautiful lady I've ever seen. Now, Levi is supposed to be your chaperone. They already left so find him when you get there."

Anna clasped her hands together in front of her—an unchaperoned carriage ride would be a first. On days like these, she wished her parents were still alive to see how grown-up she was.

A horse-drawn coach pulled up. From the window, she watched Connor jump out with a spring in his step. He wore a tailored black suit with a black tie and crisp white shirt—certainly an attractive man. As he stepped onto the porch, he took off his top hat and knocked on the front door three times.

A few minutes later, as she descended the stairs, he stood to greet her, with a crooked smile. "Breathtaking."

Once in the coach, she waved goodbye. Peeking out the window, she saw the sun setting and clouds outlined in a soft pink. Connor sat across from her and appeared distracted as he straightened his suit coat—what was on his mind? This was the first time they'd ever been alone. Soon they'd be at the dance hall, surrounded by people.

He cleared his throat. "You truly look lovely."

"Thank you." She glanced down at her white-gloved hands in her lap then out the window where the Madison Street trolley passed their carriage on the right, making the horses huff in protest. "I forgot to tell you—we found a clue from the book inscription."

He shook his head. "That scribbled mess inside the French book?"

Anna's gaze didn't falter, but she felt a small laugh building in her chest. "Russian."

Connor cleared his throat awkwardly.

"I just don't want you to be disappointed." He fixed his gaze out the window. "I love how smart you are, but you might be unnecessarily preoccupied with this. Do you think it might be because you've spent too much time reading novels?"

A light layer of sweat rose onto Anna's chest and back. Drawing in a deep breath, she looked out the carriage window toward the mountain, hoping to find comfort, but the street was practically at sea level. She focused on the stone arches above the windows of a tall building to her left and the wooden balcony below it, bright with summer flowers.

"Can I tell you something special?" she asked, tingling with nerves.

"Of course." Connor leaned toward her, reaching his hand toward her arm, then pulling it back as if remembering they were alone.

"I keep picturing myself climbing Mount Rainier. I know it's peculiar, but even just imagining it, I feel...happy."

She could feel the heat rising off her cheeks as she watched his face for a response. Suddenly, the idea meant more to her. The possibility of making an ascent seemed even more intriguing than she'd imagined before.

What if he said she should try? She wasn't sure what she hoped for in Connor's response, but everything hung on what his words might be—if he might believe in her and be supportive.

CHAPTER THIRTEEN
THE INCIDENT

"Can I be frank?" Connor ran a hand over his neatly greased hair. "It wouldn't be physically possible for the fairer sex to summit the mountain, especially one of that altitude, with such treacherous glaciers. It has nothing to do with your intelligence, and I know you're tenacious, and I adore that about you. But I certainly wouldn't advise you or any lady to attempt that feat. There's a reason only men are included in mountaineering groups."

Anna narrowed her eyes slightly then turned away.

He bit his lip. "Does that upset you?"

She sat back, unsure how to respond. "A little."

The jostling carriage felt suddenly suffocating, her stomach tossing with every bump.

He nodded. "I'm sorry."

He reached for her hand after all, but she pulled it away to fix her hair.

Clasping his hands together instead, he spoke soothingly. "You should know how serious my intentions are. I'd love to have you on my arm for every event in town. I could buy a big house for us wherever you like. You could have a baby soon to fill your time. And pick out large window panes for our house, and we could order furniture and paintings from Paris. Whatever you like."

He liked her pretty face, but thought she was as fragile as a china doll. As much as she'd hoped that Connor would encourage her plans, her desire to do something great was bigger than lace curtains and a place in society. She studied his eyes, which were full of affection, and longed to be held in his arms. He *did* say he liked that she was smart and tenacious—that was something.

But not enough. Connor was a gentleman who wanted an intelligent yet agreeable wife by his side—someone traditional.

And then the desire to settle down felt distant, unimportant— something shifted inside her. It was time to follow the growing energy drawing her toward the mountain.

She turned back to the window—they were next in line to be dropped off at the grand entrance. The white columns stood regally, reaching the third floor of the brick dance hall. Connor hopped out and sheepishly held his hand up to her.

Anna stepped down from the carriage without accepting it.

"Your face is pale. Do you feel faint?" He folded his arms and looked as if he might examine her as a patient.

"I'm not sure we'd be happy together," she said, walking up the marble steps toward the entrance, searching for any sign of her brother.

Connor gripped his top hat with both hands. "Please don't do this."

She squared her shoulders. "What would you say if I told you I have an Indian friend...and I'm planning on learning how to hunt...and I will absolutely solve this riddle even if you do think it's ridiculous?"

She put a hand on her hip and lifted a delicate eyebrow. "And what if I told you that I deeply want to be on the top of that mountain one day, just to see how it feels?"

He stared at her with his mouth agape. Anna held his gaze stoically until his face turned red.

He leaned toward her and whispered, "You're creating a scene."

She narrowed her eyes in determination. "Goodbye, Connor."

As she turned on her heel and hurried inside the dance hall, out of the corner of her eye, she caught a glimpse of June flirting with two men on a settee.

"Anna!"

Emily came up behind her in a flowing gown with large puffy sleeves. Her musical voice had an immediate calming effect on Anna.

Anna gave her friend a quick embrace. "Oh Emily. I actually had the worst ride here. Have you seen my brother?"

"Levi's back? He's here?" Her face flushed pink as she glanced around the foyer. "I'm so sorry things aren't going well. I'll look for him."

She kissed Anna's cheek, then spun around and hurried into the dance hall.

Anna hurried back outside where the sun had set and the lamp posts dimly lit the streets. She rushed down the steps, dodging couples sauntering toward the entrance. On the sidewalk, men stood around the building smoking and talking loudly. She found a quiet spot around the corner down an alley and turned to face the wall of a wood-paneled drugstore to cry. Her emotion surprised her, but the tears didn't last long.

Instead, anger rose up in her chest. Where was Levi? She spun around to find a man standing over her.

His handlebar mustache was greased at the edges, and he stumbled toward her smelling like whiskey. "How much?"

She put her hands on her hips, glaring at him. "What do you mean?"

The man's black suit coat was tailored perfectly, and he smirked as he reached behind her, interlocking his fingers behind her back.

"Come here, beautiful." He crushed his stomach against hers.

The blood drained from her face as he bent closer, his breath hot. She stomped on his toe with her heel then shoved him. He stumbled backward.

She gave him a disapproving look. "You're mistaken, sir."

"Well, what are you standin' 'round out here for, all by yourself? Seems like ya wanted it."

"Back off," Ben said from behind her. "You must have confused her with someone else."

He stepped closer, unbuttoning his suit coat.

His presence was a relief, but she was suddenly embarrassed to be found this way.

"I've handled things," she said, straightening her skirts.

The drunk man reached for her waist again. "Oh come on, sweetie. I'll pay whatever—"

Ben lunged, shoving the man, who stumbled and this time fell to the ground. Anna gasped as he grabbed the lapels of the man's suit coat with both hands, lifting him up to stand.

"Hey, watch the suit!" the man groaned. He pulled a starched handkerchief from his vest and wiped dirt from the seat of his pants.

"Are you going to behave now, or should I call for the police?" Ben asked, out of breath.

At that moment, Levi came around the corner. "Ben, where —what's going on here?"

Anna ran to her brother, and he put his arms around her shoulders.

The drunk man huffed and stumbled down the street toward the harbor.

Levi took his suit jacket off and put it around Anna's shoulders. "What happened? Where's Doctor Evans?"

"Let's go home," she said, too embarrassed to say more.

Ben was still catching his breath. "Some idiot propositioned your sister."

He tucked his shirt back into his pants and attempted to smooth his tousled hair to the side, then looked over to her.

"You all right? That doctor should've never put you in a position to fend for yourself." He paused, deep concern etched on his forehead. "But why did you step out here alone, unaccompanied?"

Anna glared at him, disappointment washing over her in waves. He was no better than Connor. Both men saw her as frail and fragile—in need of protection.

Levi's eyes narrowed, and he growled, "Let's chase him down."

"He was just a fool. We should find this Doctor Evans, see what his excuse is for not taking care of a lady properly," Ben said, finally breaking eye contact with Anna.

She was starting to shake. "Please, let's go home."

Levi squeezed her tighter. "Of course—right away."

She waited with Ben while Levi secured a carriage. She looked up the stairs toward the entrance and thought she saw Connor walking in with a woman in a green dress. Of course, he was already on to the next; or maybe it wasn't him, after all.

Soon, she was whisked away and riding through the city streets by lamplight. When the coach stopped in front of her house, Ben opened the door, and Levi helped her inside. Her grandfather buzzed around asking questions that sounded far away.

Levi held up his hands as if to quiet the questions.

"She needs a bath and hot tea before she answers any questions." He turned to her. "Do you mind if we go back, or do you need us here?"

Ben crossed his arms and gave Levi a steely glare. "We don't need to go back."

Anna sat at the bottom of the stairs to unlace her shoes. "You've both done enough, thank you. Please go, enjoy yourselves."

While her grandfather paced angrily, Greta filled a bucket from the boiler. Levi filled them in on the happenings of the evening, from his perspective.

Her dress rustled as she stood, then she lifted her hem to climb the stairs. The voices quieted behind her as her grandfather walked Levi and Ben to the door. Although he attempted to whisper through clenched teeth, his words drifted toward her.

"If you see Doctor Evans at the dance, tell him I need to speak with him."

CHAPTER FOURTEEN

THE MORNING AFTER

Anna woke the next morning to light rain pattering on the roof. Thinking of that man's hands clasped behind her back made her shudder.

She opened her window to catch sight of the mountain and breathe fresh air. The icy peak towered in the distance, and her newfound resolve settled comfortably within her spirit. A smile came over her lips as she savored the idea of summiting. There was nothing frail about Anna Gallagher.

She opened her drawer where she'd been collecting newspaper clippings. After finding the article about Isabella Bird, the explorer and mountaineer, she'd searched for others like it and saved them.

One article was about Lucy Walker, a British woman who'd summited the Matterhorn in the Alps in 1871. The article wasn't about her, though; it was about a male mountaineer who spoke poorly of Ms. Walker, saying surely all the strenuous exercise required to mountaineer would impede her ability to accomplish wifely duties.

She glared at the clipping. The man's ignorance seemed

inescapable—every man seemed to fall prey to some misgivings about women's strength.

She searched through the stories she'd collected for the one about a group of mountaineers who'd attempted to summit Mount Rainier the summer before, in 1888—all men. The group was made up of a reporter, a professor, and one mountaineer who'd summited years earlier. The article concluded with the contact information of the organizer, Mr. William Flannaghan of Tacoma. They had failed to summit due to weather, but he was gathering a group to try again in August 1890—next summer.

She pulled out a piece of paper, and with shaky fingers composed a letter.

Dear Mr. Flannaghan,

I am writing in hopes that you would consider including me in your attempt to summit Mount Rainier next summer. I am a woman, and I know mountaineers are traditionally men, but ever since I arrived in Washington when I was a little girl I have looked up at that great mountain and found strength.

If you are willing, and would be so kind as to include me, please let me know the cost, what supplies I will need, and what I can do to prepare myself.

Sincerely,
Miss Anna Gallagher
Seattle, Washington Territory

She had to get moving on solving the riddle. And what kind of training would be required exactly? She thought of how her family might react if they found out about any of this. It was all exhilarating.

Her grandfather knocked then poked his head inside. "Hungry?"

"No thanks."

His presence calmed her, as it always did. Greta followed him into the room and sat on her red-cushioned chair.

Greta hugged her arms around her stomach. "I'll bring coffee and warm bread later. Food for your soul."

"Do you want to tell us what happened last night?" her grandfather asked.

Anna sighed. "Connor is not the man I want to marry. And some drunk man thought I was a prostitute."

Greta put her hand on Anna's arm. "Your brother told us about the…incident. And that's quite all right if you don't like the doctor. Are you doing all right this morning?"

"I'm fine. I think I'll spend the day reading, although I've read everything in the house twice." She smiled half-heartedly.

"Well as luck would have it…" Her grandfather pulled a small book from behind his back. "I traded a bottle of wine with Pattinson to pick any new book I wanted off his shelves. This is a book of poems by Ella Wheeler Wilcox I got especially for you."

Anna inhaled sharply as she took the crisp book from his hands. *Poems of Passion*, the cover said.

"I wish I could take you back to Ireland sometimes," he said. "To the countryside, and we could read and drink Guinness until you forgot about all your problems."

A smile crept over her face. "He's not worth pining over."

Her grandfather's white hair was wild from sleep, and he stroked his beard twice. "Quite right. He's not the man for you, but another will be. Someone with passion, perhaps."

Anna hugged him tightly. "Thank you. And yes Greta, I'd love coffee if it's not too much trouble, with cinnamon please."

Her grandfather heaved himself up using the nightstand. "We wouldn't make it any other way, lassie."

He paused at the doorway, an adoring look on his wrinkled face. Greta stood and followed him out, giving Anna a quick kiss on the cheek.

As they left, her smile grew—she'd mail the letter first thing

Monday. Would telling June about the letter jinx it? It almost seemed that if she said the words aloud, everything would fall apart.

Around noon, she went to the porch to enjoy reading her new book with coffee. The poems were lovely—some sweet, some fiery, and they all reminded her how wonderful love would be when she found it one day. It would be so romantic to have a poem written for her, like Dmitri had for Natalya.

When she looked down to take a sip of coffee, she saw a small note rolled up in the corner of her chair. She unrolled it to find a child-like scrawl:

I am here. – Heather

Anna scanned the edge of the forest, and Heather waved shyly. She hurried to her through the tall grass.

Heather smiled. "*Wiiac.* This means hello…and goodbye."

Anna waved at Pisha as she peered around her mother. "*Wiiac.* Good morning."

Heather straightened the cloth carrying Pisha on her back. "Would you like to walk? I don't have time to go all the way to my home, but we can just walk together for a while."

"Yes. Let me grab the books for you and leave a note." She ran back to the house trying to come up with a good excuse to be gone all morning. A simple note would do.

Going for a walk. I'll be home this afternoon. – Anna

It was plain enough. She grabbed the books she'd set aside, then ran back to Heather. It felt good to stretch her legs—a walk in the woods would be just what she needed.

"Here's *Watson's Complete Speller* and *Swinton's Language Lessons and Primer.* Plus, my old slate and chalk. You can practice writing too."

Heather eagerly reached for the books and slate, examining them. "Good. Thank you."

"Thank you for the book you gave me," Anna said. "I'm hoping to figure out the clues in the inscription. How was fishing?"

Heather smiled. "Good. Lots of fish for the winter."

As they walked, Anna filled her in on the last few weeks—the dance, Connor's discouragement, Ben intervening—everything but the letter.

"I'm going to try and climb the mountain. Not quite sure how yet, but I'm working on it."

Heather smiled approvingly. "That's *great.*"

As she reflected on everything, Anna's shoulders relaxed. It wasn't all bad. She was certainly better off being rid of Connor —it was providential to see his true personality. It was a relief that she didn't waste any more time on him.

Levi was back in town, and she had a new book of poems to read that her grandfather had so thoughtfully gotten for her. Although they were going to be low on money for the winter, she had a plan to keep them afloat until a loan was approved. Now here she was in the forest with a new friend, and there was no one around to tell her it wasn't proper. The last remaining hint of melancholy lifted off her chest, but just as she looked up at the sky, she stepped into a small creek flowing through the undergrowth.

"Oh dear, that was clumsy," she muttered. "I'm usually more aware, especially in the forest."

"Listening carefully helps me," Heather said. "Certain sounds have brought us here. There will be others as we go deeper. Then I listen to the same sounds in reverse on the way back."

Anna nodded and followed Heather down a path leading into denser forest. At first, all she could hear was the sound of her breathing, but she tried her best to listen. Her surroundings were certainly refreshing: ferns wet with dew, a fallen log covered with moss crossing their path, roots weaving in and out of the earth. A toad croaked. Shortly after, a train whistled faintly, followed by squawking of crows to the west. As they moved farther into the forest, a hawk shrieked, and a branch rustled overhead as it landed.

They both sat on a log, and Anna put her hands on her knees. "In the past I've tuned the noises out to enjoy the silence. It's easier to pretend there aren't wild animals out here."

"They mostly ignore you," Heather said.

Anna lifted her face to the sky. Small slivers of light pierced through the treetops. She closed her eyes, and an insect buzzed. She tried to let the sound melt into her. But then, the twinge of a mosquito bite on her left arm brought her back and she slapped it.

"Not all creatures are good. Let's head back," Heather said, trying not to smile. "So, how many years did you go to school?"

Anna scratched the spot on her arm that was turning red and followed Heather back toward town. "Ten. I was sixteen when I finished, and that's when I started working at our bookstore."

"What did you learn?" Heather asked.

"Grammar, arithmetic, bookkeeping, geography—that was my favorite. I'd love to explore someday—find somewhere new. Grandfather says I'm lucky because the Territorial Board of Education formed shortly after we arrived, so when I started school everything was organized and uniform."

"Yes—lucky," Heather said pointedly as she adjusted Pisha.

As they went, Anna heard more or less the same sounds in reverse. This time she also heard the muted sound of their own footfall on dense undergrowth. A ship's horn sounded, and a few seagulls flew overhead as they reached the clearing near her home.

"Thank you for the lovely walk," she said as she came to a stop.

"I'll see you again." Heather waved goodbye.

Anna wanted to ask her when and how they would see one another again, but instead she said a simple "*Wiiac*," and waved at Pisha as the baby turned to see her.

She glanced up at the mountain—only the tip was visible above the clouds. Her gaze lingered on the snow-capped giant. Surrounded by trees, she felt unrestricted by the expectations her grandfather—and seemingly everyone—had for her. Finding love would be magical, but she could never be *just* a wife. That wouldn't be love at all. Were there no men who wanted more than a traditional wife by their sides—no one who sought a partner?

CHAPTER FIFTEEN

THE OCCIDENTAL HOTEL

17 August 1889

Anna's fingers flew over the tiny buttons as she put on a white collared shirt with a gentle puff at the shoulders. She had awoken with a tingling excitement for the day's plans—exploring the ruins of the Occidental Hotel with Levi and Ben. It had been two weeks since the dance, and the whole experience already felt like a distant memory. Ben and Levi had both been hired at the Yesler Mill the week prior, and Ben had promptly found an apartment in town. The house felt a touch quieter, almost emptier without him.

At the top button, she placed her mother's cameo, then tucked her shirt into a thick, gray linen skirt that brushed the ground. The circular buckle on her thin leather belt shined. She combed her hair and wrapped it up into a high bun with a black ribbon.

When she hurried into the kitchen, Ben was sitting at the table reading the newspaper. She smiled. "Ready? Where's Levi?"

"Napping by the fire, but we should wake him soon," he said with an amused look. "May I see the book? I want to keep the other clues in mind in case they're interconnected—I suspect they are."

Anna enjoyed watching his animated face. In fact, having her brother's friend around was much more fun than she'd anticipated. She was grateful for Ben's positivity, which was breathing new life into solving the riddle. "Of course. It's above the mantle."

He pulled the book down, examining the first page. His stomach rumbled, which made him blush.

Anna grinned. "I'm hungry too. Our raspberries are fruiting. Let's pick some while we wait for Levi."

Ben placed the book back on the mantle. "I've missed fruit. That's one thing that doesn't last well at sea. Berries sound incredible."

She laced up her boots. "If you have cash to spend, we should stop at the market. You can buy all kinds of fruit."

"Goodness, my mouth is watering now." He threw his head back with his eyes closed in a dramatic gesture that made Anna giggle. He opened an eye to see her reaction and grinned. "By the way, you smell lovely."

Her eyebrows flew up. "Oh. Thanks."

Her heartbeat sped up as she motioned for him to go through the door first. She and Greta had made a batch of brown Windsor soap the night before.

Outside, she pointed out her cherished raspberry plants, as well as the blackberry bushes near the woods. After they'd had their fill of berries, they headed back to the house and found Levi waiting at the table.

He stood, wiping his eyes. "I was afraid you two left me."

Anna kissed his cheek. "But you're my only brother—I'd never leave you behind."

Her grandfather's voice came down the stairs ahead of him.

"You kids have fun." He picked up the mail on the counter, a book under his arm. "Anna—a letter from Tacoma."

She exhaled calmly as she examined it. "I forgot my shawl upstairs. I'll be right back."

Once she stood in her room with the door shut, she tore open the letter.

Dear Miss Gallagher,

I have never considered adding a lady to our team to summit Mt. Rainier—it's never been done. However, if you are able to pay the $11.50 that is needed to rent pack animals and buy provisions, then I would be willing to include you. You will need an alpenstock, crampons, goggles, a tent, a sturdy pack, climbing boots, and warm clothing. Near the end of July, you will need to purchase a train ticket to Yelm, which is the closest city to the mountain accessible by railway.

The exact date of the climb has not been decided and will depend on weather. You should begin training now. To prepare, you can walk on frozen water with crampons, hike up and down snowy hills using your alpenstock, and spend a few nights camping in a tent in cold weather. Most importantly, you need to practice carrying a heavy pack while climbing up and down steep elevations. Best of luck. Please let me know if you are able to adequately train and acquire the necessary gear and funds.

Sincerely,
Mr. William Flannaghan

Anna stared in amazement. It had never been done? She folded the letter and hid it inside the drawer of her nightstand. A lady had never climbed the mountain and reached the top—and now, it was her chance. She almost forgot to grab her shawl off the dresser before she raced down the stairs.

"Shall we?" Levi offered his arm, which she gladly took.

The three of them took the dirt path to town. Levi and Ben chatted while she daydreamed. Her mind raced as she considered

Mr. Flannaghan's words—*would* she be able to climb snowy hills, walk on frozen lakes, and sleep under the stars? Her breath came faster as she imagined undertaking such an adventure. How would she train? And how could she go about it secretly? If they could figure out the clues in the book inscription, it could become a reality. She couldn't wait to tell Heather and June.

Levi paid their way for the trolley, and Anna settled into her seat by the window to take in the view. The streets smelled of horse droppings and sawdust, but the view of the bustling city was unbeatable. In the business district, white tents still lined streets, along with new brick construction. One recently rebuilt structure of bricks and stone blocks stood five stories high. "Butler Block" was engraved in the archway.

They got off at Madison and Front Street, walking the four blocks south to the site of the Occidental Hotel. Thin towers rose at each of the three corners where the hotel once stood. Blackened bricks, along with bent and broken cast iron, covered the ground. Much of the debris had been swept to the edges of the once extravagant lobby.

"Looks like brick and paneling, mostly, with cast iron on the inside," Ben said. "'*At first, you'll need to find a block, perhaps the kind that makes the place of occidental rest so strong against the quakes.*' Well, if it's going to be referred to as a block, he must be referring to bricks—don't you think, Anna?"

She scooped up a charred brick and examined it, then surveyed the piles. "Could the ring have been hidden here somewhere?"

Ben stroked his trimmed beard. "If it was, it's likely lost now."

"True." Her shoulders slumped. "Well, since it's just *one* of the clues, it's probably not meant to be the end of the riddle anyhow. Suppose it's all right if we take one?"

Levi glanced around. "You'd probably get a pat on the back for assistin' the clean-up efforts."

She laughed. "Then it's ours. I'm not sure how it fits along with the rest, but now, we've got a 'block,'" she said with a mischievous grin. "On to the next element, I guess. Before we 'put them all together.'"

"May I?" Ben reached for the brick, and she handed it to him, then rubbed her hands together to get the soot off, which didn't work at all. Ben watched her instead of examining the brick in his hands and offered her his handkerchief.

"A kerchief, my lady." He bowed slightly and peeked up at her.

She laughed. He was as silly as her brother and much funnier. It was nice to be in their company and not worry about wearing anything fancy or trying to be on her best ladylike behavior. She had soot and ash under her fingernails, mud on the bottom of her plainest skirt. And when Ben looked at her with that sparkle in his brown eyes, she felt completely gorgeous.

When she took it, their fingers brushed together, and her knees tingled with weakness, a soft sensation. She wiped her hands, then Ben wrapped the brick inside of it.

"Actually, I'd be happy to carry that for you, if you like," he said, his forehead scrunched in question.

Anna grinned and rolled her eyes playfully. "Mighty kind of you, but I can handle it. Still want to go to the fruit market?"

"Yes, ma'am, I do."

"Oh, Emily's new house is on the way," she gushed. "I haven't called on her since her marriage in May. Can we stop by?"

Their rushed encounter at the dance had been odd, and Anna planned to apologize.

Levi's face turned white. He'd always had a soft spot for Emily, but she'd had her hopes set on someone richer. He mumbled, "She'd probably prefer notice…"

Anna studied the fancy houses along Broadway, and when she got to Emily's, she walked up the steps while the boys hung back. She tapped the silver door knocker, gazing up at the three-story brick house, admiring the pink and white rose bushes on either side of the entrance.

Swinging the door wide, Emily smiled affectionately. Her curly red hair was pulled into an elegant updo with a pearl barrette. Black chiffon made up the high-necked collar of her dress, and the sleeves puffed gently before tapering down her delicate arms, with more black chiffon gathered at the fair skin of her wrists. The dress was a two-piece silk affair and clearly custom-tailored.

"I'm delighted to see you," Emily said, embracing her friend.

"I'm so sorry I was short with you at the dance. It's a long story, but it was *not* a great night."

"I'm sorry to hear things didn't work out with Doctor Evans." Emily had a concerned look on her face. "I saw Greta at the market last week—she told me."

Anna sighed and looked behind her at Ben and Levi still on the sidewalk. Emily straightened when her gaze fell on Levi, and when their eyes met, both of their faces turned pink.

Levi climbed the porch stairs, and Emily drifted closer to him. As he reached the top stair, he quickly took her hand and kissed it. Anna watched the two, embarrassed for them. She gave Ben an awkward look.

Emily had a tight-lipped smile. "It's good to see you, Levi. I'm sorry you couldn't make it to the wedding."

"We common folk have to work for a living. I was at sea. With Ben here." He motioned toward Ben, who lifted his hat in amused surprise at being mentioned.

Emily shook her head and frowned, but nodded politely toward Ben.

Anna cringed. "Just wanted to say hello. And apologize. We're off to the market."

Levi and Emily peeled their eyes away from each other, and Anna kissed her cheek before rushing down the porch steps.

"Whoa," Ben said as they walked away. "What was all that about?"

Levi scowled. "Nothing."

As they strolled toward the market, Anna took Levi's arm, eager to change the subject for him. "What did you miss most at sea?"

He perked up. "Apples, definitely. Fresh apples, apple pie, apple cider."

She bit her lip in thought. "Apples aren't quite ripe yet."

"I know. I'll settle for any fresh fruit at this point." He turned to Ben. "When do you leave for hunting?"

"Not till early spring. You should see the redwoods in California, Anna. They're hundreds of years old and taller than clouds. I love to hunt there."

Her heart swelled. "Would you teach me to shoot a bow?"

Levi raised his eyebrows. "Why? You'll be married before you know it and spending most of your time indoors."

"Well, for starters, we won't have money for meat this winter, and I'd like to help out any way I can." She had stayed home feeling useless hundreds of times while her brother and grandfather went hunting. It was time for a change.

"With your permission, Levi," Ben said. "And if you wouldn't mind accompanying us, of course, I'd be happy to teach her."

She grinned. "Thanks, Ben."

Levi huffed, then gave her a playful push with his shoulder.

As they came upon the fruit market, she admired the brightly colored fruit, but she and Levi ultimately decided not to spend any of their precious pennies. Her mouth watered as she browsed the stands, making her long for better days. Luckily, Ben bought blueberries, which he shared on the walk back.

At home, Anna found her grandfather reading a book in front of the fire while Greta worked on dinner in the kitchen.

Ben leaned in. "She's not your grandmother, right?"

Levi shook his head. "Greta married our grandfather about ten years ago. Anna sure gave her a hard time back then."

Her cheeks warmed. "I was a child. We've gotten quite close."

"What are you whispering about over there?" called her grandfather from the living room. "Come in here and give an old man some company."

"Ben, why don't you go join him?" Levi suggested. "I need to talk with my sister for a moment."

He offered his arm to her and led her to the porch. They stood at the edge of the railing as the sun set behind the tall trees and the late summer sky changed to reddish hues.

"Anna, why do you need to shoot a bow?"

She swallowed uncomfortably. "To help…"

"Grandfather and I will worry about hunting, and tomorrow you'll start staying at home to work with Greta. And Grandfather says you've been getting lost in the woods." His face was disapproving. "You don't have to marry a merchant or mill-worker if you play your cards right. Why not put foolish interests to rest and start thinking of starting a home with a gentleman from a good family, someone with an honorable profession?"

Anna exhaled and stared toward town. "I'll have no voice if I marry someone like that."She paused, thinking of Connor's cool expression as he told her not to make a scene—it made her feel invisible. "Connor seemed great, until I found that he thinks I'm weak and hardly capable of anything. It's insulting. I can't spend my life with someone like that. Anyway, a man with an established profession isn't going to want to travel."

Levi's face softened. "Well, I'm glad things didn't work out with him. There'll be someone better for you. But why do you need to travel? And shoot a bow? When we first came here it was kinda wild and women helped build houses and chop wood. But now that the city is established and we've almost been granted statehood, things are civilized. Men and women each have their

own place. I just want you to find a place that makes you happy
—on the arm of an important man, one with the means to take
proper care of a family."

It was as if he wasn't hearing her at all. Was this what
marriage was like? She had been so close to her brother when
they were younger, but as she'd grown, it was as if he saw her
growing beauty as a tool that she should use to secure a different
life. But she had always loved living on the edge of town.

"Listen, I'm not saying I want to marry someone with no
means to take care of a family, I'm just saying." She paused to
look up into the eyes that still seemed much the same as they
always had. Levi had been her constant childhood companion,
the one who'd let her crawl under the covers with him when she
was scared. "Just be on my side, whatever I choose, okay?"

He pulled her close, his chin resting on the top of her head.
"I will."

Maybe he couldn't understand the longing inside her to have
her own adventure, even though he regularly left town to have
adventures of his own. But at least it felt good to hear him say
those words.

CHAPTER SIXTEEN
THE SPARK

The next morning, Anna secured her hair tightly for her first day working with Greta. All she wanted to do was train for summiting the mountain and keep working on the inscription, but preparing for winter must come first. Otherwise, she felt as though the guilt of remaining at home and being a burden would crush her. At least she'd taken control of the food problem by planning well and utilizing Greta's knowledge.

That evening, she planned to look through their bookshelves at home to find her grandfather's books on hiking. She could spend her evenings reading those and the weekends going for long walks in the woods to get her lungs in shape. Besides, there would be plenty of time for pondering the remaining clues while her hands were busy.

For the next three weeks, she weeded and thinned the sprouts in their garden with Greta, watering it morning and night since there hadn't been any rain. They gathered berries, made soap, and dried the herbs that shot up in the garden. By the first week of September, they'd collected twenty buckets of wild blackberries and three buckets of the last of the raspberries. All over the house, berries hung from the ceiling to dry in mosquito nets; they planned to make jam next.

After dinner that night, Anna kissed her grandfather's cheek as he sat in his chair by the fire. "Can you go to the store tomorrow and get two dozen two-quart mason jars, the ones with porcelain-lined lids? That should be three dollars. And as much sugar as we can reasonably afford."

Her grandfather looked up from the wood he was carving—a new chair for the bookstore. "Yes, ma'am."

"And you already brought up all the old jars from the cellar, right?" she asked.

He nodded, this time keeping his eyes on the wood.

Greta smiled brightly at Anna and got out her quilting pieces. "Levi, would you make sure we have enough wood? We're going to burn the cookstove all day tomorrow."

Levi nodded curtly and jumped to his feet. "I'll go look."

Greta returned to her quilting, humming softly. Anna watched her and felt a growing fondness for the older woman.

"Grandfather, would you mind ordering *Crime and Punishment* for me? I've still got twenty-five cents from last Christmas. If you're right about the Raskolnikov reference, I'll need it to solve one of the clues. I already looked around town, and no one has it in stock. I know we could use the money for more food or supplies, but—"

"Of course. And no, we won't be using your Christmas money to buy food."

"I wouldn't mind, but I really need to get my hands on that book," she said.

The next morning, she found Greta awake before sunrise, the fire in the stove blazing. After her grandfather returned with the promised jars and sugar, Greta handed him a basket of freshly-baked raspberry scones and blackberry muffins to sell. With a tender smile, he donned his felt hat and waved on his way back out the door.

Levi awoke soon after and stole a handful of berries from the kitchen work table before putting on his coat and hat. "I'm off to the mill. Ben and I are going out tonight. I'll be back late."

Greta stirred a large, bubbling pot of raspberries.

"We'll still be right here." She waved to Levi as he escaped from the heat of the kitchen. "Anna, I need you to wash and dry these new jars. It's important they're as dry as possible."

They spent the entire day making jams, jellies, and syrups. Greta used the largest pot to seal the jars, immersing them then letting them boil. It was nine in the evening when they finished— the kitchen smelled heavenly, with glistening jars on every surface.

Anna kissed her grandfather on the cheek before collapsing into the cedar rocking chair near the fire. After he'd gotten home from work, he'd been put to work as well.

"We'll have to be careful with all the jam." Greta gave her husband a playful smile as she joined them. "Remember that stain from when you broke a jar of jam in the middle of the night?"

Anna shook her head, forehead scrunched in confusion. "That stain was from the accident."

Her grandfather stood noisily, the woodwork in his hands falling to the floor. "Don't ever bring that up again."

The vein in his forehead was visible, and his jaw clenched. He stormed upstairs, leaving Greta staring after him.

Anna exchanged a confused look with her but said no more. She had only been nine when the Duwamish boy had broken into their house. It was before he'd married Greta, but Anna had assumed he'd told her about it. She couldn't think of any reason he'd keep such a thing to himself, but then again, lately it seemed like there was a lot about her grandfather she didn't understand.

The women rested for a few minutes by the fire, and Anna was about to head upstairs for bed when the front door burst open.

Levi stumbled in, his words slurring together. "It smellssso good in here."

Ben laughed as Levi leaned against the wall trying to remove his boots.

Anna shot Greta a look. "I do believe Levi's drunk."

"At least he comes by it honestly," Greta mumbled.

"I heard that, an' I'm pretty sure you're mistaken." Levi sank to the floor.

Anna stood from her chair. "Will one of you fine fellas grab more wood from outside?"

Ben appeared much steadier on his feet. "Be happy to."

She followed him to the door. "Are you not much for alcohol?"

"Not my particular weakness." He tipped his hat meaningfully as he turned to the wood pile. He returned a moment later, arms full of firewood.

She put out her arms for him to fill. "I'm sure you need to get going. I can bring it in to the living room."

He peered at her questioningly then shrugged. "As you wish."

As he placed each log gently into her arms, one piece after another, her cheeks flushed at his nearness. She couldn't read his expression, but she was definitely aware that they were out of sight from the others. He put the last log on top, then stood to his full height, slowly taking a step back. She was lightheaded from the light touches of his hands on her bare arms as he'd placed each piece.

"You all right?" he asked.

"Yes, thank you for your help." Her eyes lingered on his until she made herself turn away.

"Goodnight then." He lifted his hat slightly.

Anna was grateful to have wood to stack—a task to attend to —as she closed the door. She hoped Greta would think any flush in her cheeks was from the cold, but in reality, she just wasn't sure what to make of Ben. He was handsome and charming, but her brother seemed adamant that she should keep her distance from him. He did have some inconsistencies. Did he think she was fragile and needing protection, or did he think she was strong and capable? The way he'd held her gaze after he'd stacked the wood in her arms made her cheeks warm. Was he attracted to her?

CHAPTER SEVENTEEN
THE PAST

10 December 1880

It was around midnight when Anna heard pots clinking together. Her grandfather had recently purchased some new things for the kitchen in preparation for his wedding to Greta in the spring. She wasn't sure how to feel about it, but Greta seemed like a kindhearted woman. She'd given Anna a new yellow dress for her ninth birthday.

Anna threw her covers to the side, cold air grazing her toes. As she padded down the hallway in her nightgown, she wondered what treat her grandfather might be making in the middle of the night. But at the top of the stairs, she stopped short at the sight of an unfamiliar figure in the darkness downstairs.

"What are you up to, lad?" she heard her grandfather ask as he struck a match to light the lantern.

She jumped to see her grandfather appear next to a darkskinned teenage boy, probably only a little shorter than Levi. He had long black hair, and he was pulling pots down from the wooden shelves above the stove, stuffing them into a flour sack.

The kitchen counter that had contained potatoes and dried meat was empty.

The boy spun around. Rather than fleeing as she expected, the boy spit at her grandfather, shouting in a language she didn't know, nostrils flaring. Her grandfather took two steps back, and she felt a chill settle over her.

"Get outta here, you little thief. And leave our stuff," her grandfather said, his voice shaking.

The boy scoffed and pulled out a long knife. Her grandfather quickly grabbed the steel kettle and hit the boy hard over the head. The boy crumpled.

With a painful throbbing in her chest, Anna watched her grandfather take a step toward the boy. She waited for him to stand again and fight, but he lay motionless. Blood pooled around his head, soaking into the wood floor. Her grandfather nudged the boy's shoulder, then tried to sit him upright, but he slumped like a ragdoll.

He peered behind his shoulder and up the stairs, but she ducked lower into the darkness below the banister. The front door slammed shut, and then, they were both gone.

A few minutes later, the front door knob rattled, and her grandfather tiptoed back in. He blew out the lantern, but the shadows didn't hide his look of horror.

She took a step down to reveal herself. "What happened, Grandfather?"

He jumped, then stared at her stone-faced. "I broke a jar of jam, lassie. Go back upstairs—don't want you stepping on broken glass in the dark."

"Where's the boy?"

He locked the front door and paused a moment before answering. "What did you see?"

"He was stealing, wasn't he, Grandfather? So, you hit him."

He nodded slowly. "I've propped him up against a tree for now. He'll come to soon enough and scurry home."

He balled his fists then released them. Her grandfather hadn't moved from the shadow of the doorway, but she could see the blood on his arms.

"Just a boy. Get back in bed."

The lantern flickered as he lit it again to reveal a spot of blood soaking into the wood. He lifted the iron lid of the boiler on the cook stove and ladled water into a bucket.

Anna came down the stairs and pulled a rag off the counter. "I'll help."

He sighed and shook his head. She thought he might cry, so she looked away. When the floor was as clean as it was going to get, her grandfather put his boots on.

"Now, back to bed, please."

She gave a small nod as he gathered the bloody rags then left. She should do as he said, but her heart ached to see the boy one more time, to make sure he was all right. From the window, she watched the lantern light dance across the boy's sleeping face. Her grandfather shook the boy's shoulder gently, then harder, and finally slumped to the ground in front of him. Then, all was still.

As her eyes began to droop with exhaustion, she padded back up to bed. Her grandfather had everything under control.

CHAPTER EIGHTEEN
THE ABUNDANCE

6 September 1889

The morning after going out drinking with Levi, Ben strolled
by the docks to smell the ocean breeze. He could feel the
cold air through the thick wool of his brown sweater, and the sting
made him feel alive. After the happy commotion of staying with
the Gallaghers, his apartment had felt lonely. Not only did he miss
Anna, but Greta reminded him of his own mother who he
thought of often. But he couldn't go anywhere near Berkeley now.

He was an only child. One night, he'd overheard his parents
telling their friends, *"We love our little Benjamin, but we certainly won't
be having any more children,"* followed by knowing laughter. He had
longed for siblings, if only to have other children to play with. As
a professor and librarian, his parents both believed the only
worthwhile life was an intellectual one, where one *read* about
adventures rather than actually going on them.

He wasn't sure how he belonged to them. He was forever
lonely and had learned French so he could at least play with his

nanny. She was friendly but pressured by his parents not to be too soft or affectionate toward him. They played chess, read books together, and took walks in the garden, but it was nothing like the manner of play most children enjoy—wild, imaginative, messy, loud.

Perhaps if his parents hadn't read him adventure stories, he wouldn't be so attracted to salty air on his face, or snow on a mountaintop, or watching the world disappear behind him on a train. If they knew the extent of his adventurous and nomadic life these days, they'd think it ridiculous.

He'd been to Alaska, Washington, Oregon, and all over the Pacific Ocean. The height of the mountains, the fullness of the forest, and the vastness of the ocean fed his soul, but he was always hungry for more. He still felt lonely, but had grown used to it over the years. He enjoyed the closeness between the men on fishing boats, where it was difficult to find a moment of solitude and silence—he didn't mind that one bit.

He tried to think of an excuse to visit the Gallaghers, but he couldn't think of anything reasonable, having just been there the evening before. He recalled the look on Anna's face as he'd handed her the firewood; she'd felt so strong as he placed each piece in her arms. He wondered if *Anna Karenina* had been translated into English yet, and how he might be able to get a copy. It would make a wonderful gift for Anna.

And he hoped she hadn't yet solved the inscription so he could help. It was refreshing to be around a woman who loved literature and mystery—someone with a curious mind.

ANOTHER MONTH SLIPPED AWAY while Anna worked with Greta to prepare for winter. The bookstore was half empty anyway, and she felt more useful tending the abundance of the garden. Ben hadn't visited in weeks, and she wondered if he'd forgotten about her. Everything was more fun when he was around.

One evening, her grandfather brought home a new periodical. It was a series he'd subscribed to that was being published in installments. Anna froze when she saw the title of the most recent issue thrown lazily on the table: "An Ascent of Mount Rainier" by John Muir.

After everyone had gone to bed, she snuck downstairs, pulled Esther onto her lap, and read each word hungrily.

Ambitious climbers, seeking adventures and opportunities to test their strength and skill, occasionally attempt to penetrate the wilderness on the west side of the Sound, and push on to the summit of Mount Olympus. But the grandest excursion of all to be made hereabouts is to Mount Rainier, to climb to the top of its icy crown. The mountain is very high, fourteen thousand four hundred feet, and laden with glaciers that are terribly roughened and interrupted by crevasses and ice cliffs.

She was in awe. It was at once inspiring and overwhelming. Could she really do it?

In the following days, she gazed up at the mountain often as she worked in the garden. Sometimes when she looked toward the forest, she thought she saw Heather, but when she scanned again, there was nothing. The woman drifted in and out of her mind, though, and she wondered when she might see her again. She had so much to ask her about navigating the woods, and she wanted to get her opinions on the training she was planning to do. Her friends felt like a distant memory—she hadn't seen June in forever either.

On a crisp October day, billowy clouds sagged low in the sky, and a cool wind blew from the west. Anna stood at the entrance of the root cellar as the sun rose, with Greta by her side, admiring the full shelves lined with raspberry and blackberry jams and jellies, plum preserves, pickles, and stewed tomatoes.

Some of the potatoes, parsnips, carrots, and onions had been dug up from the garden, but they were leaving others still growing in the ground until the first frost. With great satisfaction, she closed the wooden cellar door tightly before following Greta up the stairs.

Anna linked arms with her. "Thank you for making all this happen. We'll feast all winter."

"Couldn't have done it without you, dear." Greta squeezed her hand with a small smile.

As they came back in the house, they were met with the scent of all things apple. Peeled and cored apple slices hung from the ceiling to dry, and Anna immediately got busy peeling more.

"Peel the entire apple in one long slice then throw it over your left shoulder," Greta said, a twinkle in her eye. "And whatever letter it most resembles when it lands is the first name of the man you'll marry."

Greta giggled and looked back down at the apple she was coring. "That's what we did growin' up."

"That's silly." Anna couldn't help but laugh at Greta's giddiness. "All right, fine."

Anna carved the skin off a rather large yellow-red apple and made a great show of tossing it behind her. They both scrambled to where it landed to make out the letter.

"Looks like a G," Greta said. "Or maybe a C."

They were both quiet for a moment, then Anna returned to the kitchen work table as her grandfather came down the stairs rubbing his eyes.

"How long have you ladies been up? It's Saturday."

"This ought to be the last day for apples," Greta said. "Then Anna can head back to the bookstore. I know you've been missing her."

He cleared his throat and nodded before pulling a chair up to the table and grabbing an apple to peel. "Gosh, applesauce simmering on the stove, a pie in the oven, winter pies and sauces coming. I'm a lucky old man."

He paused, discarding a peel into the pile. "You know, I read in the paper yesterday about a colored man named William Grose. He sold his hotel for five thousand dollars, but it burned down in the fire. Then, he found the new owner and gave him back his five thousand. What a generous man!"

"You have no qualms with a colored business man, but Chief Seattle's daughter livin' in a tiny house in town bothers you." Greta shook her head.

"That's completely different," he said, unamused. "There are only a handful of colored men in Seattle, and they're proper and successful. Not running around barefoot like savages."

Levi joined them at the table and bit into an especially large red apple. "Can I invite Ben hunting? He's decided to stay in Seattle for the winter."

Anna's ears perked up. So, he was still in town. "What's he been up to?"

Her brother glanced at her sidelong. "We've just been working at the mill, savin' our pennies."

She nodded and turned away so he couldn't read her expression. What did her face look like anyway? Her heart was pounding.

⚜

Leaning against a bookshelf, Anna considered the furnishings of the bookstore. The same simple objects had adorned the shelves since her childhood—a worn globe, leather-bound books, her grandfather's stained-glass lamp. She sighed nostalgically. Although the rows of books had thinned, she still enjoyed the tranquility. It was good to be back.

Emily had sent an invitation to join her for tea that afternoon, so she wore a light blue cotton dress with white organza lace on the neckline—something she felt good in. She felt a little silly working at the bookstore all dressed up and wearing vanilla-lavender powder on her neck, but she wanted to look nice at tea.

After work, she knocked at Emily's door.

"I'm so glad you came!" Emily said, before leading her into the house.

As they reached the drawing room, she turned to face Anna, her ribbed silk skirt swooshing around her ankles. "It's wonderful to have you visit. It feels like old times."

"So good to see you as well." Anna accepted the delicate teacup Emily handed her and sat in an overstuffed chair.

The ornate oak coffee table beside it had intricate vines engraved in each corner. The feet were rounded into knobby spirals, and two oversized leather books sat on top, which Emily had moved to the side to set down the tray with tea and cookies. Anna peered around the room to see two vases standing on either side of the mantle and a roaring fire behind an iron screen.

She sighed at the decadence. Emily's husband was a banker, ten years her senior, already well established in his career. His house was already decorated in fine, imported furniture, but he had let Emily choose new wallpaper, rugs, and curtains for the entire house. Her eyes were drawn to the elk head above the fireplace, which made her think of Ben.

"We should invite June next time." Anna fidgeted with the buttons on her dress without looking up.

"Certainly not. My husband wouldn't allow it, and I won't put my reputation on the line just because she decided to do *that* with her life." Emily took a long sip of her tea.

"I do wish you two would get along." Anna thought it best to change the subject and pointed to the elk head. "Does your husband hunt often?"

"Quite often. He enjoys it immensely."

"Have you ever asked to join him?"

Emily laughed merrily. "Why ever would I want to do that?"

"To help." She focused on the large grandfather clock in the corner of the room, the pendulum quietly swinging back and forth, its golden circles spinning importantly behind the glass.

"I'm sure he wouldn't want a lady slowing him down, and besides, it's messy business, hunting," said Emily. "Sometimes he's gone for days. I can't imagine being gone from the comforts of the city for more than an afternoon. Is that something you'd enjoy?"

Anna set her teacup and saucer on the coffee table. "I think I might. It would be a fine skill to have—being able to find food in the wilderness."

Emily's eyebrows scrunched. She set her cup down with great care and straightened her back and neck. "I suppose I'd worry about my reputation. Might not be seen as ladylike. I'll leave the hunting and traipsing around in the forest to the fellas."

Emily hadn't always been like this.

"What do you spend most of your time doing now that you're married?" Anna wanted to playfully add "in the comforts of the city," but she thought better of it.

Emily lifted a strand of hair and twisted up into her chignon.

"Mostly cooking and sewing. Charles said we can get a housekeeper soon, so I'll be able to spend more time calling on other ladies." She glanced at Anna with a serious expression. "It's important, you know. In our station. Charles also said we'll be one of the first families in town to get one of those new twenty-dollar refrigerators we read about in the paper."

"Impressive." Anna paused, trying to read her friend. "Would you say you're happy?"

"Of course. Charles is exactly the sort of man I always hoped to marry." She lowered her voice and leaned closer. "Speaking of possible husbands, Charles's friend Mr. Jonathon Conway is unmarried and just purchased a new home on the next street over. He works at the bank, too, and Charles says he'll certainly be successful. Would you mind terribly if I invited you both for dinner sometime? You'll adore him."

A glimmer of desire surfaced in Anna. She thought of the future she'd hoped for as a young girl. But chances were that this banker had the same opinions and expectations for a wife as Connor. "Things are a little busy right now. I'd be happy to meet him soon, though."

"Certainly. Do let me know, and I'll have the invitations sent out right away." She sat upright, her eyes suddenly opening wide. "I almost forgot. Someone was shot right on our street last week!"

"A murder? Who was killed?"

Emily shook her head. "Charles said it was an Indian. They aren't allowed to be in town after dusk, you know. Perhaps the poor man was confused on account of the days being so short this time of year. He worked in town, but Charles says if they linger they're most likely up to no good. I think it's sad, though…"

Anna shook her head in disbelief. "Is that a law?"

Emily shrugged. She set her cup down and brushed a crumb off her lap. "Not sure. Seems unreasonable to me. They can work in town, sell baskets at the market, but aren't allowed to be seen here in the evening? You'd think it'd be fine for both or neither."

Anna's pulse pounded noisily in her head. She imagined Heather coming to visit her at dusk and getting spotted by a man with a gun. She shuddered. The light of the sun faded by five in the winter, earlier on particularly overcast days. What were the Duwamish to do—run home after work to escape the city? No wonder Heather refused to come to town.

After more small talk and another cup of tea, she started home, eager to be comfortable in her own cozy bedroom. It wasn't likely that she'd be able to reconcile her two childhood friends, which put a hollow feeling in the pit of her stomach, but at least they were both still in her life.

CHAPTER NINETEEN

THE BOW

The October sunshine, yellow leaves, and sunny days made for a gorgeous Pacific Northwest autumn. Normally, blue skies and mild weather put Anna in a good mood, but she was melancholy that she hadn't made any headway with the book inscription since the Occidental Hotel.

One windy but sunny Saturday morning at the end of the month, she awoke early and plopped down at the kitchen table with Muir's account of summiting Mount Rainier.

> *We passed for a mile or two through a forest of mixed growth, mainly silver fir, Patton spruce, and mountain pine, and then came to the charming park region, at an elevation of about five thousand feet above sea level.... Every one of these parks, great and small, is a garden filled knee-deep with fresh, lovely flowers of every hue, the most luxuriant and the most extravagantly beautiful of all the alpine gardens I ever beheld in all my mountain-top wanderings.*

She looked up to the mountain in wonder. All of this beauty, so near. She went out the door to get a better view, when she saw a small scroll of paper rolled up in the corner of the seat. She went back inside and grabbed her coat to meet Heather at the forest edge.

"*Wiiac,*" Anna said with a smile. "It's good to see you two."

Heather returned the greeting, motioning for Anna to follow, then winced as Pisha flung herself to one side to greet Anna. "My back hurts."

As she adjusted the chubby toddler, Anna had an idea.

"I heard back from a mountaineering team that plans to summit Mount Rainier this coming summer." She paused to read her friend's face. She hadn't said those words out loud yet, and it made her spine tingle.

Heather stopped and cocked her head. "That's good, right?"

Anna chuckled nervously. "Yes. It is—it's all new, but I'm excited. And...if it's all right, I'd love to carry Pisha on my back. Since you're sore, and I need the practice of carrying heavy weight..."

Heather nodded, already untying the mess of fabric. Pisha squealed with delight when she realized what was happening. After some careful adjustments and a few tight knots, Heather had Pisha strapped in tightly on Anna's back.

The weight seemed easy at first, but as they hiked and chatted about the reading primers Heather was working through, Anna felt the fabric dig in around her shoulders, and the muscles in her back started to ache. She obviously had a long way to go.

Heather ducked beneath a low branch. "I'll take you halfway to my home. There's a faster way than you came last time."

She nodded, and they continued south on a path she'd never taken. Pisha tapped her shoulder to get her attention then giggled, so she swung around to make a silly face, then stopped abruptly facing the opposite direction. It looked surprisingly different than what she saw facing forward. She took in the tall trees and ferns lining the path. Although she always strived to memorize her surroundings as she moved forward, she'd never thought to actually turn around and take it all in, knowing it would be the view on her way home.

As they continued, she paid special attention to the sounds— the vibrations of life. They stopped at an opening in the woods at a large thicket of blackberry bushes.

"There was a bear here earlier," Heather said in a tone that Anna felt was much too nonchalant.

The three of them enjoyed a quick snack of berries as they walked.

Anna snapped off a long branch of thorns. "I'm going to put these around a tree a little farther on. To help me find my way home."

About fifteen minutes later, Anna wrapped the thorns around a thin sapling. Then she turned and studied the way they'd come, soaking up the image. Shortly after, they came upon a small stream, ten feet down an embankment.

She was considerably out of breath from carrying Pisha. The weight felt like more than twenty pounds. Heather smiled and took Pisha out of the carrier. "This is about the middle."

Birds chirped, and toads croaked down at the water. Anna sat on a log to rest, her muscles throbbing. It had felt like a little over an hour so far, and she figured it would take about two hours to go straight to Heather's house. It was something she could work up to and make a day of in the future, especially if she left early. She could improve her time as her lungs adjusted, especially if she didn't stop to rest.

Heather nursed the girl, holding on to her daughter's chubby little hand until it suddenly shot up and pulled one of her mother's long braids. Anna sat nearby and noticed how pale the little girl's hands were compared to Heather's copper skin.

She couldn't think of a graceful way to broach the subject so she simply asked. "Who is Pisha's father?"

Heather glanced at Anna with surprise. She set Pisha down,

and the girl toddled unsteadily. "His name is Michael. He's a good man, but he doesn't think so."

Anna put her chin in her hand and glanced at the little girl who was throwing pebbles into the stream. She guessed Pisha was about a year and a half now.

"He was in the army. He saw battles that still bother him. Women and children killed because their skin was dark. He says he deserted and that's a bad thing."

Pisha wandered closer to the bank of the stream, and Heather pulled her back right before she attempted to dive in. She seemed so blasé about the save that Anna could only assume it was a regular occurrence.

"When did you meet him?"

"A few years ago. We're married now, but he refuses to live with us." Heather sat back and squared her shoulders.

Anna tilted her head to the side with interest. "Why?"

"He's angry, but he's never hurt us. Or done anything violent around us. But he's afraid he could." She picked out the pebbles from Pisha's balled up fists. "He thinks he has bad spirits following him. He calls them demons. He dreams of terrible things and thinks it's his punishment."

"I'm sorry."

"He lives in town—spends most nights in saloons for the fights." She paused, then smiled proudly. "But he works hard to take care of us. And when he holds me, all my problems seem easier to handle. I miss him so much when he's away."

Heather's eyes looked sad, but content.

"You're lucky then," Anna said.

Heather's marriage was uncommon and yet she seemed quite happy. It was inspiring to know there were different ways a marriage could be successful and bring happiness, even deep in the woods and completely outside of society.

With a devious look, Pisha bolted toward the trees behind

them. Heather ran and scooped her up, her face stern. "Be careful or Tataliya will get you."

Anna glanced toward the woods with concern. "What is Tataliya?"

Heather smiled and whispered, "Something we tell kids to keep them good—keep them safe."

Anna stood, brushing dry leaves and needles off the back of her skirts.

Heather put Pisha on her back, then put her hand on Anna's arm. "I really enjoy talking with you, Anna. Want to meet here on Sunday—halfway?"

"Likewise. And yes, next Sunday sounds perfect." She planned to pack a bag full of books to wear on her back to build her endurance.

"Good. Next Sunday when the sun is highest. We'll have lunch at my house."

Anna grinned. "I'm looking forward to it."

They parted ways, and she waved to Pisha as she bounced away on her mother's back. Levi would probably be awake by now and counting the minutes until she returned, or he might even be searching for her, so she hurried.

She soon saw the blackberry thorns wrapped around the thin tree and later the meadow with the blackberry thicket. She pulled off another branch of thorns to wrap around a tree farther on, but it sliced inside her left wrist. The sting only lasted a moment, but the bleeding was more than she expected.

From the meadow, she expected it should only take thirty minutes to get home, and the path became wider with tall grass on either side. Halfway from the meadow to her house, she wrapped the thorns around a tree so she'd recognize the path the following Sunday when they were to meet at the creek. She was pleased with herself. There was a spring in her step as she left the cover of trees and bounded up the porch steps.

Inside, she found Levi and Ben sitting at the table eating

lunch. They both stood as she entered—Levi seemed concerned. Her hair was still in a long French braid, a few large pieces falling out, her dress muddy on the hem and dirty in the back where she'd sat near the stream. Blood dripped down her wrist from her cut. She knew she looked a fright, but she didn't mind. She felt accomplished and strong.

"I'm perfectly fine, Levi. Don't look at me like that."

He pursed his lips together. "Where were you?"

"Walking." She sank into a chair and unlaced her boots.

"May I...? I mean...would you like me to look at that cut?" Ben seemed to hold his breath.

She nodded and held out her hand. His hand felt rough, and she peeked up at his concerned face.

"Looks like a thorn got you. We should wash it and tie a cloth around your hand." Ben looked up and gave her a sheepish smile when he saw her eyes on him.

She turned away in a hurry. "I'll wash upstairs and change. Are you staying for dinner?"

Did her tone reveal her hope?

Ben nodded. "Yes ma'am."

A wave of cheerfulness washed over her, her blood still pumping from the exercise—and maybe his touch. After she changed, she joined Greta to prepare Sunday dinner, which was usually quite the event at the Gallagher house. To save money, they'd been making do with simple dinners of cheese and bread, but tonight they prepared a small chicken with boiled potatoes, sweet corn, and a small lemon meringue pie. Her grandfather retrieved a bottle of his dwindling wine from the cellar and served everyone a small glass.

After everyone took their place, Anna spooned corn onto her plate. "Ben, do you like poetry? I've been reading a book of poems by Ella Wheeler Wilcox."

"I do. I'd love to borrow it when you're finished, if you don't mind." He glanced up at her briefly then adjusted the napkin on his lap. "Any progress on the inscription?"

She frowned. "Nothing new I'm afraid."

Before the meal ended, she peered over at her grandfather who was serving himself a large helping of chicken and then leaned toward Ben. "Would you still be willing to teach me to shoot a bow?"

His face lit up. "Anytime. Next Sunday good?"

She remembered her plans to meet Heather around noon on Sunday. "First thing in the morning?"

Ben's lips turned up in a grin. "Excellent. I'll be here around seven."

Levi shot him a steely look. "I'll join you."

"Of course—that's the plan." Ben gave Levi a friendly pat on the back.

Anna remembered her brother's warning, but shrugged it off.

Her grandfather exhaled loudly. "My only granddaughter, hunting with the boys. You can hold your own in the most complicated society conversations. Isn't that enough?"

Greta dismissed the suggestion with a wave of her hand. "Let the girl live the way she wants."

He grunted and pushed himself away from the table noisily.

"Why don't you give me a hand with these dishes, Anna?" Greta flashed a smile.

Anna cleared the table while Levi and Ben retreated into the living room to join her grandfather.

In the kitchen, Greta didn't look up from the dishes. "Ben sure is a nice man."

"He is." But the moment outside the dance hall flashed in her mind, and his words afterward—that she was foolish for being alone. "I'm not sure how long he'll be around though. And in some ways, he seems much like all the other men in town, don't you think?"

Greta glanced up at her. "If you say so, darlin'."

CHAPTER TWENTY
THE LESSON

After a hearty breakfast of eggs and potatoes, Anna braided her hair then coiled the end to pin at the nape of her neck. After an uneventful week at the bookstore, Sunday had finally arrived, and she couldn't wait to learn archery. It was a warm day for early November, but a coat was still necessary. She packed bread and ham, tucking them into a cloth.

Levi had found his old bow that he said would be a good size for her, and she was finishing her coffee when there was a light knock. On the porch, Ben stood with his bow slung on his back over a brown sweater and leather vest.

They set off immediately, and as they moved through fir trees, orange and burgundy leaves carpeted the path.

"*The autumn wood robed in its scarlet clothes,*" she said with a whimsical smile. "That's from a poem I read last week."

"The book of poems you were telling me about?" Ben asked.

She nodded, happy he remembered. She stepped over large ferns growing like oversized flowers at the bottom of evergreens, and he soon found a thick trunk for a target. He drew on it with chalk—a large circle with a smaller circle in the middle.

Anna put her hands at her side, ready. "When did you learn, Ben?"

"Starting about eight, my dad took me out every weekend," he said. "It's an art—you have to practice so it becomes natural. Let me show you first with my bow, then you can try with yours."

Levi plopped onto the ground, leaning against a nearby tree, and dropped his hat over his face. "I don't know why we had to rise with the sun."

Ben stood with his feet perpendicular to the target, and in one graceful motion, he pulled an arrow from the quiver, put it to the bow, and drew back the string. He hesitated for a moment before releasing the arrow—bullseye.

Anna clapped. "Well done, sir."

A light blush colored his face. "Your turn."

He gestured for her to come to him. "Here, point your feet in the same direction as mine... Good."

He handed her Levi's old bow and stood behind her. "No arrows for a minute. Just get everything lined up for practice. May I direct your arms?"

Levi lifted his hat to peek at them.

"Of course." Anna tried to relax her shoulders and focus on the target.

Ben lifted her left arm, which held the bow, then put his right hand over hers, pulling the string back toward her shoulder. She could feel his chest against her back and his right bicep against the back of her right arm.

Her heart pounded, and she hoped he couldn't feel it. "I think...I have it—thank you."

He handed her an arrow. "All right, you want it to rest on your left hand while you're taking aim. Here—I'll pull back and release it this time."

He stood behind her again and somehow it was more comfortable than before. She relaxed against his touch, and the arrow shot out of their hands, landing right next to the first arrow.

"How did that feel?" He immediately stepped away.

Her heart still pounded. "Good."

His face was hard to read. That concern in his eyes on the night of the dance—maybe he hadn't thought her weak—maybe he was just afraid of what might have happened.

Levi stood, brushing needles off the seat of his pants. "I'm sure she's got it now."

Ben handed her an arrow, which she tried to line up by herself. He let her struggle for a minute before making one adjustment to her right hand. She let the arrow fly, and it fell short, five feet in front of the tree.

Levi laughed, and Ben gave him a look. Levi cleared his throat and picked up a fallen branch. He pulled out a pocket knife and whittled at the bark, still smiling.

Ben turned back to her. "That was good. You were holding it right—there's just one thing."

He came up behind her again and lifted her right elbow higher. "Now, be still."

Anna didn't move, her back resting against his chest as he placed another arrow into her hand, his right hand returning to her right elbow, keeping it high.

"You should…" he trailed off, and she studied his face, inches away. He stood mute, as if he were about to say something.

His soft touch against her elbow and his breath against her face sparked a warmth in her chest. She lifted her eyebrows, hoping he would speak.

Ben glanced up at Levi, then stepped back from her. "Now release it as you exhale."

Anna inhaled then released the arrow with her breath. This time, the arrow skimmed the tree trunk about two feet above the large circle.

"Great job!" Ben threw his hands in the air. He rushed to her, then stopped short with a pat on her back.

After more practice shots, he set down his bow. "Let's take a break. I'm sure your arms are tired. Are your fingers sore?"

She nodded and found a fallen tree to lean against. The forest floor felt cold and damp through her skirts, but the moss on the tree made a soft place to recline. Ben sank down beside her, and Levi joined them, still working on his branch. They shared the bread and ham, along with water from Ben's canteen.

What would Ben think of her interest in climbing the mountain? He didn't seem to think less of her for wanting to learn archery, but she wagered it would be too risky to bring it up now.

Afterward, Anna did ten more practice shots and one time hit inside the larger circle, at which they both shouted in celebration. Levi looked up and smiled, shaking his head.

To celebrate her success, she and Ben plopped down again against the log. Then, to her surprise, Ben pulled out a chocolate bar.

"It's from Belgium, and I'll only share if you fully appreciate the luxuriousness." He gave her a playful grin.

Levi scowled. "I hate chocolate."

Anna nodded slowly with mock seriousness. "I shall enjoy every bite."

But as soon as she tasted it, she melted—it was decadent, a luxury she wasn't used to, especially lately. They didn't speak for nearly a minute while they both enjoyed their large pieces.

"Thought anymore about the clues?" asked Ben.

"Yes, but I've no idea how to figure out which ship he and Natalya came to America on. That's the clue Connor tried to convince me was impossible, and I fear he might have been right."

Ben grunted and shook his head.

"I wouldn't put much stock in what that man said." He stood, picking up his bow. "Well, they likely came on a passenger ship from Russia—it's a regular route. And we know the year he wrote it, 1880, so that'll narrow it down to ships in commission before then."

"Yes, excellent. I wonder if there are public records of those ships." She stood facing him.

He rubbed his jaw thoughtfully. "It would help if we knew his last name."

"Where did you say you found the book?" Levi asked.

Just then, a branch cracked behind them, and in one fluid motion, Ben lifted his bow and readied an arrow in the direction of the noise.

CHAPTER TWENTY-ONE
THE REALIZATION

"Don't shoot." Heather came out from behind the tree with her hands in front of her. "It's just me."

Ben lowered his bow. "Pardon me...miss. I thought it was an animal. Do you need help?"

Anna exchanged glances with Heather. "Actually, she's my friend. Ben, Levi, this is Heather."

Ben's forehead scrunched, and he stared at her with a searching expression. "You never mentioned you have an Indian friend."

She shrugged. "You never asked?"

With his mouth hanging open, Levi glanced from Anna to Heather.

Ben cleared his throat. "Nice to meet you, Heather. Do you live nearby?"

"I don't live in town, if that's what you're asking." She looked to Anna for help. "I'm sorry, you weren't at the creek. I thought you forgot, so I came."

It was late in the afternoon already, and Anna cringed. "It's my fault, I'm sorry. I should have paid more attention to the time. We were having such a pleasant time, and..."

Ben was smiling at her. "It was the chocolate, right?"

Levi finally found his voice. "How are you friends? How long?"

Anna bit her lip and turned to Heather.

"This is my brother and his friend. We can trust them." She turned back to the men. "Heather lives in a cabin a few miles south. She's the one who gave me the book."

Heather looked them both up and down, then nodded. Anna wondered what she might be thinking—her eyes seemed doubtful. "Okay, Anna. I trust you."

She sighed with relief. "Now we're all friends."

Heather winced with a half-smile. "I guess you all can come...if you want."

"I'd be honored. Is this the cabin the book was found in?" Ben asked.

Anna nodded.

He clapped his hands together once triumphantly. "Then we might find a clue to the name of the previous owner."

They all strode toward Heather's cabin. Anna broke off a fern and started fanning Levi with it, giggling. "King Levi!"

He frowned and pulled her aside. "Grandfather would be furious."

"You won't tell him, will you?" She peered up at him with pleading eyes.

He groaned. "I'm not comfortable with this situation. Are there any more Indians living with her? Any men?"

As they walked, she hugged him sideways. "No, it's just her baby and grandmother."

She thought of Michael, but technically, he didn't live there.

Anna showed them where she'd marked the tree on the way to the meadow with blackberries. "It's where I cut my hand."

They soon came upon the meadow, but most of the berries were gone—the weather had finally turned colder and windy. By the time they arrived at the stream it was nearly dinnertime, and Anna asked Ben for another drink of his water, which he quickly got for her.

Heather watched them, and her eyes lit up with understanding. "Is this the man who stayed with your family?"

Anna blushed deeply and pretended to tie her shoelace. "Yes."

Ben tried to hide his smile.

Heather nodded and stepped onto the fallen log over the stream, indicating for the others to follow.

On the last leg of the journey, they were surrounded by moss-drenched trees—green dripping from branches like icicles. Since Anna had gone to the cabin a different way last time, she stopped a few times to look back the way they'd come, marking a few trees with Ben's chalk. Between the lush ferns on the ground, green needles and moss on the trees, it felt like walking into an emerald-hued picture book.

When they arrived at Heather's cabin, her grandmother was sitting at the table and took Pisha into her arms, her eyes wide. Heather put both hands on her grandmother's shoulders and whispered in her ear before announcing, "This is my grandmother, Kiyotsa."

The older woman said something in Lushootseed, and Heather translated. "She says 'Welcome, I acknowledge your presence.'"

Heather served up large helpings of smoked salmon with clover sprouts and flatbread.

After they had eaten, Ben asked, "Would you mind if I took a look around to see if there might be any clue to the man's last name who wrote the inscription?"

Heather fidgeted with the end of her braid. "That's fine."

He examined the fireplace and the table, before going over to the corner where the large wooden trunk sat in the shadows. "May I open this?"

It was engraved with a winding branch across the length of the trunk, small leaves and a flower here and there.

Heather nodded, and he found furs and blankets. He examined the underside of the lid, then glared at the window, which only seemed to lighten the main room. "Can someone bring me a candle?"

Anna brought the candle from the table and put it near the underside of the lid. Nearly worn thin, they found a faint engraving: *Dmitri Ivanov.*

Ben and Anna locked eyes with matching grins.

But before they could speak, a knock on the door made Anna jump. A tall, blond man in a thin coat and army-issued hat stood at the front door holding a box. It was the man she'd seen hovering in the dark at the edge of the forest.

Confusion furrowed his brow, and he glared at Ben and Levi. "What's going on here?"

Heather took his hand in her own. "This is my husband Michael. Michael, this is my friend Anna." She hesitated then turned to the men. "And this is her brother and friend."

Michael's gaze flitted around the room, then he offered a nod to both men.

Ben extended his hand, which Michael shook heartily.

Levi cleared his throat and followed suit. "Nice to meet you, Michael."

Michael turned back to Heather, lowering his voice. "I've got powdered milk, sugar, flour, chocolate, apples, carrots, and a new cast iron pot. And I'll go fish the branches out of the well. I saw some pecking out from inside."

He kissed her softly on her forehead.

Ben tipped his hat. "We should head back. Thank you for your kindness, ma'am, and nice to meet you, Michael."

As they began to walk home, Anna prepared herself for the barrage of questions.

Levi shook his head, adjusting his hat. "I honestly don't know where to start."

"You can't tell Grandfather." She grabbed his arm tightly.

"How much do you even know about these people?"

Levi's arm was stiff, but she knew she could wear him down.

"I've spent time with them. Well, with Heather. That was the first time I've met Michael."

"So, you might have unexpectedly gone to visit your Indian friend and found a strange man visiting? Anna, please think of your safety." He frowned and looked to Ben for agreement, but Ben held his hands out palms up as if to bow out of the sibling argument. "I won't tell Grandfather. Just promise me you won't make a habit of coming out here, okay?"

She squeezed his arm, but fell silent, glancing to Ben, who gave her a half-hearted smile. That was a promise she couldn't make.

❦

AS THE GALLAGHERS sat around the breakfast table the following Saturday, Levi put his fork down. "Met any gentleman lately, Anna?"

She didn't look up as she buttered a slice of bread. "I certainly don't want to marry just anyone. Anyway, I'm eager to get to the docks to speak to Captain Pavitt. Ben is positive he can help us uncover which ship brought Dmitri."

"There are many eligible men in Seattle. *Good* men, Anna," he added.

She exhaled with a dramatic groan.

"Emily mentioned she might know someone I could meet." She twisted her napkin then untwisted it. "But I—"

134

"Excellent. You should meet the lad," her grandfather chimed in.

Why hadn't *Ben* asked to court her? The thought jumped into her head so suddenly it made her heart skip. He made her feel alive, the same way she felt when she was in sight of the mountain. She doubted her grandfather would allow it, but the idea put a thrill inside her.

Levi put his elbows on the table and leaned forward. "I know you don't think much of marrying well, but you're beautiful. Securing your future happiness with a successful gentleman won't be difficult, if you only try."

Her grandfather nodded emphatically, wiping his mouth with a napkin. "I agree. It's an excellent idea to meet him at least. She's certainly done well for herself."

Anna's face was stoic. "What if marrying a man of a certain upbringing and position won't make me happy? Is that still what you both would have me do?"

Her grandfather took a drink of coffee and slammed his cup down with a jolly smile. "Nonsense! Love is what makes the world go 'round."

He chuckled and reached for more bread.

Levi nodded at her encouragingly.

Anxiety tightened her chest—they had such high hopes for her marriage. She popped the last bite of bread into her mouth and stood, wiping crumbs off her lap. "Well, I'll meet the banker then."

Her grandfather's eyebrows flew up. "Wait, he's a banker?"

She frowned and tilted her head to the side. "Yes, but I'm not asking him for a loan."

"Yes, quite right., I was just thinking sometimes you need to know someone on the inside." He seemed quite satisfied.

Levi peered out the front window. "Here comes Ben."

Anna and Levi met him on the road, and they started toward town.

She felt her cheeks warm when Ben smiled at her and tipped his hat.

"So, the inscription was written in 1880, but it's possible they came here much earlier," she said, trying to focus on the business at hand.

Ben's face was hopeful. "I suppose we'll find out if that's enough information."

When they reached the waterfront, she could see about twenty-five ships moored as others came and went. A bald eagle rested motionless on a boulder ten feet off the rocky shore while the docks were alive with noise and commotion. They sidestepped tarps covered with fish and hoses spraying off the areas used to gut them. Wagons full of produce from Bellevue farms were being unloaded onto ships. A well-built bearded man heaved a canvas sack over his shoulder, nearly running into Anna as he turned.

They found their way to Levi and Ben's fishing vessel, which had *Troubadour* painted on the hull in black letters. A tall, thin man with white hair and beard stood on the boat directing men and looking much like an old pirate. Then he disappeared through a door in the hull.

Levi leaned in. "Stay here while we go speak with the captain."

She frowned. "Why can't I go?"

"Fine. But it'd be faster if we didn't have to explain to everyone why we brought a girl," he said sheepishly. "Just for the sake of time."

As they boarded, the sound of guitar strumming drifted from the captain's office. They followed the music and found him sitting on a stool, singing quietly.

Ben nodded then motioned toward Anna. "Captain Bob Pavitt, allow me to introduce Miss Anna Gallagher. Could we have a moment?"

He sat behind an oak desk and motioned for her to sit down

on the only other chair—a wobbly thing with a worn velvet covering. "What can I help ya with, miss?"

Anna took a deep breath. "Long story—I wondered if you could help us find out what ship might have brought Russians to Seattle in 1880 and the years before?"

He squinted his eyes at her and tilted his head to the side. "Well that's as simple as it is difficult, my dear."

She leaned forward in her chair. "How should we proceed?"

"I know a Russian captain who took over a ship about five years ago. We could check with him." The captain ushered them out off the boat, down to the next dock, and over to another boat. "You all wait here. Thompson is insufferable. I'll be right back."

About five minutes later, he hopped off the boat laughing and slapping another man on the back. "Much thanks, sir."

A smile danced on Anna's mouth as the excitement tingled down her arms, making the hair stand up in anticipation.

"He has no idea," Captain Pavitt whispered to Anna as they dodged a stack of crates on the dock.

CHAPTER TWENTY-TWO
THE RUMOR

Anna stopped abruptly, staring up at the captain in frustration. She fought the urge to stomp her foot like a child. It seemed that they were being led on a useless chase.

Ben fell into stride with them. "Did he have anything helpful to add?"

Captain Pavitt nodded. "He said his ship was just commissioned the year he took the helm, but he does know another ship that's been running that route for the last twenty years, and there have only been two captains, so the log has probably been well maintained. I'll take you to the current captain."

Once again, Anna had hope. She hurried to keep up with the three men who were more experienced in dodging fishermen and equipment on the docks; none of them had to wrangle skirts. A misting rain began again, and she pulled her shawl tighter around her shoulders, the rain soaking through.

Ben started to unbutton his coat. "Anna, would you like my coat?"

"No, I'm fine, thank you." She concealed a smile at his thoughtfulness.

When they reached the boat, Captain Pavitt explained what they were seeking, and the ship's captain pulled a large book from inside his desk and glanced up expectantly. "What name?"

"Dmitri Ivanov," she said.

The Russian captain laughed, then looked apologetic. "This is a common name, I'm afraid. Like John Smith in English. Do you know anyone else he traveled with? A relative, perhaps?"

She thought of the clue: *Remember well the ship that brought us to this wondrous place.* It said *us.* "Yes, Natalya. I don't know her last name, but I know they were on the ship together."

"And approximately how many years ago?" he asked.

She squared her shoulders. "I'm not sure exactly, sometime before 1880."

The captain grumbled under his breath as he skipped over about fifty pages. He scanned the ledger with his finger, and after two minutes, he turned the page.

"This may take a while, I'm afraid." He glanced at Captain Pavitt. "You're lucky I owe this man a favor. Is there an address I can send word to *if* I find your man?"

Anna's heart sank. Levi scribbled down their address, and they said their thanks and goodbyes to both captains. As they left, she could feel Ben's eyes on her.

"Let's be hopeful," he said. "The records should be fairly complete—it's just a matter of time. And if he doesn't, we can see if there are any public records like you mentioned."

She admired his positivity. "That might be wishful thinking. But yes, let's be hopeful."

Shouts came from a building nearby, then more yelling from down the street. Without warning, and with great force, a cannon shot toward the water from near the docks. Anna shuddered, grabbing onto her brother's arm, and the two men exchanged looks. Ben approached one of the men and asked what happened.

The man merrily patted him on the back. "President Harrison has signed the bill admitting us as the 42nd state!"

Soon, people began to spill out of buildings and into the street, sharing the news.

"I wonder if Grandfather knows?" Anna asked.

They hurried home and found him playing his harmonica and dancing around the living room while the cat watched suspiciously from the corner.

"There's gonna be a great celebration in Olympia next week," Levi said to his grandfather. "Should we take the train down to celebrate?"

The older man grabbed Anna and started dancing and singing an Irish folk song. "Why travel when we can celebrate right here?"

He twirled her, and she tossed her head back, laughing. When Greta rushed in from the kitchen, he ran to pick her up off the ground in a hug—and right there in front of everyone, he kissed her.

Levi whooped and took over on the harmonica. Greta's face flushed light pink as he whisked her into his arms to dance, and she laughed. Ben smiled at Anna, and her heart soared in anticipation of him asking her to dance, but instead, he scooped up the cat, sat near the fire, then motioned for her to join him.

"Thank you for your help today with the captains," she said over the music.

"It was nothing." He pet Esther slowly then looked up at her. "Read me a poem from your book."

She swallowed. All the poems were about love and passion. She pulled the book off the shelf and carefully thumbed through the pages. She had dog-eared and underlined her favorite lines, but none felt appropriate for sharing at the moment. Clearing her throat, she began.

The meadow and the mountain with desire
gazed on each other, till a fierce unrest
surged beneath the meadows seemingly calm breast,
and all the mountain's fissures ran with fire.
A mighty river rolled between them there.
What could the mountain do but gaze and burn?
What could the meadow do but look and yearn?

"That's beautiful," Ben said, holding her gaze steadily.

The moment was too much.

"I'm finished with it, if you still wanted to borrow it." She thrust the book toward him, which he took. "And, I know I didn't say anything specifically about it at the time, but please don't tell anyone about Heather."

He winked. "Don't worry, I can keep a secret."

"Oh really? Me too." She studied him. Did he fancy her?

With a sweet smile, she raised her eyebrows slightly, daring him to share something.

His expression became serious as he focused on the cat's fur.

"Hmm, Esther, what secrets should I share with Miss Gallagher?" Then he whispered, "I always keep a letter with me, even though it makes me sad."

Anna frowned empathetically, then she shifted uncomfortably. "From a woman who loves you?"

"Technically yes, but—"

"Well, my friend Emily is going to introduce me to a man," she blurted out. She regretted it immediately, but there was no turning back. "He's a banker and supposedly he's *successful.*"

She said the last word with sarcastic emphasis.

His face darkened. "Is that what you want?"

"It's what I'm supposed to want, isn't it?" She searched his eyes. "Love isn't as important as a proper match and a stable respectable home according to most people around here."

She exhaled. "Have you ever been in love?"

"I did fall for a gal in my British literature class. Did I tell you literature was my major?"

She felt her face blush with jealousy, both for the education and that he loved someone else. "Is that why you left Berkeley?"

He grinned. "No."

He paused suggestively, as if withholding precious information, which he was. "She wasn't for me. A difference in dreams, I guess you could say."

"What *are* your dreams?" She was afraid he could read her growing interest in him.

His expression softened as he studied her face. "Traveling, hunting, being among the trees under the stars."

Her stomach jumped at his answer. She imagined being on his arm as they traveled the world. "There's something I want to share with you, but promise never to tell any——"

"What are you guys talking about?" Levi dropped to a squatting position and put his head between them. Esther startled and jumped out of Ben's lap with a low hiss.

Ben stood and straightened his shirt. "Talking about you, of course."

Anna sighed—the moment was gone. Her grandfather and Greta joined them all in the living room, and the celebration continued, ever louder.

She took a deep breath. She had been under the spell of those brown eyes, the color of tree trunks, and now that it was broken, she was relieved she hadn't revealed anything. If he knew, he might try and stop her, or tell her brother. Or even worse, he might think her incapable.

LATER THAT NIGHT after everyone else was sleep, Ben sat in front of the fire with Levi who was about to finish off the wine. Levi had seemed glum in the days following their visit with Emily.

Ben nudged his friend. "Did you...ever kiss that girl, Emily?"

Levi's face turned red, and he sat up straight. "We were close when we were younger, but she's married now."

Ben nodded. He likely wasn't going to get any more than that out of him—a sore subject, apparently. So, his mind drifted to Anna, as it often did.

"Your sister doesn't seem to be having much luck with her courtships." Ben fixed his eyes on the fire, hoping he didn't seem too interested. He imagined her peach-colored lips and the curve of her neck. What was it she was about to tell him before Levi interrupted?

"She's young still. She needs to realize that men want a certain thing in a wife, and she's not being it." Levi glanced sideways at him.

Ben nodded once, not so much in agreement, but to acknowledge his friend's words. "What does *she* want in a husband?"

He hoped the nearly empty bottle in Levi's lap would keep his suspicion at bay. After all, many random subjects come up late at night while drinking. He wanted to be more direct, but now wasn't the time, and he wasn't sure if Levi would approve.

Levi scowled. "Money and success! What else would a lady want?"

"Of course." Ben raised his glass. "Two things with which you overflow, my friend."

Levi laughed and took a long drink to empty the bottle. "She wants to marry a man who makes more than fifteen dollars a week at a saw mill like us. That's what I'll insist on anyhow." Levi shifted in his seat and waved the thought away with a flick of his wrist. "But enough about that—how are you liking Seattle? I've never seen you stay in one place for long."

"I like it very much. But yes, I do love traveling."

He had certainly spent much of his life on the move, but not necessarily because he wanted to. He simply needed novelty in his life, and without it, he felt like he might disappear. If he didn't feel the salty ocean breeze in his hair, or smell the tall fir trees in the middle of the forest, did he even exist? Besides, California wasn't home anymore.

Levi squinted and pointed a wavering finger at him, betraying how much wine he'd had. "Ben, did you ever kill a man?"

"There it is." He shook his head. "I'm guessing you heard the rumors? I'm surprised you've waited this long to ask."

"Well?" Levi leaned forward, his face curious.

"Of course not." He grimaced. "A few years ago, when I was hunting in Oregon, I rented a cabin along a lazy river. One of my neighbors was an Indian man, went by Ed. One day, two men came to his door and started making demands—saying they needed the place and he had to get lost. I heard shouting and went to investigate. When I got there, they were both on top of Ed."

Levi's mouth went slack. "So, you killed them to protect an Indian?"

"No, I shot one of them in the leg with an arrow, and they both ran. One faster than the other." He chuckled. "The next day the sheriff came over to question me. There was talk of locking me up and having a trial for attempted murder."

He smirked and glanced sidelong at Levi. "But you know, if I'd been aiming at his heart, I would've hit it. Plus, they were attacking my friend for no good reason."

Levi scratched his head and nodded. "That's a relief. I mean, I'd still be your friend if you killed someone, if it was a good reason, but I'm glad to know you're the upright man I know you to be. Wouldn't have been right if they'd stolen the Indian's house, I suppose."

"Have you...told this rumor to your family?" Ben scratched his neck nervously.

Levi leaned his head back into his chair and closed his eyes. "Nah."

Ben sighed with relief and rested his head against his chair the way Levi had, thinking of the worn letter in his pocket.

His life in California seemed so long ago. His parents had been proud of him when he'd graduated from university, and he thoroughly enjoyed the reading and writing his degree had required. He was glad for his love of poetry and that he could share that with Anna. Surely, she saw him differently than the other eligible bachelors in Seattle, but he was fairly certain that wasn't a good thing.

He was no stranger to luxury. Glass wine goblets, maids preparing meals, and three-story brick houses downtown—these were familiar things. The sounds of clinking glasses and drunken laughter while his parents mingled with the Berkeley elite still made his skin crawl—as a child he had always been stuck upstairs alone.

As he grew up, his true desires came into focus, and he decided that as much as he'd grown to love stories, a vast world existed out there, and the time had come to explore it. His parents had suggested a semester at Oxford, which had been a wonderful and much needed adventure for twenty-year-old Ben, but it had only lit a fire inside him.

He wanted more—more travel, more newness. After graduation, he'd practically run home to pack his things and board the next train out of Berkeley. His parents had planned an extravagant graduation party, but pressure squeezed around his chest, making it harder to breathe by the minute. He knew that if he didn't leave the city right then he would have exploded, so he'd left town before the party, leaving his parents upset and confused.

Levi's soft snoring brought him back to the present, and he snuck out to walk back to his apartment. He tucked Anna's book of poems under his arm with special care, and as he passed through town, the celebrations continued. He returned the smiles of every person he passed, all the while thinking of Anna, eyes flashing with determination, and how she'd given everything she had when learning to shoot a bow.

She spent a lot of time in the woods and was good friends with a Duwamish woman, and she'd thrown herself heart and soul into solving a mystery from an old book. It was endearing. He imagined her lips and how they parted delicately whenever she was deep in thought—which was often. What would her kiss taste like?

He shook the thought away—she definitely had a spark of adventure inside her, but no doubt her brother knew her best. If Levi said she wanted a successful man to give her a peaceful city life, then he wasn't going to be selfish and tempt her away. Even though he had plenty to offer.

That she had agreed to meet the banker betrayed the fact that Levi was probably right. She had been interested in a doctor before—perhaps that was the only type of man she wanted. He remembered the night of the dance, finding her in the hands of a worthless drunk, and his blood ran hot. He squeezed his fists until they ached. If he ever saw Connor again, he'd have to work hard not to let his anger get the better of him.

CHAPTER TWENTY-THREE
THE NAME OF THE SHIP

Anna sent word to Emily about meeting the banker, and a week later a dinner had been arranged. She still had feelings for Ben, but it seemed like he wasn't being entirely forthcoming about his past and old love interests. Anyway, it wouldn't hurt to have an innocent dinner with a well-off man. Her stomach was bubbly in anticipation for the dinner that evening.

The day flew by, and Anna soon found herself at Emily's front door, adjusting her hat as she entered. The house smelled of roast duck and baking bread. There were flower arrangements on every surface, and candles glowed throughout the house. Emily came to seat her right away.

"Are the candles too much? I just wanted to set the mood," she whispered as Anna sat.

"It's lovely." And it truly was. She smoothed her napkin onto her lap.

Jonathon Conway had stood when he saw her and waited to sit until she did. "It's truly a pleasure to meet you, Miss Gallagher."

He was only slightly taller than her, with reddish brown hair and light brown eyes. Not unattractive.

"It's a pleasure to meet you, too." She took a sip from the glass of white wine Emily had just poured. "Everything smells absolutely wonderful."

Emily blushed. "Thank you."

It was evident she'd worked tirelessly to create a lovely dinner. She went to the kitchen and brought out a platter with four steaming platters.

Not only did the salmon with hollandaise come on the fanciest glass plates Anna had ever seen, it also melted in her mouth.

As they began to eat, Jonathon broke the silence. "Anna, tell me about yourself."

"I like to read and…I enjoy hiking in the forest. And I'm fond of the mountain."

Jonathan smiled warmly. "Delightful. I'm not much of an outdoorsman myself, not like Charles here. I mostly stay indoors and work with numbers."

"He's very smart," Emily chimed in.

Anna smiled. "I suppose you've been inundated with loan applications after the fire."

Jonathon nodded. "We have, but we're starting to catch up. Seattle is booming."

His voice was soothing. She couldn't quite figure out why, but there was something about his tone. He seemed like a nice man, and maybe he'd be a supportive partner if she shared her dreams. It was impossible to say from these small interactions, though.

After the main course, Emily stood. "I have plum pudding for dessert."

She hurried into the kitchen, returning with another tray. "Would anyone like coffee? I can make some?"

Everyone shook their heads politely, then praised her delicious offering.

"Quite possibly the best plum pudding I've ever had, ma'am," Jonathon said.

Anna noticed he had dimples when he grinned like that.

After they finished, Emily stood. "Should we play—"

"Emily," her husband interrupted sternly. "Jonathon and I would prefer to have our after-dinner cigars now. We've gone over this."

Emily's face reddened. "Yes of course, Charles, I'm sorry. You fellas must be exhausted from all our chatter."

Jonathon smirked. "I think they mean well, Charles. It just takes time for women to learn their place."

Anna's stomach dropped. She watched the men leave without another word. Emily clumsily stacked dinner plates, and she stood to help.

"Charles is a good man." Emily knocked a wine glass over as she reached for a plate.

Anna nodded quickly as she put a napkin over the spilled wine. "Of course."

"Sometimes it's better not to talk much around your husband, you know?" Emily said, almost to herself.

Anna tilted her head, her eyebrows knit together. "Is it?"

Emily rolled her eyes. "I don't know. My mother told me it always exhausted Father to hear a woman go on and on all the time. She said in marriage it's best not to speak unless spoken to."

She sat back down, giving up on stacking the plates. "I do feel rather lonely sometimes. Visitors make my days more enjoyable, Anna. Thanks for coming."

Patting her friend's hand, she smiled. "I understand."

But she truly did not understand. She feared Emily's fate would be her own if she married a man who wanted that kind of submission and silence. "Consider meeting up with June sometime. You don't need to meet at the brothel; invite her here, or what if we all went for a walk in the woods? Or met at my house for tea? It would do you good to be with old friends. The people who know you best."

"I really don't know." Emily rubbed her temples, her elbows on the table. "I'll think about it."

At the end of the evening, Anna insisted on walking herself home, and on the way, she thought of Heather. She and her husband had an unusual marriage, but Anna was certain that Heather and Michael talked often. And she got to live in the woods, for goodness' sake.

Summiting the mountain had seemed like such an epic goal for so long that she hadn't spent much time thinking about what she would do afterward.

Would she find someone to marry when she returned? Would she be able to keep the trip a secret from potential suitors? She could practically hear the criticism in her head; Emily, Levi, everyone would think her reckless. With their family business failing, she'd have no way to make money of her own. She might become an old, poor spinster by the time she reached her twenty-fifth birthday, and never be able to have children or a family to call her own.

But if her only other option was to marry a man like Jonathon, her future seemed dim. Nevertheless, she couldn't continue to be a burden on her family.

She shook her head as if to dissipate the fear. The only thing that mattered was seeing if she was even capable of summiting the mountain. Everything else came after.

At home, she pulled out John Muir's account.

The view we enjoyed from the summit could hardly be surpassed in sublimity and grandeur; but one feels far from home so high in the sky, so much so that one is inclined to guess that, apart from the acquisition of knowledge and the exhilaration of climbing, more pleasure is to be found at the foot of the mountains than on their tops. Doubly happy, however, is the man to whom lofty mountain tops are within reach, for the lights that shine there illumine all that lies below.

She sighed with contentment, dreaming of seeing the city illuminated below her.

The next morning, a heavy frost covered everything outside her bedroom window. The sky was a sheet of dark blue without a cloud for insulation, the temperature below freezing. It would be a good time to try walking on a frozen pond. She hoped to get there early, before anyone might be around to see her look foolish.

Wrapped in her warmest winter cloak, she set off for the pond before breakfast. Mr. Flannaghan had told her to use crampons, but she didn't have a clue what they were, nor did she have the money to purchase any. When she arrived at the frozen pond, she was pleased to find it surrounded by a thick fog. She was the only one there.

She stepped one foot onto the reasonably sturdy ice. She shuffled her other foot onto the sparkling pond and held out her arms for balance. The outer rim appeared thicker than the middle, and seemed like the safest place to stay, so she took small steps, making her way around. By the time she got back to where she started, a few children had arrived and watched her with interest.

"Be careful children," she said across the pond. "It's quite slippery."

Just as she said "slippery," she lost her footing, and both feet slid forward, throwing her body backwards onto the ice. Small cracks formed where she sat stunned on the cold pond. The children turned and ran away laughing.

Anna's face reddened as she struggled to stand. On her hands and knees, she moved the small distance to solid ground and raised herself up on the grass. She laughed, her breath coming out in white puffs. It was a good try, but she needed to get some gear soon. The slow walk home only caused a little pain on her backside.

Just as she was about to open the front door, the sound of footsteps rushed up behind her. She spun around to see a boy of about thirteen at the bottom of the steps.

He came to an abrupt halt in front of her. "Are you Miss Gallagher?"

"I am."

"Capt'n sent me, miss. He wanted to tell ya he found your friends in our passenger ledger. They came here in January 1880." He tipped his hat and started back toward town.

"Wait!" she called. "What's the name of your ship?"

"The *Compass Rose*, miss."

She grinned to herself, hardly able to wait until she could tell Ben.

CHAPTER TWENTY-FOUR
THE TRUTH ABOUT THE LETTER

Anna warmed hot cocoa, twirling peppermint sticks in the pot. A big Sunday lunch had already been served, and Greta was making their favorite Christmas treats. The men sat in the dining room discussing Seattle's greatest export: coal.

"They have it down to a science," Ben said. "Railcars on the piers go all the way to Renton and back on a line exclusively shipping coal to steam colliers and sailing ships."

Levi chewed the inside of his cheek. "We should find ourselves jobs in the mines after Christmas."

Anna saw her grandfather's nostrils flare.

"Absolutely not. It's the most dangerous job young men can do and I shan't allow it."

"Peppermint hot cocoa is finished!" she chimed. "And chocolate crinkles too. I just dusted them with powdered sugar."

"This smells amazing," Ben said. "Thank you, ladies."

Levi turned his attention back to his grandfather. "But it's where all the money is right now. And we can't exactly go fishin' in the middle of winter unless we want to cut a hole in the ice."

"I read an article in the *Post-Intelligencer* about ice fishing," Anna said. "'A Fascinating Cold-Weather Sport for Washington Boys, in Case it Freezes This Winter.' I bet you could make a fair amount of money ice fishing if you had a mind to."

"I don't mind working at the mill through the winter," Ben said. "It's hard work physically, but it's easy mentally."

She nodded as her grandfather took a sip of cocoa then hugged Greta tightly and kissed her on the cheek. For the last few weeks, ever since the day Washington statehood had been announced, her grandfather and Greta had been especially affectionate with each other.

A knock sounded at the door, and June was ushered inside out of the icy cold.

Anna grinned with delight. She couldn't remember the last time she'd seen her. "I'm so glad you're here. You *must* stay for the evening."

June glanced around. "Can't stay long. Just wanted to say Merry Christmas."

Her usually flowing curls were pulled back into a low bun.

"Are you sure you can't stay? I've missed you." She squeezed June's hand in her own.

"I'm just not feeling well."

Greta patted June on the back. "You look pale, dear. Let me wrap up a plate of cookies and peppermint sticks for you. Go home and get some rest."

She scurried to the kitchen.

"Thanks, Greta," June called after her. She looked around the room with a touch of irritation. "It's so warm in here. Let's wait for Greta outside."

Anna's smile faded. She hesitantly followed June out, disappointed the visit was apparently over.

June leaned against the frame of the patio.

"Things have been...eventful. I'll visit again after the New

Year. I'm sorry I haven't come around much lately." She eyed Anna curiously. "Is everything all right with you?"

Anna peered over her shoulder to make sure the front door was shut completely, then lowered her voice. "I'm going to climb Mount Rainier with a mountaineering group this summer."

June's eyes went wide. "You're really doing it? I can't believe it, and yet I can."

"It's just something I have to do. And there's this man Levi brought home. He's refreshing, and wild, but…he's impossible to read." She felt her cheeks warm, and she couldn't stop smiling. "Why are things always so complicated with men?"

June laughed. "I should tell you everything'll work out?"

"Yes, that's exactly what I needed to hear." She kissed her friend on the cheek.

Greta appeared with a plate. "Merry Christmas, June."

June winked and popped a peppermint stick in her mouth. "Thank you."

"Are you sure everything's okay?" Anna's concern mounted as June prepared to leave.

June glanced at Greta then fiddled with the buttons on her black coat. "I should head out. Merry Christmas, ladies, and thanks for the treats."

Anna stood next to Greta and watched her friend disappear down the road.

"Well, if we're handing out gifts…" her grandfather said with a twinkle in his eye when they returned to the kitchen. He pulled out a package wrapped in brown paper and handed it to Greta.

"What's all this?" Greta wiped her hands together, and powdered sugar floated down. She opened the package, and her face turned bright. "Christmas plum pudding and preserved Louisiana figs. How delightful! But, we didn't need to spend money on this."

She kissed him on the cheek, and he shrugged like a boy, a jolly smile playing on his lips.

Levi walked into the kitchen, and Anna slipped into the living room where she found Ben sitting with Esther.

"You never told me any more about your letter. The one from the woman who loved you." She lowered herself to sit next to him, smoothing her skirts in front of her.

Ben glanced at her with a curious smile. "Well that's not quite what I said. The woman I once loved turned out to be obsessed with money, and not much of a conversationalist. And the letter I carry around wasn't from her anyway. Here, you can read it."

He pulled out the worn envelope and pressed it into her hand.

Anna's eyes widened, and she looked toward the kitchen, but no one seemed to pay them any mind, so she unfolded it and read it to herself.

Dearest Benjamin,

How could you leave like that without even saying goodbye to your mother? I've been planning this party for weeks—you should be ashamed of yourself. I suppose I knew this day was coming, though.

Please come back to me and visit soon. Your father and I want the best life for you, and I'm sorry we haven't been as involved as you might have hoped. Even still, my love for you is never-ending. If this letter ever finds you, please be safe and know that I still think of you as my little Benjamin.

Your loving mother,
Samantha Chambers

"Oh—I see…. I'm sorry, I misunderstood." She had butterflies in her stomach. "Your mother sounds very sweet."

Ben scooted closer. "My parents didn't exactly want children."

"Well, it sounds like your mother misses you very much." She couldn't help but feel relieved that the letter wasn't from a lover.

Esther was curled up contentedly in Ben's lap, and he was quiet.

She didn't want their conversation to be over yet. "You camp a lot under the stars, right? Do animals ever get in your tent?"

"Most of them leave you alone." An amused smile danced on his lips. "Deer, foxes, rabbits…they don't want to bother you. You do need to mind the cougars and coyotes though. They're everywhere around here."

He smiled at her again with a tenderness that made her want to ask him questions all night. "Why do you ask?"

She sat back, straightening her posture. "No reason. I just like to learn."

"There are breathtaking places to camp near Mount Rainier. Rivers, fjords, spectacular glaciers."

He said the last part with a great flourish of his arm as if he was giving an imaginary tour. Esther flicked her tail and darted away.

"You've been there?" Her connection with Ben was strange and exhilarating. She longed for his arms to drape over hers as they had in the forest when he was teaching her to shoot.

He leaned back and rested both hands on the floor, stretching his legs in front of him, crossing them at the ankles. "Not on the mountain itself, but near there. It's dangerous once you gain elevation. Ice, glaciers, avalanches, and drop-offs. You'd need crampons and an alpenstock."

Her stomach flipped as she recognized the terms. "I've been reading John Muir's account of summiting and he mentioned those. What are they exactly?"

"An alpenstock is a walking stick with a spike in the bottom to go through ice and snow. Keeps you steady, and you can use it to plunge into the ground if you start sliding. Crampons fit over your boots and have long metal spikes for hiking over ice." He cleared his throat and leaned closer. "Are you hoping to see a glacier up close one day?"

Levi suddenly appeared and plopped down next to them, speaking in a cool voice. "I keep finding you two alone together. What are you talking about?"

CHAPTER TWENTY-FIVE
THE GIFT

"Nothing," Anna blurted out, trying not to look guilty.

"Anna was quizzing me on classic literature so my brain doesn't get rusty." Ben winked at her with a playful grin.

She shot him a thankful look. "What are you giving Grandfather for Christmas, Levi?"

"A stocking full o' coal—his favorite thing." He chuckled.

"Shall we find our perfect Christmas tree while everyone's here?" Greta's voice chimed from the kitchen.

"Yes, great idea," Anna said, thinking of trudging over icy hills.

Her grandfather donned his felt hat and grabbed his coat off its hook. "And then we can open our last bottle of wine for the holiday dinner."

As was tradition for the Gallaghers, they brought a steel canteen of hot chocolate along with cookies wrapped in cloth. Levi suggested many fine trees, but they couldn't all agree—too short, too thin, not green enough.

Anna made sure to walk on every snowy hill she could find. She intentionally suggested one tree after another on top of various hills fifty or so feet away, making the whole group trudge up several icy embankments. She was pleased to find herself quite steady on her feet. Although, an alpenstock would certainly make things easier.

After about an hour, they all agreed on a perfect Douglas fir. It stood about eight feet tall, taller than their ceiling, but her grandfather suggested he could cut the bottom to make it fit in the house.

The men took turns chopping at the trunk with an axe, until finally it fell. To celebrate, Anna passed out cookies, and they handed the hot chocolate around. Then the men carried the tree back to the house and set it on the porch to dry out for the next day. At the top of the porch stairs, wrapped in brown paper and twine, was a package.

Greta picked it up and read the note. "It's for you, Anna."

Her grandfather brushed the needles off his hands. "I bet it's from that Mr. Conway fella."

"No," said Greta. "Says it's from Heather. Who's that, Anna? Have we met her before?"

Anna blinked, willing her face not to betray her fear.

Ben cleared his throat loudly. "Let's get inside before it starts raining again."

Greta nodded. "You should open the gift now, Anna. I can't wait to see what it is."

She knew Heather hadn't meant to cause all this commotion. There would be no way to sneak the package to her bedroom, and she couldn't think of a good lie. She pulled the green ribbon and found a vest of fox fur inside the parcel—smooth and red-brown, with neat leather stitches.

"Why, this looks like somethin' I've seen Duwamish women wear," Greta said. "Why on earth would someone give you this? How odd."

Anna swallowed hard. She loved Heather. And she loved her gift. She tried it on over her sweater, and it was a perfect fit.

"Now *that* will definitely keep you warm this winter," Ben said, admiring the vest.

"Anna?" asked her grandfather. "What's the meaning of this?"

She turned to look at him squarely. "Grandfather, I need to tell you something. I have a Duwamish friend in the woods. Her name's Heather, and I met her a couple of months ago. She isn't anything like you say they are. She's charitable and kindhearted."

Levi frowned. "You promised not to go out there again."

She bit her lip. "I never promised that."

Her grandfather's face grew an almost crimson shade of red. "You knew about this, Levi? Where in the woods?"

Levi pursed his lips together, running a hand through his hair. "'Bout five miles south. Looked like an old pioneer cabin on a land claim."

Anna's jaw dropped. Her grandfather slammed his fist on the table and stormed out of the house.

She turned to glare at her brother. "I can't *believe* you did that."

How could he? She chased after her grandfather, fuming at her brother the whole way.

Fifty feet in front of her, her grandfather stumbled over a tree root. By the time she caught up with him, nearly ten minutes later, they were standing in front of the Land Office of Washington on Second Street.

"I'll certainly not allow *those people* to be my neighbors, and most definitely not on government land," he said through a clenched jaw.

Before she could respond, he burst through the door where two men sat behind desks, a receptionist decorating a small Christmas tree in the foyer. All three of them looked up with surprise.

"I'd like to report savages living on government property," he said breathlessly.

"Sir, we don't really deal with tribal disputes," said the younger gentleman. "As long as their main residence is on the reservation, there's not much——"

"I'll not have savages as neighbors," he spat. "It was originally claimed by settlers, and *they* took over. Who knows with what violence?"

"They're not violent." Anna's mind raced. She struggled to fight back her growing anger, keeping her face as calm as she could muster.

The older man lifted his eyes from his typewriter and waved him over to his desk. "I'm sure we can settle this. Let's take a look at the map and show me where you suspect they're livin'."

Her grandfather pointed to the location based on Levi's description, five miles south.

"Now that *is* claimed land, sir," said the older man. "If they're truly livin' on a surveyed and purchased parcel of land, and the original claimer has abandoned it, then it would fall back to the ownership of the territory—er, I mean of the state."

The man smiled at that last part, but her grandfather ignored it.

"Excellent. Can you look it up?"

"I can." He put on his glasses and reached for a large book off the shelf behind him. "Let's see here. One moment, sir."

Anna's chest ached with the heavy pounding of her heart. If Heather was kicked out of her home, she would never speak to Levi again—or her grandfather for that matter.

"Hmm, it looks like that land was surveyed and purchased three and a half years ago, June 25th 1886. By a Michael Smith. The land was surveyed and deemed to be vacant or abandoned and available to purchase from the state. After his application was certified, he purchased forty acres at fifty dollars plus a ten-dollar filing fee. I imagine by now he's received the land deed from the General Land Office in Washington. And that's all the information I have, sir."

"Well, we need to let Mr. Smith know about this situation," her grandfather said, his eyes wild. "Or maybe they've killed Michael Smith and are living on his land."

"Sir," said the older man. "If you suspect violence, you'll need to go to the police."

"Michael is Heather's husband. He's not Duwamish," Anna said breathlessly. "So you see, it's her cabin, after all."

"Bloody hell! You're forbidden to go there again." He tipped his hat and marched out of the office.

"Why are you doing this?" As she caught up with him, tears clouded her vision.

"I've been a good man, for the most part," he said, seemingly to himself. He marched through the empty streets, ice crunching beneath him.

"Ever since that day," she said nervously, lowering her voice. "You assume the worst in every Duwamish person."

It was impossible to keep up with him as he marched; his legs were far longer than hers. He was silent until they reached their dirt path.

"Would you have them breaking into our home? Risking our safety?" His face was bright red, his eyes darting everywhere but at her. "I'm angry—angry it happened to me, angry I have to carry the guilt of...hurting a boy who broke into our home—to steal from us!"

His fists were tight against his body.

Anna finally caught up with him, out of breath. "This has been their land for as long as they can remember. Maybe he was just angry about that."

He snarled and waved her away, walking briskly toward the house. "I won't speak of it, lassie. Don't bring it up again."

CHAPTER TWENTY-SIX
THE AWKWARD CHRISTMAS

"Merry Christmas everyone!" Greta exclaimed.

She had set the table with meatballs, sausage, cheese, and baked slices of potatoes layered with cream and onions—a Christmas feast in the Swedish tradition.

Anna stood at the front door watching her grandfather stomp up the stairs.

Levi bit his lip. "I'm sorry, Anna. I don't know why I told him—"

"I'll not hear any of it." She marched to the kitchen and grabbed her apron. She seethed as she rolled chocolate crinkles in her hands, preparing them for the oven.

"Anna?" Ben poked his head into the kitchen. "What happened out there? Are you all right?"

"My grandfather and brother were just attempting to throw my dear friend into the snow on Christmas Eve." She sniffled—the cold air and the emotions were catching up with her.

Ben reached for the other apron hanging—Greta's apron. "May I?"

She almost smiled then nodded, wiping a tear from the corner of her eye.

"I'm not so bad at rolling cookie dough myself." He tied the bow behind his back.

"I just wish I could *talk* with Grandfather about all this. He refuses!" She grabbed the powdered sugar and began dusting. "And Levi! He's supposed to be on my side. I'll never forgive him."

She heard her grandfather coming down the stairs and glared in his direction. He began speaking loudly in the living room, so she rushed in to hear.

"I guess it's time for dinner, then we can open presents," her grandfather said, all trace of anger gone. "Greta, this spread looks fantastic!"

Anna rolled her eyes and began untying her apron.

"You have a bit of powdered sugar on your cheek," Ben said, trying to hide a smile.

She rubbed both cheeks quickly with the back of her hands then went to the dining room, Ben following behind her.

Greta passed the potatoes to Levi. "It's so nice having everyone together."

Levi looked up sheepishly at Anna, but she ignored him.

Ben shifted in his seat. "Thank you all for inviting me. It's nice to have a family meal on a holiday."

"Oh darling, you're welcome anytime," Greta said, then popped a meatball into her mouth.

Levi pulled a small bag out of his pocket and handed it to Greta. "I'll just give you your gift now. It's burning a hole in my pocket."

"Goodness, I'm getting spoiled this year!" Greta cooed as she examined the gift. "Saffron! Where ever did you get this, Levi?"

"A merchant ship. I thought you might like to bake lussekatts for Christmas morning."

"Ben have you ever had lussekatts?" Greta asked. "It's a

Swedish pastry in the shape of an 'S' with raisins, cinnamon, nutmeg…and saffron!"

"Sounds delicious," Ben said, cutting a sausage with his knife. "I think I'll let you Gallaghers have Christmas morning as a family. Save me a piece though, will you Greta?"

Greta beamed. "Absolutely. This has got to be the best Christmas I've had in a while. It's a good one, right Oscar?"

He huffed and glanced sidelong at Anna with a hint of guilt.

After dinner, Ben said his farewells, and Anna was the last to tell him goodbye. Everyone else moved back to the living room while her grandfather began "O Holy Night" on his harmonica and Greta sang sweetly.

"Merry Christmas, Ben." She leaned against the doorframe, her hands behind her back. "I'm sorry things were so strange tonight."

He handed her a small velvet bag. "I got you something—I hope that's all right."

She opened it with shaky hands. A compass shined in her palm, mountains engraved in the silver. She took in a sharp breath.

"I wasn't sure if the second clue meant you actually needed a compass to figure out the rest, or if it's a metaphor. But just in case, I got you one." He tilted his head, watching her reaction.

"It's beautiful," was all she could say, and it was enough.

Ben smiled, tipped his hat, and set off to town. She watched him move toward the city lights, wishing she could go with him.

TWO DAYS AFTER CHRISTMAS, the men began preparations. Ben arrived first thing in the morning wearing a leather vest, bow slung behind his back, and his brown hair free of the grease most gentlemen used. As they gathered supplies, Anna watched everything they packed: a tent, blankets, water canteens, rifles, bullets, knives, a compass, and a small map. She slipped away to her bedroom to write it down.

"What are you doing, dear?" asked Greta from the doorway.

She spun around to face her, still holding her notebook. "Nothing."

"How are things goin' with Mr. Conway?" she asked. "He's nice, right?"

She chewed the inside of her cheek. "I haven't seen him since the dinner at Emily's, but I didn't quite feel...anything for him."

Greta chuckled. "I suppose we won't hear back about our new loan application. No matter, we can try another bank."

Anna exhaled loudly. "I'm sorry."

"Now, there's nothin' wrong with decidin' you don't care for a man. At least you didn't already agree to let him court you."

"No. I mean I'm sorry I'm still a burden on the family."

Anxiety constricted her chest. She daydreamed of being on the mountain. How many colors would glisten as the sun hit the different angles of the glacier? Would the northern lights cover the whole sky, and would they dance like she imagined?

"Well that's just the silliest thing I've heard. If it wasn't for you and all the hard work we did this autumn, this family would be a lot hungrier, I can tell ya that." She paused, sitting at the edge of the bed. "It's an awful thing, feeling like your marriage and happiness is the family's business, a financial transaction of sorts. I feel for you, I do."

Anna sighed, relieved to be understood.

Greta raised one eyebrow. "I wonder why there hasn't been any talk of Ben courtin' you."

She laughed nervously. "I can't imagine Grandfather or Levi allowing that to happen. They see him as a poor man with no money or house."

Greta watched her carefully. "Is that what you think of him, dear?"

Her pulse pounded in her ears. "I suppose it doesn't matter what I think. It matters who asks to court me."

"Of course it matters what you think."

Anna set her notebook down and started arranging things on her dresser. "Well, Ben isn't even sure if he's going to settle in Seattle."

Greta rose to her feet. "All right then. Didn't mean to fluster you."

"I'm not flustered. Confused, mostly." She straightened and attempted to look serene.

"That's normal," Greta said as she turned the corner.

"No, I'm not confused about Ben," she said softly, but Greta was already halfway down the stairs.

Anna lay back on her bed and pulled out the compass Ben had given her, which she'd been carrying in her pocket since Christmas Eve. It was such a lovely thing, and she liked having it on her. If he had feelings for her, and if he wasn't leaving Seattle right away, she was curious where things might go.

She grabbed *Anna Karenina* off her nightstand to get the butterflies out of her stomach. She reviewed the third clue and groaned—she'd not yet received *Crime and Punishment*.

As the men prepared to leave, she came back downstairs, but made sure to ignore Levi.

She gave her grandfather a stiff hug. "I'll see you soon."

"You and Greta stay safe as best you can, lassie." He seemed to have trouble looking at her.

She nodded then watched them walk into the forest, breathing a sigh of relief. When Greta left for the market, Anna went up and down the stairs with Levi's pack on her back filled with books. That evening her legs were alarmingly sore, and she curled up with Muir's account. Not only did she find comfort in knowing what lay ahead in a practical way, but his words were lovely.

We arrived at the Cloud Camp at noon but no clouds were in sight, save a few gauzy ornamental wreaths adrift in the sunshine. Out of the forest at last there stood the mountain, wholly unveiled, awful in bulk and majesty, filling all the view like a separate, new-born world.

The descriptions of alpine plants and glaciers continued to inspire her. When she finally had the opportunity to look down from the heights, she'd be among the few to have ever done so—an equal of men.

☙❦☙

ON THE MORNING of the third day, shouts of panic came from the clearing behind Anna's house. She ran out the door to see her grandfather and Ben carrying Levi—his bloody shirt plastered against his stomach.

"Fetch Greta! Tell her to get clean towels and hot water," her grandfather shouted. "Coyote got him!"

She raced back to the house and relayed the news. They set him down by the fire, and her grandfather ran back out the front door, yelling behind him, "Getting the doctor. Be careful cleaning the wounds."

Greta rushed into the living room with a small bowl of water and towels. She cut his shirt carefully to expose the wound. There were two deep scratches from his chest to his waist, but the area where thick blood had started to dry was the left side of his lower back. After Greta cleaned it off, they saw the bite mark.

"What happened?" Anna asked Ben.

"We followed a deer for miles, all separate, keeping about fifty feet between us," he said. "The coyote must have been starving and following the deer as well, or else he'd been following us all along. All I know is, he came out of nowhere and we heard Levi shout. We came running, scared the coyote away, but not before it bit him."

Ben seemed as if he might cry.

"This bleeding is gettin' heavier," Greta said. "Can't we do a tourniquet or…I don't know. Ben?"

He grimaced and wiped the sweat off his forehead. "Not on his back. I'll put pressure on it with towels until the doctor arrives. I've never in my life seen a coyote attack a man."

He shook his head in disbelief.

"Anna?" Levi's eyes fluttered open. "Is that you?"

She held back tears. "I'm here."

Levi's breath was labored. "Don't be afraid. We'll get this all sorted and I'll be fine. Can't believe a bloody coyote got me."

His lips and face were losing color.

Her mind flashed back to the day she'd found her parents lying in bed with fever. Her father had told Levi to run and get their grandmother. Anna and Levi had stayed with their grandfather while their grandmother tried to nurse their parents back to health. But instead, hours had turned into days, and eventually all three of them had succumbed to smallpox.

"Don't leave me." She closed her eyes, gripping her brother's hand.

By the time the family doctor arrived, Levi had lost consciousness again. Anna wrapped her arms around him while Ben held steady pressure with blood-soaked towels.

The doctor kneeled down to examine Levi, and she stepped back. Pushing his spectacles up his nose, he drew close to the wound. His unhurried manner made her want to scream.

"Doctor Wright?" she asked. "Will he be okay?"

He glanced up at her over his spectacles, pulling a few instruments out of his bag, placing each of them on the table separately. "It got him good. I'll stitch him up, though."

He poured alcohol on the wound then threaded a needle, before making countless, deliberate sutures along the wound.

Afterward, he rinsed his hands in the kitchen sink. "That

coyote might've been rabid. You'll need to keep a close eye on him. Come get me right away if he gets a fever."

Greta nodded wordlessly. Anna cleaned the blood off her hands, then ran upstairs to get clean blankets for Levi to sleep by the fire. When she returned, Greta relieved her of them and got Levi situated under the covers, neatly tucking him in.

It wasn't until she was in her bedroom, under her own quilt, that she finally began to weep.

CHAPTER TWENTY-SEVEN
THE CRIME

Ben strolled into the saloon looking for Michael—everyone was either drunk or halfway there. After meeting him at Heather's cabin, he'd realized he recognized Michael, who also worked at Yesler Mill. They'd been friendly since.

It was eleven in the evening on New Year's Eve. A cherry wood piano played a tune of its own volition, and prostitutes in low-cut silk dresses mingled with customers. He usually didn't spend much time in saloons and wasn't quite sure where to sit until he spotted Michael.

With his hands in his pockets, he sauntered up to the bar, and Pavlov welcomed him. He ordered whiskey and pulled the glass close to him, exhaling slowly through pursed lips as he lowered himself onto a stool.

"Somethin' heavy on your mind?" asked Michael. His blond hair wasn't combed, and he held a mug of coffee.

Ben took a drink, which burned more than he expected. "You could say that."

"I got demons too, brother." Michael leaned in close to him. "I come here every night."

He nodded a cautious acknowledgement. "Why?"

Michael ducked his head closer to Ben. "I see the same faces every day. A young boy clingin' to his mother, an old woman with a long braid down her back, defiant face, a skinny teenage boy, dressed like a warrior—all shot without question."

Tears glistened in his eyes.

Ben shook his head, his mouth slightly agape. "I can't imagine."

"General Sheridan told me, 'The best Indian is a dead Indian.' I didn't kill those people, but I stood by while they died. I'm guilty enough." He dropped his voice to a whisper and glanced around. "The government's probably still lookin' for me. Can't tell anybody, all right?"

"I won't. Promise." Ben nodded then cleared his throat, wondering how to change the subject. "So, how did you meet Heather?"

A grin came over Michael's face, along with a slight blush. "I had just arrived in the territory. Camping out near this big, wide river and saw the most beautiful creature I'd ever seen laying strips of salmon over a smoky fire."

He smiled. "Did you go up and talk to her?"

"Not at first. Didn't want to scare her off. Little did I know, pretty much nothing scares my girl." He roared with laughter. "I was starving, though, and the next day I went up to her and asked to buy a meal. The rest you know."

He nodded, eying Michael's empty coffee. "Can I get you a whiskey?"

"Nah, I don't drink. Just makes me feel worse." He paused. "What's eatin' you, anyway?"

Ben ordered two coffees. "Levi almost died, and I blame myself. I can't shake that feeling."

Michael shook his head as if to acknowledge the power of remorse. "Guilt is somethin', isn't it? It'll eat you alive, more than whiskey. I'm thinkin' it wasn't your fault, was it, brother?"

Ben sipped from his steaming mug then turned to Michael. "Don't know—feels like it. I should have protected him."

A tall man in the corner stood, yelling angrily and towering over another who held cards and laughed tauntingly. The tall man balled his hands into fists and spit on the floor.

Michael's face lit up, and he turned to face the exchange. He was just standing when a prostitute moseyed by the commotion, distracting the men. Pavlov mumbled something about a close call, and Michael grunted in what sounded like disappointment. He returned his attention to Ben and shrugged. "Hasn't been any action tonight."

Ben traced the edge of his mug with the tip of a finger. "I'm not a big fighter myself."

"Lots of men around here don't mind a good fight. Soon as I hear angry voices, the demons creep up my arms, and I jump into the fight. I don't know…I guess it releases the tension."

He shuddered at the image. "That's tough."

"Saw too much, which led to feeling too much, I guess." Michael shrugged. "Anyway, do you have a girl, Ben?"

He laughed, unsure how much to share. "What's it like having a family? Is it as good as it sounds?"

"Better," Michael said, a twinkle in his eye. He scanned the bottles of liquor on the shelf behind the bar. "But life's tricky sometimes, ain't it?"

"That it is." Ben lifted his mug. "Cheers."

"To the women we love, who probably deserve better," Michael said, chuckling.

"Happy New Year." He clinked his mug against Michael's.

ON THE FIRST day of January 1890, Anna picked up Levi's old harmonica. She was cleaning his room and finally putting away his camping supplies from the trip, which Ben had retrieved from the forest the day after they'd returned. The first few nights had been distressing, listening to Levi writhe in pain, and they had all decided it was best for him to stay on the first floor while he healed. They watched for fever, which would signal rabies or infection, neither of which would bode well for Levi. Overall, he had been making gains in his recovery.

Her gaze fell on the small bow he'd let her use, leaning on the wall inside his closet. Peering behind her shoulder, she checked that she was alone. A quiver with ten arrows rested near his small canvas tent and tightly rolled sleeping mat. Her heart pounded as she considered the possibility of using his gear for her own trip. If all went well, he'd be recovered by then and fishing in Alaska, so he'd never even know they were missing.

It was time—time to get serious about training. Her brother was a savvy hunter and spent much of his time in the wilderness. Yet he'd been seriously wounded by a wild animal. Levi had been surrounded by other strong and skilled men when a coyote had attacked. How would she, a small woman, with little experience or strength, be able to survive through glaciers and avalanches on a mountain? And how much more vulnerable would she be slowed down by ice and snow?

She peeked down the stairs and saw Levi's mattress, which now took up a corner of the living room. He sat propped up with pillows, reading the newspaper. Greta worked in the kitchen, humming while she kneaded dough.

Anna slipped past them both and outside into the woods, wearing her fox-fur vest, the bow and arrows slung on her back. Using chalk, she made a target on a tree and went to work practicing her aim. She found it easier to shoot without the pressure of the boys watching her, and after the first few shots, she hit the tree every time. Not the target, but at least she was hitting the tree consistently. All ten arrows, one after another, flew from the bow, then she retrieved them, gearing up to go again.

A twig cracked about thirty feet away, and she spun around,

her bow aimed in the direction of the noise, as she'd seen Ben do. Dread filled her, and she wanted to run back to the house, but her feet stayed planted. A moment later, a hawk rose into the air with something in its talons.

Her muscles relaxed. Coyotes didn't usually wander the forest mid-day, but she remained on high alert. She closed her eyes for a moment and listened. Seagulls cried, and ship horns sounded. Birds tweeted, branches rustled above her, and after she'd been still for a while, a small brown squirrel came waltzing down a nearby tree onto the forest floor.

She blew out the breath she'd been holding, seemingly for days. On her way home, she aimed at a tree as she moved away from it. Some arrows ricocheted off the bark, but she hit it five times out of ten. An exhilarating burst of energy shot through her—she was getting better, and now had an understanding that whenever she was in the woods, whether hunting or not, she should be acutely aware of what might be hunting her.

THE MUCH-FEARED FEVER NEVER CAME, and so Levi's danger of rabies was over. Three weeks after the accident, he still had a difficult time going up the stairs and bathing. The healing process had been slow. Anna had spent much of the cold, dark days of January working at the bookstore, searching through newspapers and books to find tips on preparing to climb the mountain. She had also sent a letter to Mr. Flannaghan informing him of her intentions to join them, but had left out the part that she had no idea if she'd be able to come up with the funds.

Her grandfather hadn't been himself, and although she was still frustrated with him, she didn't want to visit Heather openly. Once, after everything had happened, she'd gone to see her secretly, thanking her for the fur vest and telling her of Levi's attack. Obviously, she wasn't going to stop seeing her friend because of her grandfather's ridiculous opinions.

But she wanted to make sure Heather was getting along with the reading primers and to give her the light blue sweater she'd knitted for her as a Christmas gift. She hadn't mentioned her grandfather's embarrassing outburst and hateful words.

One bitterly cold day, Anna slumped over the counter of the bookstore, reading *Crime and Punishment* which had finally arrived. Trying to recall the clue, she set down the book and grabbed her copy of *Anna Karenina*, opening to the page of the inscription.

> *To craft with wood or game alike, a tool one can't refuse.*
> *The tool that Raskolnikov possessed but didn't use.*

She was already enjoying *Crime and Punishment* more than she thought she would, and she was interested to see what tool Raskolnikov had but didn't use, even without the riddle as motivation. At first, she and Ben had thought it might be an axe or an ice pick, but in truth, it could be almost anything.

Distracted, she stared out the window. Jonathon Conway had come to ask her grandfather about courting her a few days after Levi's injury. Her grandfather had managed to turn him down gently, and she hoped it wouldn't have any ill effects on their new loan application. Other than looking down on women, he did seem like a decent man, so hopefully he'd do them the kindness. Money had become unbearably tight in the Gallagher home.

She returned to *Crime and Punishment*, curious to see if this murder was going to happen after all. As she read between customers, she finally happened upon the sentences she'd been searching for.

> *That the deed must be done with an axe he had decided long ago. He*
> *had also a pocket pruning-knife, but he could not rely on the knife*
> *and still less on his own strength, and so resolved finally on the axe.*

So not an axe, indeed, but a simple knife—she had always wanted a knife of her own. Heather had one she always kept with her, and it often came in handy. But how many times had she been told that no lady should ever carry a knife on her person? Sure, she'd handled many kitchen knives, but she wanted a foldable pocket knife, one with an ornate handle. She had seen some of ivory and others of whale bone, which were beautiful.

An excitement rose in her chest, and she longed to tell Ben, to see the light in his eyes. He'd probably also have an uncanny gusto for figuring out the last clue now that they were close. She couldn't bear waiting any longer.

"If you don't mind, I'll take a walk near the water before I head home for dinner," she said to her grandfather, keeping her eyes on her hands.

He nodded. Before closing the bookstore door behind her, she took one last glance at the end of the inscription.

The first of men discovered this, the magic orange and red
to keep it here inside the house, it's made of brick instead.
Combine these all together now—you'll need each little part
to find the emerald ring, and then, forever have my heart.

A cold maritime breeze blew as she neared the entrance to Yesler Mill. Men in flannel shirts and felt hats lifted logs on strong shoulders and laughed with each other. These were the men of lesser importance according to her grandfather—not the type she should consider marrying—not like a doctor or a banker who would buy her a fancy house with imported furniture and glass tea sets.

The sort of man who would encourage her to stay indoors to arrange flowers and embroider things, anything to keep her busy and safely in the home. These men in the mill—the kind like her brother—seemed strong and funny, and dreamed of a future that might never take place. Still, they were full of hope. Did these kinds of men expect their wives to be quiet and stay home, too? Perhaps all men were the same.

And then, she saw Ben. She recognized him by the shape of his back and his thick brown hair. He wore a black flannel shirt and lifted one large log at a time onto a conveyor belt. She inhaled sharply as her pulse quickened, watching his handsome face smile and say something to the man next to him.

As he turned to pick up another log, he locked eyes with her, and she saw, in that one look, everything she needed to know.

CHAPTER TWENTY-EIGHT
THE REASON

Ben jogged to Anna where she waited outside the mill's fence.

"Anna," he said, breathless. "Is everything all right?"

"Yes, I'm good." She soaked in his presence.

"How've you been?"

His eyes were filled with concern, and he offered her his arm as he turned and gestured toward a small path they could walk.

"I'm well. I've been working at the bookstore and taking care of Levi." She looked back toward the mill. "It looks like quite a few Duwamish men work there."

"Don't tell your grandfather." He winked. "How's Levi's recovery?"

"He's doing fine. Better by the day."

His face darkened. "It was my fault, what happened with the coyote. I should've been paying better attention. It was his deer, and he was focused on that, and your grandfather and I were spotting him—"

"That's ridiculous." She shook her head. "I won't have you blaming yourself for a coyote attack."

He shook his head and scanned the horizon. "I usually spend late winter and spring hunting. I'll be making my way to Oregon soon, then meet up with Captain Pavitt in Astoria on his way north in May."

"But we haven't finished solving the inscription..." She trailed off, hoping her desire to keep him in Seattle wasn't obvious. "That's why I came. I found the part in *Crime and Punishment* the riddle refers to."

He raised his eyebrows. "And?"

"And, it was a knife he had but didn't use," she said triumphantly.

Ben's face lit up the way she knew it would.

"Interesting.... Have you already got a knife?"

"No. I'm not sure what respectable gentleman would sell me one that's not meant for the kitchen." She pursed her lips together in a tight frown.

"Perhaps if I'm with you?" He tilted his head to the side.

She took in a sharp breath at the idea of walking around town on his arm.

"I'm sure you don't want to be seen with a man like me anyway." Ben's face steeled, and he looked back toward the mill. "How are things with...the man you met? Are you halfway to marriage already?"

His attempt at a half-hearted laugh came out oddly loud.

Levi must not have told him.

"Not even close." She grinned. "Why do you care anyway?"

She peered up at him, sensing the closeness of his chest, clutching his arm as they stopped, her face inches from his.

"I want you to be happy. I hope you know that," he said.

Anna could feel the warmth of his breath. She wanted to tell him what would make her happy: climbing the mountain, and perhaps knowing he'd be waiting for her when she returned. But she was too afraid he'd think she was incapable—she couldn't bear to hear those words from him.

She cleared her throat and looked away. "Well, I have a brick, a compass, and now I need a knife. But what of the last clue?"

He gazed at her with clear fondness.

"This mystery calls for deep thinking near a fireplace…or perhaps a stove?" He chuckled. "Anna, I love talking with you, but I'd better get back to work."

"Of course," she said. "I'm sorry to steal you away."

His eyes turned serious. "Anytime you need me, I'm yours."

As his gaze intensified, she blinked.

He cleared his throat. "Like I said, I want you to be happy, whatever that looks like for you."

"I want to climb the mountain," she whispered.

A smile grew on Ben's face as he pulled her hand into his own. "That's why you asked so many questions about it. Why didn't you tell me sooner?"

With her hand in his, she felt a new sense of strength.

"I wasn't sure what you'd think. Or how much I meant to you," she said breathlessly, finally meeting his eyes.

Ben ran his hand along his jaw with a half-smile. In front of the mill's entrance, the saws buzzed angrily, so he leaned in close to her ear. "You're the reason I'm still in Seattle."

Just then, a short man with a clipboard motioned for him to return.

"I'm sorry—I'll come by your house this evening—we can talk more."

She squeezed his hand before letting go. "All right, tonight then."

As she hurried away, her mind raced, and she longed to speak with June. When she reached Third and Washington, she knocked on the front door of the brothel. The young woman who appeared gave her a doubtful look.

"Can I speak with June?" Anna whispered, keeping her face down.

"June's not here anymore," the woman huffed, then turned to leave.

Anna grabbed her arm. "What does that mean? Where is she?"

She shrugged. "Not my concern. Not yours either if she didn't bother to tell ya, wouldn't ya say?"

"May I speak with Lou Graham, then?" Anna was starting to panic.

The door slammed in her face, and confusion clouded her mind. Where would June go? And what might have happened that would cause her to disappear? She quickened her pace, sick to her stomach. Perhaps the woman just meant June was out for the day. Or perhaps June had packed her bags and was waiting at the Gallagher house. Or maybe—her stomach dropped—June's father had come calling.

When she arrived home and didn't see June, her nervousness increased. Out of habit, she helped Greta prepare dinner, chopping potatoes and parsnips. Meanwhile, all of the reasons June might have left the brothel ran through her head.

"June isn't at the brothel anymore."

Greta stopped mid-slice. "Perhaps she finally has enough money to get her own place."

"Maybe...or maybe she moved to a different brothel?" Anna's stomach twisted. "I'm worried about her."

Greta nodded. "The poor dear. I hope she's all right... I'll stop by the new brothel on Fourth Avenue this week and ask about her whereabouts. Please don't stop in yourself, Anna. You have a reputation to maintain."

"Thank you, Greta."

Anna had planned to do it herself, but it was probably better this way. Greta might seem more commanding. Slightly relieved already, she willed the fear away, and as soon as she did, Ben filled her mind again.

You're the reason I'm still in Seattle.

The thrill of his words and the anticipation of seeing him that evening were almost too much to bear. As she headed toward the cellar for carrots, she saw him striding toward the house. She abandoned the cellar and made her way toward him. When they met on the dirt road, he handed her a small package wrapped with brown paper.

She turned it over in her hands. "What's this?"

"You might need it." He grinned.

She unwrapped it to reveal a small pocket knife with an iridescent white handle.

He pointed at the handle excitedly. "Whale bone."

"It's exquisite. Thank you. I feel bad though. You've gotten me two gifts, and I haven't gotten you anything."

Anna admired the knife, longing to ask him questions—about his past and what he wanted for the future.

Ben shrugged, but his eyes were serious. "I want you to find what you're looking for. Don't give up—I'm sure you can figure it out. You're more intelligent than most of the women in my classes were, and certainly more interesting."

The air escaped from her lungs in a little sigh as she tried to respond, but then she saw her grandfather coming up the road.

"Best put that away before he gets here. I wouldn't want to be on his bad side." He winked and glanced down at her lips.

When her grandfather joined them, he had a wide grin on his face. "Staying for dinner, Ben? It's a night for celebration—I have good news!"

Ben agreed, flashing a delighted grin at Anna as they followed him up the porch stairs. She accepted the arm he offered. With one hand, she gathered her skirt; the other, she rested on his arm. Her heart jumped at the enamored look in his eye.

"Do I smell potato and parsnip soup?" her grandfather asked merrily.

Once inside, Ben hurried to Levi, helping him to get propped up at the table.

They all sat for dinner, and Anna jumped when her grandfather shouted.

"Good news!" He pointed a finger at the ceiling with gusto. "Our new loan application was approved."

Greta hopped to her feet with a squeal of delight. "Wonderful!"

Levi grinned. "Great news, Grandfather. I'm sure you've been itching to order new supplies."

Anna stood and hugged her grandfather, relieved that Jonathon hadn't held her lack of interest against them. Then her grandfather picked Greta up off her toes while she giggled. Ben grinned at Anna and gave her arm a gentle squeeze.

"I'm grateful you ladies provided food to last the winter. And Levi still has some of his savings in the bank to build his own house soon." He turned to Levi. "I appreciate the help you gave us, but I'm also glad I didn't let you pull out as much as you'd wanted to."

Levi nodded, and they exchanged meaningful looks.

"Tomorrow I'm finally putting in the big order for books and paper," her grandfather said. "And I'm getting wine. It's about time."

"I'd like to buy *real* brown Windsor soap," Anna said, waving her nose in the air as if she smelled something delicious.

After dinner, Greta made hot cocoa, and Anna invited Ben to sit on the porch with her. The stars glowed, and the air smelled like it might snow.

She wrapped her coat snugly around her. "I can see my breath."

"Would you like to go back in?" Ben asked with disappointment in his voice.

"No, not at all." She wished they were holding hands.

"I'm sure you've noticed how much I like to be around you."

He blew on his mug of steaming cocoa. "You're always on my mind, to be honest. Is there any chance…you think of me too, and maybe return my affections?"

The suddenness of the question caught her off guard, but her immediate smile betrayed her answer. "Your affections?"

He peeked behind his shoulder before reaching for her hand. "And I love that you learned how to shoot a bow, and now you want to climb a mountain?"

Anna cringed, lowering her voice. "They don't know anything about the mountain. I'm still trying to figure out the logistics, but I won't tell them beforehand—they wouldn't allow it."

Ben ducked his head, lowering his voice. "Sorry. It's just impressive. I've never met any woman like you—you have my full attention."

"I do think about you." She could feel her cheeks warm. "I admire your spirit of adventure—hunting, traveling, fishing. I have the same desires. And I never thought I'd find someone to share those things with."

As she said the words, it felt like flying. She leaned toward him, enjoying the feeling of her hand in his.

"Write to me. Let's not tell your family yet—we have a lot to talk about before they need to know." He paused. "Let me talk to Levi when the time's right."

Anna remembered her brother's hesitation again, but smiled as she nodded.

"And after hunting I'll catch the boat in Oregon. I'll see you on our way through Seattle."

"Great."

She looked toward the mountain, but it was hidden in the night. She could never be someone's housewife, not anymore, not even Ben's. Although she didn't think that was his desire either, her attraction to him depended on how he acted when she shared her concrete plans to summit. It wasn't a far-off dream; it was happening soon.

She paused, worried again about June. "June isn't…where she usually is. It's not like her to just disappear."

"That's not good." Ben touched her forearm. "Can I help?"

"I don't think so, but I'll let you know."

Surely June would send word if she was in trouble. Or stop by. It was more likely that she'd switched brothels and forgot to send word.

Relaxing a little, Anna reached into her pocket for the knife. "And just think how close we are with the riddle. Part of why I wanted to solve the clues was in hopes I could sell the ring to pay my way. I'll head out to Heather's soon—"

Greta's voice startled her. "Cookies are done. Want some?"

Anna hurried inside with Ben, imagining being on his arm at a town dance, waking up next to him in the middle of the night to hear his soft breathing, kissing him gently after the birth of their first child—a lifetime of possible memories flashed through her mind.

The way he looked at her, their spark, had awakened something inside her that made her long for his presence and the sound of his voice. All the time she'd spent wondering if he noticed her, and now he'd confessed that he'd been watching her all along. It all seemed better than she'd ever imagined. Would they travel the world together?

CHAPTER TWENTY-NINE
THE COMPASS ROSE

I t was the third day of February, and it had rained almost every day of 1890. Wearing a thick wool skirt, a walking coat, and her fox fur vest, Anna slung Levi's old bow, which she now considered her own, on her back and walked to Heather's cabin through the rain. It had been over a week since Ben had held her hand in his own and said he admired her. The thought of writing to him and receiving his letters in return warmed her from the inside despite the frigid weather.

Striding confidently, she paused at random to turn and aim her bow behind her. It was an exercise that left her breathless, but it was good for getting her body ready for summiting. The faster she went, the warmer she got, keeping the frosty air from chilling her blood.

As she pulled an arrow out of a tree, she thought of June again, and a shudder went through her. Greta had turned up nothing by stopping at two different brothels. She'd also inquired at the police station, but hadn't uncovered anything. Hopefully June would stop by soon.

When she arrived at the cabin, Heather hurried to open the

door to let her in as the cold air rushed around them. She was soaked completely, and as she took her boots off, she poured out a small puddle of rainwater.

"Sorry." Anna tried to sop up the puddle with her wet petticoat. "I don't want Pisha to slip."

"She's not well, actually. She's sleeping." Heather gestured to the corner where the girl lay curled up on the bed, covered with a quilt.

"Oh no." Anna crossed her arms over her chest. "Does she need medicine?"

Heather didn't take her eyes away from her daughter. "My grandmother left yesterday to ask one of the Duwamish men on Ballast Island to take her to the reservation by canoe to get medicine. She should be back soon."

Anna smiled at the sleeping toddler. "You're taking good care of her."

"How's your training going?" Heather picked up the dripping boots.

"I've been climbing the stairs with a terribly heavy pack full of books. Walking up hills and valleys—even a frozen pond. I think that'll go much more smoothly when I have the proper gear. But I feel stronger. I know it improves my lungs coming all the way out here."

Heather had a far-off smile. "You've done well."

"I've learned about other women who've climbed mountains, too. Isabella Bird, Lucy Walker. It's so inspiring to know there are women all over the world like me—it makes me feel less lonely." She pulled the brick, compass, and knife out of a handbag she'd brought along. "I have much to tell you, Heather."

Heather wrung the wet socks and coat out and put them near the fire to dry. She put a quilt over Anna's shoulders and poured boiling water into a cup, adding tea leaves to steep.

"I haven't seen you in such a long time," Anna said. "Well, you knew we collected the brick from the Occidental Hotel.

Then we figured out the name of the ship Dmitri and Natalya came to America on. And then I finally received the copy of *Crime and Punishment* I ordered months ago and discovered the third clue is a knife. Now here they all are."

Heather nodded. "You've done a lot."

"The last clue is a fireplace, I think." Anna picked up the knife and set it on top of the brick, then she opened the compass, and the wheel moved slightly as she adjusted it in her hand. "Maybe if I put these three things in the fireplace, an emerald ring will appear."

Anna laughed and leaned closer toward the fireplace, admiring the brick. "Actually...these are awfully similar to the one I have from the hotel. I wonder if Dmitri was part of the construction crew at the Occidental Hotel and purchased leftover brick to make his own fireplace?"

Heather shrugged. "I have no idea."

Anna examined the fireplace, searching for one as similar as possible to the one from the Occidental Hotel. She moved closer, dragging her finger along the bricks. They were smooth with rough spots between each where they'd been plastered together. For the first time, she saw something small drawn on a brick—a tiny black circle. Her heart pounded as she kneeled down for a closer look, and the circle became a small compass with each of the four cardinal directions marked with their abbreviations, the "N" being the largest of all on the top.

Heather came to stand behind her. "What is it?"

"A compass rose." Adrenaline rushed through her veins like lightning. *"And then, you'll need to find a rose, but not in thorny space. Remember well the ship that brought us to this wondrous place.* Could it have been here all along?"

She grabbed her knife, nearly dropping it in her excitement, then slid the blade around the edges of the brick with the small compass on it.

As she worked the knife, she thought of Ben offering to hold the brick at the Occidental Hotel. She'd just met him back then, and already she'd sensed a connection. He'd offered his coat on the docks as they'd searched for the name of the ship—the Compass Rose. And the knife in her hands had been a beautiful gift from him. She sensed the whole mystery sliding into place, along with the realization of how strong her feelings were for the man who'd been with her every step of the way.

She pulled the brick out of its place and looked up at Heather with a hopeful grin. Heather shook her head with a half-smile, clearly amused the ring had been so close all these years. Deep in the back of the hole, Anna felt something soft with her fingers. It was a small velvet bag, and she pulled it out and placed it in her hand.

"The ring," Heather said triumphantly.

Anna laughed giddily, then pulled the string of the bag and tipped it upside down above her hand. An emerald ring silently landed on her palm. The large rectangular stone sparkled, with engraved leaves winding around the golden band. All at once, she imagined herself on the top of the mountain, joy flooding over her like a waterfall. She saw herself being congratulated by all the men surrounding her, thanking her for her hard work and dedication to such a historical feat.

A moment later, when she found herself back in reality holding the antique ring in her hands, she stood and hugged Heather. She wished Ben could have been there to share the moment—he would have hollered and raised his arms up in dramatic celebration. He would have grinned so deeply, so genuinely, then kissed her, sending a shock wave through her, making the solved mystery something for the history books.

"We found it," she whispered, smiling at Heather.

Heather nodded emphatically. "*You* found it."

"This is your cabin," Anna said. It was right to give it to her.

"But you did all the work. I couldn't even read the inscription. Let it take you up the mountain."

Anna's heart pounded at how much money she might get from selling the ring. Ten dollars? Fifteen?

"We should sell it and split the money," Anna said. "I would've never found it if you hadn't given me the book."

"It's yours," Heather said firmly. "We have all the salmon we can eat. Our garden does well, and the forest has berries. Michael brings anything we need from town. Please, it's yours."

Anna's eyes filled with tears of excitement, but she forced them away. "I don't know how to thank you for everything—giving me the book, becoming my friend. My life's taken an unexpected turn since I met you. I don't know what the future holds, but I'm already happier."

Heather smiled, but it soon faded as she checked on Pisha. She put the back of her hand against the girl's forehead, then leaned down to put her cheek against her forehead.

"If I sell this ring, I'll have enough to buy supplies and a train ticket," Anna said.

"Good. The mountain is dangerous, but you're strong." She picked Pisha up from a deep sleep, and the girl hung limp in her arms. "She's burning hot."

Heather stared out the small window, worry clouding her face. "*Where* is my grandmother with the medicine?"

It took Anna a moment to come down from her emotional high and realize the severity of Pisha's situation. She felt a twinge of confusion that anything bad could be happening during such an exciting moment for her—an unlikely discovery, one that had taken so long and required so much time and thought.

"How can I help?"

Heather didn't respond but brushed the sandy brown hair away from Pisha's closed eyes.

"I could fetch a doctor from town? Our family doctor is an old man, but he could come on his horse."

"Your doctors would never come here to give a Duwamish child medicine. Getting help from the reservation is our only choice," Heather said matter-of-factly. "Will you get Michael? I can tell you his address."

"Of course."

Anna's coat and boots were still wet, but she put them back on and ran out the door. She was still soaring with the joy of solving the riddle and wanting badly to tell Ben, but she was worried for Pisha and feared she might truly need a doctor.

She hurried back to town as fast as she could, running then walking when she got too tired. It took her a little over an hour to get back, but she quickly found Michael's apartment and informed him of the situation. He thanked her for relaying the news before running out the door toward the cabin.

She pictured the way Pisha had hung limp in her mother's arms and not opened her eyes despite all their chatting. She wrung her hands. Although it had stopped raining, night had fallen, and Doctor Wright would be home and eating dinner by now. She knew where he lived, but she couldn't imagine him caring about a sick Duwamish child. It was worth a try anyway.

It was seven in the evening when she knocked on the doctor's door, and his wife answered, inviting Anna to come inside.

"You're soaked to the bone, my dear," she said with concern, eyeing Anna's vest and the bow slung on her back. "Is everything all right? Is Levi still healing well?"

"We're all fine, thank you," she said, catching her breath. "It's my friend——"

"I'll fetch William," she said, running off before Anna could finish.

The doctor came to greet her near the doorway where his wife had left her. "How can I help, Miss Gallagher?"

"I don't want to waste your time, Doctor," Anna said. "Would you come with me five miles outside of town to see a sick Duwamish child?"

The older man stared at her blankly over his spectacles. "I don't know why there would be any Duwamish people outside the reservations. You know, there are doctors hired by the government to service the Indians, Miss Gallagher. Why don't you send them there? That's where they belong anyway, you know that."

"Her grandmother went to the reservation yesterday to get medicine, but she hasn't returned. It's too far to go with a sick child."

The doctor said nothing and shrugged indifferently.

"Thank you for your time, Doctor Wright." Anna marched away without looking back.

Anger filled her chest, and she wanted to yell into the fog settling in the streets. Pisha needed to be seen by a doctor, but what else could she do?

Her mind flashed to Connor's face, and her stomach churned at the thought of having to see him again, let alone ask a favor. She started back to her house and pulled the ring out of her pocket. It gleamed, somehow pulling light from the dim electric street lamps and the full moon through the fog. Even so, frustration consumed her by the time she arrived home, still soaked to the bone and now shivering.

She quickly stripped her clothes off and dried herself with a towel. She put the velvet bag holding the ring into the top drawer of her night stand, where *Anna Karenina* still rested. Once more, she imagined Ben's excitement at her discovery, just for a moment, but that would have to wait.

Glad to finally be dry, she quickly dressed in a pink cotton shirt and black skirt, then put her knife and compass into the pocket of her skirt. As she descended the stairs, her grandfather and Levi came in the front door.

"Going out, lassie?" her grandfather asked as he helped Levi to a chair.

"Heather's daughter is unwell," she said without wasting a moment. "She's not even two years old. I'm going to ask Connor if he'll help."

Her grandfather's face went blank. "I wouldn't want any harm coming to a wee one. Good luck."

She felt a softness in her heart for him. He was trying.

"Thank you. I don't know what time I'll be home."

"Please be safe, Anna," Levi called from the living room.

She nodded and ran out the front door toward town. It started to sprinkle again, and she was glad she had on a dry cloak with a hood this time.

As she knocked on the door to Connor's house, she couldn't help but notice the neatly trimmed hedges and recently painted white fence around his property; a reminder of the life she might have had if he'd been more understanding. He answered the door, then took a step back in surprise.

"Connor," she said in the politest tone she could manage. "Sorry to disturb you at this late hour, but I'm afraid I need your help."

"Please come in." He opened the door wider.

"First I need to ask: Would you help a sick Duwamish child? They're five miles away in the forest. She's had a high fever for too long, and we're worried."

"I'll get my coat and supplies. We can leave right away." He nodded importantly and disappeared back into his house.

Anna stared after him, mouth agape.

"It's cold and dark," he said from the other room. "We should take my horse. She's in a stable in the back. I'll get her saddled, and we can be on our way."

Her eyes widened. "I've never ridden a horse."

"Just don't fall off," he said, smiling. "I thought you were all about adventure, Anna. You do want my help, right?"

She wanted to glare at him, but her appreciation for his immediate help won out. "Absolutely—thank you."

They made their way to the stable, which was just behind his residence. It was made of timber fine enough for a house and elegantly constructed. Anna wrapped her cloak around her tightly in the darkness. It smelled of hay and leather, and inside the stalls Connor lifted a match to light a lantern. He quickly saddled a regal, dark brown horse who was stomping her hoofs in anticipation. Brown eyes peeked through the black strands of her mane, which fell to the side as she strained her neck toward Anna, sniffing the air, studying her.

Connor rubbed the white marking that looked like a star on the horse's forehead. "This is Ruby. I'll carry a lantern, and she can get us through the woods in no time."

He put a stool down next to the horse, and without using it, stepped up onto the horse's back in one graceful motion. "Step onto the stool and swing one leg over like I did, and you'll be sitting right behind me."

She took a deep breath and tried to do as he described. Stepping onto the stool, she took his hand and managed to get seated behind him, but it was none too graceful.

"Hold on tightly to my waist," he said, turning to look back at her.

Her stomach fluttered at his nearness, and the horse let out an impatient breath. Confused about how she ought to feel, she leaned in against his back, reaching her arms around him. He grabbed the lantern from a high hook in the stall, and they set out into the dark forest.

CHAPTER THIRTY
THE DEPARTURE

Anna lifted her voice above the sound of the galloping hooves. "Just past this clearing is the path."

The trail was wider since the deciduous trees had lost their leaves for the winter. The full moon and lantern guided them. Connor kept his horse at a slow canter, picking up speed on straighter areas.

"All right back there?" he asked a few minutes later, turning his head again.

She was still surprised with how close his face was to hers.

"Yes, I'm fine." She swallowed her nerves to give him an encouraging look so he'd turn back around.

They arrived at Heather's cabin in about twenty minutes—faster than Anna had ever gotten there, yet it still felt too long with her worry.

She brought Connor inside, and they found Michael and Heather leaning over the bed watching Pisha. They looked up in surprise at the intrusion. After quick introductions, Connor brought his bag over to the bed.

"May I examine her?" he asked Heather.

She watched him carefully. "Yes, thank you."

Connor listened to her breathing and put his hand to her forehead. The girl was lifeless, cheeks flushed, and dark hair wet against her forehead. He lifted her eyelids, checking her pupils, then searched her torso, finding a faint pink rash on her stomach and back.

He frowned and covered her back up. "What have you tried to bring the fever down?"

"Sipping water, warm baths," Heather said. "We ran out of yarrow, and the shaman is at the reservation."

"I have dried meadowsweet and willow tree bark with me," Connor said.

Heather nodded her consent and put out her hand to receive it. She made a strong tea then waited for it to cool before offering it to Pisha.

Michael shook Connor's hand with vigor. "I'm mighty grateful you came out here, especially at this hour, Doctor. Can I get you something to eat, or do you need to get going?"

"I'd be happy to stay for a while," Connor said. "To keep an eye on her fever. It's tough when the young ones are sick, isn't it?"

"This is my first," Michael said, his voice unsteady. "But I imagine you see it all the time."

Michael poured coffee for them at the table, and Anna glanced in the direction of the fireplace, at the brick with the small compass.

"Is there anything else we can do for her, Doctor?" Michael asked.

"At this point, I'm afraid not," Connor said. "But as long as her fever comes down in the next couple hours, she'll be all right."

Michael took a deep breath and exhaled it shakily, bringing his coffee cup to his mouth.

Connor and Michael chatted about the cold and rainy weather and the political matters of the recent statehood for

Washington. All the while, Anna remained quiet—she was worried and tired. It was well past midnight when Heather came over to them with a wide awake and hungry Pisha. Connor listened to her breathe a few times, then fetched a miniature cat figurine out of his bag and offered it to her.

"I think this little one is going to be fine," he said happily. "We should be going and let you all rest."

Michael pulled out a few large bills and handed them to Connor.

"That's not necessary. I'm happy to help the friend of a friend," Connor said.

Michael held out the bills with a determined look in his eye. "Please—I'm glad to pay."

"Much obliged, sir," Connor said reluctantly, accepting the cash then awkwardly tucking it into his pants pocket. "If anything changes, send for me."

As Anna and Connor rode back into the forest, the fog lifted, and the clouds began to part, the full moon rising higher behind billowy clouds. Anna held on tightly, trying to ignore the way Connor's chest rose and fell with his breath. She focused instead on her balance.

By the time they rode up to her house, the sky was slate blue with the first light of the sun nudging over the horizon. Connor dismounted and helped her down, holding onto her waist and setting her on the ground in a motion that felt like floating.

He smoothed his hair to the side. "I need to apologize for the way things ended on the night of the dance."

She held up her hand and waved away his words silently, but her heart pounded. Did he still have feelings for her?

His shoulders slumped, and he blew out a disheartened sigh. "Your grandfather gave me an earful and told me what happened after you went outside. I should never have let you walk away upset. I should have taken you home like a proper gentleman, no matter what we disagreed on that night. For that, I'm sorry."

She offered him a crooked smile. "Apology accepted. Thank you for your help tonight. Truly—I don't know how to tell you how much I appreciate it."

"My pleasure," he said, making a slight bow. "I ought to get going. I'm sure you're exhausted."

"I am," she said, blinking up at the sky. The indigo skyline was getting lighter along the horizon.

Connor mounted his horse. "Goodbye, then."

He rode away at a gallop, and she watched him go, surprised by a side of him she'd never seen, and relieved he hadn't wanted anything from her in return.

And then, the full measure of her tiredness settled upon her. With heavy steps, she climbed the stairs to her bedroom. She laid her cloak on her chair and pulled her boots off with great effort, then finally lay down to sleep still fully dressed.

❦

THERE WAS a light knock on Anna's bedroom door, and she raised her head to see her grandfather cracking it open and holding a tray of coffee, cinnamon rolls, and a bouquet of fresh flowers.

"Can I come in?"

She rubbed her eyes against the bright sunlight streaming through her bedroom window. "What time is it?"

"About one in the afternoon." He set the tray on her nightstand, then sat at the edge of her bed. "How'd everything go? Is the little lassie all right?"

She sighed. There was no point in trying to shoo him away so she could get back to sleep. "She's much better. We got to Heather's very late, but Connor brought medicine to help get the fever down and it worked."

He folded his arms across his chest. "Doctor Evans, eh?"

"Well, I tried Doctor Wright, but he didn't want anything to do with a Duwamish person, even though she's a small child." She watched his face closely.

"Hmph." He uncrossed his arms and stood. "Glad the wee one is all right."

She picked up the flowers and took a long inhale, smiling dreamily. "These are delightful. Did you get them at the market?"

"Yes, along with beef, flour, sugar, and chocolate." He raised one eyebrow. "And our first shipment of books is set to arrive in two weeks. Feels good, doesn't it?"

She smiled brightly and took a sip of coffee. The ring and the solved mystery swirled circles in her head, and she had the impulse to spill it all to her grandfather, but she wanted to wait until dinner when Ben was coming by for the last time before he set off. Sharing the moment of celebration with him would be the best part.

She got dressed in a flurry and went to McLaughlin's jewelry store to get the ring appraised. The store owner considered the ring carefully, putting it under a magnifying glass and turning it over in his hands, then said he would purchase it for ten dollars.

Her heart leapt. Even so, she wanted to see if she could get a better offer from a different store; she would only have one shot at selling such a valuable item. Plus, she wanted to show the ring to everyone at dinner. There was no rush to sell it because she didn't plan to start purchasing supplies for her trip until closer to summer—that way she wouldn't have to hide them.

Back at the house, the day dragged on while she waited for Ben's arrival. She played chess with Levi in the living room, then helped Greta in the kitchen, and ultimately decided to rearrange the knick-knacks on her dresser. Finally, a knock on the front door made her jump—it had to be him. She couldn't help but grin as she raced down the stairs and swung the door wide.

"Hello, Ben," she said, feeling her cheeks flush with the wave of adrenaline.

"Hello." He lowered his voice. "You look beautiful, by the way."

Anna could only imagine how pink her cheeks were getting. She motioned for him to enter and mumbled a thank-you.

He took off his hat and coat, hanging them on a hook by the door. When he turned, he had a look of desire in his eyes. Would he have kissed her if they were alone? With a sigh, she simply touched his arm.

"It's good to see you," he said quietly, his voice low.

She grinned. "You too."

As they joined her family in the dining room, her grandfather poured wine for everyone.

She lifted her glass. "I have something important to tell everyone."

Ben's mouth parted in surprise, a touch of betrayal written on his face. She shook her head at him, as if to say not to worry, then pulled out the velvet bag and handed it to him. He tipped it over and gasped when the ring tumbled into his hand.

"Amazing! Anna, you did it. Well done," Ben said.

"It was in Heather's fireplace. One of the bricks had a small compass drawn in black ink. I used my knife to pull the brick out and voila—the ring." She turned to Greta. "What a romantic proposal Dmitri planned, don't you think?"

Greta appeared to enjoy watching Anna tell her story with such animation. "I think it sounds very romantic, indeed."

"Your *knife?*" Levi asked.

Anna winced with a hint of amusement.

"I'm not sure it has much of a happy ending though," Ben said. "Here you are with a ring meant for someone else."

She frowned. "That's a sad way to think of it."

He laughed. "But it *could* have been a wonderful story. Let's drink to that."

Everyone raised their glasses, and Levi lifted his to toast

Anna. "I can't believe you solved the mystery after all. Well done."

"Of course she did," her grandfather said, pulling Anna in for a bear hug.

It felt good to be on better terms with Levi and her grandfather. Everyone took a turn examining the ring, then they took their seats for dinner.

Anna placed the white linen napkin in her lap. "Oh, Ben, I almost forgot to tell you. Pisha was really ill."

"The little one?" He glanced from her to her grandfather, perhaps expecting a reaction. "Is she okay now?"

Anna hesitated. She didn't quite know why she felt uncomfortable telling Ben that she'd asked Connor for help, but she did. "Yes, she's much better now, thank goodness."

Greta stood to refill water with the glass pitcher in the middle of the table. "Ben, we're sure going to miss you around here."

"Thank you, ma'am. I'll certainly miss the Gallaghers. And your fine cooking."

Greta beamed.

After dinner, Ben put on his hat and coat. "I'd better be leaving. I'll think of you all during my travels and hope to stop by briefly in the spring."

"I'll see you soon. Be safe out there," Levi said, shaking Ben's hand and putting his other on his shoulder. Ben nodded meaningfully.

"I'll see you out." Anna wrapped a shawl around her shoulders and stepped out the door with him.

For a moment, the two stared at one another in silence. Ben seemed melancholy, as if he might change his mind and stay after all, but he didn't say a word. His absence was going to be more difficult than she'd realized, but she was happy for him that he was going to spend time in the forest. This close, he smelled like cedar from a day at the mill, and she longed to be in his arms.

"I can write to you from trading posts and anytime I'm near a city," he said, taking both her hands in his.

What did that mean that he'd be writing her? Were they courting, but just not officially because he hadn't asked permission? Now that he was leaving, she longed for him already —to finally put her hands in his dark hair or feel the touch of his hand against her back.

He knew about her desire to summit the mountain, but should she mention the planned trip? Perhaps he'd try and stop her, but still she ached to share that part of her heart with him, and not in a letter. She turned to face him and wanted to speak, but the words caught in her throat. The heat coming off his body made her lightheaded.

As she held his gaze, he leaned down and put his cheek against hers and whispered, "And I swear by the stars and my soul and say, that I will have you and hold you and kiss you, though the whole world stands in the way."

It was from one of the poems in the book she'd let him borrow. One that she'd underlined.

He put one hand on her neck, and the other held her face, his thumb enticingly close to her lips. Her knees were weak as he moved his whole body closer, until his chest touched her own. He closed his eyes, leaning in, and she squeezed her eyes shut too, ready for her first kiss.

But the handle of the front door jiggled, and she felt his hands drop away as he stepped back.

Her grandfather swung the door open with a stunned look on his face.

"Oh, I thought Ben had already left and you were out here alone." Her grandfather rubbed the back of his neck with one hand.

Ben tipped his hat and started down the steps. "I'm actually just leaving. Thank you for all your generosity, Mr. Gallagher. Good evening."

Without looking back, he hurried away. Anna wanted to watch him go, but the cold February evening without him gave her a sudden chill, and she didn't want her grandfather to see her disappointment. She rushed inside the house, ran up the stairs, and wrapped her quilt around her.

Her head spun with the thought of the kiss that should have been—she could still feel his breath against her lips. Pulling out the ring from her pocket, she tried it on her finger for the first time. It fit perfectly, and she imagined what it might feel like to have Ben propose. A deep and sudden desire filled her, and she longed to run down the street and tell him that she couldn't bear to see him go.

CHAPTER THIRTY-ONE
THE RIGHTFUL OWNER

25 December 1880

"He should've come by now." Natalya sat cross-legged on her bed, running her fingers through her dark hair.

Her roommate gave her a pitying look. "I'm sure he got stuck in the snow and thought it best to stay put until the storm ends. You're welcome to have Christmas dinner with my fiancé's family."

Natalya's shoulders slumped, and she rubbed her arms to keep warm. "No, I'll wait. He's trying to get here as soon as he can, and it's not easy trudging through the forest in two feet of snow. Thank you though."

Once she was alone in their room, she busied herself straightening the sheets on her bed and rearranging her few belongings in her wooden trunk. All day she stole glances through the small window at the street below while snow continued to fall. Dmitri never appeared.

She had come to America with a small group of Russian travelers. It had been a long and treacherous crossing of the northern Pacific, but it was on that boat that she met Dmitri. He had traveled alone while she was accompanied by her great-aunt. She had found him kneeling on the deck, hunched over a book. Dmitri had asked her if she wanted to learn English, to which she replied in English that she'd already been studying it. Their connection had been instant, and that little conversation had blossomed into a friendship, and then a romance.

Shortly after they'd arrived in America, her great-aunt had died, and she had been forced to find a small boarding house for young women. Whenever she had free time, she spent it with Dmitri, and she hoped they'd marry soon, but until then, she worked as hired help in the kitchen of a restaurant.

Natalya put her hand to her stomach and smiled. A new baby —what a surprise to tell him on Christmas in the warmth and comfort of his log cabin in the woods. But, where was he?

Two more days of heavy snowfall and high winds went by, and on December 27th, the storm finally ceased. The sun shined down on the white-dusted town, and she bundled up and started toward Dmitri's cabin. It was a path she'd taken many times, but usually with less snow. Perhaps the pregnancy made her winded, or the traipsing through the snow, but when she arrived, her whole body was spent.

She found the place tidy but empty; the only things missing were his boots, coat, and rifle. She searched outside the cabin, but there was only snow, and more snow, among the trees.

Frustrated, she made a fire and sat at the table, wondering where he might have gone. It had been almost a full week since she'd seen him last. He had no family in town or anything else to draw him away so suddenly. She couldn't imagine him simply leaving and moving elsewhere.

He was the kind of man a person just knew had a heart of gold. His eyes followed her around every room, making her feel like a Russian aristocrat. She knew beyond a doubt that he loved her and wanted to marry her. He'd written her a poem for every special occasion, and she couldn't wait to see what he'd write about expecting a child.

She searched the cabin, tearing sheets off his bed, dumping a bag of flour onto the table, and lifting up rugs, trying to find any clue as to why he would unexpectedly go missing. Searching through his trunk, she found mostly blankets and bedding, but she wasn't able to lift the heavy thing to dump it entirely. Then, without warning, a great wave of nausea hit, and she ran to the door for fresh air.

After the icy air had soothed her, she returned to lie on the bed, pieces of straw poking into her back. A small lump under her legs made her jump up to examine under the mattress, where she found a brown envelope full of money. She counted sixty-seven dollars. Surely, he hadn't abandoned her and left his savings behind. Or did he mean for her to find it as an apology for leaving her? Exhaustion seized her as dusk settled, and she put the blankets back on the bed to wait out the night in case he returned.

The next morning, Natalya rubbed her belly. She was falling in love with the baby growing inside her, but it crushed her that the love of her life had disappeared. She also knew, as an unwed pregnant woman, she would be unwelcomed at the young ladies' boarding house once she started to show.

Some of the Russians she'd traveled with had gone south to Tacoma, where it was suspected the Northwest Pacific Railway would end. With Dmitri's money, she'd have enough to rent a small room of her own, and if she could find a small group of friendly Russians, it might one day feel like home.

With trembling hands and tears threatening to fall, she closed the cabin door and set off to the boarding house to gather her few belongings before heading south.

CHAPTER THIRTY-TWO

THE GRAVE

Tacoma, Washington
18 April 1890

Natalya gazed out the window into Commencement Bay to see another steamer coming into port, full of passengers. She hurried to grab the clean sheets from the line before the afternoon drizzle started. Tacoma had been buzzing ever since Washington's statehood had been granted a few months ago, and many new families were settling in the area.

People came from all over the world, especially since the Northern Pacific Railway had made Tacoma the official end of the line in 1887. She didn't quite understand that, since it did make one more stop north in Seattle now, but nevertheless, Tacoma was growing rapidly. She lived close to the railway terminus and within walking distance from the piers, and she enjoyed working for one of the finest dressmakers in the city.

When she'd arrived in Tacoma in the cold January of 1881, she hadn't known where to go. An old German woman, Mrs. Schwarz, had seen her on the street and scolded her for not being dressed warmly enough in the snow. At first, Natalya had ignored her, annoyed the woman thought she was willingly and carelessly freezing herself, but Mrs. Schwarz had invited her inside for schnitzel and told her to warm herself by the fire. When she had told the old woman she'd just arrived in town alone and pregnant, Mrs. Schwarz had offered to let her stay in her spare room for a modest boarding fee.

One night had turned into a week, and they got along quite well. Mrs. Schwarz owned a small dress shop that she and her husband had run before he passed. She taught Natalya how to sew and soon hired her at the dress shop. Natalya had told her about Dmitri and that he was likely dead, but not that she wasn't quite convinced of his death. She hoped he was out there somewhere, looking for her. She sent letters periodically to Seattle —no address, just his name in case he ever stopped by the post office.

She brought a wide-eyed baby girl named Cara into the world in the autumn of 1881. Mrs. Schwarz proved to be a great help; by that time, Natalya (and now Cara) had become permanent tenants in her home, and together the two women took care of the baby as she grew.

Over the years, the shop became a flourishing business with as many as five seamstresses employed. Natalya became skilled at tailoring, and she also took care of all the purchasing of fabric, materials, and patterns while Cara, now eight years old, split her time between school, learning to sew with Mrs. Schwarz, and helping her mother with chores. They'd been happier than many, even if Natalya had never been able to shake her nagging fear that Dmitri had simply left her.

Her mind returned to the present as she folded the sheets from the line, placing them neatly in a basket. Since their shop was running low on fabric, she had decided to make a large purchase in Seattle. She packed her and Cara's things, everything they'd need for a weekend away, and left for the station. As the train pulled out of Tacoma, Cara looked up at her mom with big brown eyes.

"Mama, can we buy new lace for my Sunday dress?"

"Perhaps." Natalya watched the trees go by in a blur. "You know, I haven't been to Seattle since I was pregnant with you."

As she said "you," she touched the tip of her finger on Cara's nose and smiled.

"Seattle is where Pa died, right?" Cara grabbed her mother's hand and traced the edges with her finger.

Natalya hesitated. She touched the end of one of Cara's braids and kissed the top of her head. "Yes. Let's get you a new bonnet as well."

The train slowly made its way through a deep valley with water on one side and a large, tree-covered hill on the other. The bright green buds on the trees seemed to light the countryside in a soft glow as they whizzed past. Deer stood motionless in the distance until the train blew its horn, sending them sprawling through the fields of yellow flowers and tall grass. When they arrived in Seattle nearly three hours later, it began to sprinkle, and they hurried to find the boarding house Mrs. Schwarz had recommended.

The next morning, they found a new bonnet and the lace for Cara's dress. As they took the trolley, Cara's eyes were wide. "It's even busier here than Tacoma!"

Just before lunch, as they were about to go into Aurora Textiles on Second Avenue to look at fabric, the sky opened, and the sun finally shone through. Natalya longed to visit the place where Dmitri's old cabin used to be. She wondered if it still stood or if it had been cleared for new settlers.

"How about a little adventure in this lovely weather?" she asked her daughter with a gleam in her eye.

Cara nodded enthusiastically. "Yes!"

They purchased sandwiches and wrapped them in a cloth before starting in the direction of the cabin. It had been ten years, and so much of the town had changed, but she remembered the way she'd taken so many times that first year they'd arrived in America. But the forest was all new to her daughter, who had spent much of her life in the city. Cara was in wonder, carefully stepping over tree roots and jumping at foreign noises.

They stopped in the meadow of naked blackberry thorns to have lunch, then crossed the stream, eventually finding the cabin around three. When she saw the cabin in the distance, she told Cara to stay behind a tree while she inched forward to make sure it was safe.

As Natalya peered into the yard, a tan little girl with wild brown curls played with a doll while a copper-skinned woman worked in a garden planting seeds. She watched for a while and didn't see anyone else, so she motioned for Cara to join her. Everything appeared mostly the same, and it was clear the property had been well maintained. The garden was new.

Heather walked out as they grew closer. "Are you lost?"

Straightening her shoulders, Natalya offered a friendly smile. "Not exactly. I knew the man who used to live here. Actually, he built it."

Heather pulled a braid over her shoulder. "Oh, I see. Please, come in."

They followed Heather into the cabin. Cara waved at Pisha, and the girl held out her corn husk doll for Cara to admire.

"My papa used to live here," Cara said proudly.

As Natalya moved across the threshold of the cabin, memories flooded her—the ones she'd cherished through the years. They returned to her in vivid detail. The smell of the log cabin, the fireplace, the small window.

The two women spoke for quite some time while the girls played on the floor near the fireplace. Natalya told Heather how Dmitri's land claim hadn't been complete before he'd gone missing and how, without him, she'd had no reason to stay in

Seattle. Heather told her about the changes and improvements they'd made to the cabin and about Michael purchasing the land from the government years ago.

Natalya wasn't sure how to phrase her next question—the most important one—with the girls close by. She leaned in to Heather. "Have you ever found a body or remains nearby?"

Heather nodded solemnly. "A man's body. I found him a half mile from here. His boots were showing under a large pile of snow. I searched the area and found this cabin. Brought him here and waited, but no one else ever came. I buried him. That was the end of January, many years ago."

Tears brimmed in Natalya's eyes. "Thank you. Where is he buried?"

"I'll show you." Heather brought them to a shaded area with wildflowers carpeting the ground, then left Natalya and her daughter there.

Natalya kneeled in the dewy ferns. She expected to cry, but a great relief flooded her instead. She finally knew the truth. "Your father's buried here, Cara. He adored us, but he wasn't able to be with us."

Cara stood still, then knelt next to her mother. "I wish I could have hugged him, Mama. Just once."

Natalya wrapped her arms around her daughter, kissing her neck and noticing how her skin still smelled as it did when she was a baby. But Cara was turning into a young lady before her eyes. "Me too, sweetheart."

After a while, they returned and found Heather waiting outside the cabin. She motioned for them to come back inside. "I found a book. It was for you, but it's not here anymore. My friend has it."

How could she have missed it? "For me?"

"Yes. It was in the bottom corner of the trunk wrapped in brown paper. Beneath blankets. I didn't see it right away—it blended into the shadows and wood."

Natalya remembered sifting through the trunk, not being able to lift everything, pregnant as she'd been.

"Let me give you directions to Anna's house. There's more now than just a book. She can explain it all."

Cara's jaw dropped. "We aren't going all the way back tonight, are we? That was such a long walk."

Heather laughed softly. "Please, stay here tonight."

Natalya agreed, and Heather made a bed of furs in front of the fire.

The next afternoon, Heather took them as far as the meadow and offered a heartfelt goodbye. Natalya held her daughter's hand, hoping the girl couldn't sense her nerves. What book had Dmitri meant for her? Was it supposed to have been her Christmas gift? Cara smiled up at her, squeezing her hand, and she felt a deep love for both her daughter and the man she still loved.

CHAPTER THIRTY-THREE
THE CONFESSION

Anna answered a knock at the door and found a small woman and a little girl, both with brown hair and timid smiles. "Can I help you?"

She gave a quick wave to the little girl who waved back.

"I met your friend Heather—I mean if you're Anna?"

She bit her lip. "Yes, I am."

"My name is Natalya and this is my daughter, Cara."

She stared at them as if they were ghosts from the past. When she finally found her voice, she shook her head. "I'm sorry, you've surprised me. Please come in."

Her chest tightened as she invited them to sit by the fire, then went to get *Anna Karenina*. Before she could even form the idea in her mind, she felt the loss of the ring.

She had to give it to Natalya—it was her ring, after all—but without it, she had no chance of making it to Mount Rainier that summer. She took a deep breath and grabbed the book off the nightstand. With much disappointment, she tucked it under her arm as she pulled the black velvet bag out of the drawer.

Back in the living room, she put a smile on her face. Steeling herself, she looked into Natalya's brown eyes and saw such hope that she lost all sadness for her own misfortune.

"This book was meant for you." She flipped to the first page. "Here. Read this."

Natalya read the inscription and laughed as she ran her finger along the words, the clues Dmitri had meant for her to solve.

"And this." She dropped the ring into Natalya's hands. "This is where it all led. Back to a brick in the fireplace of the cabin—it was meant for you."

"Oh my!" Cara exclaimed, looking to Anna. "It's beautiful, Miss Gallagher. This was from my Papa?"

Anna nodded excitedly.

"He was a clever man." Natalya's eyes were shining. "It's been hard to let him go, but knowing all this is such a comfort."

She slipped the ring onto her finger and held her hand out to admire it. Wiping tears away, she handed the book back to Anna, who shook her head.

"They're both yours," Anna said. "Absolutely."

Natalya touched her hand to her chest. "Thank you for everything."

They talked a bit more about how Natalya had spent the last decade, then as mother and daughter gathered their things to go, they exchanged addresses to keep in touch.

"Next time you come up to Seattle," Anna said, "please stop by and say hello."

"We'd be delighted to have you some time in Tacoma as well."

After they left, Anna felt the gravity of the loss pull at her limbs as she sat at the table, her head in her hands. The money was gone. But it felt good knowing that without her interest and time spent on the riddle, Natalya might never have known how much Dmitri had loved her, and that rather than abandoning her, he'd actually created a beautiful riddle to propose to her. She couldn't fathom what that knowledge must mean to the woman, but it was for the best.

The dampness of the rainy April evening finally got to her. Ben wasn't in Seattle, so she couldn't even share the joy of meeting Natalya with him.

What did she have left?

June still hadn't visited, which made her sick with worry. And now, climbing the mountain seemed too great of a dream to give up, but she couldn't see a way to make it happen anymore.

In the last two months since Ben had left, she had only received one short letter from him postmarked from Astoria. It was brief, although he'd made his continued affections clear. She felt a nagging gap in her life with him gone, and she wished he'd told her where she could send one in return. He hadn't put his name on the letter, so their communication was at least a secret still.

She had spent many hours each day hiking up and down the hills around town and in the forest to get her lungs used to vigorous exercise. After work, she spent most of her time reading books about mountaineering and teaching Heather to read. In return, Heather had taught her some of the Duwamish language.

Heather was sewing a warm outfit for her to wear, which included leather, animal furs, and thickly knit cotton. It wouldn't be ladylike, but that was the least of her concerns. She had planned to change into her "adventure clothes" as soon as she got to the foot of the mountain.

Whenever possible, she had also stolen opportunities to climb the stairs with the pack of books. In the beginning, she could only last ten minutes before collapsing, but now she could last over an hour. It was much easier with her skirts tied up, and it would be even easier once she ditched them.

She remained at the kitchen table long after Natalya had left.

Feeling listless, she walked by the kitchen table on her way to find a snack when she noticed the postman had delivered letters. One particularly dirty envelope was addressed to her from an address in Oregon she didn't recognize—no name. Her heart squeezed as she realized it might be from Ben...or June.

> *Dear Anna,*
>
> *I have spent these last two months traveling and hunting my way down to Oregon, and my heart is refreshed. I think about you every day, and I have to write the words: I love you. I see a side of you I don't think many others appreciate.*
>
> *You are strong and confident and capable of things most women are not, or men for that matter. Would you consider a life of travel and adventure with me? We could learn new languages, read books, travel, and meet Indians all over the Pacific Northwest. This is the life I want, and I want it with you. I can't wait to see you in May, even though it will just be an afternoon.*
>
> *Yours,*
> *Mr. Benjamin Chambers*

He *loved* her and was imagining their life together in the same way she was. Heat flushed her face, and she opened the front door, imagining his face in the moonlight the way it looked on the night he'd almost kissed her. An overpowering thrill consumed her as she pictured traveling with him—just being with him.

It was happening. A man loved her, just as she was, and she was falling for him. She had never imagined that the love of a man could be the most intense feeling of all, but as she stood with the letter in her hand, an electric happiness radiated from deep inside her.

Mrs. Anna Chambers.

Would they marry one day? She spent the rest of the evening in her room, skipping dinner with her family. She had a heavy knot in her stomach, which contrasted with her lightheadedness. She lay on her bed daydreaming, staring at the ceiling until the room faded into golds and pinks as the sun set through her white curtains.

If only she could talk about all of this with June. Her no-nonsense friend would tell her the right thing to do. She'd say: *Here is this man, right in front of you, who loves you exactly as you are, and he wants to give you a life of travel, love, and adventure—you could have it all!* Where had June gone?

After a fitful sleep, Anna awoke the next morning, grabbing her bow, which she kept hidden in her closet, and set out for Heather's cabin. Ben was a dream come true, but in reality, it would be so long until she saw him again, and even longer until he was back from fishing. Perhaps it would be best to hide the letter away. She treasured its message, but she needed to focus on the mountain for the time being. Without the ring, she was back to having no idea how to get enough cash to summit.

She took aim at trees, shooting as she walked toward them. Then, after collecting the arrows, she aimed at trees behind her as she stepped backwards away. Her hand had grown steadier. Often, the arrow landed exactly where she aimed, and her spirit soared with accomplishment.

When she arrived at Heather's, she was welcomed with a delighted grin.

"You look…" Heather said, trailing off.

"What?" she asked. "Silly?"

"Ready." Heather grinned at her with pride. "You look confident and capable."

Anna hadn't even realized how much she wanted to hear those words. In that moment, she wished her parents could see her, and tears formed in her eyes. For the first time in her life, she felt entirely sure of herself. She smiled back at her friend, feeling alight with a soft glow of happiness.

"She came," she said meaningfully.

Heather put her hand on Anna's arm. "I know."

After a moment of silence, in which neither woman needed to speak, Anna exhaled and flopped into a chair at the table.

"But...Ben." She grinned, glancing sidelong at Heather, then giggled.

Heather folded a small towel. "You love him?"

"He loves *me*. I think I love him, but how would I know for certain?" She searched Heather's eyes.

"Do you feel more alive when you're with him? Do you feel drawn to him like a magnet?"

"Yes to both." She laughed and twirled a lock of hair that had fallen around her shoulders.

Heather grinned knowingly.

"But, I'm sorry you won't have money for the mountain." She stood and moved toward the kitchen, preparing tea. "I leave again for fishing with my family soon. I'm nervous, actually."

"Why?" Anna was surprised to hear anything other than her usual calm confidence.

"I love them. But they try to bring us to the reservation. Every year. They say it's wrong for Pisha to grow up away from her tribe, her family."

She frowned. "That sounds hard."

Heather's eyebrows lifted as if she'd thought of something. "Why don't you come? Usually, we split the salmon and take home baskets full, but I could ask Owiyahl if she could give you cash instead. Or you could sell your share to a grocer. It's in a couple months—in July."

"You would do that? Would I be welcome?" Anna took a deep breath.

Could the moment get any better? Not only would that solve her problem of buying the train ticket to Yelm, but she could also buy the last of the supplies she needed. She also loved the idea of meeting Heather's relatives from the reservation. She wondered if other white people were ever invited, and if she truly would be welcome. Regardless, it was an honor to be invited to experience their special salmon fishing season.

"How many fish do you catch? How do you fish for salmon? Could I earn enough?"

Heather laughed. "Plenty. Patiently. And yes."

Laughter filled the cabin, and Anna sighed with the relief that came with finding the perfect solution. She had no idea how she'd broach the subject with her grandfather, or sneak away if it came to that, but what mattered was her secret adventure officially happening. The desire to get out of the city and see something new—something awe-inspiring—seemed to be burning through her like a fever.

On her walk home, she went as fast as her legs would carry her, climbing every hill she could find. Finally, she stopped to catch her breath in front of a large Sitka spruce, and as she leaned her back against it to rest, the bark crackled behind her. Its limbs were thin, and they gave her an idea. She searched for a sturdier tree and found an old maple with large leaves fanning themselves across its branches.

In one of her newspaper clippings, she had discovered that a good way to gain strength and agility was to climb trees. She had always climbed the apple and cherry trees near their house, but there were only a few good climbing branches, so it was easy. Standing in the shade of the enormous maple tree, she knew she needed to climb it.

As she did when she climbed the stairs with weight on her back, she tied her skirt up around her knees. She jumped and grabbed hold of the lowest branch above her head. With both hands clutching the dark branch, she swung her legs and pulled herself up.

Branch by branch, she climbed, until the ground below

began to blur. Carefully, she sat on a thick branch, leaning the back of her head against the wide trunk. Her lungs burned, and the muscles in her arms ached, but her heart soared like the hawks that glided above her.

CHAPTER THIRTY-FOUR
THE REQUEST

At the end of May, Anna held Levi's arm tightly on their way to the wharf to say goodbye for the fishing season. She hoped to see Ben, as he'd promised, but the closer they got to the harbor, the queasier her stomach became. She hadn't received another letter since his first, and that had been weeks ago.

She clung to her brother's arm as he maneuvered them around a wood-planked sidewalk in front of a busy grocer. His recovery had been slow, but now he seemed as strong as ever, although more somber. She was glad that he'd be out at sea with Ben for a couple months, and she hoped it would lift his spirits.

Thinking of Levi's childhood love for Emily, she couldn't help but ask. "Do you miss her? I mean, as a friend. Now that she's married."

He cleared his throat. "No. No, I'm glad she married a wealthy man. It's good for her—for the best."

She nodded, stealing a glance at him. She hoped he meant it.

"Why did you tell me not to fall for Ben?" she asked. "It's because you want me to marry a wealthy man, too, isn't it?"

He put his hand on hers and nodded. "Ben's a great man, but he has no house and no family nearby. I'm still holdin' out hope that you'll settle here in town, with someone already established and respectable."

She nodded, then they fell silent. She let out a nervous breath and straightened her mother's cameo brooch at the top of her white collared shirt, then tucked a brown curl into her high bun. She pinched her cheeks to add color and straightened her shoulders. She couldn't believe she was going to see Ben after so long. How would it feel to look into his eyes again?

Levi cleared his throat. "Actually, I met a young lady. Her name is Elizabeth, and she's going to write to me while I'm fishing."

She leaned toward him, examining his expression. He seemed pleased, but not quite in love. "Why haven't you brought her over to meet us?"

"I will. She's spending the spring and summer in Oregon with her aunt, but she'll return in the fall. I'll introduce her to the family then."

She couldn't quite read him, but decided not to pry. She had so many questions about the girl floating around in her mind, but at the moment, all she wanted to think about was Ben.

When they arrived at the dock, Levi threw his bag onto the deck and greeted the captain and fishermen, climbing aboard. Waiting impatiently on the dock, Anna scanned the faces for Ben, and her chest began to tighten when she realized he wasn't there.

"Anchor's up in an hour, boys," shouted the captain. He tipped his hat at Anna, and she returned the greeting with a friendly bow of her head, panic rising.

How long had they already been in port? Why did they need to leave so soon? She tried to get Levi's attention to ask him where Ben might be, but he was at the far end of the boat with his back turned. An aching lump formed in her throat and made her turn on her heel.

Her brother's voice called after her as she turned the last corner on the dock.

"Leaving without saying goodbye?"

She didn't want to call out a farewell in case the tremor in her chest made her voice crack, so she simply blew him a kiss and waved her arm in a dramatic goodbye.

Levi nodded and put his fingers to his lips before turning back to his friends, looking a little choked up himself.

Clusters of bright pink and purple rhododendrons filled the streets with the scent of late spring. They usually brought her great joy with their short-lived blooms, but instead she felt angry as she marched home. She knew it was unfair; she hadn't been sure she would see him. Still, it hurt. Sulking with her head down, she nearly collided with a large man as he rounded the corner running.

"Anna!" Ben said breathlessly.

She looked up and shook her head in disbelief, then reached out to touch his arm as if to make sure he was real. His hair was disheveled, his eyes focused on her as if she might disappear.

"Where were you?" she asked. "I mean, why are you running?"

"Captain said we could only stay in port a short time. Bad weather coming in," he said, still trying to catch his breath. "Soon as we docked I ran to your house. But you'd already left with Levi, so I rushed back."

He put both of his hands on her back and slid them to her waist, sending a shiver up her spine.

She could feel the joy creeping onto her face. "I really missed you."

He glanced down at her lips, then away. After pulling her around the building into the alleyway, he kissed her cheek. He lingered there—longer than she expected—and the feel of his lips made her cheek tingle.

"I have to tell you something." She felt her breath come

faster. "I'm going to attempt to summit the mountain this summer with a mountaineering group. I wrote to the leader who said I'm welcome to come if I can come up with the money—"

"When?" Ben cocked his head to the side and ran his hand over his beard. "*This* summer?"

"Yes, I've been training—climbing snowy hills, carrying heavy weight—and I plan to keep getting stronger."

He put his hand behind her neck gently. "*When* this summer?"

Her muscles relaxed against his warm hand cradling her head. Her movements slowed like molasses. "End of July."

"I won't be back by then." He frowned. "Why don't you wait for me, then we can train together and plan a trip for next summer?"

It wasn't the worst idea, given that she still didn't even know how to use the equipment, let alone own any. Doing it together would be exhilarating, but she felt her throat tighten at the idea of waiting another year. His eyes melted her, though.

"I don't know."

He leaned down and kissed her softly—just lips, mouth closed. After a few moments, he stepped back, dropping his hands away from her neck.

Her heart raced. She looked around to see if anyone had seen, but the sliver of sidewalk visible from the alley was empty. Everything inside her wished he would do it again, but she knew better, and so did he apparently.

"Wait for me. I promise we'll do it," Ben said with a twinkle in his eye. "Anna, I love you."

Her heart squeezed. "I love you, too."

"Then let's do it together."

She hesitated. "I need to tell you something. When Pisha was ill, and our doctor refused to see her...I asked Connor for help. And he did."

"Oh." Ben stiffened. "How did he help exactly?"

"Well we took his horse to the cabin." She felt the blood rush to her face as she remembered holding Connor's waist.

Nothing happened.

"He brought medicine to bring the fever down—Kiyotsa had gone to the reservation for medicine but hadn't returned—"

"I see," Ben said, his voice low. "I mean, I'm glad she's okay. That's the most important thing."

He cleared his throat and looked toward the street. "I need to run back. So they don't leave without me."

"Oh, all right." Emotion welled up in her throat.

He kissed her hand with a strained smile. "Bye, Anna."

CHAPTER THIRTY-FIVE

THE SECRET

Off the Coast of Alaska
6 June 1890

B en leaned over the bow of the ship as they sailed through
Glacier Bay, letting the fresh ocean air blow across his face
and through his hair. What was he to make of Anna asking
Connor for help? He felt nauseated imagining them riding a
horse together—Connor saving the day, healing the sick child.

He rolled his eyes.

His beard had grown longer than the neatly trimmed way he
preferred, but the added warmth brought comfort in the
Northern Pacific, and they had just reached Alaska. Levi had
fully healed, and Ben was glad to have him along for the trip. At
the same time, having him around made it nearly impossible to
stop thinking about Anna—and the idiot doctor.

At least there was always plenty of work to do on a fishing
vessel. Every ten days they returned to sell halibut in a small
fishing village in Elfin Cove, where he'd planned to mail letters to
Anna. Now he wasn't even sure she wanted them.

All that time he'd spent in Seattle, hoping she'd fall for him.

At twenty-three years old, he'd acquired plenty of money from his various jobs, especially since he always took cheap rents whenever he was in a city, and he mainly cooked for himself. He now had a bank account in Seattle, in addition to the small fortune left in a trust for him in an account in Berkeley. He had always assumed his parents would withdraw those funds after he left, but recently he'd sent a letter of inquiry to the bank to check on the status of his account and had been told it was still being held for him in the original amount, plus interest.

Truth be told, at this point, it might be possible to travel the world over and not spend half the money he'd acquired. He was constantly advised to find a wife, but he was quite uninterested in the thin, fragile women he'd been told were the desirable sort. He found such women were often fairly uneducated and timid. But not Anna—she challenged him intellectually. Her determination and fire stoked a light in him.

He'd found a copy of *Anna Karenina* in English, but couldn't decide when would be the perfect time to give it to her. He'd also purchased a few dozen books for himself and spent most of his lonely evenings reading novels by candlelight near the fireplace, inspired by Anna's love of stories and poetry. He was the one with a degree, but she could analyze them better than anyone he knew.

The book of poems was in his coat pocket. He'd meant to give it back to her before he left, but was glad he had something of hers to keep with him. He pulled it out and re-read a passage that felt a little too fitting for the time being.

Not quite the same
the spring-time seems to me,
since that sad season when in separate ways
our paths diverged.
There are no more such days

as dawned for us in that lost time when we
dwelt in the realm of dreams, illusive dreams;
spring may be just as fair now, but it seems
not quite the same.

He exhaled forcefully and watched the white puff of air dissipate. Anna was the woman he wanted to spend a lifetime with. As he scanned the ocean, an iridescent tip of floating ice came into view—probably broken apart from an iceberg.

"That's a good size," the captain shouted as they drew nearer. "Make sure it's not a full iceberg and we don't hit anything, then pull it up!"

Ben nodded, and a few men came to help. After they hauled it on deck, they smashed it into chunks they could carry and brought it to the hold to keep the fish fresh.

He searched for Levi and found him in the hold stacking the large fish between layers of ice. Surely, he knew his sister well enough to know the truth.

"Need help?" he called down.

"Not now," Levi said. "I'm done and exhausted. Going to bed."

Ben followed him to their room, and Levi flung himself onto his bed, grabbing an old newspaper. Ben sat tentatively by his feet.

"Levi," he said nervously. "I'm sure you've noticed my affections for your sister."

Levi lowered his paper with a frown. "I mean, you two seem to get along, sure. Lots of chatting about books and whatnot."

"What I'm saying is, I'd like to court Anna when we return."

Levi's face betrayed his apprehension. His tone was firm. "I don't think that's a good idea. She's looking for a man of a certain upbringing, social status, and a place in Seattle's society. That's what we're all hoping for her, anyhow."

Ben expected some resistance from his friend, but the immediate rejection stung.

"That's what I was afraid of," he said, almost to himself. "She mentioned that she spent time with Connor."

He peeked up at Levi, afraid for his response.

"Well she definitely doesn't fancy *him*, I can tell ya that for sure. She just really likes that little girl, and she needed help."

"Oh." Ben exhaled loudly. "Hmm."

Levi paused, and his voice softened. "But, what do you have to offer her?"

Ben straightened. "I have money and nothing to spend it on, my friend. She doesn't know that yet, but I'm not even sure that's what she wants. She enjoys being in the forest, shooting a bow. She wants to see the world."

Levi looked back at his friend thoughtfully.

"I hadn't thought about it like that." He paused and set down the newspaper. "How long do you even plan to stay in Seattle, though? We're the only family she has left, and it would break Grandfather's heart if she moved away or spent most of the year traveling with you."

Ben hadn't considered this. He didn't like the idea of being tied down to one city for the rest of his life, but he realized they hadn't spoken about where they might live if they married. He had no idea what Anna's take on it would be.

"I don't mean to discourage you. If you love her and truly have enough money to take care of her, I'd be honored for you to join the family." Levi nodded meaningfully and picked the paper back up.

Ben was moved by the approval. "Thank you, Levi. It means a lot."

He patted his friend on the shoulder then left.

Back on deck, he put both hands on the railing of the ship to inhale a deep breath of salty air. Anna wanted to climb the mountain, she had a secret Indian friend, she wanted to hunt and sleep under the stars—he knew it.

His knees went weak thinking about the moment on her porch, her soft face against his and the way a dark lock of hair had fallen in her eyes and he'd brushed it away, how her eyes had searched his in the moonlight before she'd closed them tightly. Had she ever kissed a man? Had she kissed Connor on the night of the dance? His jaw tightened—he didn't want to know or think about it. He only knew how much he wanted to kiss her again.

Late that night, after Levi was snoring in his bunk, Ben got out a pen to write her. His heartbeat grew louder in his ears as he pulled out a new sheet of paper.

Dearest Anna,

I'm sorry for my rushed goodbye. I understand why you reached out to Connor to help Pisha. Forgive me. You know my heart is yours. I do need to ask, though: Are you hoping for a life of society in Seattle? Or do you want to travel? We should have spoken about this before, but you can write me now. Also, I hope you'll still wait for me to summit.

All my love,
Benjamin William Chambers

He would mail it that weekend when they offloaded fish, then spend the next few weeks wondering if she loved him or if she truly wanted an established Seattle gentleman. But he'd spent his entire childhood pondering things—he could do so once more. And so, he fell easily into a routine for the fishing season, hoping and wondering if Anna would wait for him.

Anna stamped her letter to Mr. Flannaghan confirming her attendance for the summit attempt. It was decided, then—no turning back now. It was the beginning of June, and the planned ascent was less than two months away. Hopefully she'd make enough money fishing with Heather, but how was she going to slip away from Greta and her grandfather for days to fish? She'd just have to bring it up with her grandfather and hope for the best.

Their new shipment of books had arrived, and it felt like Christmas at the Gallagher bookstore. Anna and her grandfather unwrapped the books with care and shelved each in its proper place.

After work, she stopped by the market to get cheese and oil for Greta, and she saw a familiar figure near a fruit stand. She hurried over and barely caught June before she strolled away.

"I thought it was you," Anna said.

"How've you been?" June asked, breathless. "It's been a while…"

"*Where* have you been? Is everything okay? I've been so worried." Tears of relief filled her eyes as she enveloped her friend in a hug. Then she held her at arm's length examining her. No obvious bruises, and she didn't seem alarmingly thin.

"Oh, I'm fine, you know I could survive anything, but all's well." June nodded definitively. "I'm in a different place for now. Don't worry, it's all for the best."

"Don't ever disappear like that again. It's been months, June! You've never gone that long without checking in with me." Anna wiped the tears off her face. "Your hair looks divine, by the way. It's so long now, and thicker than I remembered it."

June paid the woman working the fruit stand, refusing the change the woman offered, then turned to face Anna. "Thank you."

June folded her arms and shifted her weight to the side

carrying the bag of fruit. Her eyes softened. "How have you been, dear friend?"

"I've been spending a lot of time with Heather," she said. "Would you like to meet her? It's a long walk to her place, but the spring rains have stopped."

"I'd like that. Maybe I'll stop by your house later this week—"

Anna was determined. "How about Sunday afternoon?"

"Dare I even argue when you make that face?" June grinned.

The girls laughed, and June agreed to come by.

On Sunday, June knocked on Anna's door after lunch, and they hiked leisurely through the woods.

"This feels like such a long way," June said after a while. "You sure you know the way?"

"I do. I've been coming out here and training a lot." Anna had to intentionally shorten her strides so as not to leave June behind.

"Whatever happened with the man your brother brought around? The wild one."

"Oh, he loves me," Anna replied with a coy smile.

"I'll be," June said with a laugh.

"He's incredible. He's fishing now with Levi. We've been writing each other, and he...he kissed me." She sighed dramatically. "But then I think I messed things up by telling him that Connor helped me when Heather's daughter was sick."

June stopped. "Connor Evans?"

She nodded quickly. "It was nothing, though. I don't have feelings for him at all, I just needed help. I hope Ben can understand."

June began to walk again. "When?"

"When did I tell him? Or when was Pisha sick?"

"Never mind." June hurried ahead, and Anna had to quicken her pace to catch her.

"He's a wonderful man though. I can't wait for you to meet him," she said when she came alongside her.

"How much longer?" June stopped and slumped down against a fallen log and lifted her hair off her neck. "I feel like we've been trudging along over an hour."

"We have," Anna said apologetically. "About thirty minutes left if we walk quickly. Shall we take a break?"

June waved a hand flippantly. "No, let's get there already. How in the world did you ever meet this woman to begin with?"

Anna spent the last leg of their journey telling her how the book's riddle had been solved.

"My goodness," June exclaimed. "I can't believe that ring even existed, let alone that you were able to hunt it down. All to give it away!"

"I *returned* it to the rightful owner," Anna corrected her.

"Still. The whole thing is uncanny." June shook her head in amazement.

As they approached the log cabin, they found Heather and Pisha enjoying their lunch in the grass near neat rows of seedlings. Sprouts filled their spring garden, and the soil gleamed rich and dark. Anna was pleasantly surprised to see Heather's grandmother squatting between rows of carrot sprouts, thinning them and neatly piling the discarded ones. She hadn't seen Kiyotsa in some time. Her weathered face smiled a greeting, then she returned her attention to the carrots. Dimples appeared in Pisha's plump cheeks as she spotted Anna and ran to her with bare feet beating the earth, then jumped into her arms.

"You're getting so big, my girl." Anna put the little girl on her hip. "June, this is Pisha, she's my favorite two-year-old, and this is Heather, who I told you about."

Heather stood and brushed crumbs off her skirt with a pleasant smile. "Nice to meet you."

June looked sideways at her friend with an amused smile. "I

wasn't sure how far out into the woods Anna was gonna bring me."

"Anna is very good at finding her way," Heather said. "She can travel safely long distances."

Anna blushed, glancing down at her feet.

June winked. "She could pretty much do anything she'd like if she set her mind to it."

"She also learned to shoot a bow," Heather said.

Anna squirmed and shrugged under the compliments.

Heather laughed and gave her a shoulder to shoulder nudge. "Come inside."

Heather tried to take Pisha by the hand, but the girl ran into the garden yelling "No!"

"It's okay," Kiyotsa said in English. "I'll watch."

Heather lifted her hands in the air as if to say 'I give up.'

The older woman returned to the garden, dirt between her bare toes, and Anna turned to Heather. "I've never thought to garden barefoot."

Kiyotsa spoke in Lushootseed, and both Anna and June looked to Heather to translate. "She says dirt is the ashes of our ancestors. The soil is rich with their life. We walk gently on it with our bare feet."

Anna nodded solemnly.

The three women went inside, and Heather motioned for them to sit at the table. She set out small cookies on a plate in the middle.

"Thanks, I'm starving." June plopped into a chair, putting a hand to her stomach. "My feet are killin' me, too."

Heather watched her with interest. "Perhaps…. Do you have a baby on the way?"

June's face turned white, and she started to say something but then shut her mouth.

Anna leaned toward her. "Are you pregnant?"

How could she have missed the signs?

June sighed and rubbed her belly. "Yes. Expecting in August, I think."

She looked at Anna and shrugged as if to say sorry.

Heather grinned with satisfaction. "I knew when my sister was pregnant, too."

Anna gripped the table and looked deep into June's eyes. "Will you keep the baby?"

"Yes," June said proudly, her hazel eyes sparkling. "My situation has changed."

"Do you know who the father is?" She unconsciously rubbed her own flat stomach and thought of Ben—how it might feel to start a family. But pregnant women can't climb mountains. She pushed the thought away.

June bit her lip and traced her finger along the cookie she'd taken from the plate.

Anna wrinkled her forehead. "What is it? Did something bad happen?"

"Bad things happened to me all the time at the brothel." June's eyebrows furrowed. "But this is different, he loves me."

"That's good. Do you love *him*?"

June smiled broadly. "I do."

"How wonderful!" Anna hugged her friend. "Are you going to get married? Oh June, I'm delighted for you. What's his name?"

But at that, June burst into tears, and Heather jumped up to get a blanket to put over her shoulders.

Anna rubbed June's back silently. "What is it? You can tell me, June."

Without looking up, June said, "It's Connor."

CHAPTER THIRTY-SIX
THE DOCTOR

Anna's hand froze on June's back mid-stroke. "Doctor Connor Evans is the father of your baby?"

Her palms became moist with sweat, and she moved her hand away.

June finally looked up at her, and they locked eyes. "Yes."

"How did that.... I mean, when—" Anna realized it must have been Connor and June she'd seen together at the dance, even though she hadn't trusted her eyes. June wasn't allowed to refuse customers, but it still stung.

"I'm so sorry. He asked me to dance, and he was upset. We ended up at the brothel that night, then he started coming regularly." June took a small bite of cookie.

"You don't need to apologize!" she said incredulously. "I never loved him. It's fine. But how do you know for sure it's his baby?"

"Shortly after the dance, in September, he got me an apartment, and I moved out of the brothel." June relaxed back into the chair. "He didn't want me to be with other men, so now he takes care of me."

Anna tilted her head to the side. "Is he...courting you?"

"Don't be ridiculous." June crossed her arms over her chest. "He's a respected doctor, and his family would be mortified if he was so much as seen with me. They'd cut him off from the family inheritance."

Her gaze darted from Anna to Heather then down at her hands, which were busy playing with the yarn at the hem of the blanket.

Anna looked to Heather for help, but she just listened stoically, still standing next to June after putting the blanket on her.

"But he loves me," June said. "And, believe it or not, he's overjoyed about the baby. I found out I was expecting in November, and I'd been with no other men, only him, for two months before that. So, we know without a doubt—'tis his."

A knot formed in Anna's stomach as she wondered what Connor's true intentions were with her friend. He obviously hadn't told June about coming out to this very cabin to help Pisha that night. That meant he probably didn't want June to know he'd spent time with her. Here was June, in love with him, and Anna cringed at the possibility that her love might not be reciprocated.

She gathered herself. "How are you doing with all this? How are you feeling?"

June looked relieved and hugged her friend.

"I'm sorrier than I can say—that I entertained him on the night things ended between the two of you. But he said you were finished, and that it was your decision." She blew a strand of hair away from her face. "I'm all right. He can't be seen in public with me for fear of word gettin' back to his family a few blocks away."

"That must be hurtful," Anna said with a soft voice, her hands clasped in her lap.

"That's not even the worst of it." June's eyes filled with tears. "His father's pressurin' him to settle down and suggested a young lady who just came out. I don't know what I'm gonna to do if he marries her."

She covered her face with her hands, and a few soft sobs escaped between deep breaths.

"It'll be all right," Anna said. "The best part is you're going to have a baby. And you're being taken care of outside the brothel, so there's nothing keeping you from being together and keeping it. It just sounds like it won't be in…a traditional way. But since when are you traditional?"

June nodded and wiped her tears away with her fingers. "I've suggested moving away to start over. Maybe California. We could be a family, and he wouldn't have to worry about his father or what anybody thought because they wouldn't know about my past in a new town."

Anna forced a smile. How could June stand it? Her lover was embarrassed to be seen with her. But she didn't want to hurt her friend, and there was no easy solution, so she simply took her hand. "I'm delighted for you."

⚜

AROUND LUNCHTIME THE NEXT DAY, after a busy morning at the bookstore, Anna told her grandfather she needed something at the market. Instead, she went to Connor's office and marched up to the receptionist who sat behind a small desk, papers piled in front of her.

"I need to see the doctor immediately." She glanced around the waiting area, which was empty and painted a soft blue.

"All right," the old woman said, her glasses low on her nose. "Regarding?"

"It's private." Anna folded her arms defiantly.

The old woman took her glasses off and rubbed her eyes impatiently. "All right then, dear."

She poked her head into the back room and told Connor he

had a visitor. When he came to the door, his eyebrows raised slightly before he quickly recovered with a friendly smile.

He gestured for her to go through the door. "Do come in."

Anna glared at him and strode into the room, letting her skirt twirl around her as she turned to face him. "How *could* you?"

"I'm sure I don't know what you're talking about." The apprehensive look on his face suggested otherwise.

"Stop it," she said. "I'm talking about you having a baby with my dear friend and telling her you love her."

He cleared his throat. "Please lower your voice."

She cocked her head to the side. He was afraid of their conversation being overheard, and it was her move. "Are you going to deny it?"

"No." He lifted his chin. "I've put her up in an apartment because I didn't want her staying in that wild place where anyone could…hire her. She's mine now, and I'll take care of her."

"Yours?" asked Anna, her voice cracking. "Well, the *baby* is yours, she certainly believes that."

"Indeed," Connor said coolly, taking a seat at his desk and motioning for her to sit.

She looked down at the chair but remained standing.

"Heather and I appreciated your help when Pisha was sick." She paused and sat. "But you didn't tell June about that night, did you?"

"No. She's in a weakened state on account of her condition, and she gets upset when I talk about other women. Pregnancy is hard on a woman's countenance. Concessions must be made."

"Hmm." She narrowed her eyes.

"No need to mention it to her, of course." He glanced around the room uneasily. "Or, at least, if you don't mind not mentioning it, I'd appreciate it. Nothing uncouth happened."

"Certainly not." She wondered if he was as afraid of June knowing about his goings-on as he was of anyone finding out that he was keeping June. He hardly deserved her.

Connor scratched the back of his head and left his arm there, cupping his neck. "My parents try to control my life. They want me to marry a prudent woman and contribute to society."

"It must be nice to have living parents," she said with a brief wry smile.

"Yes," he said quickly. "It is, of course, but they're extraordinarily controlling. It's hard to explain. Word already got out that I treated a Duwamish child in the woods, and some of my patients have started seeing other doctors."

"Oh, I'm sorry to hear—"

"It's fine. I don't regret it. But when my parents found out, they made a huge ado about it and made me promise to maintain a sterling reputation. They even asked me to lie about treating the child if I was confronted directly about it. Which of course is silly, but these are the demands they make."

Anna could see his chest rising and falling. She couldn't imagine her own parents behaving this way. Even her grandfather, with his faults, had understood the importance of helping a child. She was quite glad she'd never met his parents.

"That's your cross to bear," she said finally.

He gave her a weak, one-sided smile.

"It is, and I manage fine." He paused and looked up at her with tired eyes. "Would you please not mention anything about this—June, the baby, Heather's family. I know that's asking much from you, but it would be appreciated."

"I haven't, and I don't plan to." She raised her eyebrows pointedly and added, "I'd never do anything to hurt *June*."

Connor clapped his hands together and stood. "Much appreciated."

"One last thing," she said as she turned to leave. "June said you were going to start courting a young lady. Is it true?"

"My parents continually suggest young ladies," he said, shaking his head. "Sometimes they invite me to dinner, and there's magically a lady visiting at the same time, but nothing serious, not since you."

"Right...all right. Thank you for your candor."

She nodded curtly then moved toward the door, but Connor reached out and stopped her gently by placing a hand on her shoulder.

"I *will* need to marry eventually," he said solemnly. "I do love June—I need you to know that. And I'll always take care of her and my child, but I can't marry her, my parents would never allow it. Plus, I'd lose all my patients in the process. They'd definitely protest my marrying a prostitute. I don't see how I could ever have a real family with her. You must understand."

"Well shame on you for being so concerned about your reputation, when this is June's *life* we're talking about. She loves you with everything she has, and she thinks you're going to take her away. And you should!"

Anna slammed the door behind her.

⌘

OVER THE NEXT WEEKS, Anna spent much of her free time with June, hoping for a letter from Ben. On a warm Friday afternoon, the aroma of lilacs hung in the air, and they decided to visit Heather for dinner. As they walked through the forest in the heat, June pushed a lock of hair out of her face and lifted the rest from the back of her neck. She wore a lightweight plaid dress that Greta had made her to accommodate her growing abdomen. Only a weak breeze came off the sound, and it was rather hot for the third week in June.

Anna brought her bow and hoped to shoot moving targets on their walk, perhaps a squirrel for Kiyotsa, who loved their fur. She had started stashing the bow and arrows in the nook of a tree trunk in the woods near her house so she didn't have to sneak them out every time.

"He brings food and stays most nights," June said, letting her hair fall back down over her shoulders.

Anna was a few steps ahead, and she turned around to nod. "That's good. Heather will be happy to see you. She asks about you every time I stop by."

June stopped mid-stride, putting a hand to her stomach. "This can't be right."

"What is it?" Anna asked.

"I've had small pains, but this is heavy pressure." June rubbed her stomach, then waved her hand dismissively. "I'm sure it'll go away. The baby isn't expected till August—I've still got two months to go if Connor's calculations are correct."

"Oh dear." Anna watched her friend breathing deeply.

June straightened and strolled forward. "It's nothing. Let's just hurry and get there."

But, every few minutes, June stopped to grab Anna's hand, hunching over. By the time they arrived at Heather's house, Anna was panicked.

As soon as she saw her, Heather helped June sit down and started tea.

June pulled Anna in close. "Will you fetch Connor? I don't understand what's happening, but I feel like this baby is coming soon."

Anna nodded and left the cabin, setting off toward town at a jog. When she arrived, she rushed straight into Connor's office, past his secretary, and interrupted a consultation with a patient.

"June's having the baby right now, and she wants you." She held her hand to the cramp in her side as she caught her breath.

"Where?" Connor's face lost color. "It's too early."

She wiped a layer of sweat off her forehead with the back of her hand. "At Heather's cabin. You should get your medical things and come right away."

"Mrs. Barth, I'm afraid I need to leave," Connor said to his patient. "It's an emergency…with…another patient."

Anna rolled her eyes but said nothing.

Connor looked through his medicine cabinet, clumsily knocking over bottles. "I've never delivered a baby—that's a job for midwives. I briefly learned about the new field of obstetrics, but I never imagined I'd need the information for a live birth."

She shrugged. "Are you going to take your horse?"

"Yes. You can ride with me. Chloroform, forceps, keep things sanitary—that's all I remember. I don't have forceps, but I have chloroform in my bag."

Mrs. Barth sat dumbfounded in her chair as they ran out of the office. He threw the saddle on his horse and mounted, offering his hand to Anna.

The horse seemed to remember the way and galloped swiftly, perhaps sensing his rider's desperation. At such a fast pace, she had no choice but to hold on tightly. His body felt tense and hot with sweat. She wondered briefly if the baby wasn't in fact early at all, if June might have lied about when she conceived to let Connor think he was the father. They might have a clue based on how big the baby was. Did Connor wonder the same thing?

But lying like that, a lie that big, wasn't in June's character. Surely it was his baby.

He let the horse take a flying leap over the river, and soon they were back at the cabin. Anna was anxious to get back to her friend, but she had a suspicion Connor was even more so.

From the outside, the cabin seemed quiet, and she ran inside with Connor following closely behind her. They found June on the bed, Heather stroking her hand. Kiyotsa stood in the kitchen with Pisha, boiling water and hanging wet towels to dry on a line indoors.

Connor rushed over to June and gently brushed a golden strand of hair from her forehead. "I'm here."

She opened her eyes to take him in, then turned sideways as another wave of pressure consumed her.

"Anna, go sit with her," Heather said.

Heather took Connor's arm and brought him into the kitchen, speaking in low tones. "She's doing well. But she's losing energy. I hope your presence brings her strength."

He cleared his throat. "I don't know what to do."

"I've seen many births—my sisters and cousins." Heather poured water into a bucket. "My grandmother has seen more. We'll do our best. Usually men aren't present, but she needs you."

He nodded, his face obedient. They returned to June who lay still, eyes closed.

"How's my girl?" Connor encompassed her white hand in his.

June leaned her head in his direction and smiled weakly. "It's too early. He's not gonna make it."

He grinned at her with a confident warmth. "Seems like this baby wants to come right now. There isn't much we can do about that. He's a stubborn one. Or she."

June offered a strained smile, her face riddled with fear. She inhaled with difficulty and looked up at his face, seeming to soak in his presence. "Don't you have work today, Doctor?"

He scooted his chair closer to the bed and patted her hand, still in his. "I thought it might be nice to spend the afternoon with my favorite person."

Anna had been sitting in the chair next to June, but stood to walk away amidst this new conversation. She had watched June's face turn from distress to love-struck, and as she turned her back on the two lovers, she was unsure what to think. The sunbeams shining through the window pitched light across the room delicately, and she sighed, her backside still a little sore from the horseback ride, her nerves as frazzled as ever.

CHAPTER THIRTY-SEVEN
THE BIRTH

Anna moved into the kitchen and whispered to Heather, "You sure it was right to bring him?"

She remembered Connor's words about how weak and incapable women were. Did he suppose birthing a baby was easy?

As another contraction came, Connor's eyes grew panicked, but he held June's hand. As her body relaxed again, he rubbed her arm and said, "I love you."

Heather squeezed the hot water out of a rag and turned toward Anna. "Yes. She kept asking for him while you were gone."

Anna sat stiffly and shook her head. "Just don't want him upsetting her, I guess."

Connor had June's face in his hands and leaned in to kiss her on the forehead.

Heather tilted her head to the side. "Probably not upsetting her. It's important for her to feel calm. She needs strength, because this baby is coming."

"I don't think I can do this." June sat upright with sudden force and threw her covers off.

Connor looked to Heather with concern, who came over to the bed with her grandmother.

"You strong," Kiyotsa said.

Heather held June's hand gently. "The baby is almost here. You're doing fine."

"I just want to be done." June began to cry softly.

Connor offered her a cup of water, and she threw up into it and handed it back to him. Heather tried not to smile and watched Connor's reaction with interest, but there wasn't much to see. Apparently, vomit was something with which he was familiar.

"I was thinking," Connor said, as he set the cup of vomit down on the floor, "about taking you and the baby to California. What do you think?"

His smile was tranquil as he leaned toward her, reaching up a hand to brush a strand of hair away from her face.

A smile came over June's exhausted and sweaty face. "Do you mean it?"

He nodded and grinned. "You, me, and the baby. We can start over like you said. But you have to pull your strength together and help our baby come into the world. What do you say?"

"Yes," June said, her face full of relief.

Another wave of pressure overtook her, and she seemed to disappear into another world.

Anna took a deep breath and looked away. He was only saying those things to help June get through labor.

Heather peeked under the blankets. "I see a head."

June was already lying on her left side, so Heather and her grandmother helped her pull her legs up around her stomach and told her to push with the next wave. Anna moved closer, hesitant to get in the way, but unable to resist the importance of the moment. With Connor at June's side, she stood on the other side.

June grabbed Anna's hand and looked up at her with an expression she couldn't read. Her face was tense and covered with perspiration—it brought tears to Anna's eyes that she couldn't do more to help.

Within minutes, there was a crescendo of shouts and moans, and then, when the wail of an infant should have filled the small cabin, there was only silence. Anna's stomach turned as she watched Heather pull a small, bluish baby into her hands. Her grandmother grabbed the slippery, lifeless body, holding its face up to her own, inspecting it. She pulled a small tool from her apron and put it inside the baby's mouth, pulling out fluid that she dumped to her left. Then she wrapped the baby in a clean sheet and rubbed it furiously with both hands.

A horrified look came over Connor's face. He muttered something to himself and moved as if to take the baby away from what looked like violent rubbing. A painful stillness hung in the room as Anna and Heather stared at each other, not knowing what to say. After the noisy birthing, the unexpected silence was agony.

June remained facing away from the scene, lying on her side.

"Boy or girl?" she asked whimsically. She started to roll over, but Heather grabbed both her hands and held her there gently.

"A boy," Heather said, tears in her eyes. "You did good."

June smiled and rested her head back. "Can I hold him?"

Connor paced back and forth with his hands on the top of his head. He kept leaning over Kiyotsa as the rubbing seemed to drag on.

Finally, a faint cough and a whimper sounded. Kiyotsa immediately lifted the baby upright, supporting his tiny head then laughed with joy. "He lives!"

Connor gasped with tears in his eyes, then kissed June on the mouth. "It was close, darling, but he's all right!"

Tears filled June's eyes. "Oh my!"

Her face was a mixture of relief and pure exhaustion. She reached toward the baby, and Kiyotsa laid the crying, naked infant on June's chest, covering him with a fresh blanket.

Connor and June kissed again, then she kissed her baby's head—his hair still wet and plastered against his skin.

"He's so small." Connor touched the baby's hand. "I've never seen such a small baby."

June's face was full of wonder and she turned the baby's head up to see his face. Soft blond hair became visible as she rubbed his head dry. He looked up at her with wide, dark blue eyes and tiny blond eyelashes. His lips were still purple, but slowly turning pinker. She ran her finger along the side of his cheek in awe, then gasped suddenly, reaching for her stomach with a look of shock. The placenta came out with a gush of blood, and June's eyes fluttered shut. Connor watched the blood begin to soak through the sheets, then jumped to action taking the baby. "What's happening?"

"She needs to rest," Heather said, giving her grandmother a look. Kiyotsa rushed out of the cabin.

"Where's she going?" he asked.

Heather lifted the tiny baby into her arms and brought him over to the sink. "There's a moss that helps with the bleeding afterward. She knows where it is. Stay with June."

He exhaled loudly as he collapsed into the chair next to an unconscious June, slumping forward to put his head in his hands, then reached a hand toward her still shoulder.

Anna followed Heather to the sink with the baby. "What can I do?"

Heather wrinkled her brow. "We wait."

She pulled the pot of water off the stove and added cool water from a bucket already sitting in the kitchen. She washed the baby from head to toe with the warm water and a cloth—his hair becoming a fluffy halo. Then she swaddled him tightly with a clean blanket and brought him back to Connor.

"So much yellow hair," Heather said, smiling as she placed the baby in his arms.

Connor looked down at his son and pulled in a sharp breath. The baby locked eyes with him and made a small sound that made Connor laugh and look up to see if everyone had heard it. He sat back in his seat carefully, his shoulders back as he nestled the infant into his chest. Then he looked over to June, and his forehead crinkled with worry.

Twenty minutes later, Kiyotsa burst through the door with a basket full of green moss. Heather took it from her and picked out a few choice pieces.

"I'm going to clean her up and change blankets. Why don't you take the baby over by the fire to stay warm?" she told Connor.

He looked longingly at June then reluctantly nodded. "Thank you for taking such good care of her."

Heather and Connor maintained eye contact, then Heather nodded, pulled a braid over her shoulder, and turned back to her work. Connor took the baby to the fire, and Anna sat beside them.

"He's heavenly," she said. "Do you know what you're going to name him?"

His eyes glistened, and he let out a contented breath. "I think we've decided on a boy's name.... I'll let June announce it when she wakes."

"Of course. He's so small." She leaned closer to get a better look at the newborn.

"Well he's premature. It's to be expected." Connor grinned. "He'll be tall and strong soon enough."

Heather hurried by with dark red sheets.

Connor's jaw dropped. "Is that normal?"

Heather offered a strained smile, and Anna followed her outside. "Is she going to be all right?"

"I hope." Heather returned to the kitchen and washed her hands. She came up to Connor and reached for the baby. "May I?"

Connor didn't move at first, then reluctantly handed her the baby, who was starting to cry. Heather brought the baby to June who was still lying still and white. Heather unbuttoned June's shirt, exposing her chest. "June, your baby is hungry."

Connor gawked. "What are you doing? Can't the baby have cow's milk?"

Heather frowned.

"No. When the baby sucks, things fix inside." She said something in Lushootseed. "It's hard to explain in English. Trust me."

Heather unwrapped the baby and laid him on June's warm chest, putting the blanket over his back and legs. She guided the baby's tiny mouth to June's breast, and he started to suck.

June began to stir, then looked down at the baby.

"Hello, little one," she said with a hoarse voice.

Connor's face lit. "I'm so glad you're awake."

He leaned down and gave her a long kiss.

"My Joseph." She beamed at her nursing baby, then looked up at Anna with a grateful expression. "Thank you for getting Connor."

Anna nodded with a smile, admiring the baby. June's life had been difficult, and here she was in love with the father of her child. She hoped Connor sincerely planned to take June and the baby to California. But after the conversation they'd had in his office, she feared it wasn't likely.

CHAPTER THIRTY-EIGHT
THE DECISION

When Anna arrived home, a wavy and ink-blotched letter addressed to her sat on the kitchen table. It looked as if it had been soaked then dried. There was no name, but the return address was Alaska. She tore it open, and tears of happiness formed as she read Ben's words.

He understood. It was as if he'd known her for years and accepted everything about her. She sat down immediately to write him back.

Dear Ben,

So much has happened since you left, but I'll tell you everything when you return. You asked if I want a life in society, and I'll be honest: a fancy house with lace curtains and not worrying what I'll eat over the winter sounds nice.

But more than that, I long to be free, like you—free to travel and explore. Also, I must make a confession. I have decided to go ahead with my plans to summit this summer, before you return. I hope you're not angry. Don't say anything to Levi—it remains a secret from my family.

I'm sorry if this hurts you, but it's something I must do for myself—to see if I have what it takes.

Always yours,
Anna Gallagher

ANNA WASN'T sure how to broach the subject of fishing with Heather to her grandfather. She assumed he would explode in anger, but she needed the money, and it was essential that she try camping for the first time before she was on the mountain.

She had waited until the last possible hour to bring it up. As they opened the bookstore on the day she was expected at Heather's, she started with some facts to see if it might elicit any empathy from him.

"Did you know the Duwamish had over eighty huge longhouses along the Duwamish River that were burned down? The government wanted them to move to the reservation, so they…encouraged them by burning down their homes."

He grunted. "Doesn't seem quite right, I s'pose."

"At the end of the month, Heather's family is going to camp along the river to fish. Right where their homes used to be."

"Is that right?" He straightened his shoulders and stroked his beard. "Does that mean you've continued visiting her? I assumed so, but…I *really* wish you wouldn't."

"Her daughter is healthy and growing beautifully. I've been checking in on her, of course." She smiled convincingly.

"Hmm," he mumbled as he leaned over the counter, examining the ledger balance.

She gathered courage for the big question. "You've mentioned before that we might be able to hire a new person to help out at the bookstore occasionally. Would you mind if I joined Heather next week? We could find someone to help you while I'm gone."

He set down his pen and blew out his breath. "If you want to put aside your propriety to fish with savages, you can't expect proper society to excuse your behavior. You're ruining your marriage prospects, and I won't allow it!"

She glared at him. "Savages? Is that why you hit that boy then left him in the woods? He must have been so afraid when he came to. We could have cared for him inside and cleaned him up at least."

Her grandfather's face grew white, and he assumed the height of an angry bear. "If you go fishing with them, I'll never forgive you."

Her stomach dropped, and she slammed the large door of the bookstore behind her, hurrying away.

At home, she ignored Greta's greeting and packed her bag with Levi's sleeping mat and canvas tent. She slung her bow across her back and headed straight for the woods. As she turned toward the path to Heather's, the bag weighed heavily on her shoulder.

Her grandfather's anger toward the Duwamish made no sense, and even if she didn't need the money to summit the mountain, she might have wanted to join Heather for salmon fishing anyway. How could he be so hateful?

Would people *really* think it was such an awful thing to spend a week with Duwamish people? She wondered what Emily might think, but she knew Ben wouldn't think a thing of it.

When she arrived at the cabin, she set down her bag and tent. Her arms had grown muscular in the last few months, and her walks to Heather's cabin had become fast and easy—her body and lungs strong.

"I'm so happy you're here," Heather exclaimed as she burst out the front door to greet her. "This is going to be fun."

Anna laughed and hugged her friend. "Shall we?"

Heather nodded and called to Kiyotsa and Pisha, who were still in the cabin. As soon as they came out, they all left, and Pisha insisted on wandering by herself, which made them all walk a little slower. Anna took the slower pace as an opportunity to shoot at squirrels and rabbits as she went. She was inches away from hitting a squirrel before it made a sharp turn behind a fern. Kiyotsa seemed impressed with her good aim.

They finally arrived at a wide, winding river. As they drew closer to the camp, Anna saw tents against the tree line and canoes moored along the riverbank. About fifty Duwamish people were already there setting up camp. Some men were bare-chested, wearing breechcloths around their waists, while others were dressed in denim and cotton. Women wore stiff dark brown skirts with different types of cotton shirts, and many had layers of shell necklaces.

She felt a sudden rush of nerves as they joined a group of dark-haired women.

"You'll introduce me, right?" Anna whispered.

Heather grinned and linked arms with her as they came to join the circle. She said a few words in Lushootseed, then turned to her. "This is my dear friend, Anna. She's going to help."

One old woman spit on the ground and shuffled away. Most of them smiled politely then hugged Heather, talking again in Lushootseed.

"It's very nice to meet you," said one younger woman. "I'm Heather's cousin Lana."

Shell earrings adorned her ears, and her skirt hit around her knees, revealing what looked like brown paintings on her legs.

Anna beamed. "The pleasure's all mine."

Lana nodded shyly, then joined the others chatting with Heather. Kiyotsa patted Anna on the back and nodded encouragingly.

Later, she fumbled through setting up Levi's tent, glad for the practice.

Heather set her things up next to her. "So tonight, the first salmon will be caught and prepared. It's special, so there's a ceremony."

Anna looked up from tying off one end of the tent. "Oh, that sounds neat. Why is the first one special?"

"Salmon souls never die. It's important to treat each one with respect, because each year they return in new bodies, to feed us." Heather peered wistfully upriver. "If we don't treat them with dignity, they won't return."

Anna nodded seriously and took in her surroundings. Pisha went to the riverbank to play with her cousins and watch the older women weave baskets. It was a grand celebration with so many of Heather's relatives and friends there. The musical sounds of Lushootseed surrounded them.

After making camp, Heather brushed her hands off on her skirt and sat at the riverbank near the basket weavers. One loose, black braid hung down her back, which for the first time in a while did not have a child attached to it.

"The baskets are magnificent," Anna said, joining her on the ground. "Are they weaving animals into the pattern?"

Heather smiled easily and leaned back on the grass, resting on her elbows and crossing her feet at the ankles. "Yes. My family does animals on baskets. Ravens are clever and represent our people, who helped white men and women when they first got here."

Anna picked a daisy out of the grass, admiring the bright white of the petals. "I'm sure they'd have starved to death without them. Perhaps the Duwamish regret helping them now."

Heather looked out at the river, then over at the basket weavers again. "They also weave the eagle who rules the sky. He's the most respected bird. We use cedar and spruce roots and the inner bark of cedar as well. Some women weave them so tightly, water can't get in. Not mine, though."

She looked at Anna with a smile, and they both giggled.

"Pisha, can you bring me that bag?" Anna asked as the girl pranced by it.

The girl came running. "Here. For you."

"Thank you, darling." She scooped Pisha into her arms.

An old woman weaving baskets huffed and said something in Lushootseed, speaking over the other voices.

Heather blushed. "She says Pisha should only speak our language for now. See? The older generation has opinions."

"Oh…" Anna set the girl down. "*Wiiac*, Pisha," she added for good measure.

That evening, by the light of the moon and torches, the first salmon was caught and prepared. After that, men of all ages scooped salmon out of the river with nets. They erected upright logs in a line through the water to trap fish. Anna watched one young boy struggle with a full net as a frail old man sat next to him in the canoe. The smile on the old man's face made her glad to witness such an occasion.

The next day, she and Heather tended smoky fires while salmon hung suspended over the flames. Some of the sliced salmon was pounded in flour, which she found odd.

Men in canoes used nets to scoop out the salmon that were trapped behind the weir screens. There were fires all over the makeshift camp, where gutted fish were hung or pierced with sticks and leaned over fires to smoke.

She thought of Ben and her brother, fishing in a different way in a faraway place, and she couldn't help but long for his presence. It would be so great if he were here with her, holding her hand. Her chest clenched at the thought, and she grinned, looking forward to seeing him again, hoping he would understand why she had to leave for the mountain without him.

For the next several days, they worked under the summer sun, keeping the fires hot, rotating fish, then rinsing themselves in the cool river in the evening. The daylight hours were long, but they took breaks often and spent much of the time chatting.

On the last evening, the stars sparkled, and the water lapped quietly against the shore, with all the fish traps removed. Anna could see large salmon in the clear water making their way unbothered. Heather told her that they had caught all they needed and allowed the rest to pass through to spawn.

She hadn't been able to do any of the fishing herself, as she'd imagined. It was a little disappointing, but now she had lots of experience sleeping in her brother's tent, putting it up herself, and soon taking it down. Plus, she'd had the privilege of meeting so many of Heather's relatives.

When they awoke the next morning, many people had already packed up and left, having said their goodbyes the evening before. Lana sat at the edge of the river finishing a basket, so they joined her for breakfast.

"Does your whole family live with you at the reservation?" Anna asked.

"Two sisters and my parents," Lana replied. "My older brother went missing when I was nine. He was always getting in trouble. We looked for days, but he vanished. Maybe he was captured by a tribe to the east. To be a slave. Or his behavior finally caught up with him."

Heather nodded solemnly. "Kiyoque was a mischievous boy, but one of my favorite cousins. He'd be about your brother's age now, Anna."

"I'm sorry," she said. She thought of the man who was shot in town for being there in the evening and shuddered—hopefully that hadn't been the fate of Heather's cousin.

Heather stood, wiping the dirt from the back of her brown skirt. "You want cash only, no smoked salmon, right?"

"If that's okay," she said hopefully as she rolled her sleeping mat.

Heather nodded and joined an older woman who was still weaving baskets as everyone packed. After a moment, the older woman looked over at her and shook her head stiffly. Anna exchanged glances with Lana who looked apologetically doubtful.

Heather returned with a frown. "Owiyahl says she can't give you cash, but if you take it to Meyer's Grocer, he'll give you fifty cents per pound. That should be all you need."

Anna hugged her friend with tears in her eyes. "That's completely fine—my heart is full. I could never have made this dream come true without you, my dear friend."

Heather nodded happily then said her final goodbyes to her friends and relatives. Lana kindly stayed with Anna until Heather was finished.

"Thank you for helping me feel welcome, Lana," Anna said, taking her hands in her own. "I know it was probably...odd for everyone to have me here. *Wiiac.*"

"*Wiiac,* Anna." Lana smiled then turned back toward her family.

After the walk back to Heather's cabin, Anna said goodbye to Pisha then hugged Heather tightly. "I leave soon. Probably won't see you again until I return."

"Be safe on the mountain." Heather put her hand on Anna's shoulder. "Safe and happy."

Anna's mouth widened into a smile as she walked away. She turned to wave a thank-you to Kiyotsa who was examining the garden. The older woman returned it with a toothless grin.

She wondered how her grandfather would receive her when she came home, and how, even if the homecoming went better than she expected, he might refuse to see her altogether after she returned from Mount Rainier. Even so, this was something she needed to do. And she was proud of herself for earning the money on her own.

And after everything that had happened throughout the past year since she'd met Heather, one question remained in her mind, the one that had been there all along.

Do I have enough grit to climb my mountain?

CHAPTER THIRTY-NINE
THE REPLY

B en stopped abruptly as he left the Elfin Cove post office, Anna's letter in his hands. Upon finishing it, he fought the urge to catch another boat home to stop her. He understood her desire to attempt the summit and admired her for it, but why did she need to go so soon, and without him?

Back on the boat, he leaned over the handrail on the bow, where Captain Pavitt joined him with a pleasant nod. "Good afternoon, son."

"Afternoon, sir. Looks like we're almost to Juneau. Do you have business there before we head out?"

The captain winked. "A little. Are you out here pondering life, or is there a specific woman on your mind?"

Ben cleared his throat awkwardly and looked out into the sea. "Is it that obvious?"

"Every man on this boat is thinking about a woman, son." Captain Pavitt patted him roughly on the back, laughing. "Tell me about yours."

"Well, she's beautiful and not afraid of anything." He shifted his weight and ran his hands through his hair.

The captain grunted an approval. "She married?"

Ben's chest tightened with the desire to call her Mrs. Chambers—wake up next to her, hold her hand as they hiked the forest together. "Not yet."

"Levi's sister? The lady you brought by who asked about Russian ships?"

Ben nodded.

"I see. You love her?" asked the captain.

"She's the most enchanting woman I've ever met. Smart and clever, tough and strong. I *absolutely* love her, sir," Ben said with a half-smile.

"Atta-boy," said the captain. "Send her a letter next time we're in town. When you get home, you sweep her up and away forever, you hear? This life is almost over before it begins. No time for waffling."

Ben smiled at the old captain and nodded seriously. That was already his plan. He went back to his bunk to pen a letter.

Dearest Anna,

I'm falling so deeply for you, and I hope you're thinking of me. As for the mountain, I don't understand why you need to embark on this adventure without me. However, I love you, and I wish you the best of luck.

Has Mount Rainier ever been summited by a woman? I don't believe so, which would make you the first. I would be so proud of you. Please be safe and take every precaution. I will think of you each moment between now and the time I hold you again.

Yours completely,
Benjamin Chambers

He waited for the ink to dry, then addressed it and put it in his coat pocket. Hopefully she'd receive it before she left on her trip. He wanted her to know as she trudged up that mountainside that he wished her well and that he loved her absolutely. There was nothing left to be done but mail the letter and hope.

CHAPTER FORTY

THE PREPARATIONS

18 July 1890

Anna made her way quickly and easily from Heather's cabin toward town, carrying her supplies and fish, her body muscular and limber. She couldn't wait to send a telegram to Mr. Flannaghan to tell him she had every penny she needed. The plan was to leave from Yelm in ten days' time, and all she had left to do was gather supplies.

As she neared the meadow of blackberries, a brown rabbit sat fifteen feet away. She slowed, setting her heavy basket of fish on the ground, and became completely silent, pulling an arrow back. Just as she released it, she remembered Ben's hand on top of her own that first time she'd shot it, and she exhaled as the arrow shot true and the rabbit fell.

After she'd finished selling her share of salmon at the grocer, night fell quickly. She was famished. She had saved a small portion of fish to give Greta along with the rabbit, so she decided there was no point in hiding the bow anymore. She burst in the front door out of breath, hands full.

"Oh my!" Greta exclaimed. She took in the vision of Anna, a bow slung over her shoulder and a rabbit dangling from her belt. "I'm so glad you're back, darling."

Greta rushed over, embracing her in a tight hug.

Anna breathed in the scent of home, still holding on to Greta after the older woman had let go. All along, Greta had been a quiet supporter every time she had attempted to do anything independent that made her brother or grandfather cringe. When Anna pulled away and looked into her eyes, there was a soft pride shining back at her which made her heart swell.

"I got this rabbit for you," she said quietly.

"This'll make a fine stew, and what a soft coat." Greta's eyes were misty. "I imagine the boys'll take you hunting next Christmas. I'm mighty proud of you."

Anna beamed and leaned her bow against the wall. "A little smoked salmon too."

"Mind that you don't tell your grandfather any details. He's a tired old man. And he drank himself silly while you were gone. He put an ad in the paper, and a young lady answered—been working with him in the store. She's a fine worker, but he misses you."

"Any mail for me?"

Surely Ben had written her since she'd been gone.

Greta turned to a pile on the counter, then handed her a single letter. "This. Came this mornin'. And before I forget, can you pick the cherries off the highest part of the cherry trees tomorrow? I need to make sauce, and I can't manage to get as high as you."

A thrill of excitement hit Anna—both for the letter and the opportunity for more climbing practice. It had been a while since she'd climbed the tree in the forest, and she was eager to see if she was even stronger than ever. She grabbed the letter and moved toward the stairs when she noticed her grandfather sitting in the living room, eyes down at his woodwork. Her heart plunged into her stomach—he hadn't even come over to greet her.

"Hello, Grandfather."

He lifted his eyes and gave her a nod.

Once in her room, tears formed in her eyes. Things were only going to get more complicated between them after she left for the mountain. She breathed deeply, hoping that Ben's words would be a comfort.

She opened the letter and found that it wasn't from Ben at all —it was from Mr. Flannaghan, saying he'd meet her at the train station at nine in the morning on Saturday, July 28th in Yelm. She exhaled sharply and threw herself onto her bed, suddenly exhausted from the day.

Later that night, she lay in bed. In the last moments before she fell asleep, she saw Ben's face and his warm brown eyes; he'd be back from fishing by the time she returned, and she already missed him so much.

The next morning, she bought her ticket at the train station. She had the outfit Heather had made for her wrapped in brown paper and tucked into her closet. It included two pairs of wool socks and mittens. She needed to purchase boys' climbing boots, crampons to fit over them, and an alpenstock. She also needed a wooden packframe, but Mr. Flannaghan had mentioned there might be extras, and she hoped she could borrow one. The last thing he'd said was to bring goggles, which would help block out the rays of the sun amplified against white snow.

Anna shut her closet and took out a couple of bills to buy the goggles, crampons, and alpenstock. A secret shopping trip was in order.

But first she wanted to stop in at June's apartment to check on her.

June had been staying at Heather's house for a few days after the birth, and Heather had helped her learn to breastfeed. Anna couldn't wait to see how she and the baby were getting on now.

With a small breakfast to share, she arrived at the address June had given her and inquired with the doorman. Her room was on the second floor, and Anna knocked softly, worried the baby might be sleeping.

June opened the door with her hair cascading around her shoulders and an exhausted look in her eye. She had the tiny baby wrapped in a long fabric against her chest.

Anna set down a basket of cinnamon bread, strawberries, and cream. "How's everything going?"

June threw her hands up in the air. "Pretty good—I think. He nurses constantly and sleeps and cries a lot. Is that normal?"

Anna shook her head with a questioning look. "I don't know."

She shrugged. "Connor says it's normal...I guess it's fine."

Anna dished up small plates for both of them, smothering the berries with cream and putting a small pat of butter on slices of cinnamon bread. "Does he...come by much?"

"Yes, every night since Joseph and I returned home," June said with a proud smile. She sighed happily as Anna handed her a plate of food.

"Good. May I hold him?"

"Of course." June unwrapped the long cloth from her neck and bundled the baby inside it.

Anna used her gentlest touch with what felt like a weightless baby. He yawned and looked up at her with an expressionless face, before letting out a tiny coo. The sound spread warmth through her, and she couldn't help but smile. What would it be like to have a tiny baby of her own, with a man she loved? Throughout the last couple months, she'd been so focused on her plan to get to the mountain. These days, she felt so far removed from her childhood dream of a happy family of her own. Ben was so far away and hadn't written in weeks.

What if she could be a wife, a mother, and a mountaineer? It wasn't as if having a family made her a weaker person. As long as she had a supportive partner—as long as Ben still loved her—perhaps she could have both.

She ran her fingers gently over the fluffy baby hair. His blond locks seemed even thicker than when he was born. "As soft as goose down. He's so precious—I can't believe how much I love him already."

Her eyes filled with tears as the surprising emotion seized her.

"Thank you." June had a spark of pride in her expression. She ran her hands through her curly hair and twisted it into a bun. When she let go, it fell back around her shoulders in bouncy waves. "Connor's such a proud father. I love seein' him with Joseph."

Anna shifted in her chair uneasily. She wanted to ask if they still planned to move to California but didn't want to upset her. It would be best not to bring it up unless June did. She laid the baby in the wooden cradle near his mother and picked up her plate of food. They ate together in comfortable silence while the baby cooed then fell into a light sleep.

After they finished, Anna put her hat on and kissed her friend. June was aglow, but she looked positively weary.

"I'm leaving soon to attempt summiting the mountain—without Ben. I'll be the first lady to do it, June, the first one to summit Mt. Rainier if I succeed."

"You will," June said with a confident smile. "I'm glad you're doing it now. Why wait, right?"

"Although…" Anna shifted uncomfortably in her seat. "Of course, there's the possibility that I don't make it home."

"Don't be ridiculous," June said with a dismissive wave of her hand.

"I'm serious, June. There are glaciers, ice cliffs, strong winds…" She sighed heavily. "I just want you to know: You're the best friend I've ever had."

June put both of her hands on Anna's cheeks. "You can do

this. And I'll be right here waitin' to hear all about it when you return."

She squeezed Anna in a hug.

"Thank you." Anna's heart soared as she shut the door behind her.

On her way home, she stopped by a store she hoped would have everything she needed. She examined each aisle, stopping at the boys' boots. Her palms were moist as she tried on a pair.

Two men with thick beards gave her quizzical looks.

The boots fit a little loose, but she moved on to the next item. She tried to imagine the way Ben had described alpenstocks and eventually found some leaning against a wall near the goggles.

She had to ask the young clerk to help her find crampons. He was thoroughly amused at her trying them on.

"Ya sure ya know what you're doin', miss?" he asked. "I could fetch my Pa from the back. Don't usually have ladies buyin' this sort of thing…"

"It's quite all right, these'll do," Anna said, fumbling with her cash.

She flushed with embarrassment as she left. The young man's words bothered her, and even though she tried not to care, the men who'd watched her try on the boys' boots made her skin crawl with paranoia. Would they tell her grandfather?

CHAPTER FORTY-ONE
THE SECRET DEPARTURE

Anna's grandfather still refused to speak with her or let her come to the bookstore. Her train was leaving at half past five the next morning, so she'd be long gone before he awoke.

She looked up from the dough she was kneading as he left for the morning without even glancing in her direction. Her face grew hot.

Folding her arms over her stomach, she looked to Greta. "Is he just working by himself, then?"

Greta didn't look up from her own handful of dough. "Last week he hired that temporary gal full-time."

Throwing off her apron with a huff, Anna grabbed a basket before heading outside. She climbed the cherry tree, and her eyes strained to see the mountain. But a light summer rain had rolled in for the afternoon, and clouds obscured the view. The limbs of the tree were mossy, but she managed to hold on tight while she reached for the farthest branches to fill her basket with the biggest, ripest cherries.

A bright red cluster at the end of a thin branch caught her eye. She leaned forward to grab it, but her feet slipped from underneath her on the slick branch. She reached for the trunk of the tree, but it was too far away.

Her stomach sank, and her hands grasped at air. Finally, she lunged for the last branch on the way down and clung to it with both hands. She dropped the few feet to the wet ground and wiped her dirty, shaking hands on her skirt. With her heart pounding in her chest, she imagined having to send word she couldn't make the excursion on account of a broken leg. She rushed back to the house feeling the gravity of all she'd worked for and nearly lost.

Inside, she slammed the basket of cherries onto the kitchen counter, still shaken. She went to her room to towel off her face and arms, then opened her closet to survey her gear. Everything was ready to go, including the letter she'd planned to leave for her grandfather to find. She was already sorry for how hurt and worried he'd be, but she didn't want to lie about where she would be.

Then she thought of Greta. All of her support and goodwill throughout the years seemed suddenly obvious. What would Greta think of her disappearance?

At the dinner table that night, Anna was abnormally quiet.

"Met a strapping gentleman today," her grandfather said, looking up at her for the first time in days. "He's just moved to town and asked about places to purchase a home. A lawyer and unmarried."

He raised his eyebrows.

"He sounds nice," Anna said, looking into his eyes and trying to find forgiveness.

Greta frowned. "What about that Ben? Is he comin' back?"

"Ben's a charming young man," her grandfather said. "I half expected him to ask to court you."

She folded the napkin in her lap and didn't respond.

Greta nonchalantly buttered a slice of bread. "Did you fancy him?"

Had she caught on? Ben's soft lips on her hand filled her mind, and she sighed. "Ben's a fine man."

Her grandfather shot Greta a look.

Greta changed the subject. "How's June's baby?"

Anna sat back in her chair and sighed, relieved to talk about something else. "He's doing well. June's all right too. I'm not sure what her plan is moving forward, but Connor has assured me he plans to take care of them both indefinitely."

Her grandfather cleared his throat. "I don't know how long I can keep quiet about this. I ran into his father yesterday and he told me his plans to set Connor up with a nice young lady for dinner this weekend. That family is full of secrets. Good thing you didn't get caught up in it."

After they finished, she helped Greta clear the table and wash dishes. As they worked, she stole glances at Greta. She had a few more soft wrinkles since she'd first joined their family, but she still looked much the same. Her cheerful spirit had breathed life into the Gallagher family back then, and still did. Anna's breath caught as she realized she probably should have confided in her about the mountain, but now it was too late—telling her was too great a risk.

Cozied near the fire, she spent the rest of the evening composing a letter to Greta. Her grandfather worked on carving some details on the arm rests of a new rocking chair he'd made while Greta knitted.

Dearest Greta,

I hope you're not terribly disappointed in me, but I'm leaving to summit Mt. Rainier. I've written more details in Grandfather's letter, but I wanted to tell you personally. I wonder now if I should have told you about all of this.

If I succeed, I'll be the first woman in American history to summit. I hope this might make you proud. Thank you for the years of love and the grace you've given me. It means so much, and I know my parents would be grateful for the tenderness you've shown my brother and me.

Fondly,
Anna Gallagher

It was just what she needed to calm her nerves before the big adventure. Lastly, she studied Muir's words once again, trying to commit the distances to memory so she'd be prepared.

The distance to the mountain from Yelm in a straight line is perhaps fifty miles.... The distance from the Soda Springs to the Camp of the Clouds is about ten miles.

As she tried to sleep that evening, she wondered what Ben might be doing and if he dreamed of her. Would he be proud of her for summiting, or would he think she was irresponsible? She couldn't quell her anxiety until she imagined his face inches from her own, the way he'd looked when he leaned in that night. As her image of him sharpened, she relaxed her shoulders, finally fading into sleep.

She woke every hour that night, checking her small bedside clock to make sure she hadn't overslept.

At three in the morning, she was wide awake and got dressed, even before the early summer sun had risen. She tiptoed around, eating a hearty breakfast, filling her canteen with water, and bringing her bag down the stairs as quietly as she could.

Just as she was heading for the kitchen, a noise at the top of the stairs stopped her cold. Swinging around, expecting to see her grandfather, she found Esther, who purred and weaved her way through the banister.

She sighed with relief, kissed the cat goodbye, and put her things on the porch under the dark blue sky before dawn.

It would have been such a comfort to receive a letter from

Ben before leaving. All she could do was hope he understood and that he'd forgive her for attempting to summit the mountain without him.

She pulled the letters out of her pocket and set them on the table—one for Greta, and one for her grandfather. Then, with doubt in her heart, she strode through the thick silence of the sleeping city to catch the train to Yelm.

CHAPTER FORTY-TWO

THE PAST

Five Miles South of Seattle, Washington Territory
24 December 1880

The snow fell lightly at first, dusting the tops of the towering evergreens that surrounded the small frontier town of Seattle. For a single snowflake to land on the dark forest floor, it had to slip past hundreds of branches. A young deer stepped carefully through the high snow banks near a single cabin in the woods where a thin wisp of smoke escaped the chimney. Hunched over a book, a young man with brown hair and dark green eyes sat at a wooden table, writing a poem by candlelight.

Dmitri planned to ask Natalya to marry him the next evening. He had saved his money for a year, enough to start a life with her. To prepare for moving to America, he'd spent three years studying Russian books translated into English. It had been lonely living alone this past year in the small log cabin he'd painstakingly built, but hopefully Natalya would be his wife soon, and the cabin would become a cozy home. Everything was planned for the following day—Christmas—which he'd end by giving her his great-grandmother's emerald ring. An heirloom, the rectangular green stone sparkled, with carefully engraved leaves winding along the gold band.

He concentrated on a crack in the cabin wall, trying to conjure the perfect final line to inscribe within Natalya's Christmas gift—Anna Karenina—words that would give her cryptic clues to find the ring. She was so smart and loved a good mystery. Dmitri never felt so alive as when he was with her.

They had been attempting to speak English as much as possible, and so his brain was muddled trying to compose elegant words in his second language. His hands were moist with sweat, and the surprisingly loud beat of his heart unsettled him. The snow blew sideways across his window, playing on his nerves. With his old quill pen in hand, he carefully wrote the final line in the bottom corner on the first blank page, then blew on the ink impatiently. With the pages left open to dry, he dressed in his warmest fur coat to hunt before the sun set.

Before leaving, he closed the book, wrapped it with brown paper, and carefully placed it below the blankets in the bottom of his trunk for safekeeping. He blew out his candle and shut the heavy, ill-fitting door of his cabin. As he trekked in the opposite direction of town, his feet sank much deeper than normal with each step. The path before him was white, but he was determined to have fresh meat for Christmas dinner with his bride-to-be. Fresh deer droppings rested on top of the snow—he could find the deer before nightfall.

Far above, snow fell on ancient firs, weighing heavily on their branches. The winter of 1880 had been unusually cold, and a deep layer of ice coated each branch. As the full moon rose over the horizon, an owl flew to the tallest branch of the highest tree. The moment it landed, the great branch snapped and crashed down to the snow-covered earth.

Dmitri looked up just in time to see a mountain of ice and branches hurtling toward him.

CHAPTER FORTY-THREE

THE ADVENTURE

28 July 1890

B rick buildings and tall sails disappeared, fading away through the train window. There was a brief stop in Tacoma, then the whistle blew as they lurched away, traveling another thirty miles farther to Yelm.

Anna had never traveled past Tacoma, and the sights mesmerized her. She peered through the window, hungrily taking in the views of small towns, farmlands, and new forests. This was really happening, and the complete freedom made her giddy.

She was nervous to meet Mr. Flannaghan at the station, then ultimately put her life into his hands, but she knew of his previous expeditions and that he had a wife and three daughters.

He received her with a hearty handshake and a pat on the back. "You must be Miss Gallagher—welcome to Yelm. Ready for an adventure?"

He was a tall man with black hair and green eyes. His skin was tan and leathery from what she guessed were many years of mountaineering. He wore a black suit with vest and tie, along with a tall black top hat, which he'd tipped on her arrival. Is that what he was wearing for the trip?

She looked around the station. "Looking forward to it. Happy to finally meet you. Where is everyone?"

A family and a couple of businessmen went about their business, but she didn't see a sprightly group of mountaineers with piles of gear.

Could it be that this man had conned her?

She glanced at Mr. Flannaghan and held tightly to her bag. She was already nervous about being the only female in the group, but there was no other way to be the first woman to summit Mt. Rainier. If there was going to be another woman in their group, she'd have to share that title.

"We've made camp for the evening," he said with a reassuring tone. "There are only two houses nearby, and they're full, so we have tents set up and a few beds of fresh hay in the barn. You have your own tent, correct? You can set up near the others so you're safe, but still have some privacy."

Anna nodded in agreement, glad she'd managed to borrow Levi's. He offered to take her bag, but she respectfully declined. She had carried the bag this far and would carry it miles farther, so there was no point in letting chivalry rob her of the full experience or let it dictate how much her fellow mountaineers respected her ability to pull her own weight.

When they arrived at the camp, a few tents were set up in a semi-circle around a fire.

"Anna, this is John," said Mr. Flannaghan.

John looked up from the notebook he was writing in and flashed a quick smile. "Pleasure, ma'am. Glad to have you with us."

That was a relief.

"I'm so excited to be here. Wonderful to meet you, John." She shook his hand heartily.

Mr. Flannaghan took his hat off and wiped a sweaty forehead. "And this is Lou and Peter."

Peter nodded and shook her hand cordially, his camera in the other hand.

Lou glanced up from his gear and took a long look at Anna with his jaw clenched, arms folded. "You're not gonna slow us down, are ya, woman?"

Lou was of medium build with light brown hair, streaks of gray starting near his temples. He might have been a handsome man when he was younger, and even now if he chose to smile.

Anna mustered a polite smile. "I've every intention of keeping up with you fine gentlemen. If I start to slow you down, please let me know and I'll do my best to pick up my pace. And if there comes a time——"

"That's a whole lotta talkin, miss." He turned back to his pack, checking his gear, tying things tightly.

The conversation was clearly over, but Anna did not want to give him the satisfaction of turning away yet, so she stood watching him adjust his gear with an unimpressed frown.

"Let me show you the ponies," Mr. Flannaghan said enthusiastically.

In the barn, he whispered, "Don't fret about ol' Lou, he's harmless. A crusty ol' grump—he's summited twice already, though, and he's our best guide."

She shrugged, trying to exude indifference. She had certainly never climbed a mountain before, so she expected it to be a grueling, demanding challenge—the biggest of her life. But she was ready; she'd trained.

She just hoped she was as prepared as she thought.

Mr. Flannaghan showed her the five ponies that would serve as their pack animals. Anna stroked the nose of the smallest one, and it nipped back at her. She took a hasty step back, giving the grumpy animal some space.

"We have a three days' journey ahead of us before we get to

the springs." Mr. Flannaghan looked toward the mountain with a smile, putting his hands on his lower back and leaning as far as he could go for a stretch.

She set up her tent as fast as she could, sweat forming on her brow as she realized they were all watching. When she finished, she set her things inside then rested on a log next to John.

"Hey there, Miss Gallagher." He pushed his black-rimmed glasses up his nose.

He had orangish-red hair, and she guessed he was about her age, maybe a year older.

She straightened her skirts in front of her. "You can call me Anna."

John eyed her dress then made a face that said it was none of his business. "It's my first time attempting to summit. Yours too, I'm assuming, since no lady has, I don't think."

"Yes. First time." She relaxed a little. He seemed easy to talk to, albeit distracted with his note taking.

"Well I'm a journalist, and I'd love to write an article about you if we succeed," he offered, finally making eye contact.

She nodded, her cheeks warming. "Oh, you don't have to do that, but you could if you want."

"You got a fella?"

Her chest squeezed as she thought of Ben. "I do."

She wished he was with her. Or at least that he'd written her one last time. John nodded and went back to his writing.

It was a warm evening, and everyone went to sleep before sundown to get an early start the next morning. Anna had a difficult time falling asleep, and, in the end, simply closed her eyes, waiting for sleep to come.

At dawn, she emerged wearing the outfit she and Heather had put together.

"Now that's a much better choice than a dress," John said, scribbling something in his notebook with a grin.

Mr. Flannaghan nodded in approval. "Indeed."

Peter appeared amused, and Lou simply laughed and shook his head.

She wore men's pants, boys' climbing boots, and her own cotton shirt with her mother's cameo brooch pinned at the top button. Her shirt was tucked into the pants, with a slim belt to keep everything in place. She marveled at the sensation of pants —something she never in her life imagined she'd wear in public. She had tried them on briefly to make sure they fit, but it was another thing entirely to be seen in them. They felt loose, but fitted, not unlike her bloomers. The coarse material was much stiffer and seemed to entomb every inch of both legs, whereas her bloomers and petticoats had a floating effect.

Still, it was liberating. It was too warm still for the wool sweater and fur vest, so she left them in her bag. The boots were still a little loose and stiff. As she attempted to curl and straighten her toes, she wondered if she would have been better off bringing her own walking boots.

She hadn't yet given Mr. Flannaghan the money she owed for her provisions and the cost of using the ponies. As they packed up camp, she pulled out the bills and handed them to him, counting each one.

"Quite right, thank you dear," he said cheerily. "The first pony is carrying the food, and I did scrounge up a pack for ya."

That morning, they guided the ponies through meadows with winding creeks. It was thrilling to finally be on the adventure she'd long imagined. The men were mostly quiet as they made their way, all spread about by a few feet each.

"This is by far the most exciting thing I've ever done," Anna whispered to Mr. Flannaghan when they stopped for lunch.

He chuckled. "Well, your excitement is contagious, dear. I'm getting pretty eager to get there myself." He paused. "How's the traveling treating you so far? You getting on all right?"

She grinned. "Oh yes. Quite enjoying it."

"Time to get movin'," Lou said gruffly.

Why didn't he like her?

They set out through a valley covered in white flowers and short, yellowish grass. Peter was a few feet behind her, and Anna wondered if it would be unwelcome if she struck up a conversation.

She turned to smile at him, and he returned it so she went for it. "Such beautiful country."

"Yes, ma'am." He fell silent as his eyes scanned the trees lining the other side of the valley.

He looked about thirty, with light blond hair and a barrel chest.

She swallowed and turned her head around again. "Is your family going to miss you while you're away?"

"No family," he said with a frown. "You married?"

"Oh, no, I'm not." Perhaps she didn't need to get so personal with her chitchat. "My family didn't even know I was coming, so…"

Peter lifted his eyebrows in surprise. "Well, hopefully they don't turn ya out."

He smirked, and she wished he hadn't said anything.

The day was tiring, and by the time they set up their tents for the evening, she was ready to collapse on her sleeping mat. Six hours in the scorching sun had made her face tender.

The next day, she didn't strike up any unsolicited conversations and found that everyone mostly preferred hiking in silence. They did talk around the fire at dinner, and afterward they made camp beside Forked Creek. By lunchtime the next day, they arrived at Succotash Valley, a place known for wild raspberries.

They only passed a few scattered farms. Anna found it easy to sleep after these long travel days, her body completely exhausted, giving her mind little time to worry before closing her eyes.

CHAPTER FORTY-FOUR

THE SHADOW

As she moved through unfamiliar surroundings, she wondered what Levi might think of the fact that she'd fallen for his friend after all. His initial warning had felt silly and unnecessary—she'd never expected Ben to be as kind, intelligent, and adventurous as he'd turned out to be.

They reached Longmire Springs at 2,700 feet elevation on the morning of the third day, which meant they'd already traveled fifty miles. Anna crinkled her nose at the strong sulphur smell, then looked behind her, as was now her habit. A bald eagle swooped down toward the springs then back up into the sky with something in his talons. With strong, graceful motions, it ascended to the tops of Douglas firs. The branch it chose bent slightly from its weight as it perched near the top, nearly in the clouds.

As they approached the roaring Nisqually River, she caught her breath at its hugeness and the power with which the water flooded down the valley. She had never seen anything like it, with logs and boulders sweeping by with great speed, water rushing with all the force of the melted snow and glaciers in summer. It was nothing like the wide, peaceful river the Duwamish fished in. She remembered Muir's words from his account, that it "goes roaring by, gray with mud, gravel, and boulders." The air felt cooler with the water rushing by, and it was impossible to see how deep the river was.

They formed a line, holding on to the ponies, who were not impressed with the notion of crossing, and they waded into the river until everyone stood nearly chest deep.

Anna began to panic as the water rose toward her neck. It was freezing, and although it was quite hot out, she was suddenly chilled to the bone, submerged in icy water. The pressure against her chest took her breath away.

She looked to Mr. Flannaghan for encouragement, but he was having just as much trouble, clinging to a pony for balance. Her own pony bucked and attempted to turn back, but she yanked on the reins until he followed.

Slowly, they made it across to the other side. She was grateful she wasn't wearing a dress and petticoats as it would have taken the rest of the day or longer for them to dry thoroughly.

"Up here to the left is a bona fide glacier, Anna," John said, scribbling something in his notebook. "You ever seen a glacier up this close?"

She shook her head in wonder. "No."

She tried to soak in the immensity of ice and rock, the whiteness of the blinding ice, the intimidating jagged edges.

"Ten miles to go before we get to base camp," Peter said, coming up behind them. "I'll race ya there!"

He lunged between Anna and John, racing past them. John took chase.

For a second, she considered running after them, but her wet boots squished uncomfortably. She stopped for a moment to retie the laces as tightly as possible, but her wet socks sloshed around, and the friction from the fabric against her skin began to burn.

She quickly caught up with Peter and John who waited at the

bottom of a steep path. With one eye out for loose gravel and downed trees, they slowly climbed. Dirt and dust billowed, reaching her nostrils and making her mouth dry—the taste reminded her of gardening. Monarch butterflies flitted past, along with flies that seemed to favor the ponies. The muscles going up the back of her legs were tight as they marched onward.

She could hear Mr. Flannaghan's heavy breathing and Peter grunting along. They were on a steep hill then, what looked to her like the face of a cliff, and they hiked back and forth from side to side, weaving their way upward.

"This here's a sixty-five-degree angle," said John, putting a shiny tool back in his pack and pushing his glasses up the bridge of his nose.

Then he dropped his notebook and let out a terrible yelp as it fell down the steep gravel.

Anna gasped and was surprised to see that no one else stopped. She waited while John slid carefully on the seat of his pants to retrieve it, then slowly wound his way back up to the caravan.

The air smelled of warm pine sap and sweet meadow grass. Miniature pine trees stood along the path next to her, around two feet tall. The taller pines had needles of dark green with fresh, light green needles on the tips of the branches—new growth. Amidst the healthy trees were large skeletons, with branches broken off, looking like they'd been sanded and polished, their bark completely gone with a white skin covering every inch. A tapping noise came from the fields around them—probably an insect.

About two hours later, as they drew nearer to base camp, a vast meadow of flowers came into view. Anna gasped at the bright array of colors, brighter than any rainbow. Purples, yellows, golden orange, and deep reds—all dancing in the soft breeze. She thought of all the women stuck in their houses arranging small, dead flowers. It was no wonder so many people she knew in Seattle society seemed muted. Perhaps the soul longed to have a slice of the beauty and wonder so often left unexplored—the gorgeous natural world, with every color and texture and sensation.

A silence fell over the group as they passed through a paradise of perfectly shaped Christmas trees and soft green grass below their feet. A small bunny, no larger than a squirrel, watched the party advance from nearby, twitching its nose then bounding away when a pony huffed. They soon came to a lake surrounded by sparse trees and a garden of purple daisies and small white flowers.

"This here lake is as smooth as a glass-pane window," said John, scribbling down his words into his notebook, now covered with dust.

Anna nodded in agreement. They stopped for a minute to let the ponies drink, and she leaned over to see the reflection of the mountain in the lake.

Just as she reached toward it with her fingers, Lou came up behind her and said gruffly, "Almost there, no time for gazing at our reflections."

She rolled her eyes before standing.

Patches of snow and ice appeared, and twenty minutes later, they arrived at base camp for the evening. They'd reached 6,000 feet elevation. The camp was filled with tents of different sizes in a long line, and people lounged around enjoying the wondrous view. Stalls and makeshift arenas made of zig-zagged logs held mules and ponies.

Clouds were beginning to roll in and obscure the heavens, but between them stood the most outstanding view of the mountain Anna had ever seen—it filled the sky.

She stood in amazement as everyone dropped their bags and sprawled out on the grass. It wasn't true, but even so, she imagined she was one of the first humans to ever see this mountain—to see it this close. It was in that moment she knew she wouldn't be the first woman to summit Mt. Rainier, because surely men and women had been climbing it since the beginning. She'd be the first American woman to summit, and that would be an amazing feat, but it wasn't something a woman hadn't done before; all at once, she was sure of that fact.

Peter craned his neck, staring up at the sky as he pulled his tent out. "It's bad luck for clouds like this to come and hide the mount'n before a summit. Bad weather's comin'."

A hollowness settled in Anna's stomach. They didn't need any bad luck.

A light rain began, and everyone hurried to make camp. The animals were given over to a man at the checkpoint to be watched over until their group returned down the mountain. There was no way to take them farther. Just beyond the camp was a major elevation jump; there was solid ice and glaciers to climb. They would need to carry everything on their backs.

Anna sat alone in her tent as the rain poured. She gingerly took her boots off and found blisters covering the back of her heels and around her ankles—in some places the skin was rubbed so raw that blood stained her socks. The skin on her feet throbbed. The fresh air did not make them feel better, and she had no bandages.

In order to maintain a light load, she hadn't brought any books or letters to read, and now, without anyone to talk to or anything to look at, she lay on her back and closed her eyes, listening to the pattering of rain on canvas. She breathed in deeply and felt the decrease of oxygen in the air. Her legs were sore, and her feet ached from the days of travel, but her heart was full. She'd risen to meet every challenge thus far with rigor. She felt exhilarated about what lay ahead and proud of how far she'd already come.

She pulled out the compass Ben had given her, tracing the engravings with her fingertip. It was a lovely thing. Remembering his soft brown eyes, and the comfort of his arms, she tried to imagine what it might be like to kiss him again, his body against her own, what it might be like to wake up in the middle of the night and hear his soft breathing. She loved him and hoped he still loved her. She rolled to her side, and the dial on the compass adjusted accordingly.

By her calculations, it was the first day of August. At this point, her grandfather would be terribly worried. In her letter, she'd left the address of Mr. Flannaghan's wife, so he might visit with her if he needed reassurances. Other than that, she wasn't sure what else he might do.

What else *could* he do? It would be impossible for him to follow her any farther than the Yelm railway station. Would he refuse to see her when she returned? Would Ben be emasculated by her success, or would he be thrilled for her?

Please be happy for me.

As she pulled her blankets close around her, she decided not to think of Ben anymore. Everything in her life had led her to this place; the next morning would bring one of the hardest parts of the climb. She was doing everything on her own as much as possible and only relying on the group for the same things any of the men also left to teamwork—packing up camp, making fires, carrying water. She didn't need the thought of Ben to give her strength or the stamina she needed. She calmed her nerves by breathing slowly and letting her body relax, praying she'd find sleep.

After nearly an hour squeezing her eyes shut, she began to dream of what her next adventure might be—sailing to Alaska, or perhaps mining in California. Anything was possible.

Hours later, with rain pounding down and high winds tearing at her tent, Anna awoke as a large shadow the size of a man came over the canvas. The howling of the wind through the peaks and valleys of the mountain at night put a chill deep inside her, and her chest squeezed so tightly it felt as if the blood couldn't reach her heart. The dark figure bent down and fumbled with the opening of the tent, which she'd tied from the inside. She pulled her knife out, and the iridescent handle shone in the darkness.

She gripped it tightly, turning toward the opening of the tent. But as quickly as it had appeared, the shadow stumbled away. She sank back under her blanket and slept the rest of the night with her knife in hand.

CHAPTER FORTY-FIVE
THE MISSED CONNECTION

B en arrived back in Seattle on the morning of August 2nd, a full week earlier than expected. He wanted to run straight to the Gallaghers' house to ask Oscar's permission to court Anna, but he thought it best to bathe, get a haircut, and trim his scraggly beard before seeing her grandfather. He was the first to jump off the boat, and as the other men tied off, Levi waved him away with a grin.

He checked into the renovated Occidental Hotel, for sentimental reasons, and as he bathed and trimmed his hair and beard, he thought with fondness of the time they'd come to the ruins to collect a brick. The memory of Anna happy as a schoolgirl, solving a book mystery, made him giddy with excitement to see her. She hadn't mentioned when she'd return from the mountain, and he could only hope she'd already returned safely with stories to share.

It was only three in the afternoon, so he had time to purchase a clean outfit. He found a dark blue suit with a brown tie, both of which the young man at Pearl Brothers assured him were quite in fashion. As the clerk carefully counted the bills, Ben became irritated at the slowness and wished he'd gone straight to Anna's house so that he'd already be there, hopefully kissing her.

He took the Madison Street trolley that dropped him right in front of the road leading to her house. With a deep breath, he looked up at the big sky and said a small prayer.

Oscar answered the door immediately and greeted him warmly. "That's a dashing look. You're as handsome as I've ever seen you."

His eyes were bloodshot.

"Hello, sir," Ben said, his voice more serious than he intended. "Is Anna home?"

Oscar's face grew dark, and he waved for Ben to follow him inside. "Levi arrived twenty minutes ago, then ran off to find you."

Oscar shook his head and couldn't seem to get any more words out, so he handed him the letter Anna had left behind.

With each sentence Ben read, he tried to appear surprised, and his left knee bounced as he attempted to stand still. "When?"

"Less than a week ago," said Oscar, his eyes filling with tears.

"Did she get my letter?" he asked, his voice strained.

Oscar handed him a battered, unopened envelope from the table. "This one?"

"Oh." Ben frowned.

"It arrived the day she left."

It seemed like a blow to his chest. He sprang up, opening his mouth to speak, but decided against it. Was it too late to follow her up the mountain and hire a team to accompany him?

"I know what you're thinking," Oscar said, "and I assure you I've had the same thoughts. Greta's convinced me to leave it be. I've been in contact with the wife of the lead man, and she's done her best to convince me Anna's in good hands. There's a group of four men accompanying her—one has summited the mountain twice already."

Ben's cheeks grew hot—she was alone, surrounded by rough

mountaineers on an icy trail. His chest was tight thinking of how the men probably weren't giving her the credit and respect she was due. She was tough as nails. He shook his head and turned to Oscar.

"Sir, I wish I was there with her."

The summer sky was clear, and Oscar folded his arms, looking out the kitchen window, glaring at the mountain. "Me too, lad."

Ben's face softened, and he shook his head.

"I can't believe she did this on her own, and yet, I can. Honestly, I admire her even more." He turned to face Oscar. "I love her, sir. You may have guessed that by now. I come from a good family in California, and I want you to know that I have all the money I'll ever need to take care of her. Can't promise we'll stay in Seattle, but from the looks of it, my own desire to travel won't be the issue. I don't think anyone or anything could keep Anna tied down."

"Well." Oscar rubbed his chin. "I have to say, I'm quite relieved to hear about your financial situation. I've always liked you, lad. You certainly have my blessing, but first she needs to return home to us."

Oscar sighed and motioned for Ben to follow him to the kitchen. "Let's go out for a drink, shall we? I'm sure I can double some money if we find a poker game."

Ben shrugged uneasily as he watched him fumble to open the box of cash above the sink.

Greta peeked her head out of the pantry. "What are you doing, dear?"

Oscar jumped. "Thought we might head to the saloon—have a drink."

He opened the box where only three dollars lay. "Where's all the cash I brought home from the bookstore yesterday?"

"In my coin purse as I'll be needin' it for meat and milk tomorrow." Greta's voice was firm, but friendly.

Relieved, Ben put his hat on and nodded for Oscar to follow him. Oscar grunted and grabbed the three dollars, slamming the box shut before following him out the front door.

CHAPTER FORTY-SIX

THE ASCENT

W hen she awoke after eight, Anna was groggy with fatigue
and the effects of the altitude. The blisters felt slightly
better, but she was hesitant to entomb them in her boots once
again. She tore off pieces from her petticoats she'd packed in her
bag, using them to wrap her heels and ankles. Hopefully the
added bulk would make up for the extra room in the boots—less
movement around the raw skin. She stepped outside of her tent
to find that most of the others had already packed up.

"There's no rush, my dear," said Mr. Flannaghan, seeing her
panic. "We won't leave till these clouds clear. Hoping they will as
the day goes on."

She nodded and began to pack up, the air cool against her
face. She joined her group at the fire, and John handed her a
bowl of warm grits with nuts. His orange hair was disheveled,
and he grinned boyishly.

"It's a big day," he said brightly. "Nine thousand feet more to
climb at a forty-degree incline. Maybe two days left until you are
the first lady to summit this great mountain!"

Anna grinned with as much confidence as she could muster.

She ate her breakfast and mulled over what had happened the night before. Who had tried to come into her tent? She looked around at the men in her group as they were all engrossed in their meals. Peter looked up and offered a tired smile. She smiled back, then looked around at the other tents and clusters of people.

Really, it could have been anybody.

By half past nine, the clouds still hung low. As they prepared to leave anyway, another group descended toward the camp.

The tallest man greeted Lou with a hearty handshake. "Good luck to you, brother. It's stormy, and I've never seen so many avalanches. We didn't get to summit this time."

Anna's heart sank. She watched Lou nod seriously then pat the other man on the back.

"Thank ya for the warning, Edward. I imagine y'all need to get some rest now."

"That we do, old man," he replied. "We'll stay here two or three nights to recover from the elevation."

Two of the men had blisters surrounded by deep sunburns on their faces, and another still seemed dizzy from the elevation and vomited at his feet before plopping down near a fire.

"Such a shame," John whispered to her. "All that way and through all that. Didn't even get to summit."

She nodded, making every effort to keep her face expressionless.

They set out and encountered icy ground as soon as they rounded the first bend. Since they wouldn't have their pack animals for the rest of the way, they'd left most of their supplies, and Anna only had her blanket, knife, compass, crampons, and her ration of food for the next few days in her pack. Their tents were left behind as well.

She wore her goggles on the top of her head until she needed them. They each hiked along with their alpenstocks, Lou leading the way. It was slow going, and each step brought her discomfort from the raw skin and blisters tearing, but by midday the sensation had dulled. She wasn't sure if her body had gotten used to the pain or if her feet had swollen to fill out the boots better.

Despite her uncomfortable feet and the exhaustion, pure joy welled up inside her. It was the familiar comfort she'd always felt looking up at the mountain, even as a frightened child arriving from Ireland. The rich pleasure of fresh air and a novel undertaking energized her. She felt the world was opening up to her.

The snow crunched beneath her feet, and for almost an hour no one spoke. Above, large gray billows of clouds contrasted sharply with the cobalt sky. The dark green of the trees in the distance blurred against the marigold of hay fields.

Then, out of nowhere, a loud shout rang out as a man came sliding down the large snow hill in front of them. At first Anna was alarmed, until he came close enough for her to see the smile on his face. He slid on the seat of his pants down what looked like a slide carved into the snow.

"Snow chute," Lou said. "That'll be us in a day or so. Good thing ya wore pants."

John chuckled and pulled out his pen to scribble more notes.

Anna watched two more men slide down. They weren't going disturbingly fast, and it seemed like they were enjoying themselves.

She whispered to John, "How much of the descent is sliding do you suppose?"

John shrugged, and the corners of his lips turned down. "I reckon the only places that have a chute carved out are from other people slidin', and that'd only be where it's not too steep or close to a drop off."

She nodded. They climbed over three distinct snow hills, all including a snow chute. She tried to imagine the thrill of sliding down, having already summited, and a grin stretched across her face. For a moment, she turned back to face the way they'd come

—three large hills rested below her. She memorized the scene, the way the snowfield angled slightly west to a precipitous drop-off onto a glacier below, the spot they'd emerged from around the bend, and where they'd return in a couple days, depending on weather.

As she turned to rejoin the group, she felt a snowflake land on her cheek. The sky had darkened to a light gray, the blue disappearing behind low clouds.

Lou's scowl became progressively more pronounced as the winds picked up, slapping across their faces. A large boulder lay beside the path, looming above Anna's head, and she paused to lean against it and catch her breath. With her mittened hand, she wiped snow off the boulder to see gray and white striations cutting horizontally through it.

What beauty and history hid inside this rock? Inside the mountain?

"We're almost at ten thousand feet!" Mr. Flannaghan announced as the wind grew sharper.

"Won't make it much farther tonight with this weather," Lou said with a huff.

Anna squinted into the freezing wind as snow blew sideways. The skin on her face was already sensitive with sunburn, and now it stung with each gust that brought sleety snow peppering across her cheeks.

Before night fell, they chose a spot against a tall cliff to camp for the evening. Anna's stomach churned as it had on the boat ride to America, and she could feel the sunburn on her face. She declined dinner, but drank as much water as she could manage before it started sloshing around angrily inside her.

This time she didn't even bother taking her boots off to see the damage. The pieces of cloth from her petticoat were no doubt sticking to the raw skin, and she wasn't going to be tearing them off any time soon.

With no campfire for the evening, she wrapped her blanket

tightly around her to sleep, laying on the icy rock. She stayed as close as possible to Mr. Flannaghan and hoped the open air and easy viewing would discourage any ill-meaning advances from anyone. Hopefully whoever had tried to get in her tent was a random man floating around the base camp and not one of her own team.

The other men were just a few feet away, huddled near each other and against the rock cliff face. The wind howled all night, and Anna was sure she didn't sleep at all, as she was freezing and nauseated from the altitude. Somehow the men all fell asleep, and she could hear them snoring along with the howling of the wind. Although she was grateful the snow had finally stopped, she still shivered until dawn.

The next morning, everyone awoke at sunrise to a miraculously clear sky. The view from the ridge, hidden the evening before by the storm, was astounding. Vast areas of golden fields and farms with zigzag log fences spread as far as she could see—mountain ranges and lone peaks in the distance, and blankets of evergreens covering the base of the mountain. From that height, she felt like she was suspended in air, flying.

As they ate a small, cold breakfast, they all sat facing the overlook off the ridge, soaking up the sight of cities in the distance and trains winding across the valley as smoke rose into the sky.

"We're quite lucky the weather cleared, aren't we, Miss Gallagher?" Mr. Flannaghan smiled warmly at her.

"Very much so," she said between bites.

Isn't it wonderful, Ben? If only he could hear her.

They set out as soon as they finished eating. When they reached the trail, she was pleasantly surprised to see an icy but flat area.

"This here is where we need our spikes." Lou flung his pack around to the front of him.

As Anna strapped her crampons in place, she felt a swell of

pride. She was doing it. A lady—a woman—strapping on her crampons with the boys to summit a mountain. They were so close, only four thousand feet to go, but the hardest sections lay ahead.

The sun's glare off the ice was dizzying, so she put her goggles in place. For the better part of an hour, the group trod over the Cowlitz Glacier, which provided a compact, icy path. Her hands and feet were freezing, but heat from the exercise and the sun warmed the rest of her.

Mr. Flannaghan told stories about his family to keep their spirits up, and many of them made the group laugh.

"What's the name of your fella?" John turned behind him to look at Anna. Everyone else turned to look at her as well.

She grinned awkwardly. "Ben. He's fishing now, with my brother. Should be back around the same time we are."

"I'd never let my woman go climbin' a mountain without me," Peter said, shaking his head.

She smirked at him. "Well, he knows how strong I am."

She forced herself to look more confident than she felt.

The sound of ice crushing beneath their feet was rhythmic. Mr. Flannaghan had grown silent, his breath heavy with exertion.

"Well, I'm sure he'll be mighty proud of you," John said between breaths.

Another hour passed, and soon the ice thinned, then disappeared. In its place, rocks, pebbles, and small boulders made up their path. Lou instructed them to remove their crampons so as not to dull them.

John pushed his glasses up the bridge of his nose as he consulted his notebook. He leaned toward Anna to say, "I believe this here rocky area is called Cathedral Gap."

The path was now unstable, the rocks and pebbles loose under their feet. Anna's first step took her foot sliding farther than she expected to the right, stretching her interior leg muscle. She took smaller strides and glued her eyes to her feet to maintain her balance as the elevation climbed again. Her chest heaved from the exhilaration and the altitude. The sound of slipping, grinding rocks echoed around them as if water rushed through the path. She gripped her alpenstock, using it to find a steady place before taking each step.

They soon came upon another icy section, and everyone strapped their crampons over their boots.

Lou came up to her and attempted a smile. "Only ice, snow, and glaciers from this point. Comin' up on eleven thousand feet, and I need to secure the rope around each of us."

She nodded, and he looped the thick rope around her waist with a special knot. Then he let out a few feet before looping John in.

Once they were all connected, they began slowly, the deep spikes helping with their footing. She shivered, both from cold and fear of sliding to her death.

"Dependin' on weather," said Lou, looking back at the group from where he led in the front. "We might be able to summit tonight. No promises though, might be tomorrow. Let's keep at 'er as best we can. Comin' up on the Ingraham Glacier."

Her lungs burned. The icy air swirled around, making her cheeks ache. The compound soreness in her upper legs and the tightness in her calves from days of gaining elevation was affecting her more than she'd expected. But despite the pain, her spirits were high—she could almost burst with pride that she'd made it so far.

It was ten in the morning, and this might be the very day that her dream of climbing the biggest mountain she'd ever known would be realized. All this time, wondering if she was capable, wondering if she was strong and tough enough—this was the day she could prove her own doubts wrong by reaching the top of the mountain she'd always admired. If only her mother could see her now!

With glaciers rising on either side of them, the team made

only very careful movements on the icy ridge. A thin layer of snow from the storm the night before covered the ice.

Just then, a great thundering sound filled the air, and Lou turned to them. "Avalanche! Stay put."

As it grew closer, Anna's heart pounded. She imagined being covered in ice and rocks. It wasn't visible, but she guessed it was two or three hundred feet away. Rocks crashed in the distance, and she turned behind her to see John's reaction. He was squeezing his eyes shut behind his goggles and white-knuckling his alpenstock.

As the sound faded, they all breathed a sigh of relief, and Lou signaled for them to keep moving. They reached the edge of the ridge, with glaciers on either side of them. White and dark blue swirled together in the ice surrounding them.

As she marched firmly for each icy step, Anna thought of the day she'd attempted to walk on the frozen pond in her walking boots.

She smiled and took a confident step onto what looked like a mound of snow, but there was a sharp scratching noise as she stepped down. Her ankle twisted, and she lost balance, causing her to fall to her left. Her heart pounded rapidly, and a shot of pain jolted through her as she slid toward the edge of the shallow path.

CHAPTER FORTY-SEVEN

THE ALPENSTOCK

A nna plunged her alpenstock into the ice to secure herself as the rope around her waist tightened. Her mind raced, and she tried to make sense of what was happening.

The spikes in her boots must have come right down on a boulder covered by snow, her crampon coming loose as her foot landed sideways. She let out a small whimper before sitting to catch her breath.

John caught up from his place ten feet behind her, the rope lagging between them. "What happened?"

Everyone circled around her.

"I'm fine, just slipped," she said, trying not to wince. "The tip of a rock or something."

Lou had already turned around, heading in her direction. She dreaded whatever he'd have to say. He gingerly took her foot in his hands to examine the damage.

"Crampon was too loose," he said definitively. "Take your boot off."

She shook her head in disbelief. "They were…on as tight as they could go."

302

Her eyes were wide, searching Lou's face for a sign that everything was going to be fine. It wasn't the crampons being too loose that had caused her to stumble—it was the boots being too big. Why had she even cared if anyone saw her trying them on in the store? Everyone would know she'd hiked the mountain soon enough.

Lou pointed at her foot with his eyebrows raised in question. She loosened the laces, and with great difficulty, removed her boot. Mr. Flannaghan gasped. Both fresh and dried blood covered her socks, and her foot was already beginning to swell—she could feel the heat through the wool. Her foot throbbed, and her eyes filled with tears that she blinked back.

"It's fine," she said. "The blood is just from blisters, not the fall. No need to make a big fuss over a little twist of the ankle."

Her breath came faster as she attempted to put the boot back on. Lou took a deep breath, watching her fiddle with the crampon, tightening it over her boot. He held out his hand to help her up, and she stood swiftly. But as she took her next step, she clearly favored one side.

Lou's expression was full of genuine concern. "How's it feel?"

It felt like there was a knife in her ankle.

She didn't respond, because if she did, everything would come crashing down. Her breath was fast and hot as she took three tender steps, then brushed the snow off the seat of her pants and elbows. Warmth spread on her cheeks, and she hoped her face didn't look as flushed as she felt. "Good as new."

"I knew something like this would happen," Lou said, running his hands over his beard. "Looks like we'll have to turn around, boys."

She glared at him then looked away, her arms hanging limp at her sides. All the possibilities of things she could say filled her mind, but she knew better. Best to keep things civil with this man. "I'm sure I'm fine."

"It's only gonna get more difficult and icy from here. Ya need all your appendages to summit, because if ya go tumblin', ya need to be able to sprawl out like a flying squirrel to catch yourself."

"Are you worried I'm going to slow you down?" she asked.

Lou shook his head. "This is much bigger than slowin' our pace. You'll put us all at risk of bein' injured. This is a game-ender right here."

His words cut to her core, and she shook her head in disbelief. All of the preparation, all of the money spent, all of the grief she'd caused her grandfather, would now be for nothing. Light-headed, she adjusted her goggles. Her foot was throbbing —he wasn't overreacting.

Lou turned to address everyone. "We need to return to the place we camped last night—"

"What? Why?" Peter's face was red with anger. "I didn't come all this way to turn around because *she* got hurt. We paid good money to summit."

"I'm in charge here, boy," Lou said firmly. "Y'all will stay at that campin' place for the rest of the day while I take her back to base camp. I'll bring back more food and return by first light. Not a discussion."

"No," Anna said, blood rushing to her face.

Lou repeated her menacingly. "No?"

"I mean, no you don't need to walk me down to base camp. I can get there on my own."

"Like hell you can," he scoffed.

"I can, and I'll slide down the snow chutes for the last bit anyway, just like those men we saw, so my ankle will hardly slow me down. I'll be back before nightfall." She breathed heavily— her desire not to take up extra space warred with her need to assert her capacity.

"Absolutely not, dear," Mr. Flannaghan said, putting his hands gently on her shoulders. "I promised to take care of you, and I shall. I propose we all return to base camp together and set out again tomorrow if the weather allows. It's not the end of the world if we can't summit on this trip."

"Please," Anna urged.

She turned to Lou and looked at him imploringly. "I *do* know the way. It must be half past ten now, and we're at eleven thousand feet, correct?"

Lou nodded grimly.

"It's about thirty minutes back on this icy path until I'll reach the rocky trail. I'll take off my crampons for that, then after the loose rocks I'll be back on the compact ice where I'll put my spikes back on. I'll rest for a bit at the ridge we camped at last night, then head out onto the path that had the large boulder with striations. Shortly after that, I'll come across the three large snow hills where we saw the men sliding. And from the bottom of those, it should only take me another hour or so to get back to camp. I'll be there before dinner."

Lou made a grunting noise that sounded both angry and a little impressed. Mr. Flannaghan rubbed his hand across his forehead, clearly concerned.

"Please, I can do this," she pleaded. "You all can summit today, and I'll see you at base camp when you return."

After a long pause, Lou lifted his head to the sky, then fixed his eyes on her. "I think she can do it."

Mr. Flannaghan groaned and began to protest.

"I'll be safe." Anna felt nearly as confident as she sounded.

She knew that weather conditions could change drastically in an hour, or another injury could happen suddenly. But there was no time to dwell on the dangers. It felt as if her very existence hung on the mystery: Could she do this on her own?

"Oh yes, I suppose you can. I'll just be quite worried over it. But yes, you are as capable as any of us. Actually, I don't think I could find my way back down on my own, but clearly you were paying attention. Well done, dear. Your talents will allow the rest of us to summit after all."

Anna breathed a sigh of relief.

"Just be careful." Lou pointed at her ankle. "It's just a twist, but it'll continue to swell."

She smirked. "At least my boot will fit better."

Lou stared at her with a steely expression then offered a half smile before turning to the group. "I'm gonna go with her roped up back to the rocky path while y'all eat lunch. I'll be back in an hour or less."

John patted her softly on the back. "Ya did good, Anna. Sorry this is the end for ya."

Mr. Flannaghan gave her a weak smile. "I'm sorry too. Don't be concerned about delaying us, we'll be fine resting for a bit. In fact, I'm glad for it."

Anna nodded and waved as she and Lou set out while the men pulled jerky out of their packs. Before she turned to walk down the mountain, she paused to take in the disappointment. It was a small victory that they trusted her ability to descend solo, but missing the summit stung, more than she could even admit to herself.

Pain already stabbed her with every step. She wasn't sure how much was from the twisted ankle or the raw skin rubbing against wool socks, but she did her best to keep up with Lou as they silently moved away from the glaciers.

Fear settled in her mind. The way ahead might be more painful and dangerous than she'd imagined.

When they reached the rocky path, he removed the rope from around her waist and gave her a long look that she couldn't quite read.

He nodded gruffly. "Well ya didn't slow us down after all. I'm impressed ya know the way back and that ya have the fortitude to do it on your own. Now, ya better make it back to camp safely 'cause if I have to return to town with a woman's corpse, I'll be in a heap o' trouble."

He gazed intensely then broke eye contact. "Off ya go, then."

With a wave, he turned to leave without looking back. He wasn't a charming man, but she appreciated the vote of confidence. She needed it right now.

CHAPTER FORTY-EIGHT
THE WOMAN

Anna removed her spikes and returned them to her pack. It wasn't easy keeping the sadness at bay, but she refused to acknowledge it. All the quiet walks alone to Heather's house, all the practice looking back, had prepared her for this day, but none of it could prepare her for the heartache she felt. The loss of the achievement she could almost taste.

Her footing over the pebbles, rocks, and dirt was even worse with a twisted ankle. She hadn't realized how much harder going downhill would be on the unstable rocks. The alpenstock helped steady her, but every step caused discomfort, and she had difficulty finding balance. Small step after small step worked best.

After a minute, she began to slide and fell squarely on the seat of her pants. The jolt of pain shot up through her back, then subsided after a few throbs. Tears burned at the edge of her eyes, but she had to press on; there was a long way to go.

After a grueling two hours on the rocky path, twice what it had taken them to climb it, she finally reached the compact icy trail and returned the crampons to her feet. She was grateful for the general flatness of the icy path and found she was much steadier on her feet on the flat, slippery surface compared with the steep rocky trail.

Examining her surroundings carefully, she recognized everything. It was as if her mind had absolute clarity and the path was a picture-perfect memory. This gave her something to focus on besides the mixed feelings blossoming in her chest.

With cautious steps, she marched toward the ridge where they'd spent the evening. That would be a good place to rest her foot and eat lunch—if jerky and stale bread counted as lunch.

When she reached the ridge, she sat to enjoy the highest lookout point she'd see on this attempt. The tops of evergreen trees carpeted the mountain below, and farther in the distance, rivers carved through foothills, heading toward the sound. And nestled against the water was her beloved city. How many times had she looked up at this mountain from there? Now she looked down from the heights. She took a deep breath, releasing it slowly. Did she still have a place in Seattle? What sort of life lay ahead of her?

The air had grown warmer, but cool gusts still brought the scent of snow. It was midafternoon already, so she soaked in as much of the sight as possible then turned toward base camp. It wasn't the summit, where she would have seen steaming craters and an even more glorious view of hundreds of miles of the Cascade Range, but it was still the grandest sight she'd ever seen.

The striated boulder she recognized from the ascent poked out of the snow about a hundred feet below, so she headed toward it. Her foot throbbed, but she tried to distract herself with the view. Large, white clouds settled above her, creating the illusion of fog. She wasn't sure if the sky was getting darker because the sun was on the other side of the mountain, or if another storm was coming.

The boulder stood regally right where she remembered, a fresh dusting of snow coating it. She brushed some snow away and admired the strata that represented different eras. It seemed like the right place to begin sliding down the snowy hills. Her ankle was killing her. But as she looked around, she couldn't see any of the defined snow chutes that had been there before. Perhaps they were just covered with fresh snow and she'd need to make new ones. She sat at the top of a snow-covered hill and pushed off with her alpenstock.

She slid about five feet, but went at an angle rather than straight down, then came to an abrupt halt. It must have been a poor push off. With a shove against the crisp snow behind her, she was off again, only to stop immediately. The ridges of snow were wind-swept like whipped cream, rippled ridges every couple feet that would likely prevent her from sliding at all. It didn't make sense. Where were the existing sliding paths?

Her eyes filled with tears as she pushed off again, this time harder. She careened sideways to the end of a snow cusp and came to another stop. She moved her goggles to her forehead as hot tears rolled down her cheeks. She brought her hands out of her mittens to cover her face as she cried. Her ankle was warm and throbbing. All the energy she'd put into the last few hours had been in hopes that she could at least slide the last two thousand feet back to camp. She rolled onto her side and wept.

Once she started to cry, she felt as though there'd be no end to it. She had never felt so profoundly empty. She couldn't summit the mountain—not like this. Her goal had not been achieved, and she still needed to go home to her family who would be terribly worried and upset she'd kept everything a secret and put herself in danger. Even her tears were reckless—dehydrating herself at a high altitude, with only a little water left in her canteen.

She dreaded telling Heather of her failed attempt. The money was all gone, and she hadn't made it, after all. Perhaps she wasn't as tough as she'd thought. As her shoulders shook from crying, the muscles in her shoulders stiffened.

Alone and sitting in the silence, she remembered when she'd

first met Heather. It was as if it had been another lifetime—how strong and skilled she'd grown since then. Even now, her legs and arms felt solid beneath her.

So, she wouldn't go home the first woman to summit Rainier, but then, she already knew she wasn't the first. At least she'd be the first white woman to get close. And it was possible she could return. She forced herself to stand and steady herself with her alpenstock. If she needed to walk the rest of the way, so be it.

Hobbling in pain, she could again feel the raw skin rub against her socks and torn petticoats, but she was relieved it wasn't numb from frostbite. She thought of Ben and how his presence would have been a comfort to her on this first summiting attempt. She dreaded telling him of her failure.

Sunbeams slipped through the low-hanging clouds, bouncing off the next snow hill which caught her eye. There—the three perfectly round hills standing exactly how she remembered them. She laughed as she realized she'd simply attempted sliding too early. Straining to see against the bright reflection, she made out a carved-out chute going down the next hill. She picked up her pace, leaning on her good foot and alpenstock. There was still something to be salvaged from this.

When she arrived at the first of the hills, she plopped down with anticipation. It was steeper than she remembered, so she held out her alpenstock and pressed her good leg against the snow in preparation to stop herself if she sped up too quickly. An inexplicable sensation bubbled in her chest, which gave her a burst of energy. She pushed herself away from the top and began sliding down the mountain.

The cold wind rushed by her, and the ribbon flew out of her hair. As she slid, she couldn't stop giggling, and her hair fluttered behind her. She picked up speed, grateful for pants. What exhilaration!

Another group waved to her as they hiked up the snowfield toward the summit, and she shouted a hello. As she whizzed past them, she thought she saw a woman in the group, and her heart sank. Perhaps she was mistaken—paranoid.

She stood to brush herself off at the bottom of the first hill and looked up toward the group she'd passed, but they were gone. Twice more she slid down the snow chutes created by other mountaineers—others that had gone before her, knowing there would be so many after.

At the bottom of the third hill, she estimated she'd been sliding for the better part of an hour, and by now she must be only a thousand feet above base camp. She giggled every now and then just from the delight of the speed.

Patches of grass poked through the snow, and mountain flowers appeared occasionally along the sides of the path—purples and yellows. Pressure began to mount in her ears, and she swallowed hard, causing popping noises in her ears.

Adrenaline coursed through her, and all her pain and discomfort faded as she saw the tents of the Camp of the Clouds come into view. She walked the rest of the way, then as she got closer she started to run, which turned into a lopsided hobble.

A man ran up to her, his face aghast. "What happened, miss? Everything all right?"

Anna could smell dinner cooking over campfires, and a grin spread on her face. Not only had she survived the descent alone, she'd also made good time.

"I'm fine, thank you. The rest of my group should be back in a day or two."

Once she reached the privacy of her own tent, she took off her boots with care, then her socks, and finally she peeled away the cloth that clung to her raw skin. She used water from her canteen to soften the hold of the cloth, and as soon as it was free, blood flowed.

She tore off more cloth from her petticoats, wrapping her feet again, then peeked out the flap of her tent to see a small group huddled around a fire. She listened in for a minute to see if they might make good company for the evening.

"Did you see the woman?" asked a short man with dark hair. "Why, if she summits, she'd be the first woman I know of to do it."

"I ain't never heard of a woman summiting," said another man stoking the fire.

She hated to disappoint them, but she might as well get used to practicing her story. She hobbled over to them.

"Actually," she said, sadly. "I injured myself and had to return. Won't be making history this time, I'm afraid."

"No disrespect, miss," said the dark-haired man. "We wasn't talkin' 'bout you. There's another group that left from this here camp this morning with a lady."

She folded her arms over her chest. Heat flooded her face, and she nodded, sitting near the fire, resting her foot. The men quickly changed the subject and started talking about the new mountaineering gear one of them had purchased from Europe.

Anna stared into the fire. It had been a woman in the group she'd passed while coming down the mountain, after all. A woman would summit Mount Rainier, tomorrow, most likely. She let out a deep sigh and reminded herself it would be great for women everywhere to hear about this news—if she succeeded. She had to be content knowing she hadn't slowed her group down. Plus, she'd had the opportunity to prove her mountaineering capabilities and skill by finding her own way back to base camp. That was something.

By the next morning, the swelling had gone down considerably. She wondered where on the mountain her group was by now. Would they be successful? She tried to push away the hope that a great storm might come, pushing all the groups downward and back to the safety of the camp. If no one summited, then it would hardly be news that her injury had forced her to stay behind. A moment later, she blushed with guilt for even entertaining the thought.

Only one day after that, her team returned from the summit, and she greeted them heartily.

"Glad to see you alive," Lou mumbled as he patted her on the back.

Mr. Flannaghan's face was covered in a bright red sunburn, much worse than anyone else's. "Oh, my dear, you're safe and sound, thank goodness."

"How did it go? I'm assuming the weather held, and you summited?"

John pushed his glasses up his nose. "Sure did! Wish you'd been there with us."

She nodded with emotion, glad her team had succeeded. "What was it like up there?"

"Unlike anything I've ever seen," John marveled. "I'll let you read my notes if you like."

The next morning, Anna packed her tent, preparing to leave with her group after lunch. A honeybee buzzed around her feet, weaving through the clovers and clusters of white flowers. A woman's voice caught her attention, and she dropped her tent to follow it.

Leaning against a tree, a dark-haired woman sat, her face blackened with what looked like coal. Anna wondered at her appearance, watching her wide, expressive eyes dance as she talked with a semi-circle of men around her. The conversation stopped when her eyes met Anna's.

"I thought I saw a woman sliding down the mountain," she said, brushing off her flannel skirts as she stood. "I'm Fay Fuller. It's great to make your acquaintance. Did you summit, too?"

Anna shook her head. "My ankle. I took a bad step in the ice —about eleven thousand feet. I came back while the rest of my group went on to summit."

There were a few gasps around the group of men.

"You made the descent from eleven thousand feet back here all alone?" one man asked.

"I did." Her lips curved into a small smile.

"Impressive indeed," Fay said, adjusting the goggles resting above her forehead. "How'd the altitude treat ya? I blackened my face with coal and still managed to get sunburned."

"It was bright. I wish I'd thought of coal," Anna said. "My face is burned too, but my blisters took most of my attention."

Fay nodded understandingly. "Wasn't easy, was it? But now I can say I've accomplished what I've always dreamed of and feared impossible. I think you should be quite proud of yourself as well."

Anna smiled before a man from the circle chimed in.

"Well, I can't say for sure, but we're thinkin' you're the first woman ever to summit this here mountain."

Fay nodded graciously. Anna couldn't deny her feelings of jealousy, but she willed herself to remain proud of her own accomplishment.

After lunch they set out with the pack animals. Her foot was much improved, and although the swelling had gone down considerably, and she barely limped anymore, Mr. Flannaghan insisted she ride a pony for the long stretches.

Much of the skin on her feet was still rubbed raw, but as both her feet were slightly swollen, the boots fit more snugly, and there was hardly any friction anymore. Instead, a new problem emerged—her toenails jammed against the front of her boots with every step down the mountain.

On the last morning before arriving in Yelm, Anna changed back into her dress and what was left of her petticoats. Her foot throbbed—it had become a constant dull ache punctuated with random sharp or burning pains. Now that she could put most of her stuff on the pony, her back was relieved, but every muscle was still sore.

When they finally arrived at the train station, it was

bittersweet for her to say goodbye to John and Mr. Flannaghan—
she saw them as new friends.

"I'm proud of how far you went," Mr. Flannaghan said,
beaming. "And I'm utterly impressed with your ability to find
your way back down the mountain on your own. What an
achievement! I'll tell my young daughters how brave you were,
and I hope they might be so brave one day."

Anna grinned with pride. "You wouldn't prefer they were
proper ladies?"

"Times are changing, Miss Gallagher," said Mr. Flannaghan.
"You'd already be allowed to vote here in Washington if that law
we voted for hadn't been overturned by the Territorial Supreme
Court. But it's coming soon, and there are other changes brewing
as well."

She gave him a serious nod with a half-smile. "I look forward
to that, Mr. Flannaghan."

Next, she shook John's hand and wished him well with his
article and his future writing.

Then she turned to Lou. "Thank you for everything."

He shrugged. "Long as everyone stays safe—that's my job.
The summit is just the cherry on top, so to speak."

Anna looked back up to the mountain. It was still such a close
presence, looming above them into the sky. Lou gave her a firm
handshake and pat on the shoulder.

Once they'd all gone their separate ways, she couldn't decide
if she should take the train straight home to see if Ben had
returned, or stay a night in Tacoma. It'd be nice to bathe before
reuniting with Ben and facing her family. She just had a single
dollar left, which would only buy her one meal, but as she
boarded the train, she remembered she had a friend who lived in
Tacoma.

CHAPTER FORTY-NINE
THE HOMECOMING

As soon as Anna got on the warm train and rested against cushioned seats with her head against the window, she fell into a deep sleep. What seemed like moments later, a shrill whistle blew, announcing their arrival in Tacoma. Natalya had mentioned their dress shop was close to the railway station, but she couldn't recall the address. She asked a newspaper boy where she might find a good seamstress close by, and he made no attempts to hide his obvious surprise at her disheveled appearance. He pointed toward a street visible from the station and said to knock on the dark blue door.

Despite her appearance, Natalya recognized her at once. "Anna!" she squealed.

Natalya's surprise was written in her face, but her smile was genuine. She whisked Anna inside and took her upstairs to their residence to serve her a meal with hot coffee. While Anna savored her dinner of oyster soup and hot biscuits in the large dining room, Cara came through the door and plopped down at the table next to her.

"You look familiar, miss," Cara said. "Do I know you?"

Mrs. Schwarz struggled up the stairs and lowered herself into a chair at the table. Her presence made Anna acutely aware of how dirty she looked.

"I met you and your mother in Seattle," she said, smiling at the girl.

"I remember now." She surveyed Anna's tangled hair and the dirt around her neck, then apparently decided not to care. "Mrs. Schwarz, this is our friend Anna from Seattle."

The old woman nodded graciously. "How do you do, my dear?"

"A pleasure to meet you, ma'am."

Natalya came from the kitchen with a cart holding three more steaming plates and joined everyone at the table.

Mrs. Schwarz glanced at Anna's dirty nails then looked up at her with interest as she took a spoonful of soup. "What brings you to Tacoma?"

"Well, I attempted to summit Mount Rainier, but I hurt my ankle and had to stop before I reached the top."

Cara dropped her spoon, and the sharp dinging of it landing against the side of her bowl was the only sound in the room until she asked, "You did what?"

"Oh my, Anna." Natalya exchanged glances with Mrs. Schwarz. "You've certainly been busy. Good for you."

"What a marvelous adventure, Miss Gallagher," Cara said.

"Did you see the newspaper this morning?" Mrs. Schwarz asked.

Anna shook her head.

The older woman pointed to the coffee table in the living room, and Cara dutifully retrieved the newspaper for her.

Mrs. Schwartz held it at a distance from her face and read it aloud. "Front page says that on August 10th a school teacher, Miss Fay Fuller, summited Mount Rainier. First lady ever. Sorry she beat you to it, young lady."

The old woman's eyebrows were scrunched in sympathy.

Anna smiled and shook her head. "Yes, I met Miss Fuller a few days ago at base camp. No need to apologize. I'm sorry I wasn't able to be the one, but I'm happy a woman succeeded. Publicity will make it more respectable for women to be mountaineers in the future."

Natalya nodded and patted Anna's hand. "You've done a wonderful and brave thing. I'm honored to know you."

Cara gazed at Anna with admiration, but Anna couldn't help but feel a deep and lasting disappointment knowing that Fay, who had gone just one day after her, had successfully summited and taken a title that had almost belonged to her.

Yet the look of wonder and admiration on Cara's face helped to soften the blow. Maybe instead of being looked down upon after returning to Seattle, she might be an inspiration to other little girls—the brave ones, the ones who dared to be different.

After her delicious dinner, she bathed and carefully washed the raw skin around her heels and ankles, patting it dry with a towel. Natalya had offered to wash her dress and what was left of her petticoats, letting her borrow a cotton nightgown. She had felt like a new person in her pants, wool sweater, and fur vest, but back in the warmth of the maritime climate, the light nightgown was airy and comfortable.

Lying in bed, she wondered how her grandfather would receive her the next day, and if Ben was longing to see her again. Part of her was in no hurry to return home and face her family, but she also missed them dearly. Perhaps they'd throw their arms around her in forgiveness.

And Ben—how she longed to kiss him. She fell into a deep sleep atop the soft pillow and dry sheets and didn't wake until nearly ten the following morning.

With a dry dress, she felt refreshed, and after a late breakfast of pancakes, berries, and cream, Natalya and Cara both accompanied her to the station.

As they waited for the train, Cara looked up at her with a grin. "I think you're really brave."

Anna's heart fluttered, and she leaned down to hug the girl tightly. "Thank you, darling. That means a lot."

She spent the train ride to Seattle reflecting. It was frustrating how the men hadn't fully embraced her as a teammate—well, not all of them, but then she remembered Cara's face looking up into hers with admiration. The young girl's words made her feel respected in a way she'd never anticipated or even imagined when she first decided on the expedition. And Mr. Flannaghan's sentiment about hoping his daughters would be like her gave her a new dignity.

No, she hadn't summited the mountain, but she was proud of herself for trying and getting as far as she had. Especially since she'd had no encouragement from her family and no one had expected such a thing of her—she'd accomplished it all herself.

Before long, the train pulled into the station. It had been over two weeks since she'd left, and although she'd failed, she'd never forget the views or how it felt to get there on her own two feet. Now that she was so close, her hesitation vanished, and she couldn't wait to get home.

Instinctively, she searched the sea of faces at the station for Ben, as if he would somehow know the very minute she arrived back in town. She noticed, as if for the first time, the tall brick buildings that had been constructed after the fire. They were sturdy and stately. The ground was dry and dusty, and all the anxiety she'd felt about going against people's expectations seemed foreign now. Although she hadn't summited the mountain, her life was changed forever.

The pain had subsided to a dull ache. She still limped slightly, but she hurried home. Her mother's cameo gleamed at her collar, and she couldn't help but wonder what her mother might have felt after surviving in the woods alone for three days. When they found her, did she wish they hadn't, so she could stay free a little longer? She slowed her pace to savor the last moments.

As she turned down the dirt road to her house, she saw her grandfather sitting on the porch, a book in his lap, stopping every few minutes to look down the hill toward town. He jumped to his feet, grinning ear to ear, and with no small effort, he ran toward her, dust trailing behind him. As he picked her up, he swung her around, petticoats flying.

Anna gushed, "I'm so sorry——"

"No. My deepest apologies. I'm afraid I pushed you away so you couldn't trust me." His face grew pink with emotion. "Trust me now. With everything."

He laughed and touched the cameo at her neck tenderly. "Dirty boots, ripped up petticoats, and a perfectly clean cameo—you are your mother, indeed. They'd be so proud of you, lassie."

She hugged him tightly, honored to be compared to her mother not just in appearance, but in spirit, too. She had prepared so many things to say—arguing for her right to do as she pleased, to choose her own path for the future, but none of it seemed relevant now. He understood—maybe not her need to summit, but who she was at her core.

She took the arm he offered—he never even mentioned her slight limp or ginger steps. On the dirt path leading to their house, they saw Greta in the cherry tree, and as they got closer, she waved enthusiastically. As she climbed down, she had tears in her eyes.

"Darling girl! Just look at you!" she exclaimed. "I'm so *proud.*"

"Really? I hope you're not mad." She squeezed Greta, reveling in the sweetness of the moment. "I didn't actually make it to the top, though."

"No matter. You followed your heart and I wouldn't expect anything less from our Anna."

The tears flowed freely down Greta's face, which made a lump of emotion catch in Anna's throat.

Inside, Levi was carving wood in front of the fire, and when he turned to see her he had a look on his face she couldn't read.

She peeked around for any sign of Ben. Why wasn't he here waiting for her?

"I'm so relieved." Levi hugged her, then held her away from him, and his voice got low. "I've never been so scared in my life. Not even when the coyote attacked me. Don't ever leave again."

She laughed despite his serious face. "I'm sorry, but I see a lot of leaving in my future. But, next time I promise I'll tell you first."

Levi groaned and shook his head.

She set down her pack and began untying her boots. "I have so much to tell you all, but let me soak my feet for a few minutes and change."

Her grandfather brought a new wine from the cellar, and Greta roasted halibut and potatoes for dinner. When Anna returned barefoot, Greta gasped at the state of her feet.

"I'll be fine. How's the bookstore?" She looked first at Greta, then her grandfather.

"I've missed you," he said quietly. "Business has been good now that we're fully stocked, and the lady I hired is helpful. But of course, you're welcome back any time."

"Cinnamon buns are most popular lately," said Greta.

"Anna, I need to apologize again," her grandfather said. "So much has happened over the last year, and I know that I haven't been as supportive as I should've been." He sighed gruffly. "And so much pressure on you to settle down. I know that's unfair."

She shook her head. "You don't have to—"

"I do though," he said sadly. "Your parents spent all their free time exploring and doing dangerous things that made me lose my head. When I saw that desire growing in you, I got scared. I had such high hopes moving here with you and your brother."

He paused and looked up to the ceiling, full of emotion. "I wanted an easy life for you, a safe one. I thought all we had to do was find you a successful man and all your dreams would come true. But you've been telling me your dreams all along, and I...I guess I stopped listening. I'm sorry, lassie. I was just trying to do right by you."

She jumped up from her chair to hug him, and Greta came over to join them.

"Let's sit for dinner, and you can tell us everything," Greta said.

"I have so many questions," Levi said with an amused grin.

Anna laughed and took her seat. "All right, ask away."

"How far did you get?" he asked, then stuffed a bite in his mouth.

"About eleven thousand feet, but I stepped on a boulder covered in snow and twisted my ankle."

"Oh dear!" Greta exclaimed. "Is that why your feet are all bloody?"

Anna frowned. "No, that was just from my ill-fitting boots. But I managed to make it back down to base camp solo, which was no easy task."

"I should think not," her grandfather said, concern clouding his face. "Well I'm just glad it's all over with. I can finally sleep again!"

She grinned and looked out at the forest. For some reason, though she usually looked right past it, her eyes fell on the tree the Duwamish boy had been propped up against on that terrible night, and she found she couldn't look away. She saw him slumped against the trunk, hoping he'd rise again. Then, she thought of Heather's cousin, the one that had gone missing.

"Grandfather, what ever happened to that Duwamish boy?" she asked with a pointed look. "You never told me. I recently learned that Heather's cousin went missing around that time."

He shrugged uncomfortably and mumbled something about getting more wine. She shook her head, determined to push him more on the subject another time.

"This halibut is amazing, Greta." She hesitated, tracing the edge of a potato with her fork. "Did Ben come by?"

A flicker of hope stirred in her as she held her breath.

"Yes," Greta replied, wiping her mouth with a crisp, white napkin. "Soon after you left. They've been back about a week."

"Ben's staying at the Occidental and wants to see you somethin' fierce," Levi added.

She took a sharp breath in and let it out slowly. Her heart began to pound with an aching to see him.

"And," her grandfather said, handing her a letter as he walked back in the room. "This is for you. He was troubled you hadn't seen it yet. Must be important."

She took the envelope gingerly. It was agony not to tear it open immediately, but she tucked it into her pocket to read in privacy later. Greta had also prepared a fine dessert of baked apples with cinnamon and sugared oats—Anna didn't want all her work to fall by the wayside. Afterwards, they all sat in front of the fire, and once her grandfather and Greta had exhausted all their questions about what food she ate and what the views were like, she went up to her room and opened the letter. Her heart beat faster as she read his words.

... I love you, and I wish you the best of luck...be safe and take every precaution. I will think of you each moment between now and the time I hold you again.

Her breath caught at the last bit.

Had he come running to her house to see her and found her already gone? Most importantly, he wasn't at all offended that she'd gone without him. Tears formed in her eyes, but she wiped them away, relieved at last.

CHAPTER FIFTY
THE RECEPTION

At half past seven, the sun still shined brightly in the summer sky. Anna dressed in an indigo and white print summer dress, with layers of white ruffles along the hem and pearl buttons from waist to collar. She found clean bandages for her feet and wrapped them before putting on her stockings and shoes.

With heart pounding, she adjusted her hat. "Would anyone like to join me?"

"I'd be happy to, dear." Greta grabbed her beaded lace shawl from the hook near the door. "Oh, and you got a letter from June. I've got it here in my bag."

Anna stood on the porch to read it, eager for news from her friend.

Dear Anna,

By the time you read this letter, you will have already gone on your big adventure. You did it! I hope it was everything you dreamed of. So much has happened in the last three weeks, and I'm so sorry I won't be able to say goodbye in person.

First, I stopped by Emily's house with Joseph. I'm not sure what prompted it, but I remembered playing with dolls together and just had to show her my real-life baby. She was so welcoming, Anna, it made me weep. She adores Joseph. I wish you could have been there. I told her where you were, and she's worried sick, so you should call on her soon.

And secondly, I've married Connor! It was a very small affair, private, and now we're off to San Francisco to start a new life. Will you come visit once we're settled?

Sincerely,
June Evans

Anna blinked in amazement. She hoped with all her heart that things would turn out well for June. She deserved a happy ending after all the difficulties she'd faced in her life so far.

They left for the Occidental, and on the way, everyone she passed interested her more than ever. She looked into each face, wondering what their dreams were and if they had accomplished them, or ever tried, and if they'd found something in their lives that brought them joy.

She glanced at Greta. "Are you happy? I mean in general."

Greta chuckled. "Of course."

She believed her, but looked forward to a time in the future, while they were baking perhaps, when she could ask Greta more about her dreams.

When they arrived at the Occidental Hotel, they asked at the front desk if Benjamin Chambers was still staying there, and the gentleman pointed to a nearby table in the restaurant. She turned to see him sitting with a book, eating dinner alone. She struggled a moment to catch her breath then strode to his table while Greta took a seat in an overstuffed settee near the stairs.

Ben looked up from his book when she was about ten feet away, and his face instantly exploded in a wide grin. He jumped to his feet.

As she reached him, he leaned down and kissed her softly on the cheek, then motioned for her to sit. "I just finished, but if you're hungry we could order—"

She shook her head. "Let's walk."

He nodded and left money on the table. As they joined Greta, he gave a slight bow and tipped his hat. Anna admired his fine new suit—he looked exquisitely handsome and refined—different than the hunter with a bow slung over his back that she remembered.

He grinned at Greta. "Care to join us?"

"I'll be fine right here." She had a spark of delight in her eye. "I trust you'll be a perfect gentleman?"

He nodded with another tip of his hat. "Yes ma'am."

As they exited the grand entrance, he offered his arm to Anna. They descended the steps onto the street and walked toward the docks as the sun colored the sky pink and gold. She stepped gingerly, so as not to disturb her carefully wrapped foot. Walking arm in arm with a man she loved sparked a thrill of delight inside her, and she looked up to read his face. His eyes were lit with an energy she'd never seen before—a fresh, inviting look in his eye.

"Are you upset I did it without you?"

Although one arm was linked with Ben's, her other hand began to tremble at her side.

He stopped cold, tilting his head.

"I wish you'd gotten my letter. Of course, I'm not upset. I'll be honest, it scared me that you were alone, but I could *not* be prouder of your spirit. I was only upset that you might be in danger, but no matter what, I'm glad you followed your heart." His smile was full of admiration. "How did it go? Did your team summit?"

"Well, yes, but I didn't get to," she said.

Forming the words and saying them out loud to him proved

even harder than she'd imagined. She explained the crampon and how she had hurt her foot.

"And now I feel as though every muscle in my body is both tight and sore. And you don't even want to see my feet..."

Ben's face was full of empathy.

"You weren't able to summit this time, but I've no doubt you will next time." He put his arm around her waist. "And all the way back to base camp by yourself? I mean, wow. I don't even think I could do that. What an accomplishment!"

She looked at him in amazement. "Really? And you don't think it was improper?"

The final walls came tumbling down—the ones she didn't even know were there, preventing her from loving him wholeheartedly. With her fears laid to rest, she saw him in a new way, and it overwhelmed her.

Ben laughed heartily and shook his head. "Perhaps you don't know me at all, even after all this time."

Anna turned to face him finally. She stared up at his brown eyes and the way he looked down adoringly at her. "Then tell me everything."

"But first, I owe you a kiss," he said.

They'd reached the hill above the docks, and as the last rays of sunlight sliced over the dark waters, Ben leaned closer. She felt an almost magnetic pull, and once his lips pressed against hers, a wave of tingles reached to her toes. His mouth parted, and the sensation of his lips moving against hers made her melt into his chest. This was the kiss she'd imagined for weeks—months—and it was as magical as she'd hoped. Out of breath, she pulled away, and Ben opened his eyes, looking like he'd just been awakened from a dream.

He cleared his throat, his arms still wrapped around her. "I love you. I suppose I should write to my parents finally. Tell them about my beautiful love."

"Invite them to Seattle for a visit. I'd love to meet them," she said enthusiastically.

She put her hands on his big shoulders and pulled herself even closer to him, laying her head against his chest. She thought the kiss might have released some tension, but instead it had only created more heat.

"Well, I'd like to make it known, I've no interest in standing quietly by your side or being stuck in the house. But if you're up for my going where I please and doing dangerous things, then I think things might just work." She looked back up at him, his brown eyes sparkling, and he picked her up off her feet and kissed her again.

"I wouldn't have it any other way. Although I'm afraid I've not, in fact, been a perfect gentleman on this walk," he said, smiling mischievously. "I guess *you* are my particular weakness."

"So that's what it is," she said, reaching for both of his hands to hold.

"I have something for you," he said, pulling her close again when she grabbed his hands. "But it's a birthday gift, and, of course, that's not until the 25th."

He paused. "I could give it to you early, though."

She laughed. "I've finally found a man who understands me. I won't have to escape to the forest alone after all. That's all the birthday gift I need."

Ben's face turned serious. "I'm proud of you—you had a dream, and you went for it. I'll escape with you into the forest or anywhere else your heart desires."

She gazed up at him, admiring his ability to see inside her heart. It would be a true pleasure to get to know him better. She laid her head on his chest and felt his heart beating. He put his hand against her cheek and pushed a loose strand of her hair back softly.

"Let me get you home before I can never let go of you," he said, his voice deeper than usual.

He leaned in for another kiss, both hands behind her head, his fingers tangled in her hair. This time the kiss was more urgent, and Anna wished it would never end.

When he pulled away, he looked into her eyes, clearly reluctant to let her go. "Can I give you your gift tomorrow? I'll come over for lunch."

She laughed giddily, still reeling from the heat of the kiss. "Of course."

They returned to the hotel to gather Greta, who read the couple correctly and grinned. The three headed home in the twilight as the warm breeze rustled through trees. When they got home, Anna seemed to drift up the stairs, buoyed by happiness and the fact that she was about to sleep in her own bed for the first time in what felt like years.

Ben saw her true heart, and he was enamored with her. In a burst of excitement, she imagined what life might be like with him by her side—riding trains, hiking forests, who knew what else. She closed her eyes and melted into sleep.

CHAPTER FIFTY-ONE
THE REALIZATION

Anna awoke feeling like she could sleep for several more hours, but she remembered Ben's touch from the night before and shot out of bed, eager to get ready for his arrival. She brushed her hair and attempted a low chignon tied with a blue ribbon, putting on her light blue pinstriped dress with white organza lace. As she ran down the stairs, she was quite surprised to see Heather, Michael, and Pisha chatting around the table with her family.

"I invited them," her grandfather said, his eyes heavy with meaning.

"Heather, I'm delighted to see you!" She rushed up to her friend and hugged her before picking Pisha up.

She looked up at Greta, who was pouring coffee, and Levi, who was popping a muffin in his mouth, then turned to her friend. "Heather, how did you know I was home?"

"Your grandfather invited us. To welcome you." She shifted in her seat, and Anna knew she was uncomfortable being so close to town.

"Thank you. It means everything."

Heather bowed her head with a gracious grin. "So, how did it go?"

Anna took in the faces of those around her—everyone loved her dearly. "It was the adventure of a lifetime, but it was just the first."

She paused, wondering where to start. "I met some interesting people, got a lot of blisters, saw my reflection in a mountain lake, almost slid down a glacier, and then hiked down Mount Rainier all by myself. I could see all of Seattle and beyond from up there—it was unbelievable."

"I'm so proud of you," Heather said admiringly. "Did you stay warm?"

She leaned toward her. "Yes, thanks to you!"

"See snow?" asked Pisha in a soft voice.

"I did, darling." Anna grinned at the little girl, who giggled.

She looked over at her grandfather to smile, but his face was white, which alarmed her. "Grandfather, are you all right?"

He cleared his throat. "Can we speak privately? On the porch. You too, Heather."

As Heather stood, Michael stood with her, but she whispered something in his ear. He sat back down uneasily, pulling Pisha onto his lap.

On the porch, Anna stared at her grandfather, who looked defeated.

"When did your cousin go missing?" he asked Heather quietly.

"My cousin? Oh, Kiyoque. It was the summer I was nine. So, about ten years ago."

Her grandfather frowned as tears formed in his eyes. When he tried to speak again, his voice cracked, and he put his face in his hands.

Anna shifted uncomfortably and took over. "When I was nine, a boy came into our home, at about midnight. He was stealing our food and pans."

She paused to read Heather's face, but it betrayed nothing. "I heard my grandfather ask him to leave. The boy was maybe fifteen or sixteen, with dark skin and hair. He pulled out a knife, pointing it at my grandfather."

A flicker of understanding passed through Heather's eyes.

Anna looked to her grandfather who cleared his throat and wiped a tear from the corner of his eye. "I hit the boy over the head with a pan, something heavy. I thought for sure he was just unconscious. Then, I brought him out to the woods—propped him against a tree and waited. For hours. I hoped for a miracle. Before morning light, I walked to the police station to tell them I'd killed a Duwamish boy, but they said to just bury him and forget about it."

He choked back another sob.

"Wait, he died?" Anna asked in disbelief.

He nodded, continuing to weep into his hands.

Heather's eyes narrowed. "You think that boy was my cousin."

Anna felt tears fill her eyes. "Could it be?"

She'd always thought the boy had woken up a while later and run home. Or she had until she was a bit older, and something about it no longer sat right with her. She asked herself when she'd first realized something about her grandfather's story wasn't quite natural, but the truth was, she wasn't sure. It had just gradually come over her. His face that night. The absurdity of leaning an unconscious boy against a tree in the first place.

"We can't know," Heather said, her voice catching. "He may have run away or been captured. But yes, it could be. The police should have identified him...and told us."

"I know," he said. "I know that now. And my heart is broken about it. Since I've come to accept Anna's friendship with you, I've started thinking about it again, really thinking, of that boy's point of view, of what might have been going on with him. I've been sick about it. And so angry—this time with myself."

333

Anna shook her head angrily. "I can't believe the police did that. Even back then. I'm so sorry, Heather. I should have realized all this sooner."

Heather was visibly shaken. "It wouldn't have mattered to our friendship. I don't think so, anyway. You were little. What could you have done?"

Anna shuddered involuntarily and looked over at her grandfather.

He cleared his throat, his eyes glistening. "Heather, may I show you where he's buried? It would bring me peace, and maybe it would to you as well."

He turned to Anna. "Lassie, I'd like to show her by myself."

Heather looked to the older man, uncertainty written on her face. "Yes, show me."

"Are you sure you don't want me to come?" Anna asked.

Heather embraced her. "It's all right."

She watched her grandfather lead Heather down the porch stairs and to the woods.

When she walked back inside, Greta was waiting at the door. "Why don't you join me in the kitchen while Levi and Michael chat?"

Anna nodded absentmindedly, distracted. As they grabbed their aprons, familiar comfort came over her, and she sighed in relief. They rolled cookie dough then placed it in lumps on a pan.

"I forgot to tell you, while I was at base camp, a woman returned from the summit. We think she might be the first to ever do it." Anna looked down at her hands covered in flour. "I wish it had been me, but it's incredible nonetheless."

"Indeed," Greta replied. "What an accomplishment. For you *both*."

Anna looked up gratefully. "Ben's coming over later to give me my birthday gift."

Greta grinned. "I knew you two were perfect for each other."

"You did not!" she exclaimed.

"Did so," Greta said with a chuckle.

She nudged Anna with her hip playfully.

When Anna pulled the cookies out of the oven, her grandfather and Heather emerged, both with tears in their eyes, and she hurried toward them.

"I don't know what to say," she said, looking from Heather to her grandfather, who sighed heavily.

His cheeks were pink and blotchy, his lips turned down and trembling. He looked away, running his hands through his white hair.

"Your grandfather showed me a special place," Heather said slowly. "Perhaps an ending for the story of my cousin. Or at least someone I knew growing up. I'm going home now."

She turned to him with a grave expression. "I'm not angry. Thank you for showing me this."

Anna searched Heather's eyes and put her hand on her friend's arm.

"I'll visit soon. I want to hear more about your cousin." She hugged her friend. "Thank you for believing in me."

Heather squeezed her hand. "I'm taking my family home now. I'll see you soon. And I have so many questions about your trip. *Wiiac.*"

Anna hugged Pisha and said goodbye, then watched them walk into the forest.

CHAPTER FIFTY-TWO
THE GIFT

L ater that morning, Anna heard a knock at the door. When she turned to see who was walking in, her eyes immediately went to Ben who had a wistful expression when he saw her.

"I'm afraid lunch isn't ready, Mr. Chambers," Greta said playfully. "You're quite early."

He nodded sheepishly. "It's so hard to be away from her."

He pulled a package from behind his back and handed it to Anna with a spirited grin. It was wrapped in brown paper, a single blue ribbon tied in a bow.

"He's been waiting impatiently for your return." Levi laughed easily and patted Ben on the back. "With nothing else to do but think about you and your birthday, apparently."

Anna beamed and took the gift, untying the ribbon. She tore the paper off to reveal a medium-sized, brown leather-bound book. On the first page, there was a handwritten inscription coloring the page with neat blue lines.

This empty birthday book you hold will someday tell our tale.
Adventure, travel, journeys to wherever we can sail.

At first, you'll see it at the end, a small shaped piece of brass,
to open doors you've never seen, surrounded by soft grass.
You'll find a house one mile south, along the edge of town,
The fireplace is sturdy brick, the mantle chestnut brown.
Now let me take you to that house, to peek behind a brick.
Inside you'll find a golden sphere, but only if you're quick.
Today's inscription might remind you of a different book,
but this new story's all our own, no emerald if you look.
The treasure lies within your choice, my darling search your soul.
I offer everything I have, my helpless heart you stole.

"My goodness," Anna said, putting her hand to her mouth. "It's just like—"

Ben was bursting at the seams. "I thought it would be fun— knowing it's meant for *you*. Makes it more fun, right?"

She nodded and laughed. "It does."

Her heart pounded, knowing full well what was likely coming at the end of solving the riddle.

The next page was blank, as was every other page in the book. When she flipped to the back, she found a key taped to the inside cover.

"My small shaped piece of brass?" she asked, smiling at him.

He shrugged good-naturedly. "First one's easy."

He took her hand, leading her to the front door. "Do you have your compass and knife?"

"Always," she said, and pulled both out of her pockets. "Let's head south?"

"I'll follow you." Ben motioned for her to lead. "Shall I carry you to save your sore feet?"

Anna laughed. "I've made it this far. I can do another mile."

They set off along the edge of the forest going south, weaving through forested land claims just outside the city.

After twenty minutes, Ben stopped at the bottom of a small hill. He led her up to a two-story cedar house with glass windows and a brick chimney. It was nestled into the edge of the forest, just like the house she grew up in, except this house looked brand new, with young apple trees lining a front walkway made of dark red bricks leading to town a hundred feet away. A wide porch wrapped around the house, with two wooden rocking chairs facing the mountain.

She turned around to face the breathtaking view. "Should I...enter?"

Her voice caught, knowing what a big moment it was.

"The door's open," Ben said with a sly grin. "Plus, I know the man who owns the place."

As soon as he said the words, Anna knew, and her knees went weak. The hardwood floors looked brand new, and she moved through the parlor into the living room, torn between elation and being so nervous she might trip. Lining both sides of the fireplace were large bookshelves, filled completely with books of all sizes and colors. She traced her fingers along the bindings with gold letters as she drew closer to the fireplace.

She pulled out the knife Ben had given her and looked at the fancy fireplace with its dark wood mantle. One brick, in the bottom right corner, had a small drawing of a mountain on it. She smiled from ear to ear and looked at Ben as she leaned down to pull it out with her knife, uncovering a green velvet bag. She carefully tipped the bag over to find a gold ring engraved with pink flowers and green leaves—a large sapphire in the center.

"I thought the blue matched your eyes better," he said, blushing. "And this house is mine. If you'll do me the honor of marrying me, it can be *ours*."

Anna was lost for words. She looked around and couldn't believe the beauty and elegance. It was as grand as Emily's house, yet everything reminded her of her childhood home. The kitchen table was made of cedar and polished to a shine. The chairs near the fireplace were remarkably similar to those in the Gallagher house, and a large rug lay in front of the brick fireplace.

"I'd love to." Her eyes brimmed with tears, and she wiped them away joyfully. It was better than she'd ever imagined.

Ben picked her up off her feet and kissed her hard. She was breathless when he finally pulled away.

"Forgive me... but how did you buy it?" There was no way a year's wages at the mill could buy all this.

"I have loads of money," he said with an amused look. "I just never thought it important to bring it up."

Anna laughed and shook her head. Things just kept getting better. "And all these *books!* It's a dream, Ben."

He pulled a wrapped gift off the bookshelf and handed it to her. "I imagine you've still hung onto your love of literature despite your new mountaineering passion."

"You know me so well."

She opened it to find *Anna Karenina*—a beautiful, brand-new edition in English. "Oh my! How did you...? This is amazing—thank you!"

"I've had it for a while. I just needed the perfect moment to give it to you." He kissed her hand. "Would you like to go on an adventure together?"

"Of course!" Anna put the book down and wrapped the other around his waist.

"I have a short honeymoon planned," he said. "We can explore the woods and mountains to the east, and there's going to be a meteor shower. That's what the journal's for—you can write about everything as we do it."

"It sounds magical."

He kissed her on the forehead and hugged her close. "I want the same life you do, Anna. I've been dreaming of it since I was a young boy reading stories of voyages and explorations."

She looked toward the table where she'd placed the blank book, already eager to fill the pages. She lifted her face to meet his eyes. "And next summer we can summit Mount Rainier together."

He laughed, nodding enthusiastically. "Yes ma'am."

Anna put both arms around her fiancé. The large windows from the living room presented a magnificent view of the mountain, and they turned to face it. She melted into his arms, soaking up the sight that was somehow even better than when she'd looked down from its heights.

ANNA'S JOURNEY CONTINUES...

In Light of the Summit
The Rainier Series, Book 2

After Anna Gallagher's first climb on Mt. Rainier, she faces a new challenge—enduring the ridicule and threats that come with breaking tradition. In 1890, being a young female mountaineer makes polite society uncomfortable, even angry. But despite the threats and inherent risk, she still has plans for another climb, even if it jeopardizes her family bookstore, and puts her in more danger than she ever imagined.

Emily Watson has always been close with the Gallagher family. As a young girl she dreamed of a wealthy husband, a fine house, and a future in Seattle society and now she finally has it. Her desires couldn't be more different than Anna's, but she's confronted with her own invisible mountain to climb when she's suddenly poverty-stricken. She must decide what matters most, and whether true love is worth waiting for.

In Light of the Summit is a captivating story of ambition, heartbreak, and redemption. It's a tale of two childhood friends navigating womanhood in the late 19th century, with as much grace as they can muster, while still figuring out how to be true to themselves.

Use coupon code ANNA20 for 20% off signed paperbacks at:
jamiemcgillen.com/shop

ABOUT THE AUTHOR

- Author portrait by Melissa Nolen -

Jamie McGillen lives in the shadow of Mount Rainier, and no matter how many times she moves away, it draws her home. Everything about large evergreen trees delights her, except how poky they are, and the sap.

Her poems and essays have been published in numerous literary journals, and she teaches English Composition at Highline College. When she's not teaching or cutting strawberries for her starving children, she enjoys writing rhyming poetry, but it's simply not as popular as it used to be.

She also loves to chat with readers, so say hello on Instagram, send her an email, or leave a review and you'll make her day! (Every time you leave a review for this book, a baby book angel gets its wings. Don't deprive them, for heaven's sake.) You can connect and find out more about her at www.jamiemcgillen.com.

instagram.com/jamiemcgillen

BOOK CLUB QUESTIONS

1. Can you relate to Anna's pressure to conform to social norms? Why do you think women put so much pressure on themselves to be what society expects them to be? What can the payoff be for not "doing as we're told?"
2. Anna is confronted with the stereotype that women shouldn't climb mountains. What modern beliefs about gender will people think are ridiculous a century from now?
3. How does Mount Rainier play a role in the story? Have you ever felt drawn to a mountain, lake, forest, state, or part of the country?
4. Oscar is a complicated character who exhibits clear racism, yet is beloved by Anna. Did you like him? At any point in the story did you feel particularly offended by his actions or beliefs? Did your opinion of him change by the end of the story?
5. The Duwamish people are still an unrecognized tribe by the U.S. government. How do you think Heather

would feel about that? Do you think that there is any merit to denying tribal land to indigenous people?

6. William Grose is mentioned briefly in the book as one of the first black men in Seattle. What do you think of Oscar's acceptance of a successful black man, but his disdain for the poverty-stricken indigenous people of Seattle? Why do you think his racism is so subjective and specific?

7. What are your initial impressions of June? Does your opinion of her change by the end of the story?

8. What kind of man is Dr. Connor Evans? Did his actions surprise you throughout the novel?

9. How did you feel when Ben asked Anna to wait and summit with him? Would you have made the same choice Anna did?

10. Would you have liked to live in the late nineteenth century?

11. Some of the scenes were set a decade earlier. Did you find that those scenes provided a deeper layer to the story? If so, how?

12. John Muir said about Mount Rainier "More pleasure is to be found at the foot of the mountains than on their tops. Doubly happy, however, is the man to whom lofty mountain tops are within reach, for the lights that shine there illumine all that lies below." Do you think this sentiment rings true for Anna?

13. What did you think of the ending? Was it what you expected? Did you think that Anna's summit attempt was ultimately a success? Why or why not?

14. What do you think is next for the characters in the story? Do you think June will find happiness? Do you think Oscar will find peace?

15. This story depicts the struggles of having a family that doesn't support one's dreams. Have you ever felt that

the people closest to you don't understand you? If so, how has that affected you?

16. When was the last time you figuratively "pulled on a pair of wool trousers" to do something scary that you've never done before?

ACKNOWLEDGMENTS

Kyle – My honeymooner, my rock, and the love of my life. For all the times you sent me upstairs to write, or took the kids on an adventure—thank you. Your encouragement and belief that any of this was possible, and worth my time, has made the process not only possible, but fun. It's a pleasure to call you mine.

Scott – I love you more than all the stars in the sky, more than the raven loves her treasure, and more than all the dinosaurs that ever lived (times infinity). Beat that!

John and Beth Hanifan – To the best parents a girl could ever dream of—thank you for everything. My world revolves around your light. (And you thought it was the other way around!) Thank you for being my constant, my North Star.

Mollie Hanifan – Thank you for being a cheerleader and an encouraging voice from the very beginning. Your strong opinions and honest feedback were both refreshing and valuable. You truly are the winner of the cats.

Barbara Pavitt – Thank you for reading my book twice before it ever saw the light of day. I hope I can be as cool as you one day. This one's for you.

Claire Cain – Thank you for going on this adventure with me. This book might have never been written if you hadn't challenged me to take a break from poetry and write a novel that fateful November. For your encouragement, excitement, commiseration, and for the million times you read Anna's story —Danke.

Caroline Sibley – The master deleter of words. You are ruthless and I love you. Thanks for your brutal honesty that was just what I needed. Your fierce encouragement has always been just a message away.

Tanya Ludlow – Thank you for asking thoughtful questions and making feminist demands of Anna. And for suggesting Oscar's bowtie. He's forever distinguished because of your fine taste.

Mr. Melton – Thank you for putting up with my naïve writing skills in high school. I could joke about Latin, or your impossibly high standards, but the truth is that being your student for all those years taught me to think for myself. Thank you for teaching me that my opinion, and my art, matters.

Jaimee – Thank you for your fine editing skills and critical eye. Your insights have shaped me into the novelist I am today, and I'm forever grateful.

Mr. McCready – Cheers to the mountaineer! Thank you for taking the time to painstakingly consider Anna's every step up (and down) the mountain. Your experience and impeccable memory helped create a truly realistic story.

The "Chicklits" Book Club – Lorri Stiefel, Jan Allen, Beth Hanifan, Pam Culver, Carole Grove, Becky Burton, Cindy Strupp, Sandy Malone, and Wendy Ray—thank you for believing in my book when it was still a baby bird. Your thoughtful ideas and questions helped to shape the story. And I can't even describe how delightful it was to have women I've looked up to all my life take the time to read and discuss my book.

Cecile Hansen – Thank you for your invaluable knowledge and insights about the Duwamish people. Your thorough answers to my questions were instrumental in my portrayal of how the Duwamish people were treated in the story, and also depicting the extreme racism they faced. I hope that one day soon the Duwamish people will get the land and respect they have long deserved.

Made in the USA
Las Vegas, NV
10 January 2021